Snow Flower
and the Secret Fan

Snow Flower
and the Secret Fan

LISA SEE

BLOOMSBURY

First published in Great Britain 2006

Copyright © 2005 by Lisa See

The moral right of the author has been asserted

Bloomsbury Publishing Plc, 38 Soho Square, London W1D 3HB

A CIP catalogue record for this book is available from the British Library

ISBN 0 7475 8066 9
ISBN-13 9780747580669

10 9 8 7 6 5 4 3 2 1

Printed in Great Britain by Clays Ltd, St Ives plc

All papers used by Bloomsbury Publishing are natural, recyclable products
made from wood grown in well-managed forests. The manufacturing processes
conform to the environmental regulations of the country of origin

www.bloomsbury.com/lisasee

IN THIS NOVEL, I HAVE FOLLOWED THE TRADITIONAL CHINESE style for rendering dates. The third year of Emperor Daoguang's reign, when Lily was born, is 1823. The Taiping Rebellion started in 1851 and ended in 1864.

It is believed that *nu shu*—the secret-code writing used by women in a remote area of southern Hunan Province—developed a thousand years ago. It appears to be the only written language in the world to have been created by women exclusively for their own use.

SNOW FLOWER
AND THE
SECRET FAN

Sitting Quietly

I AM WHAT THEY CALL IN OUR VILLAGE "ONE WHO HAS NOT yet died"—a widow, eighty years old. Without my husband, the days are long. I no longer care for the special foods that Peony and the others prepare for me. I no longer look forward to the happy events that settle under our roof so easily. Only the past interests me now. After all this time, I can finally say the things I couldn't when I had to depend on my natal family to raise me or rely on my husband's family to feed me. I have a whole life to tell; I have nothing left to lose and few to offend.

I am old enough to know only too well my good and bad qualities, which were often one and the same. For my entire life I longed for love. I knew it was not right for me—as a girl and later as a woman—to want or expect it, but I did, and this unjustified desire has been at the root of every problem I have experienced in my life. I dreamed that my mother would notice me and that she and the rest of my family would grow to love me. To win their affection, I was obedient—the ideal characteristic for someone of my sex—but I was too willing to do what they told me to do. Hoping they would show me even the most simple kindness, I tried to fulfill their expectations for me—to attain the smallest bound feet in the county—so I let my bones be broken and molded into a better shape.

When I knew I couldn't suffer another moment of pain, and tears fell on my bloody bindings, my mother spoke softly into my ear, encouraging me to go one more hour, one more day, one more week, reminding me of the rewards I would have if I carried on a little longer. In this way, she taught me how to endure—not just the physical trials of footbinding and childbearing but the more torturous pain of the heart, mind, and soul. She was also pointing out my defects and teaching me how to use them to my benefit. In our country, we call this type of mother love *teng ai*. My son has told me that in men's writing it is composed of two characters. The first means *pain;* the second means *love.* That is a mother's love.

The binding altered not only my feet but my whole character, and in a strange way I feel as though that process continued throughout my life, changing me from a yielding child to a determined girl, then from a young woman who would follow without question whatever her in-laws demanded of her to the highest-ranked woman in the county who enforced strict village rules and customs. By the time I was forty, the rigidity of my footbinding had moved from my golden lilies to my heart, which held on to injustices and grievances so strongly that I could no longer forgive those I loved and who loved me.

My only rebellion came in the form of *nu shu,* our women's secret writing. My first break with tradition came when Snow Flower—my *laotong,* my "old same," my secret-writing partner—sent me the fan that sits here on my table, and then again after I met her. But apart from who I was with Snow Flower, I was resolved to be an honorable wife, a praiseworthy daughter-in-law, and a scrupulous mother. In bad times my heart was as strong as jade. I had the hidden might to withstand tragedies and sorrows. But here I am—a widow, sitting quietly as tradition dictates—and I understand that I was blind for too many years.

Except for three terrible months in the fifth year of Emperor Xianfeng's reign, I have spent my life in upstairs women's rooms. Yes, I have gone to the temple, traveled back to my natal home, even visited with Snow Flower, but I know little about the outer realm. I have heard men speak of taxes, drought, and uprisings, but these subjects are far removed from my life. What I know is embroidery, weaving, cooking, my husband's family, my children, my grandchildren, my great-grandchildren, and *nu shu.* My life course has been a normal one—daughter days, hairpinning days, rice-and-salt days, and now sitting quietly.

So here I am alone with my thoughts and this fan before me. When I pick it up, it's strange how light it feels in my hands, for it records so much joy and so much grief. I open it quickly, and the sound each fold makes as it spreads reminds me of a fluttering heart. Memories tear across my eyes.

These last forty years, I have read it so many times that it is memorized like a childhood song.

I remember the day the intermediary handed it to me. My fingers trembled as I opened the folds. Back then a simple garland of leaves adorned the upper edge and only one message trickled down the first fold. At that time I didn't know many characters in *nu shu,* so my aunt read the words. *"I understand there is a girl of good character and women's learning in your home. You and I are of the same year and the same day. Could we not be sames together?"* I look now at the gentle wisps that compose those lines and see not only the girl that Snow Flower was but the woman she would become—persevering, straightforward, outward-looking.

My eyes graze along the other folds and I see our optimism, our joy, our mutual admiration, our promises to each other. I see how that simple garland grew to be an elaborate design of interwoven snow blossoms and lilies to symbolize our two lives together as a pair of *laotong,* old sames. I see the moon in the upper right-hand corner shining down on us. We were to be like long vines with entwined roots, like trees that stand a thousand years, like a pair of mandarin ducks mated for life. On one fold, Snow Flower wrote, *We of good affection shall never sever our bond.* But on another fold I see the misunderstandings, the broken trust, and the final shutting of the door. For me, love was such a precious possession that I couldn't share it with anyone else, and it eventually cut me away from the one person who was my same.

I am still learning about love. I thought I understood it—not just mother love but the love for one's parents, for one's husband, and for one's *laotong.* I've experienced the other types of love—pity love, respectful love, and gratitude love. But looking at our secret fan with its messages written between Snow Flower and me over many years, I see that I didn't value the most important love—deep-heart love.

These last years I have copied down many autobiographies for women who never learned *nu shu.* I have listened to every sadness and complaint, every injustice and tragedy. I have chronicled the miserable lives of the poorly fated. I have heard it all and written it all down. But if I know much about women's stories, then I know almost nothing about men's, except that they usually involve a farmer fighting against the elements, a soldier in battle, or a lone man on an interior quest. Looking at my own life, I see it draws from the stories of women and men. I am a lowly woman with the usual complaints, but inside I also waged something like a man's battle between my true nature and the person I should have been.

I am writing these pages for those who reside in the afterworld. Peony, my grandson's wife, has promised to make sure that they are burned at my death, so my story will reach them before my spirit does. Let my words explain my actions to my ancestors, to my husband, but most of all to Snow Flower, before I greet them again.

Daughter Days

Milk Years

MY NAME IS LILY. I CAME INTO THIS WORLD ON THE FIFTH DAY of the six month of the third year of Emperor Daoguang's reign. Puwei, my home village, is in Yongming County, the county of Everlasting Brightness. Most people who live here are descended from the Yao ethnic tribe. From the storytellers who visited Puwei when I was a girl, I learned that the Yao first arrived in this area twelve hundred years ago during the Tang dynasty, but most families came a century later, when they fled the Mongol armies who invaded the north. Although the people of our region have never been rich, we have rarely been so poor that women had to work in the fields.

We were members of the Yi family line, one of the original Yao clans and the most common in the district. My father and uncle leased seven *mou* of land from a rich landowner who lived in the far west of the province. They cultivated that land with rice, cotton, taro, and kitchen crops. My family home was typical in the sense that it had two stories and faced south. A room upstairs was designated for women's gathering and for unmarried girls to sleep. Rooms for each family unit and a special room for our animals flanked the downstairs main room, where baskets filled with eggs or oranges and strings of drying chilies hung from the central beam to keep them safe from mice, chickens, or a roaming pig. We had a table and stools against one wall. A hearth where Mama and Aunt did the cooking occupied a corner on the opposite wall. We did not have windows in our main room, so we kept open the door to the alley outside our house for light and air in the warm months. The rest of our rooms were small, our floor was hard-packed earth, and, as I said, our animals lived with us.

I've never thought much about whether I was happy or if I had fun as a child. I was a so-so girl who lived with a so-so family in a so-so village. I didn't know that there might be another way to live, and I didn't worry about it either. But I remember the day I began to notice and think about what was around me. I had just turned five and felt as though I had crossed a big threshold. I woke up before dawn with something like a tickle in my brain. That bit of irritation made me alert to everything I saw and experienced that day.

I lay between Elder Sister and Third Sister. I glanced across the room to my cousin's bed. Beautiful Moon, who was my age, hadn't woken up yet, so I stayed still, waiting for my sisters to stir. I faced Elder Sister, who was four years older than I. Although we slept in the same bed, I didn't get to know her well until I had my feet bound and joined the women's chamber myself. I was glad I wasn't looking in Third Sister's direction. I always told myself that since she was a year younger she was too insignificant to think about. I don't think my sisters adored me either, but the indifference we showed one another was just a face we put on to mask our true desires. We each wanted Mama to notice us. We each vied for Baba's attention. We each hoped we would spend time every day with Elder Brother, since as the first son he was the most precious person in our family. I did not feel that kind of jealousy with Beautiful Moon. We were good friends and happy that our lives would be linked together until we both married out.

The four of us looked very similar. We each had black hair that was cut short, we were very thin, and we were close in height. Otherwise, our distinguishing features were few. Elder Sister had a mole above her lip. Third Sister's hair was always tied up in little tufts, because she did not like Mama to comb it. Beautiful Moon had a pretty round face, while my legs were sturdy from running and my arms strong from carrying my baby brother.

"Girls!" Mama called up the stairs to us.

That was enough to wake up the others and get us all out of bed. Elder Sister hurriedly got dressed and went downstairs. Beautiful Moon and I were slower, because we had to dress not only ourselves but Third Sister as well. Then together we went downstairs, where Aunt swept the floor,

Uncle sang a morning song, Mama—with Second Brother swaddled on her back—poured the last of the water into the teapot to heat, and Elder Sister chopped scallions for the rice porridge we call *congee*. My sister gave me a tranquil look that I took to mean that she had already earned the approval of my family this morning and was safe for the rest of the day. I tucked away my resentment, not understanding that what I saw as her self-satisfaction was something closer to the cheerless resignation that would settle on my sister after she married out.

"Beautiful Moon! Lily! Come here! Come here!"

My aunt greeted us this way each and every morning. We ran to her. Aunt kissed Beautiful Moon and patted my bottom affectionately. Then Uncle swooped in, swept up Beautiful Moon in his arms, and kissed her. After he set her back down, he winked at me and pinched my cheek.

You know the old saying about beautiful people marrying beautiful people and talented people marrying talented people? That morning I concluded that Uncle and Aunt were two ugly people and therefore perfectly matched. Uncle, my father's younger brother, had bowlegs, a bald head, and a full shiny face. Aunt was plump, and her teeth were like jagged stones protruding from a karst cave. Her bound feet were not very small, maybe fourteen centimeters long, twice the size of what mine eventually became. I'd heard wicked tongues in our village say that this was the reason Aunt—who was of healthy stock, with wide hips—could not carry a son to term. I'd never heard these kinds of reproaches in our home, not even from Uncle. To me, they had an ideal marriage; he was an affectionate rat and she was a dutiful ox. Every day they provided happiness around the hearth.

My mother had yet to acknowledge that I was in the room. This is how it had been for as long as I could remember, but on that day I perceived and felt her disregard. Melancholy sank into me, whisking away the joy I had just felt with Aunt and Uncle, stunning me with its power. Then, just as quickly, the feeling disappeared, because Elder Brother, who was six years older than I was, called me to help him with his morning chores. Having been born in the year of the horse, it is in my nature to love the outdoors, but even more important I got to have Elder Brother completely to myself. I knew I was lucky and that my sisters would hold this against me, but I didn't care. When he talked to me or smiled at me I didn't feel invisible.

We ran outside. Elder Brother hauled water up from the well and filled buckets for us to carry. We took them back to the house and set out again to gather firewood. We made a pile, then Elder Brother loaded my arms with the smaller sticks. He scooped up the rest and we headed home. When we got there, I handed the sticks to Mama, hoping for her praise. After all, it's not so easy for a little girl to lug a bucket of water or carry firewood. But Mama didn't say anything.

Even now, after all these years, it is difficult for me to think about Mama and what I realized on that day. I saw so clearly that I was inconsequential to her. I was a third child, a second worthless girl, too little to waste time on until it looked like I would survive my milk years. She looked at me the way all mothers look at their daughters—as a temporary visitor who was another mouth to feed and a body to dress until I went to my husband's home. I was five, old enough to know I didn't deserve her attention, but suddenly I craved it. I longed for her to look at me and talk to me the way she did with Elder Brother. But even in that moment of my first truly deep desire, I was smart enough to know that Mama wouldn't want me to interrupt her during this busy time when so often she had scolded me for talking too loudly or had swatted at the air around me because I got in her way. Instead, I vowed to be like Elder Sister and help as quietly and carefully as I could.

Grandmother tottered into the room. Her face looked like a dried plum, and her back bent so far forward that she and I saw eye to eye.

"Help your grandmother," Mama ordered. "See if she needs anything."

Even though I had just made a promise to myself, I hesitated. Grandmother's gums were sour and sticky in the mornings, and no one wanted to get near her. I sidled up to her, holding my breath, but she waved me away impatiently. I moved so quickly that I bumped into my father—the eleventh and most important person in our household.

He didn't reprimand me or say anything to anyone else. As far as I knew, he wouldn't speak until this day was behind him. He sat down and waited to be served. I watched Mama closely as she wordlessly poured his tea. I may have been afraid that she would notice me during her morning routine, but she was even more mindful in her dealings with my father. He rarely hit my mother and he never took a concubine, but her caution with him made us all heedful.

Aunt put bowls on the table and spooned out the *congee,* while Mama nursed the baby. After we ate, my father and my uncle set out for the fields, and my mother, aunt, grandmother, and older sister went upstairs to the women's chamber. I wanted to go with Mama and the other women in our family, but I wasn't old enough. To make matters worse, I now had to share Elder Brother with my baby brother and Third Sister when we went back outside.

I carried the baby on my back as we cut grass and foraged for roots for our pig. Third Sister followed us as best she could. She was a funny, ornery little thing. She acted spoiled, when the only ones who had a right to be spoiled were our brothers. She thought she was the most beloved in our family, although nothing showed her that this was true.

Once done with our chores, our little foursome explored the village, going up and down the alleys between the houses until we came across some other girls jumping rope. My brother stopped, took the baby, and let me jump too. Then we went home for lunch—something simple, rice and vegetable only. Afterward, Elder Brother left with the men, and the rest of us went upstairs. Mama nursed the baby again, then he and Third Sister took their afternoon naps. Even at that age I enjoyed being in the women's chamber with my grandmother, aunt, sister, cousin, and especially my mother. Mama and Grandmother wove cloth, Beautiful Moon and I made balls of yarn, Aunt sat with brush and ink, carefully writing her secret characters, while Elder Sister waited for her four sworn sisters to arrive for an afternoon visit.

Soon enough we heard the sound of four pairs of lily feet come quietly up the stairs. Elder Sister greeted each girl with a hug, and the five of them clustered together in a corner. They didn't like me intruding on their conversations, but I studied them nevertheless, knowing that I would be part of my own sworn sisterhood in another two years. The girls were all from Puwei, which meant that they could assemble often, and not just on special gathering days such as Catching Cool Breezes or the Birds Festival. The sisterhood had been formed when the girls turned seven. To cement the relationship, their fathers had each contributed twenty-five *jin* of rice, which was stored at our house. Later, when each girl married out, her portion of rice would be sold so her sworn sisters could buy gifts for her. The last bit of rice would be sold on the occasion of the last sworn sister's marriage. That would mark the end of the sisterhood, since the girls would have all married out to distant villages, where they would be too busy with their children and obeying their mothers-in-law to have time for old friendships.

Even with her friends, Elder Sister did not attempt to grab attention. She sat placidly with the other girls as they embroidered and told funny stories. When their chatter and giggles grew loud, my mother sternly hushed them, and another new thought popped into my head: Mama never did that when my grandmother's late-life sworn sisters came to visit. After her children were grown, my grandmother had been invited to join a new group of five sworn sisters in Puwei. Only two of them plus my grandmother, all widows, were still alive, and they visited at least once a week. They made each other laugh and together they shared bawdy jokes that we girls didn't understand. On those occasions, Mama was too afraid of her mother-in-law to dare ask them to stop. Or maybe she was too busy.

Mama ran out of yarn and stood up to get more. For a moment she stayed very still, staring pensively at nothing. I had a nearly uncontrollable desire to run into her arms and scream, *See me, see me, see me!* But I didn't. Mama's feet had been badly bound by her mother. Instead of golden lilies, Mama had ugly stumps. Instead of swaying when she walked, she balanced herself on a cane. If she put the cane aside, her four limbs went akimbo as she tried to maintain her balance. Mama was too unsteady on her feet for anyone ever to hug or kiss her.

"Isn't it time for Beautiful Moon and Lily to go outside?" Aunt asked, cutting into my mother's daydream. "They could help Elder Brother with his chores."

"He doesn't need their help."

"I know," Aunt admitted, "but it's a nice day—"

"No," Mama said sternly. "I don't like the girls wandering around the village when they should be working at their house learning."

But about this one thing my aunt was stubborn. She wanted us to know our alleys, to see what lay down them, to walk to the edge of our village and look out, knowing that soon enough all we would see was what we could glimpse from the lattice window of the women's chamber.

"They have only these few months," she reasoned. She left unsaid that soon our feet would be bound, our bones broken, our skin rotting. "Let them run while they can."

My mother was exhausted. She had five children, three of us five and under. She had the full responsibility of the household—cleaning, washing, and repairing, cooking all our meals, and keeping track of the household debts as best as she could. She had a higher status than Aunt, but she could not fight every day for what she believed was proper behavior.

"All right." Mama sighed in resignation. "They can go."

I grasped Beautiful Moon's hand and we jumped up and down. Aunt quickly shooed us to the door before my mother could change her mind, while Elder Sister and her sworn sisters stared after us wistfully. My cousin and I ran downstairs and outside. Late afternoon was my favorite part of the day, when the air was warm and fragrant and the cicadas hummed. We scurried down the alley until we found my brother taking the family water buffalo down to the river. He rode on the beast's broad shoulders, one leg tucked under him, the other bouncing on the animal's flanks. Beautiful Moon and I walked single file behind them through the village's maze of narrow alleys, the confusing tangle of which protected us from ghost spirits and bandits alike. We didn't see any adults—the men worked in the fields and the women stayed in their upstairs chambers behind lattice windows—but the alleys were occupied by other children and the village's animals: chickens, ducks, fat sows, and piglets squealing underfoot.

We left the village proper and rambled along a raised narrow path paved with small stones. It was wide enough for people and palanquins but too small for oxen- or pony-pulled carts. We followed the path down to the Xiao River and stopped just before the swaying bridge that crossed it. Beyond the bridge, the world opened before us with vast stretches of cultivated land. The sky spread above us as blue as the color of kingfisher feathers. In the far distance, we saw other villages—places I never thought I would go in my lifetime. Then we climbed down to the riverbank where the wind rustled through the reeds. I sat on a rock, took off my shoes, and waded into the shallows. Seventy-five years have gone by, and I still remember the feel of the mud between my toes, the rush of water over my feet, the cold against my skin. Beautiful Moon and I were free in a way that we would never be again. But I remember something else very distinctly from that day. From the second I woke up, I had seen my family in new ways and they had filled me with strange emotions—melancholy, sadness, jealousy, and a sense of injustice about many things that suddenly seemed unfair. I let the water wash all that away.

That night after dinner, we sat outside, enjoying the cool evening air and watching Baba and Uncle smoke their long pipes. Everyone was tired. Mama nursed the baby a final time, trying to get him to fall asleep. She looked weary from the day's chores, which were still not completely done for her. I looped my arm over her shoulder to give her comfort.

"Too hot for that," she said, and gently pushed me away.

Baba must have seen my disappointment, because he took me on his lap. In the quiet darkness, I was precious to him. For that moment, I was like a pearl in his hand.

Footbinding

THE PREPARATION FOR MY FOOTBINDING TOOK MUCH LONGER than anyone expected. In cities, girls who come from the gentry class have their feet bound as early as age three. In some provinces far from ours, girls bind their feet only temporarily, so they will look more attractive to their future husbands. Those girls might be as old as thirteen. Their bones are not broken, their bindings are always loose, and, once married, their feet are set free again so they can work in the fields alongside their husbands. The poorest girls don't have their feet bound at all. We know how they end up. They are either sold as servants or they become "little daughters-in-law"—big-footed girls from unfortunate families who are given to other families to raise until they are old enough to bear children. But in our so-so county, girls from families like mine begin their footbinding at age six and it is considered done two years later.

Even while I was out running with my brother, my mother had already begun making the long blue strips of cloth that would become my bindings. With her own hands she made my first pair of shoes, but she took even more care stitching the miniature shoes she would place on the altar of Guanyin—the goddess who hears all women's tears. Those embroidered shoes were only three and a half centimeters long and were made from a special piece of red silk that my mother had saved from her dowry. They were the first inkling I had that my mother might care for me.

When Beautiful Moon and I turned six, Mama and Aunt sent for the diviner to find an auspicious date to begin our binding. They say fall is the most propitious time to start footbinding, but only because winter is coming and cold weather helps numb the feet. Was I excited? No. I was scared. I was too young to remember the early days of Elder Sister's binding, but who in our village had not heard the screams of the Wu girl down the way?

My mother greeted Diviner Hu downstairs, poured tea, and offered him a bowl of watermelon seeds. Her courtesy was meant to bring good readings. He began with me. He considered my birth date. He weighed the possibilities. Then he said, "I need to see this child with my own eyes." This was not the usual case, and when my mother fetched me her face was etched with worry. She led me to the diviner. She held me in front of him. Her fingers clutched my shoulders, keeping me in place and frightening me at the same time, while the diviner performed his examination.

"Eyes, yes. Ears, yes. That mouth." He looked up at my mother. "This is no ordinary child."

My mother sucked in her breath through closed teeth. This was the worst announcement the diviner could have made.

"Further consultation is required," the diviner said. "I propose we confer with a matchmaker. Do you agree?"

Some might have suspected that the diviner was trying to make more money for himself and was in league with the local matchmaker, but my mother didn't hesitate for an instant. Such was my mother's fear—or conviction—that she didn't even ask my father's permission to spend the money.

"Please return as soon as you can," she said. "We will be waiting."

The diviner departed, leaving all of us confused. That night my mother said very little. In fact, she would not look at me. There were no jokes from Aunt. My grandmother retired early, but I could hear her praying. Baba and Uncle went for a long walk. Sensing the unease in the household, even my brothers were subdued.

The next day, the women rose early. This time sweet cakes were made, chrysanthemum tea brewed, and special dishes brought out of cupboards. My father stayed home from the fields so he could greet the visitors. All these extravagances showed the seriousness of the situation. Then, to make matters worse, the diviner brought with him not Madame Gao, the local matchmaker, but Madame Wang, the matchmaker from Tongkou, the best village in the county.

Let me say this: Even the local matchmaker had not been to our house yet. She was not expected to visit for another year or two, when she would serve as a go-between for Elder Brother as he searched for a wife and for Elder Sister when families were looking for brides for their sons. So when Madame Wang's palanquin stopped in front of our house, there was no rejoicing. Looking down from the women's chamber, I saw neighbors come out to gape. My father kowtowed, his forehead touching the dirt again and again. I felt sorry for him. Baba was a worrier—typical for someone born in the year of the rabbit. He was responsible for everyone in our household, but this was beyond his experience. My uncle hopped from foot to foot, while my aunt—usually so welcoming and jolly—stood frozen in place at his side. From my upstairs vantage point, the conclusion was evident on all the faces below me: Something was terribly wrong.

Once they were inside, I went quietly to the top of the stairs so I could eavesdrop. Madame Wang settled herself. The tea and treats were served. My father's voice could barely be heard as he went through the polite rituals. But Madame Wang had not come to speak trivialities with this humble family. She wanted to see me. Just as on the day before, I was called to the room. I walked downstairs and into the main room as gracefully as someone can who's only six and whose feet are still clumsy and large.

I glanced around at the elders in my family. Although there are special moments when the distance of time leaves memories in shadows, the images of their faces on that day are very clear to me. My grandmother sat staring at her folded hands. Her skin was so frail and thin that I could see a blue pulse in her temple. My father, who already had plenty of aggravations, was speechless with anxiety. My aunt and uncle stood together in the main doorway, afraid to be a part of what was about to happen and afraid to miss it too. But what I remember most is my mother's face. Of course, as a daughter I believed she was pretty, but I saw her true person for the first time that day. I had always known she had been born in the year of the monkey, but I'd never realized that its traits of deceit and cunning ran so strongly in her. Something raw lurked underneath her high cheekbones. Something conniving lay veiled behind her dark eyes. There was something . . . I still do not quite know how to describe it. I would say that something like male ambition glowed right through her skin.

I was told to stand in front of Madame Wang. I thought her woven silk jacket was beautiful, but a child has no taste, no discrimination. Today I would say it was gaudy and unbefitting a widow, but then a matchmaker is not like a regular woman. She does business with men, establishing bride prices, haggling over dowries, and serving as a go-between. Madame Wang's laugh was too loud and her words too oily. She ordered me forward, clasped me between her knees, and stared hard into my face. In that moment I changed from being invisible to being very visible.

Madame Wang was far more thorough than the diviner. She pinched my earlobes. She put her forefingers on my lower eyelids and pulled the skin down, then ordered me to look up, down, left, right. She held my cheeks in her hands, turning my face back and forth. Her hands squeezed my arms in rough pulses from my shoulders down to my wrists. Then she put her hands on my hips. I was only six! You can't tell anything about fertility yet! But she did it just the same, and no one said a word to stop her. Then she did the most amazing thing. She got out of her chair and told me to take her place. To do this would have shown terribly bad manners on my part. I looked from my mother to my father for guidance, but they stood there as dumb as stock animals. My father's face had gone gray. I could almost hear him thinking, Why didn't we just throw her in the stream when she was born?

Madame Wang had not become the most important matchmaker in the county by waiting for sheep to make decisions. She simply picked me up and sat me on the chair. Then she knelt before me and peeled off my shoes and socks. Again, utter silence. Like she had with my face, she turned my feet this way and that and then ran her thumbnail up and down my arch.

Madame Wang looked over at the diviner and nodded. She stood again and with an abrupt movement of her forefinger motioned me out of her chair. After she had once again taken her seat, the diviner cleared his throat.

"Your daughter presents us with a special circumstance," he said. "I saw something in her yesterday, and Madame Wang, who brings additional expertise, agrees. Your daughter's face is long and slender like a rice seed. Her full earlobes tell us she is generous in spirit. But most important are her feet. Her arch is very high but not yet fully developed. This means, Mother, that you should wait one more year to begin footbinding." He held up a hand to prevent anyone from interrupting him, as if they would. "Seven is not the custom in our village, I know, but I think if you look at your daughter you will see that . . ."

Diviner Hu hesitated. Grandmother pushed a bowl of tangerines in his direction, so he might have a way to gather his thoughts. He took one, peeled it, and dropped the rind on the floor. With one section poised before his mouth, he resumed.

"At age six, bones are still mostly water and therefore malleable. But your daughter is underdeveloped for her age, even for your village, which has endured difficult years. Perhaps the other girls in this household are, as well. You should not be ashamed."

Until this time I had not thought there was anything different about my family, nor had I considered that there was anything different about me.

He popped the wedge of tangerine into his mouth, chewed thoughtfully, and went on. "But your daughter has something besides smallness from famine. Her foot has a particularly high arch, which means that if the proper allowances are made now, her feet could be the most perfect produced in our county."

Some people don't believe in diviners. Some people think they make only commonsense recommendations. After all, autumn is the best time for footbinding, spring is the best time to give birth, and a pretty hill with a gentle breeze will have the best *feng shui* for a burial spot. But this diviner saw something in me, and it changed the course of my life. Still, at that moment there was no celebration. The room was eerily quiet. Something continued to be terribly amiss.

Into this silence, Madame Wang spoke. "The girl is indeed very lovely, but golden lilies are far more important in life than a pretty face. A lovely face is a gift from Heaven, but tiny feet can improve social standing. On this we can all agree. What happens beyond that is really for Father to decide." She looked directly at Baba, but the words that traveled into the air were meant for my mother. "It is not such a bad thing to make a good alliance for a daughter. A high family will bring you better connections, a better bride-price, and long-term political and economic protection. Though I appreciate the hospitality and generosity that you have shown today," she said, emphasizing the meagerness of our home with a languid movement of her hand, "fate—in the form of your daughter—has brought you an opportunity. If Mother does her job properly, this insignificant girl could marry into a family in Tongkou."

Tongkou!

"You speak of wonderful things," my father ventured warily. "But our family is modest. We cannot afford your fee."

"Old Father," Madame Wang responded smoothly, "if your daughter's feet end up as I imagine, I can rely on a generous fee being paid by the groom's family. You will also be receiving goods from them in the form of a bride-price. As you can see, you and I will both benefit from this arrangement."

My father said nothing. He never discussed what happened on the land or ever let us know his feelings, but I remembered one winter after a year of drought when we didn't have much food stored. My father went into the mountains to hunt, but even the animals had died from hunger. Baba could do nothing but come home with bitter roots, which my mother and grandmother stewed into broth. Perhaps in this moment he was remembering the shame of that year and conjuring in his mind how fine my bride-price might be and what it would do for our family.

"Beyond all of this," the matchmaker went on, "I believe your daughter might also be eligible for a *laotong* relationship."

I knew the words and what they meant. A *laotong* relationship was completely different from a sworn sisterhood. It involved two girls from different villages and lasted their entire lives, while a sworn sisterhood was made up of several girls and dissolved at marriage. Never in my short life had I met a *laotong* or considered that I might have one. As girls, my mother and aunt had sworn sisters in their home villages. Elder Sister now had sworn sisters, while grandmother had widow friends from her husband's village as late-life sworn sisters. I had assumed that in the normal course of my life I would have them as well. To have a *laotong* was very special indeed. I should have been excited, but like everyone else in the room I was aghast. This was not a subject that should be discussed in front of men. So extraordinary was the situation that my father lost himself and blurted out, "None of the women in our family has ever had a *laotong*."

"Your family has not had a lot of things—until now," Madame Wang said, as she rose out of her chair. "Discuss these matters within your household, but remember, opportunity doesn't step over your threshold every day. I will visit again."

The matchmaker and the diviner left, both with promises that they would return to check my progress. My mother and I went upstairs. As soon as we entered the women's room, she turned and looked at me with that same expression I had just seen in the main room. Then, before I could say anything, she slapped me across the face as hard as she could.

"Do you know how much trouble this will bring your father?" Mama asked. Harsh words, but I knew that slap was for good luck and to scare away bad spirits. After all, nothing guaranteed that my feet would turn out like golden lilies. It was equally possible that my mother would make a mistake with my feet as her mother had made with hers. She had done a fairly good job with Elder Sister, but anything could happen. Instead of being prized, I could totter about on ugly stumps, my arms constantly flapping to keep my balance, just like my mother.

Although my face stung, inside I was happy. That slap was the first time Mama had shown me her mother love, and I had to bite my lips to keep from smiling.

Mama did not speak to me for the rest of the day. Instead, she went back downstairs and talked with my aunt, uncle, father, and grandmother. Uncle was kindhearted, but as the second son he had no authority in our home. Aunt knew the benefits that might arise out of this situation, but as a sonless woman married to a second son, she had the lowest rank in the family. Mama also had no position, but having seen the look on her face when the matchmaker was talking, I knew what her thoughts would be. Father and Grandmother made all decisions in the household, though both could be influenced. The matchmaker's announcement, although a good omen for me, meant that my father would have to work very hard to build a dowry appropriate for a higher marriage. If he didn't comply with the matchmaker's decision, he would lose face not only in the village but also in the county.

I don't know if they agreed on my fate on that day, but in my mind nothing was ever the same. Beautiful Moon's future also changed with mine. I was a few months older, but it was decided that the two of us should have our feet bound at the same time as Third Sister's. Although I still continued to do my outdoor chores, I never again went to the river with my brother. I never again felt the coolness of rushing water against my skin. Until that day Mama had never hit me, but it turned out that this was just the first of what would become many beatings over the next few years. Worst of all, my father never again looked at me the same way. No more sitting on his lap in the evenings when he smoked his pipe. In one instant I had changed from being a worthless girl into someone who might be useful to the family.

My bindings and the special shoes my mother had made to place on the altar of Guanyin were put away, as were the bindings and shoes that had been made for Beautiful Moon. Madame Wang started to make periodic visits. Always she came in her own palanquin. Always she inspected me from head to toe. Always she questioned me about my house learning. I would not say she was kind to me in any way. I was only a means to make a profit.

DURING THE NEXT year, my education in the upstairs women's chamber began in earnest, but I already knew a lot. I knew that men rarely entered the women's chamber; it was for us alone, where we could do our work and share our thoughts. I knew I would spend almost my entire life in a room like that. I also knew the difference between *nei*—the inner realm of the home—and *wai*—the outer realm of men—lay at the very heart of Confucian society. Whether you are rich or poor, emperor or slave, the domestic sphere is for women and the outside sphere is for men. Women should not pass beyond the inner chambers in their thoughts or in their actions. I also understood that two Confucian ideals ruled our lives. The first was the Three Obediences: "When a girl, obey your father; when a wife, obey your husband; when a widow, obey your son." The second was the Four Virtues, which delineate women's behavior, speech, carriage, and occupation: "Be chaste and yielding, calm and upright in attitude; be quiet and agreeable in words; be restrained and exquisite in movement; be perfect in handiwork and embroidery." If girls do not stray from these principles, they will grow into virtuous women.

My studies now branched out to include the practical arts. I learned how to thread a needle, choose a thread color, and make my stitches small and even. This was important, as Beautiful Moon, Third Sister, and I began working on the shoes that would carry us through the two-year footbinding process. We needed shoes for day, special slippers for sleep, and several pairs of tight socks. We worked chronologically, starting with things that would fit our feet now and moving to smaller and smaller sizes.

Most important, my aunt began to teach me *nu shu*. At the time, I didn't fully understand why she took a special interest in me. I foolishly believed that if I was diligent, I would inspire Beautiful Moon to be diligent too. And if she was diligent, perhaps she would marry better than her mother had. But my aunt was actually hoping to bring the secret writing into our lives so that Beautiful Moon and I could share it forever. I also did not perceive that this caused conflict between my aunt and my mother and grandmother, both of whom were illiterate in *nu shu* just as my father and uncle were illiterate in men's writing.

Back then I had yet to see men's writing, so I had nothing to compare it with. But now I can say that men's writing is bold, with each character easily contained within a square, while our *nu shu* looks like mosquito legs or bird prints in dust. Unlike men's writing, a *nu shu* character does not represent a specific word. Rather, our characters are phonetic in nature. As a result, one character can represent every spoken word with that same sound. So while a character might make a sound that creates the words for "pare," "pair," or "pear," context usually makes the meaning clear. Still, much care has to be taken to make sure we do not misinterpret meaning. Many women—like my mother and grandmother—never learn the writing, but they still know some of the songs and stories, many of which resonate with a *ta dum, ta dum, ta dum* rhythm.

Aunt instructed me on the special rules that govern *nu shu*. It can be used to write letters, songs, autobiographies, lessons on womanly duties, prayers to the goddess, and, of course, popular stories. It can be written with brush and ink on paper or on a fan; it can be embroidered onto a handkerchief or woven into cloth. It can and should be sung before an audience of other women and girls, but it can also be something that is read and treasured alone. But the two most important rules are these: Men must never know that it exists, and men must not touch it in any form.

THINGS CONTINUED THIS way—with Beautiful Moon and me learning new skills every day—until my seventh birthday, when the diviner returned. This time he had to find a single date for three girls—Beautiful Moon, myself, and Third Sister, the only one of us to be the proper age—to begin our binding. He hemmed and hawed. He consulted our eight characters. But when all was said and done, he settled on the typical day for girls in our region—the twenty-fourth day of the eighth lunar month—when those who are to have their feet bound say prayers and make final offerings to the Tiny-Footed Maiden, the goddess who oversees footbinding.

Mama and Aunt resumed their pre-binding activities, making more bandages. They fed us red-bean dumplings, to help soften our bones to the consistency of a dumpling and inspire us to achieve a size for our feet that would be no larger than a dumpling. In the days leading up to our binding, many women in our village came to visit us in the upstairs chamber. Elder Sister's sworn sisters wished us luck, brought us more sweets, and congratulated us on our official entry into womanhood. Sounds of celebration filled our room. Everyone was happy, singing, laughing, talking. Now I know there were many things no one said. (No one said I could die. It wasn't until I moved to my husband's home that my mother-in-law told me that one out of ten girls died from footbinding, not only in our county but across the whole of China.)

All I knew was that footbinding would make me more marriageable and therefore bring me closer to the greatest love and greatest joy in a woman's life—a son. To that end, my goal was to achieve a pair of perfectly bound feet with seven distinct attributes: They should be small, narrow, straight, pointed, and arched, yet still fragrant and soft in texture. Of these requirements, length is most important. Seven centimeters— about the length of a thumb—is the ideal. Shape comes next. A perfect foot should be shaped like the bud of a lotus. It should be full and round at the heel, come to a point at the front, with all weight borne by the big toe alone. This means that the toes and arch of the foot must be broken and bent under to meet the heel. Finally, the cleft formed by the forefoot and heel should be deep enough to hide a large *cash* piece perpendicularly within its folds. If I could attain all that, happiness would be my reward.

On the morning of the twenty-fourth day of the eighth lunar month, we offered the Tiny-Footed Maiden glutinous rice balls, while our mothers placed the miniature shoes they had made before a small statue of Guanyin. After this, Mama and Aunt gathered together alum, astringent, scissors, special nail clippers, needles, and thread. They pulled out the long bandages they had made; each was five centimeters wide, three meters long, and lightly starched. Then all the women in the household came upstairs. Elder Sister arrived last, with a bucket of boiled water in which mulberry root, ground almonds, urine, herbs, and roots steeped.

As the eldest, I went first, and I was determined to show how brave I could be. Mama washed my feet and rubbed them with alum, to contract the tissue and limit the inevitable secretions of blood and pus. She cut my toenails as short as possible. During this time, my bandages were soaked, so that when they dried on my skin, they would tighten even more. Next, Mama took one end of a bandage, placed it on my instep, then pulled it over my four smallest toes to begin the process of rolling them underneath my foot. From here she wrapped the bandage back around my heel. Another loop around the ankle helped to secure and stabilize the first two loops. The idea was to get my toes and heel to meet, creating the cleft, but leaving my big toe to walk on. Mama repeated these steps until the entire bandage was used; Aunt and Grandmother looked over her shoulder the entire time, making sure no wrinkles saw their way into those loops. Finally, Mama sewed the end tightly shut so the bindings would not loosen and I would not be able to work my foot free.

She repeated the process on my other foot; then Aunt started on Beautiful Moon. During the binding, Third Sister said she wanted a drink of water and went downstairs. Once Beautiful Moon's feet were done, Mama called for my sister, but she didn't answer. An hour before, I would have been told to go and find her, but for the next two years I would not be allowed to walk down our stairs. Mama and Aunt searched the house and then went outside. I wanted to run to the lattice window and peek out, but already my feet ached as the pressure on my bones built and the tightness of the bindings blocked my blood's circulation. I looked over at Beautiful Moon, and her face was as white as her name implied. Twin streams of tears ran down her cheeks.

From outside, Mama's and Aunt's voices carried up to us as they called, "Third Sister, Third Sister."

Grandmother and Elder Sister moved to the lattice window and looked out.

"Aiya," Grandmother muttered.

Elder Sister glanced back at us. "Mama and Aunt are in the neighbors' house. Can you hear Third Sister squealing?"

Beautiful Moon and I shook our heads no.

"Mama's dragging Third Sister down the alley," Elder Sister reported.

Now we heard Third Sister yell, "No, I won't go, I won't do it!"

Mama scolded her loudly. "You're a worthless nothing. You're an embarrassment to our ancestors." These were ugly words but not uncommon; they were heard almost every day in our village.

Third Sister was pushed into the room, but as soon as she fell to the floor she clambered to her feet, ran to a corner, and cowered there.

"This will happen. You have no choice," Mama declared, as Third Sister's eyes darted frantically around the room, looking for a place to hide. She was trapped and nothing could stop the inevitable. Mama and Aunt advanced on her. She made one final effort to scramble under their outstretched arms, but Elder Sister grabbed her. Third Sister was only six years old, but she struggled and fought as hard as she could. Elder Sister, Aunt, and Grandmother held her down, while Mama hurriedly applied the bandages. The whole while, Third Sister screamed. A few times an arm broke free, only to be restricted again. For one second, Mama loosened her grip on Third Sister's foot, and soon that entire leg flailed, the long bandage twirling through the air like an acrobat's ribbon. Beautiful Moon and I were horrified. This was not the way someone in our family should act. But all we could do was sit and stare, because by now growing daggers of pain were shooting from our feet up our legs. Finally, Mama finished her task. She threw Third Sister's wrapped foot to the floor, stood, looked down at her youngest daughter with disgust, and spat out a single word: "Worthless!"

Now I will write about the next few minutes and weeks, the length of which in a lifetime as long as mine should be insignificant but to me were an eternity.

Mama looked at me first, because I was the eldest. "Get up!"

The idea was beyond my comprehension. My feet were throbbing. Just a few minutes ago I had been so sure of my courage. Now I did my best to hold back my tears and failed.

Aunt tapped Beautiful Moon's shoulder. "Stand up and walk."

Third Sister still wailed on the floor.

Mama yanked me out of the chair. The word *pain* does not begin to describe the feeling. My toes were locked under my feet so that my body weight fell entirely on the top of those appendages. I tried to balance backward on my heels. When Mama saw this, she hit me.

"Walk!"

I did the best I could. As I shuffled toward the window, Mama reached down and pulled Third Sister to her feet, dragged her to Elder Sister, and said, "Take her back and forth across the room ten times." Hearing this, I understood what was in store for me, and it was nearly unfathomable. Seeing what was happening and being the lowest-ranked person in the household, my aunt roughly took her daughter's hand and pulled her up and out of the chair. Tears coursed down my face as Mama led me back and forth across the women's chamber. I heard myself whimpering. Third Sister kept hollering and trying to wrestle away from Elder Sister. Grandmother, whose duty as the most important woman in our household was merely to oversee these activities, took Third Sister's other arm. Flanked by two people much stronger than she, Third Sister's physical body had to obey, but this did not mean that her verbal complaints lessened in any way. Only Beautiful Moon buried her feelings, showing that she was a good daughter, even if she too was lowly in our household.

After our ten round-trips, Mama, Aunt, and Grandmother left us alone. We three girls were nearly paralyzed from our physical torment, yet our trial had barely begun. We could not eat. Even with empty stomachs, we vomited out our agony. Finally, everyone in the household went to bed. What a reprieve it was to lie down. Even to have our feet on the same level as the rest of our bodies was a relief. But as the hours passed a new kind of suffering overtook us. Our feet burned as though they lay among the coals of the brazier. Strange mewling sounds escaped from our mouths. Poor Elder Sister had to share the room with us. She tried her best to comfort us with fairy stories and reminded us in the most gentle way possible that every girl of any standing throughout the great country of China went through what we were going through to become women, wives, and mothers of worth.

None of us slept that night, but whatever we thought we felt on the first day was twice as bad on the second. All three of us tried to rip our bindings, but only Third Sister actually freed a foot. Mama beat her on her arms and legs, rewrapped the foot, and made her walk an extra ten rounds across the room as punishment. Over and over, Mama shook her roughly and demanded, "Do you want to become a little daughter-in-law? It's not too late. That future can be yours."

Our whole lives we had heard this threat, but none of us had ever *seen* a little daughter-in-law. Puwei was too poor for people to take in an unwanted, stubborn, big-footed girl, but we hadn't seen a fox spirit either and we believed fully in those. So Mama threatened and Third Sister temporarily surrendered.

On the fourth day, we soaked our bandaged feet in a bucket of hot water. The bindings were then removed, and Mama and Aunt checked our toenails, shaved calluses, scrubbed away dead skin, dabbed on more alum and perfume to disguise the odor of our putrefying flesh, and wrapped new clean bindings, even tighter this time. Every day the same. Every fourth day the same. Every two weeks a new pair of shoes, each pair smaller. The neighbor women visited, bringing us red-bean dumplings, in hopes that our bones would soften faster, or dried chili peppers, in hopes that our feet would adopt that slim and pointed shape. Elder Sister's sworn sisters arrived with little gifts that had helped them during their footbinding. "Bite the end of my calligraphy brush. The tip is thin and delicate. This will help your feet to become thin and delicate too." Or, "Eat these water chestnuts. They will tell your flesh to think small."

The women's chamber turned into a room of discipline. Instead of doing our usual chores, we walked back and forth across the room. Every day Mama and Aunt added more rounds. Every day Grandmother was enlisted to help. When she tired, she rested on one of the beds and directed our activities from there. When it got colder, she pulled extra quilts over her body. As the days grew shorter and darker, her words got shorter and darker too, until she rarely spoke but just stared at Third Sister, willing her with her eyes to keep up with her rounds.

For us, the pain didn't lessen. How could it? But we learned the most important lesson for all women: that we must obey for our own good. Even in those early weeks, a picture began to form of what the three of us would be like as women. Beautiful Moon would be stoic and beautiful in all circumstances. Third Sister would be a complaining wife, bitter about her lot, ungracious about the gifts that were given to her. As for me—the so-called special one—I accepted my fate without argument.

One day, as I made one of my trips across the room, I heard something crack. One of my toes had broken. I thought the sound was something internal to my own body, but it was so sharp that everyone in the women's chamber heard it. My mother's eyes zeroed in on me. "Move! Progress is finally being made!" Walking, my whole body trembled. By nightfall the eight toes that needed to break had broken, but I was still made to walk. I felt my broken toes under the weight of every step I took, for they were loose in my shoes. The freshly created space where once there had been a joint was now a gelatinous infinity of torture. The freezing weather did not begin to numb the excruciating sensations that raged through my entire body. Still, Mama was not happy with my compliance. That night she told Elder Brother to bring back a reed cut from the riverbank. Over the next two days, she used this on the backs of my legs to keep me moving. On the day that my bindings were rewrapped, I soaked my feet as usual, but this time the massage to reshape the bones was beyond anything I had experienced so far. With her fingers Mama pulled my loose bones back and up against the soles of my feet. At no other time did I see Mama's mother love so clearly.

"A true lady lets no ugliness into her life," she repeated again and again, drilling the words into me. "Only through pain will you have beauty. Only through suffering will you find peace. I wrap, I bind, but you will have the reward."

Beautiful Moon's toes broke a few days later, but Third Sister's bones refused. Mama sent Elder Brother out on another errand. This time he needed to find small stones that could be wrapped against Third Sister's toes for extra pressure. I have already said she was resistant, but now her cries were even louder, if such a thing were possible. Beautiful Moon and I thought she responded this way because she wanted more attention. After all, Mama was devoting her efforts almost entirely to me. But on the days when our bindings were removed, we could see differences between our feet and Third Sister's. Yes, blood and pus seeped through our bandages, as was normal, but with Third Sister the fluids that oozed from her body had taken on a new and different smell. And while Beautiful Moon's and my skin had wilted to the pallor of the dead, Third Sister's skin shone as pink as a flower.

Madame Wang came for another visit. She inspected the work my mother had done and made a few recommendations of herbs that could be made into a tea to help the pain. I did not try that bitter brew until the days of snow set in and the bones in my mid-foot cracked apart. My mind was in a haze brought on by the combination of suffering and the herbs, when Third Sister's condition suddenly changed. Her skin burned. Her eyes glittered with water and fever insanity, and her round face waned into sharp angles. When Mama and Aunt went downstairs to prepare the mid-day meal, Elder Sister took pity on her pathetic sibling by letting her stretch out on one of the beds. Beautiful Moon and I took a break from our walking rounds. Afraid to be caught sitting, we stood at Third Sister's side. Elder Sister rubbed Third Sister's legs, trying to give her some relief. But it was the deepest part of winter and we all wore our clothes with the heaviest padding. With our help, Elder Sister pulled Third Sister's pant leg up to her knee so she could massage the calf directly. That's when we saw the brutal red streaks that rose from underneath Third Sister's bindings, snaked their way up her leg, and disappeared back under her pants. We looked at one another for a moment and then quickly examined the other leg. The same red streaks were there too.

Elder Sister went downstairs. To tell what we'd found, she had to confess her failure in her duties. We expected to hear Mama's hand strike Elder Sister's face. But no. Mama and Aunt hurried back upstairs instead. They stood at the top of the landing and surveyed the room: Third Sister staring at the ceiling with her little legs exposed, two other girls waiting meekly to be punished, and Grandmother asleep under her quilts. Aunt took one look at the scene and went to boil water.

Mama walked to the bed. She didn't have her cane and she flapped across the room like a bird with broken wings, and as a person she was about as useless to help her own daughter. As soon as Aunt returned, Mama began to unwrap the bindings. A disgusting odor infused the room. Aunt gagged. Although it was snowing, Elder Sister tore away the rice paper that covered the windows to give the stench an exit. Finally, Third Sister's feet were fully exposed. The pus was dark green and the blood had coagulated into brownish, putrid mud. Third Sister was brought to a sitting position and her unbound feet set into a steaming bowl of water. She was so far away in her mind that she didn't cry out.

All of Third Sister's screams of the past weeks took on a different meaning. Did she know on that first day that something bad might happen? Was that why she had resisted? Had Mama made some terrible mistake in her haste? Had Third Sister's blood poisoning been triggered by wrinkles in her bindings? Was she weak from bad nutrition as Madame Wang claimed I had been? What had she done in her previous life to deserve this punishment now?

Mama scrubbed at those feet, trying to remove the infection. Third Sister fainted. The water in the bucket became murky with noxious discharge. Finally Mama pulled the broken appendages from the bucket and patted them dry.

"Mother," Mama called to her mother-in-law, "you have more experience than I. Please help me."

But Grandmother didn't stir under her quilts. Mama and Aunt disagreed about what to do next.

"We should leave her feet open to the air," Mama suggested.

"You know that's the worst thing," Aunt came back. "Many of her bones have already broken. If you don't bind them, they will never heal properly. She'll be crippled. Unmarriageable."

"I would rather keep her on this earth unmarried than lose her forever."

"Then she would have no purpose and no value," Aunt reasoned. "Your mother love tells you this is no future."

The whole time they argued, Third Sister didn't move. Alum was spread over her skin and her feet were rebound. The next day, the snow still fell and she was worse. Though we were not rich, Baba went out into the storm and brought back the village doctor, who looked at Third Sister and shook his head. It was the first time I saw that gesture, which means that we are powerless to stop the soul of a loved one from leaving for the spirit world. You can fight it, but once death has grasped hold, nothing can be done. We are meek in the face of the afterworld's desires. The doctor offered to make a poultice and prepare herbs for a tea, but he was a good and honest man. He understood our situation.

"I can do these things for your little girl," he confided to Baba, "but they will be money spent on a no-use cause."

But the bad news of that day was not yet done. While we kowtowed to the doctor, he looked round the room and saw Grandmother under her quilts. He moved to her, touched her forehead, and listened to the secret pulses that measured her *chi*. He looked up at my father. "Your honored mother is very sick. Why did you not mention this before?"

How could Baba answer this and save face? He was a good son, but he was also a man, and this business fell within the inner realm. Still, Grandmother's welfare was his most important filial duty. While he was downstairs smoking his pipe with his brother and waiting for winter to end, upstairs two people had fallen under the spell of ghost spirits.

Again, our whole family set to questioning. Was too much time spent on worthless girls that the one woman of value and esteem in our home was allowed to weaken? Had all that walking back and forth across the room with Third Sister stolen Grandmother's storehouse of steps? Had Grandmother—tired of hearing Third Sister's screams—closed down her *chi* to shut out the irksome racket? Had the ghost spirits who'd come to prey on Third Sister been tempted by the possibility of another victim?

After so much noise, and after all the attention that had been paid in recent weeks to Third Sister, all focus now shifted to Grandmother. My father and uncle left her side only to smoke, eat, or relieve themselves. Aunt assumed all the household duties, making meals for everyone, washing, and caring for all of us. I never saw Mama sleep. As the first daughter-in-law, she had two main purposes in life: to provide sons to carry on the family and to care for her husband's mother. She should have watched Grandmother's health more assiduously. Instead, she had allowed man-hope to enter her mind by shifting her attention to me and my good-luck future. Now, with the fierce determination born of her earlier neglectfulness, she performed all the prescribed rituals, preparing special offerings to the gods and to our ancestors, praying and chanting, even making soup from her own blood to rebuild Grandmother's life force.

Since everyone was occupied with Grandmother, Beautiful Moon and I were assigned to watch over Third Sister. We were only seven and did not know the words or actions to comfort her. Her torment was great, but it was not the worst I would see in my lifetime. She died four days later, enduring more suffering and pain than was fair for such a short life. Grandmother died one day after that. No one saw her suffer. She just curled up smaller and smaller like a caterpillar under an autumnal blanket of leaves.

THE GROUND WAS too hard for burial to take place. Grandmother's two remaining sworn sisters attended to her, sang mourning songs, wrapped her body in muslin, and dressed her for life in the afterworld. She was an old woman, who had lived a long life, so her eternity clothes had many layers. Third Sister was only six. She did not have a lifetime of clothing to keep her warm or many friends to meet her in the afterworld. She had her summer outfit and her winter outfit, and even these were things that Elder Sister and I had worn first. Grandmother and Third Sister spent the rest of winter under a shroud of snow.

I would say that between the time of Grandmother's and Third Sister's deaths and their burials much changed in the women's chamber. Oh, we still did our rounds. We still bathed our feet every four days and changed into smaller shoes every two weeks. But now Mama and Aunt watched over us with great vigilance. And we were heedful too, never resisting or complaining. When it came time for bathing our feet, our eyes were as riveted to the pus and blood as Mama's and Aunt's. Each night after we girls were finally left alone, and every morning before our routine began again, Elder Sister checked our legs to make sure we were not growing serious infections.

I often think back on those first few months of our footbinding. I remember how Mama, Aunt, Grandmother, and even Elder Sister recited certain phrases to encourage us. One of these was "Marry a chicken, stay with a chicken; marry a rooster, stay with a rooster." Like so much back then, I heard the words but didn't understand the meaning. Foot size would determine how marriageable I was. My small feet would be offered as proof to my prospective in-laws of my personal discipline and my ability to endure the pain of childbirth, as well as whatever misfortunes might lie ahead. My small feet would show the world my obedience to my natal family, particularly to my mother, which would also make a good impression on my future mother-in-law. The shoes I embroidered would symbolize to my future in-laws my abilities at embroidery and thus other house learning. And, though I knew nothing of this at the time, my feet would be something that would hold my husband's fascination during the most private and intimate moments between a man and a woman. His desire to see them and hold them in his hands never diminished during our lives together, not even after I had five children, not even after the rest of my body was no longer an enticement to do bed business.

The Fan

SIX MONTHS PASSED SINCE OUR FOOTBINDING, TWO MONTHS since Grandmother and Third Sister died. The snow melted, the earth softened, and Grandmother and Third Sister were prepared for burial. There are three events in Yao lives—no, *all* Chinese lives—on which the most money is spent: birth, marriage, and death. We all wish to be born well and marry well; we all wish to die well and be buried well. But fate and practical circumstance influence these three events like no others. Grandmother was the matriarch and had led an exemplary life; Third Sister had accomplished nothing. Baba and Uncle gathered together what money they had and paid a coffin maker in Shangjiangxu to construct a good coffin for Grandmother. Baba and Uncle made a small box for Third Sister. Grandmother's sworn sisters came again, and at last we held the funeral.

Once again, I saw how poor we were. If we had more money, perhaps Baba would have built a widow arch to commemorate Grandmother's life. Perhaps he would have used the diviner to find a propitious spot with the best *feng shui* elements for her burial or hired a palanquin to transport his daughter and niece, who still could not walk very far, to the grave site. These things were not possible. Mama carried me on her back, while Aunt carried Beautiful Moon. Our simple procession went to a place not far from the house, yet still on our leased land. Baba and Uncle kowtowed three times in succession, again and again. Mama lay on the burial mound and begged forgiveness. We burned paper money, but no gifts other than candy were given to the mourners who came.

Although Grandmother could not read *nu shu,* she still had the third-day wedding books that had been given to her at her marriage so many years before. These, along with a few other treasures, were gathered together by her two late-life sworn sisters and burned at her grave so the words would accompany her to the afterworld. They chanted together: "We hope you find our other sworn sisters. The three of you will be happy. Don't forget us. The fibers between us are connected even if the lotus root is cut. Such is the strength and longevity of our relationship." Nothing was said about Third Sister. Not even Elder Brother had any messages to give. Since she had no writing of her own, Mama, Aunt, and Elder Sister wrote messages in *nu shu* to introduce her to our ancestors, and then we burned them after the men left.

Though we were still at the beginning of our three-year mourning period for Grandmother, life continued. The most agonizing part of my footbinding was behind me. My mother didn't have to beat me so much, and the pain from the bindings had lessened. The best thing for Beautiful Moon and me to do now was sit and let our feet bond into their new shape. In the early morning hours, the two of us—under Elder Sister's supervision—practiced new stitches. In the late morning, Mama taught me how to spin cotton; in the early afternoon, we switched to weaving. Beautiful Moon and her mother did the same lessons only in reverse. Late afternoons were devoted to the study of *nu shu,* with Aunt teaching us simple words with patience and great humor.

Without having to oversee Third Sister's binding, Elder Sister, now eleven, went back to her studies of the womanly arts. Madame Gao, the local matchmaker, came regularly to negotiate Contracting a Kin, the first of the five stages that would make up the wedding process for both Elder Brother and Elder Sister. A girl from a family much like ours had been found in Madame Gao's natal village of Gaojia to marry Elder Brother. This was a good thing for the potential daughter-in-law, because Madame Gao did so much business between the two villages that *nu shu* letters could regularly be sent back and forth. Beyond this, Aunt had married out from Gaojia. Now she would be able to communicate with her family more easily. She was so gleeful that for days everyone could see through her smile and into the great cave of her mouth with all its jagged teeth.

Elder Sister, acknowledged by all who met her to be quiet and pretty, was to marry out to a family better than ours that lived in faraway Getan Village. We were sad that eventually we would not see her as often as we would like, but we would have her company for another six years before the actual marriage, then another two or three years after that before she left us for good. In our county, as is well known, we follow the custom of *buluo fujia,* not falling permanently into our husbands' homes until we become pregnant.

Madame Gao was not like Madame Wang in any way. The word to describe her is coarse. Where Madame Wang wore silk, Madame Gao dressed in homespun cotton. Where Madame Wang's words were as slick as goose fat, Madame Gao's sentiments were as abrasive as the barks of a village dog. She would come up to the women's chamber, perch on a stool, and demand to see the feet of all of the girls in the Yi household. Of course, Elder Sister and Beautiful Moon complied. But even though my fate was already under the direction of Madame Wang, Mama said I should show my feet as well. The things Madame Gao said! "The cleft is as deep as this girl's inner folds. She will make her husband a happy man." Or, "The way her heel curves down like a sac with her forefoot pointed out just so will remind her husband of his own member. All day long that lucky man will be thinking of bed business." At the time I did not understand the meaning. Once I did, I was embarrassed that these kinds of things had been spoken in front of Mama and Aunt. But they had laughed along with the matchmaker. We three girls had joined in, but, as I said, these words and their meanings were far beyond our experience or knowledge.

That year, on the eighth day of the fourth lunar month, Elder Sister's sworn sisters met at our house for Bull Fighting Day. The five girls were already showing how well they would manage their future households by renting out the rice their families had given them to form the sisterhood and using the earnings to finance their celebrations. Each girl brought a dish from home: rice-noodle soup, beet greens with preserved egg, pig's feet in chili sauce, preserved long bean, and sweet rice cakes. A lot of cooking was done communally too, with all the girls gathering to roll dumplings, which were steamed and then dipped in soy sauce mixed with lemon juice and chili oil. They ate, giggled, and recited *nu shu* stories like "The Tale of Sangu," in which the daughter of a rich man remains loyal to her poor husband through many ups and downs until they are rewarded for their fidelity by becoming mandarins; or "The Fairy Carp," in which a fish transforms itself into a lovely young woman who then falls in love with a brilliant scholar, only to have her true form revealed.

But their favorite was "The Story of the Woman with Three Brothers." They did not know all of it and they didn't ask Mama to lead the call-and-response, although she had memorized many of the words. Instead, the sworn sisters begged Aunt to guide them through the story. Beautiful Moon and I joined their entreaties, because this well-loved true-life tale—tragic and darkly funny at the same time—was a good way for us to practice the chanting associated with our special women's writing.

One of Aunt's sworn sisters had given the story to her embroidered on a handkerchief. Aunt pulled out the piece of cloth and carefully unfolded it. Beautiful Moon and I came to sit next to her so we could follow the embroidered characters as she chanted.

"A woman once had three brothers," my aunt began. "They all had wives, but she was not married. Though she was virtuous and hardworking, her brothers would not offer a dowry. How unhappy she was! What could she do?"

My mother's voice answered. "She's so miserable, she goes to the garden and hangs herself from a tree."

Beautiful Moon, my two sisters, the sworn sisters, and I joined in for the chorus. "The eldest brother walks through the garden and pretends not to see her. The second brother walks through the garden and pretends not to see that she's dead. The third brother sees her, bursts into tears, and takes her body inside."

Across the room, Mama glanced up and caught me staring at her. She smiled, pleased perhaps that I had not missed any words.

Aunt began the story cycle again. "A woman once had three brothers. When she died, no one wanted to care for her body. Though she had been virtuous and hardworking, her brothers would not serve her. How cruel this was! What would happen?"

"She is ignored in death as in life, until her body begins to stink," Mama sang out.

Again we girls recited the well-known chorus. "The eldest brother gives one piece of cloth to cover her body. The second brother gives two pieces of cloth. The third brother wraps her in as many clothes as possible so she'll be warm in the afterworld."

"A woman once had three brothers," Aunt continued. "Now dressed for her future as a spirit, her brothers won't spend money on a coffin.

Though she was virtuous and hardworking, her brothers are stingy. How unfair this was! Would she ever find rest?"

"All alone, all alone," Mama chanted, "she plans her haunting days."

Aunt used her finger to carry us from written character to written character and we tried to follow, although we weren't fluent enough to recognize most of the characters. "The eldest brother says, 'We don't need to bury her in a box. She is fine the way she is.' The second brother says, 'We could use that old box in the shed.' The third brother says, 'This is all the money I have. I will go and buy a coffin.'"

As we came to the end, the rhythm of the story shifted. Aunt sang, "A woman once had three brothers. They have come so far, but what will happen to Sister now? Elder Brother—mean in spirit; Second Brother—cold in heart; but in Third Brother love may come through."

The sworn sisters let Beautiful Moon and me finish the tale. "Elder Brother says, 'Let's bury her here by the water buffalo road'" (meaning she would be trampled for all eternity). "Second Brother says, 'Let's bury her under the bridge'" (meaning she would wash away). "But Third Brother—good in heart, filial in all ways—says, 'We will bury her behind the house so everyone will remember her.' In the end, Sister, who had an unhappy life, found great happiness in the afterworld."

I loved this story. It was fun to chant with Mama and the others, but since my grandmother's and sister's deaths I better understood its messages. The story showed me how the value of a girl—or woman—could shift from person to person. It also offered practical instruction on how to care for a loved one after death—how a body should be handled, what constituted proper eternity garments, where someone should be buried. My family had tried their best to follow these rules, and I would too, once I became a wife and mother.

THE DAY AFTER Bull Fighting Day, Madame Wang returned. I had grown to hate her visits, because they always meant more anxiety for our household. Of course, everyone was pleased with the prospect of Elder Sister's good marriage. Of course, everyone was delighted that Elder Brother would also be married and that our home would have its first daughter-in-law. But we had also had two funerals in our family recently. If you put emotions aside, these sad and happy occasions meant the expense of two burials and two upcoming weddings. The pressure on me to make a good marriage took on added meaning. It meant our survival.

Madame Wang came upstairs to the women's chamber, politely checked Elder Sister's embroidery, and praised her for its pleasing qualities. Then she sat on a stool with her back to the lattice window. She did not look in my direction. Mama, who was just beginning to understand her new position as the highest-ranking woman in the household, waved to Aunt to bring tea. Until it came, Madame Wang spoke of the weather, of plans for upcoming temple fairs, of a shipment of goods that had arrived by river from Guilin. Once the tea was poured, Madame Wang got down to business.

"Cherished Mother," she began, "we have discussed before some of the possibilities open to your daughter. A marriage to a good family in Tongkou Village seems assured." She leaned forward and confided, "I have already had some interest there. In just a few more years I will visit you and your husband for Contracting a Kin." She pulled herself back to an upright position and cleared her throat. "But today I have come to suggest a match of a different sort. As you may recall from the first day we met, I saw in Lily the chance for her to become a *laotong*." Madame Wang waited for this to sink in before she went on. "Tongkou Village is forty-five minutes away by men's walking. Most families there are from the Lu clan. There is a potential *laotong* match for Lily in this clan. The girl's name is Snow Flower."

Mama's first question showed me and everyone else in the room not only that she had not forgotten what Madame Wang had suggested on her first visit but that she had been scheming and thinking about this possibility ever since.

"What of the eight characters?" Mama asked, the sweetness of her voice doing little to cover her determination. "I see no reason for a match unless the eight characters are in full agreement."

"Mother, I would not have come to you today unless the eight characters aligned well," Madame Wang responded evenly. "Lily and Snow Flower were born in the year of the horse, in the same month, and, if what both mothers have told me is true, on the same day and in the same hour as well. Lily and Snow Flower have the same number of brothers and sisters, and they are each the third child—"

"But—"

Madame Wang held up a hand to stop my mother from continuing. "To answer your question before you ask it: Yes, the third daughter in the Lu family is also with her ancestors. The circumstances of these tragedies do not matter, for no one likes to think of the loss of a child, not even a daughter." She stared at Mama with hard eyes, practically daring her to speak. When Mama looked away, Madame Wang went on. "Lily and Snow Flower are of identical height, of equal beauty, and, most important, their feet were bound on the same day. Snow Flower's great-grandfather was a *jinshi* scholar, so social and economic standing are not matched." Madame Wang did not have to explain that if this family had an imperial scholar of the highest grade among its ancestors, it must indeed be well connected and well off. "Snow Flower's mother does not seem to mind these discrepancies, since the two girls share so many other sames."

Mama nodded calmly, the monkey in her absorbing all this, but I wanted to fly from my chair, run down to the riverbank, and scream my excitement. I glanced at Aunt. I expected to see that big smiling cave of a mouth, but instead she had clamped it shut as she tried to hide her delight. Her whole body was a picture of stillness and well-bred decorum, except for her fingers, which swam nervously among themselves like a bowlful of baby eels. She, more than the rest of us, understood the importance of this meeting. Without being obvious, I sneaked peeks at Beautiful Moon and Elder Sister. Their eyes glittered with happiness for me. Oh, the things we would talk about tonight after the rest of the household went to sleep!

"Although I usually make this approach during the Mid-Autumn Festival when the girls are eight or nine," Madame Wang remarked, "I felt in this instance that an immediate match would be especially beneficial for your daughter. She is ideal in many ways, but her house learning could improve and she needs much refinement to be able to fit into a higher household."

"My daughter is not what she should be," Mama agreed indifferently. "She is stubborn and disobedient. I am not so sure this is a good idea. Better to be one imperfect grape among many sworn sisters than to disappoint one girl of high standing."

My joy of moments before plunged into a black chasm. Even though I knew my mother well, I was not old enough to understand that her sour words about me were part of the negotiation, just as many similar sentiments would be spoken when my father and the matchmaker sat down to discuss my marriage. Making me seem unworthy protected my parents from any complaints that either my husband's or my *laotong*'s families might have about me in the future. It might also lower any hidden costs they would have to pay the matchmaker and lessen what they would have to provide for my dowry.

The matchmaker was unfazed. "Naturally you would feel this way. I too have many of the same concerns. But enough talk for today." She paused for a moment as if deliberating, though it was quite clear to all of us that every word she spoke and every action she carried out had long been planned and practiced. She reached into her sleeve, pulled out a fan, and called me over. As she handed it to me, Madame Wang spoke over my head to my mother. "You need time to consider your daughter's fate."

I clicked open the fan and stared at the words that ran down one of the folds and at the garland of leaves that adorned the upper edge.

Mama spoke sternly to the matchmaker. "You give this to my daughter though you and I have not discussed your fee?"

Madame Wang waved away the suggestion as if it were a bad smell. "Same as with her marriage. No fee to the Yi family. The other girl's family can pay me. And if I raise your daughter's value now as a *laotong,* my bride-price payment from the groom's family will be further enriched. I am satisfied with this arrangement."

She rose and took a few steps toward the stairs. Then she turned, rested a hand on Aunt's shoulder, and announced to the room, "One more thing you should all consider. This woman has done a good job with her daughter, and I can see that Beautiful Moon and Lily are close. If we can agree to this *laotong* relationship for Lily, which will help solidify her chance of marriage into Tongkou, then I think it would be a good thing to consider looking for a match for Beautiful Moon there as well."

This possibility took us all by surprise. I forgot about decorum and turned to Beautiful Moon, who looked as excited as I felt.

Madame Wang lifted her hand and let it arch out into a crescent-moon shape. "Of course, you may have already engaged Madame Gao. I would not want to interfere with her local"—and by this she meant inferior—"business in any way."

If nothing else, this showed that my mother could not equal the bargaining expertise of Madame Wang, who now addressed Mama directly.

"I consider this a woman's decision, one of the few you can make for your daughter, and perhaps for your niece as well. Nevertheless, Father must agree too, before we can go any further. Mother, I will leave you with one final piece of advice: Use your bed time to plead your case."

While Mama and Aunt walked the matchmaker to her palanquin, Elder Sister, Beautiful Moon, and I stood in the middle of the room together, hugging and chattering excitedly. Could all these wonderful things be happening to me? Would Beautiful Moon also marry into Tongkou? Would we really be together for the rest of our lives? Elder Sister, who could have felt bitter about her own fate, devoutly wished for everything the matchmaker had proposed to come true, knowing our whole family would benefit.

We were young girls and thrilled, but we knew how to behave. Beautiful Moon and I sat back down to rest our feet.

Elder Sister tipped her head toward the fan I still held. "What does it say?"

"I can't read everything. Help me."

I opened the fan. Elder Sister and Beautiful Moon stared over my shoulder. The three of us scanned the characters, finding those we recognized: *girl, good, women, home, you, I.*

Knowing only she could help me, Aunt was the first one back upstairs. Using her finger, she pointed to each character. I memorized the words on the spot: *I understand there is a girl of good character and women's learning in your home. You and I are of the same year and the same day. Could we not be sames together?*

Before I could respond to this girl named Snow Flower, many things had to be examined and weighed by my family. Although Elder Sister, Beautiful Moon, and I had no say in anything that might happen, we spent hours in the upstairs chamber listening as Mama and Aunt discussed the possible consequences of a *laotong* match. My mother was shrewd, but Aunt came from a better family than ours and her learning was deeper. Still, being the lowest-ranked woman in our household meant that Aunt had to be careful in what she said, especially now that my mother had total control over her life.

"A *laotong* match is as significant as a good marriage," Aunt might say to begin the conversation. She would repeat many of the matchmaker's arguments, but she always came back to the one element she viewed as most important. "A *laotong* relationship is made by choice for the purpose of emotional companionship and eternal fidelity. A marriage is not made by choice and has only one purpose—to have sons."

Hearing these words about sons, Mama would try to comfort her sister-in-law. "You have Beautiful Moon. She is a good girl and makes everyone happy—".

"And she will leave me forever when she marries out. Your two sons will live with you for the rest of your life."

Every day the two of them came to this same sad place in the conversation, and every day my mother tried to steer the subject to more practical issues.

"If Lily becomes a *laotong,* she won't have sworn sisters. All the women in our family—"

—*have had them* is how Mama intended to end the sentence, but Aunt finished it another way—"can act as her sworn sisters on those occasions when they are necessary. If you feel we need more girls when it comes time for Sitting and Singing in the Upstairs Chamber before Lily's marriage, you can invite the unmarried daughters of our neighbors to assist her."

"Those girls won't know her well," Mama said.

"But her *laotong* will. By the time those two girls marry out, they will know each other better than you or I know our husbands."

Aunt paused as she always did at this point.

"Lily has an opportunity to follow a path different from the one either you or I took to end up here," she continued, after a moment. "This *laotong* relationship will give her added value and show people in Tongkou that she is worthy of a good marriage into their village. And since the bond between two old sames is forever and does not change with marriage, ties with people in Tongkou will be further cemented and your husband—and all of us—further protected. These things will help secure Lily's position in the women's quarters of her future husband's home. She won't be a woman crippled by an ugly face or ugly feet. She will be a woman with perfect golden lilies who has already proved her loyalty, faithfulness, and ability to write in our secret language well enough to have been the *laotong* of a girl from their own village."

Variations of this conversation were endless, and I listened to them every day. What I didn't get to hear was how all this was translated to my father during Mama and Baba's bed time. This match would cost my father resources—the constant exchange of gifts between the old sames and their families, the sharing of food and water during Snow Flower's visits to our house, and the expense for me to travel to Tongkou—all of which he did not have. But as Madame Wang said, it was up to Mama to convince Baba that this was a good idea. Aunt helped too by whispering in Uncle's ear, since Beautiful Moon's future was attached to mine. Anyone who says that women do not have influence in men's decisions makes a vast and stupid mistake.

Eventually, my family made the choice I wished for. The next question was how I should respond to this Snow Flower. Mama helped me add extra embroidery to a pair of shoes I had been working on to send as my first gift, but she could not begin to advise me on my written response.

Usually the return message was sent on a new fan, which would then become part of what might be considered the "wedding" gifts exchange. I had something different in mind, which broke completely with tradition. When I looked at Snow Flower's interwoven garland at the top of the fan, I thought of the old saying, "Hyacinth bean and papayas, long vines, deep roots. Palm trees inside the garden walls, with deep roots, stand a thousand years." To me this summed up what I wanted our relationship to be: deep, entwined, forever. I wanted this one fan to be the symbol of our relationship. I was only seven and a half years old, but I envisioned what this fan with all its secret messages would become.

Once I was convinced that my response would be on Snow Flower's fan, I asked Aunt to help me compose the right *nu shu* reply. For days we discussed the possibilities. If I was to be radical with my return gift, I should be as conventional as possible with my secret message. Aunt wrote out the words we agreed upon, and I practiced them until my calligraphy was passable. When I was satisfied, I ground ink on the inkstone, mixing it with water until I achieved a deep black. I took brush in hand, holding it upright between my thumb, index finger, and middle finger, and dipped it in the ink. I began by painting a tiny snow flower amid the garland of leaves at the top of the fan. For my message, I chose the fold next to Snow Flower's beautiful calligraphy. I started with a traditional opening and then proceeded with the accepted phrases for such an occasion:

> I write to you. Please listen to me. Though I am poor and improper, though I am not worthy of your family's high gate, I write today to say it was fated that we join. Your words fill my heart. We are a pair of mandarin ducks. We are a bridge over the river. People everywhere will envy our good match. Yes, my heart is true to go with you.

Naturally I did not mean *all* these sentiments. How could we conceive of deep love, friendship, and everlasting commitment when we were only seven? We had not even met, and even if we had, we didn't understand those feelings one bit. They were just words I wrote, hoping that one day they would come true.

I set the fan and the pair of bound-foot shoes I had made on a piece of cloth. With nothing now to occupy my hands, my mind worried about many things. Was I too low for Snow Flower's family? Would they look at my calligraphy and realize just how inferior I was? Would they think my break with tradition showed bad manners? Would they stop the match?

These troubling thoughts—fox spirits in the mind, my mother called them—haunted me, yet all I could do was wait, keep working in the women's chamber, and rest my feet so the bones healed properly.

When Madame Wang first saw what I had done to the fan, she pursed her lips in disapproval. Then, after a long moment, she nodded knowingly. "This is truly a perfect match. These two girls are not just sames in the eight characters, they are alike in their horse spirits as well. This will be . . . interesting." She said this last word almost as a question, which in turn made me wonder about Snow Flower. "The next step is to complete the official arrangements. I suggest that I escort the two girls to the Temple of Gupo fair in Shexia to write their contract. Mother, I will take care of transportation for both girls. Little walking will be required."

With that, Madame Wang took the four ends of the cloth, folded them over the fan and shoes, and took them away with her to give to my future *laotong*.

Snow Flower

OVER THE NEXT FEW DAYS, IT WAS HARD FOR ME TO SIT STILL and let my feet heal as I was supposed to when all I could think about was that I would soon meet Snow Flower. Even Mama and Aunt got caught up in the anticipation, making suggestions about what Snow Flower and I should write in our contract even though neither of them had ever seen one. When Madame Wang's palanquin arrived at our threshold, I was clean and dressed in country-simple clothes. Mama carried me downstairs and outside. Ten years later when I got married I would make a similar journey to a palanquin. On that occasion I was fearful of the new life that lay before me and sad to be leaving all I had known behind, but for this meeting I was giddy with nervous excitement. Would Snow Flower like me?

Madame Wang held the door to the palanquin open, Mama set me down, and I stepped into the small space. Snow Flower was far prettier than I had imagined. Her eyes were perfect almonds. Her skin was pale, showing that she had not spent as much time outdoors as I had during my milk years. A red curtain hung down next to her, and a rosy-hued light glinted in her black hair. She wore a sky-blue silk tunic embroidered with a cloud pattern. Peeking out from beneath her trousers were the shoes I had made her. She did not speak. Perhaps she was as nervous as I was. She smiled and I smiled back.

The palanquin had just one seat, so the three of us had to squeeze together. To keep the palanquin balanced, Madame Wang sat in the middle. The bearers picked us up, and soon they were trotting over the bridge that led out of Puwei. I had never been in a palanquin before. We had four bearers, who tried to run in a manner that would minimize the swaying, but—with the curtains drawn, the heat of the day, my own anxieties, and the strange rhythmic movement—my stomach felt sick. I had never been away from home either, so even if I could have looked out the window I would not have known where I was or how far I still had to travel. I had heard about the Temple of Gupo fair. Who hadn't? Women went there each year on the tenth day of the fifth month to pray for the birth of sons. It was said that thousands of people went to this fair. That idea was beyond my comprehension. When I began to hear other noises coming through the curtain—bells jingling on horse-drawn carts, the shouted voices of our bearers telling people, "Move out of the way," and the calls of street vendors beckoning customers to buy their joss sticks, candles, and other offerings that could be placed at the temple—I knew we had reached our destination.

The palanquin came to a stop and the bearers set us down with a hard thump. Madame Wang leaned over me, pushed open the door, told us to stay put, and got out. I closed my eyes, grateful not to be moving and concentrating on calming my stomach, when a voice spoke my thoughts. "I am so happy we're still again. I felt like I was going to be sick. What would you have thought of me then?"

I opened my eyes and looked at Snow Flower. Her pale skin had turned as green as I imagined mine to be, but her eyes were filled with frank inquiry. She pulled her shoulders up under her ears conspiratorially, smiled in a way that I would soon learn meant that whatever she had in mind was going to get us in trouble, patted the cushion next to her, and said, "Let's see what's happening outside."

Key to the matching of our eight characters was that we had both been born in the year of the horse. This meant that we both should long for adventure. She looked at me again, weighing the depths of my bravery, which, I must admit, were quite shallow. I took a deep breath and scooted to her side of the palanquin; she pulled back the curtain. Now I was able to put faces to the voices I'd heard, but beyond that my eyes filled with amazing images. Yao-nationality people had set up fabric stands decorated with billowing pieces of cloth, all much more colorful than anything Mama or Aunt had ever made. A troupe of musicians in flamboyant costumes passed by, on their way to an opera performance. A man walked along with a pig on a leash. It had never occurred to me that someone would bring his pig to a fair to sell. Every few seconds another palanquin veered around us, each, we assumed, holding a woman who had come to make an offering to Gupo. Many other women walked on the street—sworn sisters who'd married out to new villages and had reunited on this special day—dressed in their best skirts and wearing elaborately embroidered headdresses. Together they swayed down the street on their golden lilies. There were so many beautiful sights to absorb, all of which were heightened by an incredibly sweet smell that wafted into the palanquin, enticing my nose and calming my stomach.

"Have you been here before?" Snow Flower asked. When I shook my head no, she rattled on. "I've come with my mother several times. We always have fun. We visit the temple. Do you think we'll do that today? Probably not. That would mean too much walking, but I hope we can go to the taro stand. Mama always takes me there. Do you smell it? Old Man Zuo—he owns the stand—makes the best treat in the county." She had been here *many* times? "Here's what he does: He fries cubes of taro until they are soft on the inside but firm and crisp on the outside. Then he melts sugar in a big wok over a large fire. Have you had sugar, Lily? It is the best thing in the world. He melts it until it turns brown, then he throws the fried taro into the sugar and swirls it around until it is coated. He drops this on a plate and places it on your table, along with a bowl of cold water. You can't believe how hot the taro is with that melted sugar. It would burn a hole in your mouth if you tried to eat it like that, so you pick up a piece with your chopsticks and dip it in the water. *Crack, crack, crack!* That's the sound it makes as the sugar goes hard. When you bite into it, you get the crunch of the sugar shell, the crispiness of the fried taro, and then the final soft center. Auntie just *has* to take us, don't you agree?"

"Auntie?"

"You *talk*! I thought maybe all you could do was write beautiful words."

"Maybe I don't talk as much as you," I responded quietly, my feelings hurt. She was the great-granddaughter of an imperial scholar and far more knowledgeable than the daughter of a common farmer.

She picked up my hand. Hers was dry and hot, her *chi* burning high. "Don't worry. I don't care if you're quiet. My talking always gets me in trouble because I often don't think before I speak, while you will be an ideal wife, always choosing your words with great care."

You see? Right there on that first day we understood each other, but did that stop us from making mistakes in the future?

Madame Wang opened the door to the palanquin. "Come along, girls. Everything is arranged. Ten steps will get you to your destination. More than that, and I would break my promise to your mothers."

We stood not far from a paper goods stand decorated with red streamers, good luck couplets, red and gold double-happiness symbols, and painted images of the goddess Gupo. A table in front was piled with the most colorful items for sale. Aisles on either end allowed patrons to enter the stand, which was protected from the hubbub of the street by three long tables on the sides. In the middle of the stand, a small table was set with ink, brushes, and two straight-back chairs. Madame Wang told us to select a piece of paper for our contract. Like any child I had made small choices, like which piece of vegetable to pick from the main bowl after Baba, Uncle, Elder Brother, and every other older member of our household had already dipped their chopsticks into the dish. Now I was overwhelmed by the selection, my hands wanting to touch all the merchandise, while Snow Flower, at just seven and a half, was discriminating, showing her better learning.

Madame Wang said, "Remember, girls, I will pay for everything today. This is only one decision. You have others to make, so don't dawdle."

"Of course, Auntie," Snow Flower responded for both of us. Then she asked me, "Which do you like?"

I pointed to a large sheet of paper that by its very size seemed the most appropriate for the importance of the occasion.

Snow Flower ran her forefinger over the gold border. "The quality of the gold is poor," she said; then she held the sheet up toward the sky. "The paper is as thin and transparent as an insect wing. See how the sun shines through it?" She set it down on the table and stared into my eyes in that earnest way of hers. "We need something that will show for all time the precious nature and durability of our relationship."

I could barely comprehend her words. She spoke a slightly different dialect than I was familiar with in Puwei, but this was not the only reason for my incomprehension. I was coarse and stupid; she was refined, and already her house learning had extended beyond what my mother and even my aunt knew.

She pulled me deeper into the stand and whispered, "They always keep the better things back here." In her regular voice, she said, "Old same, how do you find this one?"

This was the first time that anyone had ever asked me to look—really *look*—at something, and I did. Even to my uneducated eye, I could see the difference between what I had chosen on the street side of the stand and this. It was smaller in size and less gaudy in its decoration.

"Test it," Snow Flower said.

I picked it up—it felt substantial in my hands—and held it up to the sunlight just as Snow Flower had done. The paper was so thick that the sun came through only as a dull red glow.

In wordless agreement we handed the paper to the merchant. Madame Wang paid for it and for us to write our contract at the center table in the stand. Snow Flower and I sat down opposite each other.

"How many girls do you think have sat in these chairs to write their contracts?" Snow Flower asked. "We must write the best contract ever." She frowned a little and asked, "What do you think it should say?"

I thought about the things my mother and aunt had suggested. "We're girls," I said, "so we should always follow the rules—"

"Yes, yes, all the usual things," Snow Flower said, a little impatiently, "but don't you want this to be about the two of us?"

I was unsure of myself, while she seemed to know so much. She'd been here before and I'd never been anywhere. She seemed to know what should be included in our contract, and I could only rely on what my aunt and mother *imagined* should be in it. Every suggestion I made came out like a question.

"We're to be *laotong* for life? We will always be true? We will do chores together in the upstairs chamber?"

Snow Flower regarded me in the same forthright way she had in the palanquin. I couldn't tell what she was thinking. Had I said the wrong thing? Had I said it in the wrong way?

A moment later she picked up a brush and dipped it in ink. Quite apart from seeing all my shortcomings today, she knew from our fan that my calligraphy was not as good as hers. But as she began to write I saw she had taken my suggestions. My sentiments and her beautiful phrasing swirled together, taking two girls and creating one common thought.

We believed that the sentiments on that piece of paper would last forever, but we could not foresee the turmoil that lay ahead. Still, I remember so many of the words. How could I not? They became the words of my heart.

We, Miss Snow Flower of Tongkou Village and Miss Lily of Puwei Village, will be true to each other. We will comfort each other with kind words. We will ease each other's hearts. We will whisper and embroider together in the women's chamber. We will practice the Three Obediences and the Four Virtues. We will follow Confucian instruction as found in *The Women's Classic* by behaving as good women. On this day, we, Miss Snow Flower and Miss Lily, have spoken true words. We swear a bond. For ten thousand *li,* we will be like two streams flowing into one river. For ten thousand years, we will be like two flowers in the same garden. Never a step apart, never a harsh word between us. We will be old sames until we die. Our hearts are glad.

Madame Wang watched us solemnly as we both signed our names in *nu shu* at the bottom. "I am happy with this *laotong* match," she announced. "Like a marriage between a man and woman, the kind ones go with kind ones, the pretty ones go with pretty ones, and the clever ones go with clever ones. But unlike marriage, this relationship should remain exclusive. No"—and here she allowed herself a small cackle—"concubines allowed. You understand my meaning, girls? This is a joining of two hearts that cannot be torn apart by distance, disagreement, loneliness, better marriage position, or by letting other girls—and later women—come between you."

We took our ten steps back to the palanquin. For so many months, walking had been agony, but right then I felt like Yao Niang, the first tiny-footed lady. When that woman of legend danced on a golden lotus, she gave the illusion of floating on a cloud. Every step I took was cushioned by great happiness.

The bearers carried us to the center of the fair. This time when we stepped out, we were in the heart of the marketplace. On a slight rise I could see the red walls, gilt decorative carvings, and green-tile roof of the temple. Madame Wang slipped us each a piece of *cash* and told us to buy gifts to celebrate the day. If I had never had the opportunity to make a choice for myself, I certainly had never been given the responsibility of spending money. In one hand I held the coin; in the other I held Snow Flower's hand. I tried to think of what this girl beside me could want, but with so many wonderful things around me my mind dulled with the possibilities.

Thankfully Snow Flower took charge again. "I know just the thing!" she squealed. She took a couple of quick steps as if to run and hobbled to a stop. "Sometimes I still forget my feet," she said, her face tight with pain.

My feet must have been healing slightly faster than hers, and I felt a shiver of disappointment that we wouldn't be able to explore as much as we—I—would have liked.

"We'll go slow," I said. "We don't have to see everything this time—"

"—because we'll come here every year for the rest of our lives." Snow Flower finished for me, and then she squeezed my hand.

What a sight we must have been: two old sames on their first excursion, trying to walk on remembered feet with only exhilaration to keep them from falling, and an older woman dressed in a gaudy outfit yelling at them, "Stop that bad behavior, or we'll go home right now!" Fortunately, we didn't have far to go. Snow Flower pulled me into a stall that sold embroidery necessities.

"We are two girls in our daughter days," Snow Flower said, as her eyes scanned the rainbow of threads. "Until we marry out, we will be in the women's chamber, visiting together, embroidering together, whispering together. If we buy carefully, we will have memories we can make together for many years."

In the embroidery stall we were of the same mind. We liked the same colors, but we also chose a few that we agreed did not speak to our hearts but would be good nevertheless to create the detail of a leaf or the shadow of a flower. We handed over our *cash* and went back to the palanquin with our purchases in hand. Once we were back inside, Snow Flower implored Madame Wang for one more treat. "Auntie, please take us to the taro man. Please, Auntie, please!" Assuming that Snow Flower was using this honorific to soften Madame Wang's stern demeanor, and once again emboldened by my *laotong*'s daring, I joined in. "Please, Auntie, please!" Madame Wang could not say no with a girl on either side of her pulling on a sleeve, each begging for another extravagance as only a first son might do.

She finally gave in with warnings that this sort of thing could not happen again. "I am just a poor widow, and spending my money on two useless branches will lower my esteem in the county. Do you want to send me into poverty? Do you want me to die alone?" She said all of this in her usual abrupt manner, but actually everything was ready for us when we reached the stand. A short table had been set up, with three small barrels for seats.

The proprietor brought out a live chicken and held it up. "I always select the best for you, Madame Wang," Old Man Zuo said. A few minutes later, he carried out a special pot heated by coals in a bottom compartment. Broth, ginger, scallions, and the cut-up chicken we'd seen just moments before bubbled inside the bowl. A dipping sauce of chopped ginger, garlic, scallions, and hot oil was also set on the table. A platter of fresh pea greens sautéed with whole garlic cloves rounded out the meal. We ate with relish, fishing for delectable pieces of chicken with our chopsticks, chewing happily, and spitting our bones on the ground. But as wonderful as all this was, I still kept room for the taro dish that Snow Flower had mentioned earlier. Everything she said about it was true—the way the hot sugar crackled as it hit the water, the irresistible crunch and softness in my mouth.

As I did at home, I picked up the teapot and poured tea for the three of us. When I set the pot back down, I heard Snow Flower suck in air reprovingly. I had done something wrong again, but I didn't know what. She put her hand over mine and guided it to the teapot, so that together we could turn it so the spout no longer pointed at Madame Wang.

"It's rude to aim the spout at anyone," Snow Flower said mildly.

I should have felt ashamed. Instead, I felt only admiration for my *laotong*'s upbringing.

The bearers were asleep under the palanquin's poles when we returned, but Madame Wang's clapping and her loud voice roused them and soon we were on our way home. For the return trip, Madame Wang let the two of us sit together, even though this upset the weight balance in the palanquin and made it harder for the bearers. I think back and see that we were so young—just two little girls giggling at nothing, sorting our embroidery thread, holding hands, sneaking peeks out the curtain when Madame Wang dozed off, and watching the world go past the window. So involved were we that this time neither of us felt the movement sickness brought about by the bearers jogging and jostling over the bumpy road.

This was our first trip to Shexia and the Temple of Gupo. Madame Wang took us back the next year, and we made our first offerings in the temple. She would escort us there almost every year until our daughter days were over. Once Snow Flower and I married out, we met in Shexia each year if circumstances allowed, always making offerings in the temple so that we might have sons, always visiting the thread merchant so we could continue with our projects in similar color schemes, always reliving the details of our first visit, and always stopping to have Old Man Zuo's caramelized taro at the end of the day.

We reached Puwei at dusk. On that day I had made more than just a friend outside my natal family. I had signed a contract to be old sames with another girl. I didn't want the day to end, but I knew it would as soon as we reached my house. I imagined myself being dropped off, then watching as the bearers carried Snow Flower down the alley, with just her fingers daring to sneak under the flapping curtain to wave a final goodbye before she disappeared around the corner. Then I learned my happiness was not yet over.

We stopped and I got out. Madame Wang told Snow Flower to step out too. "Goodbye, girls. I will be back in a few days to retrieve Snow Flower." She leaned out of the palanquin, pinched my old same's cheeks, and added, "Be good. Don't complain. Learn through your eyes and ears. Make your mother proud of you."

How can I explain what I felt with just the two of us standing outside my family's threshold? I was beyond happy, but I knew what waited inside. As much as I loved my family and our home, I knew Snow Flower was accustomed to something better. And she had not brought any clothes or toiletries with her.

Mama came out to greet us. She kissed me; then she put an arm around Snow Flower's shoulders and guided her over the threshold into our home. While we were gone, Mama, Aunt, and Elder Sister had worked hard to tidy the main room. All trash had been removed, hanging clothes taken down, and dishes put away. Our hard-packed dirt floor had been swept and water sprinkled on it to tamp it down and make it cooler.

Snow Flower met everyone, even Elder Brother. When dinner was served, Snow Flower dipped her chopsticks first in her cup of tea to clean them, but other than this small gesture, which showed more refinement than anyone in my family had ever seen, she did her best to hide her feelings. But already my heart knew Snow Flower too well. She was putting a smiling face on a bad situation. To my eyes, she was clearly appalled by the way we lived.

It had been a long day and we were very tired. When it came time to go upstairs I had another sinking feeling, but the women in our household had been busy there as well. The bedclothes had been aired and all the clutter associated with our usual activities organized into orderly piles. Mama pointed out a bowl of fresh water for us to wash up, along with two sets of my clothes and one of Elder Sister's—all freshly cleaned—for Snow Flower to wear while she was our guest. I let Snow Flower use the water bowl first, but she barely dabbed her fingers into it, suspicious, I think, that it was not pure enough. She held the sleeping garment I gave her away from her body with two fingers, scrutinizing it as though it might be a rotting fish instead of Elder Sister's newest piece of clothing. She looked around, saw our eyes on her, and then, without a word, stripped and put on the garment. We climbed into bed. Tonight, and for all future nights when Snow Flower came to stay, Elder Sister would sleep with Beautiful Moon.

Mama said good night to the two of us. Then she leaned down, kissed me, and whispered in my ear, "Madame Wang told us what we needed to do. Be happy, little one, be happy."

So there we were, the two of us side by side with a light cotton quilt over us. We were such little girls, but as tired as we were we couldn't stop whispering. Snow Flower asked about my family. I asked about hers. I told her how Third Sister had died. She told me that her third sister had died from a coughing disease. She asked about our village and I told her that Puwei meant Common Beauty Village in our local dialect. She explained that Tongkou meant Wood Mouth Village, and that when I visited her I would see why this was so.

Moonlight came in through the lattice window, illuminating Snow Flower's face. Elder Sister and Beautiful Moon fell asleep, but still Snow Flower and I talked. As women, we are told never to discuss our bound feet, that it is improper and unladylike, and that such conversation only inflames the passions of men. But we were girls and still in the process of our footbinding. These things were not memories, like they are for me now, but pain and suffering we were living at that time. Snow Flower talked about how she had hidden from her mother and begged her father to have mercy on her. Her father had almost given in, which would have consigned Snow Flower to the life of an old maid in her parents' home or a servant in someone else's.

"But when my father started smoking his pipe," Snow Flower explained, "he forgot his promise to me. With his mind far away, my mother and aunt took me upstairs and tied me to a chair. This is why I, like you, am a year late in my footbinding." This didn't mean—once her fate had been sealed—that she embraced it. No, she struggled against everything in her early months, even tearing off her bindings completely one time. "My mother bound my feet—and me to the chair—even tighter the next time."

"You can't fight your fate," I said. "It is predestined."

"My mother says the same thing," Snow Flower responded. "She untied me only to walk to break my bones and to let me use the chamber pot. All the time, I looked out our lattice window. I watched the birds fly by. I followed the clouds on their travels. I studied the moon as it grew larger, then shrank. So much happened outside my window that I almost forgot what was happening inside that room."

How these sentiments scared me! Snow Flower had the true independent streak of the horse sign, only her horse had wings that carried her far above the earth, while mine had a plodding nature. But a feeling in the pit of my stomach—of something naughty, of pushing against the boundaries of our preordained lives—gave me an internal thrill that in time would become a deep craving.

Snow Flower snuggled close to me so that we were face-to-face. She put her hand on my cheek and said, "I am happy we are old sames." Then she closed her eyes and fell asleep.

Lying next to her, looking at her face in the moonlight, feeling the delicate weight of her small hand on my cheek, listening to her breathing deepen, I wondered how could I make her love me the way I longed to be loved.

Love

WE WOMEN ARE EXPECTED TO LOVE OUR CHILDREN AS SOON as they leave our bodies, but who among us has not felt disappointment at the sight of a daughter or felt the dark gloom that settles upon the mind even when holding a precious son, if he does nothing but cry and makes your mother-in-law look at you as though your milk were sour? We may love our daughters with all our hearts, but we must train them through pain. We love our sons most of all, but we can never be a part of their world, the outer realm of men. We are expected to love our husbands from the day of Contracting a Kin, though we will not see their faces for another six years. We are told to love our in-laws, but we enter those families as strangers, as the lowest person in the household, just one step on the ladder above a servant. We are ordered to love and honor our husbands' ancestors, so we perform the proper duties, even if our hearts quietly call out gratitude to our natal ancestors. We love our parents because they take care of us, but we are considered worthless branches on the family tree. We drain the family resources. We are raised by one family for another. As happy as we are in our natal families, we all know that parting is inevitable. So we love our families, but we understand that this love will end in the sadness of departure. All these types of love come out of duty, respect, and gratitude. Most of them, as the women in my county know, are sources of sadness, rupture, and brutality.

But the love between a pair of old sames is something completely different. As Madame Wang said, a *laotong* relationship is made by choice. While it's true that Snow Flower and I didn't mean all the words we'd written to each other in our initial contact through the fan, when we first looked in each other's eyes in the palanquin I felt something special pass between us—like a spark to start a fire or a seed to grow rice. But a single spark is not enough to warm a room nor is a single seed enough to grow a fruitful crop. Deep love—true-heart love—must grow. Back then I didn't yet understand the burning kind of love, so instead I thought about the rice paddies I used to see on my daily walks down to the river with my brother when I still had all my milk teeth. Maybe I could make our love grow like a farmer made his crop to grow—through hard work, unwavering will, and the blessings of nature. How funny that I can remember that even now! *Waaa!* I knew so little about life, but I knew enough to think like a farmer.

So, as a girl, I prepared my earth—getting a piece of paper from Baba or asking Elder Sister for a tiny scrap of her dowry cloth—on which to plant. My seeds were the *nu shu* characters I composed. Madame Wang became my irrigation ditch. When she stopped by to see how my feet were progressing, I gave her my missive—in the form of a letter, a piece of weaving, or an embroidered handkerchief—and she delivered it to Snow Flower.

Nothing can grow without the sun—the one thing completely outside the farmer's control. I came to believe that Snow Flower filled that role. For me, sunshine came in the form of her answers to my *nu shu* letters. When I received something from Snow Flower, all of us gathered to decipher the meaning, for she already used words and images that challenged Aunt's knowledge.

I wrote little-girl things: *I am fine. How are you?* She might respond: *Two birds balance on the top branches of a tree. Together they fly into the sky.* I might write: *Today Mama taught me how to make sticky rice wrapped in taro leaf.* Snow Flower might write back: *Today I looked out my lattice window. I thought of the phoenix rising to find a companion, and then I thought of you.* I might write: *A lucky date has been chosen for Elder Sister's wedding.* She might write back: *Your sister is now in the second stage of her many marriage traditions. Happily, she will be with you for a few more years.* I might write: *I want to learn everything. You are smart. Can I be your student?* She might write back: *I am learning from you too. This is what makes us a pair of mandarin ducks nesting together.* I might write: *My meanings are not deep and my writing crude, but I wish you were here and we could whisper together at night.* Her response: *Two nightingales sing in the dark-ness.*

Her words both frightened and exhilarated me. She was clever. She had much more learning than I did. But this was not the scary part. In every message she spoke of birds, of flight, of the world away. Even back then, she flew against what was presented to her. I wanted to cling to her wings and soar, no matter how intimidated I was.

Except for the initial delivery of the fan, Snow Flower never sent any-thing to me without my sending something to her first. This did not bother me. I was coaxing her. I was watering her with my letters, and she always reacted by giving me a new shoot or a new bloom. But one obsta-cle confounded me. I wanted to see her again. She needed to invite me to her home, but an invitation did not come.

One day Madame Wang came to visit, this time bringing the fan. I did not open it in one motion. Instead I clicked open only the first three folds, revealing her first message to me, my response next to it, and now a new communication next to that:

If your family agrees, I would like to come to you in the eleventh month. We will sit together, thread our needles, chose our colors, and talk in whispers.

In the garland of leaves, she had added another delicate flower.

On the chosen day I waited by the lattice window, watching for the palanquin to come around the corner. When it stopped before our thresh-old, I wanted to run downstairs and out onto the street to greet my *laotong*. This was impossible. Mama went outside and the door to the palanquin swung open. Snow Flower stepped down onto the street. She wore the same sky-blue jacket with the cloud pattern. In time I came to think of it as her traveling tunic and believed she wore it for every visit so as not to embarrass my family for our lack.

She had brought neither food nor clothes with her, as was the custom. Madame Wang offered the same admonition she had given Snow Flower the last time. She should be good, not complain, learn through her eyes and ears, and make her mother proud. Snow Flower answered, "Yes, Aun-tie," but I could tell she wasn't listening, because she was standing on the street, staring straight up to the lattice window, searching the shadows for my face.

Mama carried Snow Flower upstairs, and from the minute her feet hit the floor of the women's chamber she couldn't stop talking. She chatted, whispered, teased, confided, consoled, admired. She was not the girl who upset me with her thoughts of flying away. She just wanted to play, have fun, giggle, and talk, talk, talk, talk, talk, talk, talk about little-girl things.

I had told her I wanted to be her student, so she started that day to teach me things from *The Women's Classic,* like never to show my teeth when I smiled or raise my voice when talking to a man. But she had written that she wanted to be my student too, so she asked me to show her how to make those sticky rice cakes. She also asked strange questions about hauling water and making pig feed. I laughed because every girl knows those things. Snow Flower swore she didn't. I decided she was teasing me. She insisted she really was ignorant. Then the others began goading me.

"Maybe *you're* the one who doesn't know how to haul water!" Elder Sister called out.

"And maybe you don't remember how to feed a pig," Aunt added. "That learning was tossed out with your old shoes."

This was too much and I got to my feet. I was so mad, I put my fists on my hip bones and glared at them, but when I saw sunny faces staring back at me my anger melted and I wanted to make them even happier.

It was quite an entertainment for everyone in the women's chamber to watch me toddle on my still-healing feet back and forth across the room, acting out pulling water from the well and hauling it back to the house or stooping for grass and mixing it with kitchen scraps. Beautiful Moon laughed so hard she said she needed to pee. Even Elder Sister, so serious with all her dowry work, tittered into her sleeve. When I looked over at Snow Flower, her eyes were gay as she clapped her hands in delight. You see, Snow Flower was like that. She could come into the women's chamber and with a few simple words make me do things I would never dream of doing on my own. She could be in that room—which I saw as a place of secrets, suffering, and mourning—and turn it into an oasis of bright times, good cheer, and silly fun.

For all of her talk about speaking in a low voice to men, she babbled to Baba and Uncle during dinner, making them laugh too. Younger Brother climbed on and off Snow Flower as if he were a monkey and her lap a nest in a tree. She had so much life in her. Everywhere she went, she entranced people and made them happy. She was better than we were—anyone could see that—but she turned that into an adventure for my family. To us, she was like a rare bird that had escaped its cage and was roaming through a courtyard of common chickens. We were amused, but so was she.

The time came for us to wash our faces before bed. I remembered the awkwardness I felt during Snow Flower's first visit. I motioned for her to go first, but she refused. If I went first, then the water would not be clean for her alone. But when Snow Flower said, "We'll wash our faces together," I knew that all my common farmer's work and willfulness had produced my desired crop. Together we bent over the basin, cupped our hands, and scooped water onto our faces. She nudged me with her elbow. I looked into the water and saw our two faces reflecting back through the ripples. Water dripped off her skin just as it dripped off mine. She giggled and splashed a little water from the basin at me. In that moment of shared water, I knew that my *laotong* loved me too.

Learning

DURING THE NEXT THREE YEARS, SNOW FLOWER VISITED EVERY couple of months. Her sky-blue tunic with the cloud pattern gave way to another outfit of lavender silk with white trim—an odd color combination for a girl so young. As soon as she entered the upstairs chamber, she changed into an outfit that my mother had made for her. In this way we were old sames on the inside and on the outside as well.

I had yet to go to Snow Flower's home village of Tongkou. I didn't question this, nor did I hear the adults in my home discuss the strangeness of the arrangement. Then one day when I was nine, I overheard Mama query Madame Wang about the situation. They were standing outside the threshold, and their conversation carried up to me at my spot by the lattice window.

"My husband says we are always feeding Snow Flower," Mama said that day in a low voice, hoping no one would hear. "And her visits cause us to haul extra water for drinking, cooking, and washing. He wants to know when Lily will visit Tongkou. This is the usual way."

"The *usual* custom is for *all* eight characters to be matched," Madame Wang reminded my mother, "but we both know that a very important one was not. Snow Flower has come to a family that is below her." Madame Wang paused, then added, "I did not hear you complain of this when I first approached you."

"Yes, but—"

"You clearly don't understand the way things are," Madame Wang continued indignantly. "I told you from the beginning that I hoped to find a match for Lily in Tongkou, but a marriage could never happen there if a potential bridegroom happened to glimpse your daughter before the wedding day. Furthermore, Snow Flower's family suffers because of the girls' social imbalance. You should be grateful that they haven't demanded an end to the *laotong* agreement. Of course it is never too late to make a change, if that is what your husband truly desires. It will only mean more awkwardness for me."

What could my mother do except say, "Madame Wang, I misspoke. Please come inside. Would you care for some tea?"

I heard Mama's shame and fear that day. She could not jeopardize any aspect of the relationship, even if it placed an added burden on our family.

Are you wondering how I felt, hearing that Snow Flower's family didn't feel I was her equal? It didn't disturb me, because I knew I didn't deserve Snow Flower's affections. I worked hard every day to make her love me as I loved her. I felt sorry—no, embarrassed—for my mother. She had lost a lot of face with Madame Wang. But the truth is, I didn't care about Baba's concerns, Mama's discomfort, Madame Wang's stubbornness, or the peculiar physical design of Snow Flower and my relationship, because even if I could have visited Tongkou without my future husband seeing me, I felt I didn't need to go there to know about my *laotong*'s life. She had already told me more about her village, her family, and her beautiful home than I could ever have learned just by seeing them. But the matter didn't end there.

Madame Wang and Madame Gao always fought over territory. As the go-between for people in Puwei, Madame Gao had negotiated a good marriage for Elder Sister and had found a suitable girl from another village for Elder Brother. She had expected to do the same for Beautiful Moon and me. But Madame Wang—with her ideas about my fate—had changed not only my course and that of Beautiful Moon but Madame Gao's as well. Those moneys would no longer go into her purse. As they say, a miserly woman always nurses revenge.

Madame Gao traveled to Tongkou to suggest her services to Snow Flower's family. It didn't take long before word of this reached Madame Wang. While the disagreement had nothing to do with us, the confrontation took place in our house when Madame Wang came to pick up Snow Flower and found Madame Gao eating pumpkin seeds and discussing the logistics of Elder Sister's Delivering the Date ceremony in the main room with Baba. Nothing was said in front of him. Neither woman was *that* unrefined. Madame Gao could have avoided the quarrel altogether if she'd simply left when her business was done. Instead, she walked upstairs, plopped down on a chair, and began bragging about her matchmaking expertise. She was like a finger poking at a boil. Finally, Madame Wang couldn't take any more.

"Only a she-dog in heat would be demented enough to come to my village and try to steal one of my little nieces," Madame Wang snapped.

"Tongkou is not *your* village, Old Auntie," Madame Gao answered smoothly. "If it is your village to master, why do you come sniffing around Puwei? By your reckoning, Lily and Beautiful Moon should be mine. But do I cry *waa-waa* like a baby over this?"

"I'll make fine matches for those girls. I will for Snow Flower too. You couldn't do better."

"Don't be so sure. You did not do so well for her elder sister. I'm better suited, given Snow Flower's circumstances."

Did I mention that Snow Flower was in the room hearing these words, being talked about as if she and her sister were bags of inferior rice being haggled over by unscrupulous merchants? She had been standing by Madame Wang, waiting to go home. In her hands she held a piece of cloth she had embroidered. She twisted it in her fingers, stretching the threads. She didn't look up, but I could see that her face and ears had turned bright red. At this point, the argument could have escalated. Instead, Madame Wang reached out a veined hand and placed it gently on the small of Snow Flower's back. Until that time I hadn't known that Madame Wang was capable of either pity or backing down.

"I do not speak to gutter women," she rasped. "Come, Snow Flower. We have a long journey home."

We would have put this episode from our minds, except that those two matchmakers were at each other's throats from then on. When Madame Gao heard that Madame Wang's palanquin had arrived in Puwei, she'd dress in her overly bright clothes, rouge her cheeks, and come nosing around our house like a—well, like a she-dog in heat.

BY THE TIME Snow Flower and I turned eleven, our feet had completely healed. Mine were strong and noticeably perfect at just seven centimeters long. Snow Flower's feet were slightly larger, while Beautiful Moon's feet were larger still but exquisitely shaped. This, along with Beautiful Moon's good house learning, had made her very marriageable. With our footbinding behind us, Madame Wang negotiated the Contracting a Kin phase for all three of our marriages. Our eight characters were matched with our future husbands' and engagement dates selected.

Just as Madame Wang predicted, the perfection of my golden lilies led me to a fortuitous betrothal. She arranged for me to be married into the best Lu family in Tongkou. My husband's uncle was a *jinshi* scholar, who had received much land from the emperor as an enfeoffment. Uncle Lu, as he was called, was childless. He lived in the capital and relied on his brother to oversee his holdings. Since my father-in-law served as headman of the village—renting tracts to farmers and collecting rents—everyone assumed my husband would become the future headman. Beautiful Moon was going to marry into a lesser Lu family nearby. Her betrothed was the son of a farmer who worked four times as many *mou* as Baba and Uncle. To us, this seemed prosperous, but it was still far, far less than what my future father-in-law controlled on his brother's behalf.

"Beautiful Moon, Lily," Madame Wang said, "you two are as close as sisters. Now you will be like my sister and me. We both married into Tongkou. Though we have both suffered misfortune, we are lucky to have spent our whole lives together." And truly, Beautiful Moon and I were grateful that we would continue to share everything, from our rice-and-salt days as wives and mothers to sitting quietly as widows.

Snow Flower had to marry out of Tongkou, but she would be close by in Jintian—Open Field Village. Madame Wang guaranteed that Beautiful Moon and I would be able to see Jintian and possibly even Snow Flower's window from our new lattice windows. We didn't hear much about the family Snow Flower was marrying into, except that her betrothed was born in the year of the rooster. This concerned us, because everyone knows this is not an ideal match, since the rooster wants to sit on the horse's back.

"Don't worry, girls," Madame Wang assured us. "The diviner has studied the elements of water, fire, metal, earth, and wood. I promise this is not a case where water and fire will have to live together. Everything will be fine," she said, and we believed her.

Our grooms' families delivered the first gifts of money, candy, and meat. Aunt and Uncle received a leg of pork, while Mama and Baba received an entire roasted pig, which was cut up and sent to our relatives in Puwei as gifts. Our parents reciprocated with gifts to the grooms' families of eggs and rice to symbolize our fertility. Then we waited for the second stage to begin, when our future in-laws would Deliver the Date for our weddings.

Imagine how happy we were. Our futures were settled. Our new families were higher than our own. We were still young enough to believe that our kind hearts would win over any difficulties with our mothers-in-law. We were busy with our handiwork. But most of all we were glad to be in each other's company.

Aunt continued to teach us *nu shu,* but we also learned from Snow Flower, who brought new characters with her every time she visited. Some she got from sneaking peeks at her brother's studies, since many *nu shu* characters are only italicized versions of men's characters, but others came from Snow Flower's mother, who was extremely well versed in our women's secret writing. We spent hours practicing them, tracing the strokes with our fingers on each other's palms. Always Aunt cautioned us to be careful with our words, since by using phonetic characters, as opposed to the pictographic characters of men's writing, our meanings could become lost or confused.

"Every word must be placed in context," she reminded us each day at the end of our lesson. "Much tragedy could result from a wrong reading." With that admonition expressed, Aunt then rewarded us with the romantic story of the local woman who invented our secret writing.

"Long ago in Song times, perhaps more than one thousand years ago," she recounted, "Emperor Song Zhezong searched through the realm for a new concubine. He traveled far, finally coming to our county, where he heard of a farmer named Hu, a man of some learning and good sense who lived in the village of Jintian—yes, Jintian, where our Snow Flower will live when she marries out. Master Hu had a son who was a scholar, a very high-ranking young man who had done well in the imperial exams, but the person who most intrigued the emperor was the farmer's eldest daughter. Her name was Yuxiu. She was not an entirely worthless branch, for her father had seen to her education. She could recite classical poetry and she had learned men's writing. She could sing and dance. Her embroidery was fine and delicate. All this convinced the emperor that she would make a fine royal concubine. He visited Master Hu, negotiated for his clever daughter, and soon enough Yuxiu was on her way to the capital. A happy ending? In some ways. Master Hu received many gifts and Yuxiu was guaranteed a courtly life of jade and silk. But, girls, I tell you that even someone as bright and cultivated as Yuxiu could not avoid that sad moment of departure from her natal family. Oh, how the tears poured down her mother's cheeks! Oh, how her sisters wept in sadness! But none of them were as sad as Yuxiu."

We'd learned this part of the story well. Yuxiu's separation from her family was just the beginning of her woes. Even with all her talents, she could not keep the emperor amused forever. He grew tired of her pretty moon face, her almond eyes, her cherry mouth, while her talents—as noteworthy as they were here in Yongming County—were insignificant compared to those of the other ladies of the court. Poor Yuxiu. She was no match for palace intrigues. The other wives and concubines had no use for the country girl. She was lonely and sad but had no way to communicate with her mother and sisters without others finding out. An incautious word from her could result in decapitation or being thrown into one of the palace wells to silence her forever.

"Day and night, Yuxiu kept her emotions to herself," Aunt went on. "The wicked women of the court and the eunuchs watched her as she quietly did her embroidery or practiced her calligraphy. All the time they made fun of her work. 'It's too sloppy,' they'd say. Or, 'Look how that country monkey tries to copy men's writing.' Every word that came from their mouths was cruel, but Yuxiu was not trying to copy men's writing. She was changing it, slanting it, feminizing it, and eventually creating entirely new characters that had little or nothing to do with men's writing. She was quietly inventing a secret code so she could write home to her mother and sisters."

Snow Flower and I had often asked how Yuxiu's mother and sisters had been able to read the secret code, and today Aunt wove her answer into the story.

"Perhaps a sympathetic eunuch slipped out a letter from Yuxiu that explained everything. Or perhaps her sisters didn't know what the note said, tossed it aside, and in its skewed state they saw and interpreted the italicized characters. Then, over time, the women of that family invented new phonetic characters, which they grew to understand from context, just as you girls are learning to do right now. But these are the kinds of particulars that men would care about." She delivered this reprimand sternly, reminding us that these questions weren't our concern. "What we should carry away from Yuxiu's life is that she found a way to share what was happening beneath her happy surface life and that her gift has been passed down through countless generations to us."

For a moment we were quiet, thinking of that lonely concubine. Aunt began to sing first and the three of us joined in, while Mama listened. It was a sad song, one reputed to have come straight from Hu Yuxiu's own mouth. Our voices poured out her sorrow:

"My writing is soaked with the tears of my heart,
An invisible rebellion that no man can see.
Let our life stories become tragic art.
Oh, Mama, oh, sisters, hear me, hear me."

The last notes floated out the lattice window and down the alley. "Remember, girls," Aunt said. "Not all men are emperors, but all girls marry out. Yuxiu invented *nu shu* for the women in our county to keep our ties to our natal families."

We picked up our needles and started embroidering. The next day, Aunt would tell us the story again.

THE YEAR SNOW Flower and I turned thirteen our learning came at us from every direction, and we were expected to help in all the usual ways. Where Snow Flower's womenfolk had excelled in teaching her the refined arts, they had failed miserably with the domestic arts, so she shadowed me as I did my chores. We rose at dawn and started the cooking fire. After Snow Flower and I washed the dishes, we mixed the pig's meal. At midday, we went outside for a few minutes to pick fresh vegetables from the kitchen garden; then we made lunch. Mama and Aunt once did all these tasks. Now they supervised us. Afternoons were spent in the women's chamber. When evening came, we helped prepare and serve dinner.

Every minute of every day involved lessons. The girls in our household—and I include Snow Flower in this—tried to be good students. Beautiful Moon was best at making thread and yarn, tasks that Snow Flower and I had no patience for. I liked to cook but was less interested in weaving, sewing, and making shoes. None of us liked to clean, but Snow Flower was terrible at it. Mama and Aunt didn't chastise her as they did my cousin and me if we didn't sweep the floor well enough or didn't get all of the dirt out of our fathers' tunics. I thought they were lenient with Snow Flower because they knew she would have servants one day and would never have to do these things herself. I looked at her failure differently. She would never learn to clean properly, because she seemed to float above and apart from the practicalities of life.

We also learned from the men in my family, though not in the way you might expect. Baba and Uncle would never teach us anything directly. That would have been improper. What I mean is that I learned about men through Snow Flower's actions and the way Baba and Uncle reacted to them. *Congee* is one of the easiest things to make—just rice, a lot of water, and stirring, stirring, stirring—so we let Snow Flower make this for breakfast. When she saw that Baba liked scallions, she made sure that an extra handful was added to his bowl. At dinner, Mama and Aunt had always silently put the plates on the table and let Baba and Uncle serve themselves; Snow Flower circled the table, keeping her head lowered and offering each dish, first to Baba, then Uncle, then Elder Brother, then Second Brother. She always stood just far enough away not to be too intimate but at the same time to exude graciousness. I learned that through her small attentions to them, they refrained from shoveling food in their mouths, spitting on the floor, or scratching their full stomachs. Instead, they smiled and talked to her.

My desire for knowledge went far beyond what I needed to know in the upstairs women's chamber, in downstairs areas, or even with the study of *nu shu*. I wanted to know about my future. Fortunately, Snow Flower loved to talk, and she talked a lot about Tongkou. By now she had traveled often between our two villages and had learned the route well. "When you go to your husband," she told me, "you will pass over the river and through many rice paddies, heading for the low hills that you can see from the edge of Puwei. Tongkou nestles in the arms of those hills. They will never falter and neither will we, at least that's what my baba says. In Tongkou, we are protected from earthquake, famine, and marauders. It is *feng shui* perfect."

Listening to Snow Flower, Tongkou grew in my imagination, but this was nothing compared to how I felt when she talked about my husband and my future in-laws. Neither Beautiful Moon nor I were present at the discussion that Madame Wang had with our fathers, but we were familiar with the basics: Everyone who lived in Tongkou was a Lu, and both families were prosperous. These things interested our fathers, but we wanted to know about our husbands, our mothers-in-law, and the other women in our upstairs chambers. Only Snow Flower could give us the answers.

"You are lucky, Lily," Snow Flower said one day. "I have seen this Lu boy. He is my cousin twice removed. His hair is the blue-black of night. He is kind to girls. He once shared a moon cake with me. He didn't have to do that." She told me that my future husband was born in the year of the tiger, a sign that is as spirited as mine, which made us perfectly suited. She told me things I would need to know to fit into the Lu family. "It is a busy household," she explained. "As the headman, Master Lu receives numerous visitors from inside and outside the village. Beyond this, many people live in the house. There are no daughters, but daughters-in-law will marry in. You will be daughter-in-law number one. Your ranking will be high to start. If you have a son first, your ranking will hold true forever. This does not mean you won't have the same sorts of problems as Yuxiu, the emperor's concubine. Even though Master Lu's wife has given him four sons, he has three concubines. He must have them, because he is the headman. They help show the people his strength."

I should have worried more about this. After all, if the father took concubines, the son probably would as well. But I was so young and innocent, this didn't cross my mind. And even if it had, I wouldn't have known the conflicts that could arise. My world was still just Mama and Baba, Aunt and Uncle—simple, simple.

Snow Flower turned to Beautiful Moon, who, as always, attended to us quietly, waiting for us to include her. Snow Flower said, "Beautiful Moon, I am happy for you. I know this Lu family very well. Your future husband, as you know, was born in the year of the boar. His characteristics are to be sturdy, gallant, and thoughtful, while your sheep nature will cause you to dote on him. This is another perfectly suited match."

"What about my mother-in-law?" Beautiful Moon inquired tentatively.

"This Madame Lu visits my mother every day. She has a kind heart, kinder than I could ever tell you."

Tears suddenly welled in Snow Flower's eyes. It was so strange that Beautiful Moon and I giggled, thinking it was some sort of joke. My *laotong* blinked quickly.

"A ghost got in my eyes!" Snow Flower exclaimed, before joining in our laughter. Then she picked up where she left off. "Beautiful Moon, you will be very content. They will love you wholeheartedly. And the best part is every day you will be able to walk to Lily's house. That's how close you will be to each other."

Snow Flower cast her eyes back to me. "Your mother-in-law is very traditional," she said. "She follows all the women's rules. She is careful in what she says. She is well attired. And when guests come, hot tea is always at the ready." Since Snow Flower had been teaching me to do these things, I was not afraid of making a mistake. "There are more servants in the house than I have had in my family," Snow Flower continued. "You will not have to cook, except to make special dishes for Lady Lu. You will not have to nurse your baby unless you want to."

When she told me these things, I thought she was crazy.

I questioned her further about my husband's father. She thought for a minute and answered, "Master Lu is generous and compassionate, but he is also smart, which is why he is the headman. Everyone respects him. Everyone will respect his son and his wife too." She looked at me with those penetrating eyes of hers and repeated, "You are so lucky."

With Snow Flower's word pictures how could I not imagine myself in Tongkou with my loving husband and perfect sons?

MY KNOWLEDGE BEGAN to extend well beyond my own village. Snow Flower and I had now gone to the Temple of Gupo in Shexia five times. Each year we climbed the stairs to the temple, placed our offerings on the altar, and lit incense. Then we walked to the marketplace, where we bought embroidery thread and paper. We always ended the day with a visit to Old Man Zou to have his burnt-sugar taro. Going to and fro, we peeked outside the palanquin when Madame Wang slept. We saw little pathways leading off the main road to other villages. We saw rivers and canals. From our bearers we learned that these waters gave our county contact with the rest of the nation. In our upstairs chamber, we saw only four walls, but the men of our county were not so isolated. If they wanted, they could travel almost anywhere by boat.

All during this time, Madame Wang and Madame Gao were in and out of our house like a pair of busy hens. What? Do you think, because our engagements were set, that those two would leave us alone? They had to watch and wait and conspire and cajole, protecting and securing their investments. Anything could go wrong. Obviously they were apprehensive about four marriages in one household and whether Baba would come through with the promised bride-price for Elder Brother's wife, adequate dowries for the three girls, and, most important, the matchmaking fees. But in my thirteenth summer, the battle between the two matchmakers suddenly escalated.

It started simply enough. We were in the upstairs chamber when Madame Gao began complaining that local families were not paying their fees in a timely manner, implying that our family was one of them.

"A peasant uprising in the hills is making things difficult for all of us," Madame Gao opined. "No products come in and no products go out. No one has *cash*. I have heard that some girls have had to give up their betrothals because their families can no longer provide dowries. Those girls will now become little daughters-in-law."

That things had become so difficult in our county was not news, but what Madame Gao said next surprised us all.

"Even Little Miss Snow Flower is not safe. It's not too late for me to look for someone more appropriate."

I was glad that Snow Flower was not here to hear this insinuation.

"You are speaking of a family that is among the best in the county," Madame Wang countered, her voice sounding not like oil but like rocks rubbing together.

"Perhaps, Old Auntie, you mean *was*. That master has seen too much gambling and too many concubines."

"He has done only what is right for his position. You, on the other hand, must be forgiven your ignorance. High station is foreign to you."

"Ha! You make me laugh. You tell lies like they are truth. The whole county knows what's happening to that family. Take trouble in the hills and combine it with bad crops and inattention, and nothing can be expected but that a weak man will take to the pipe—"

My mother rose abruptly. "Madame Gao, I am grateful for the things you have done for my children, but they *are* children and should not hear this. I will see you to the threshold, for you have others to visit, I'm sure."

Mama practically lifted Madame Gao out of her chair and nearly dragged her to the stairs. As soon as they were gone from sight, my aunt poured tea for Madame Wang, who sat very still, deep in thought, her eyes far away. Then she blinked three times, looked around the room, and called me to her. I was thirteen and still afraid of her. I had learned to call her Auntie to her face, but in my mind she was always the intimidating Madame Wang. When I neared, she yanked me close, held me between her thighs, and grabbed my arms like she did the first time we'd met.

"Never, *never* repeat what you've heard here to Snow Flower. She is an innocent girl. She does not need that woman's filth rotting her mind."

"Yes, Auntie."

She shook me once very hard. "Never!"

"I promise."

At the time I didn't understand half of what was said. Even if I had, why would I have repeated that evil gossip to Snow Flower? I loved Snow Flower. I would never hurt her by repeating Madame Gao's venomous remarks.

I will only add this: Mama must have said something to Baba, because Madame Gao was never allowed inside our house again. All further business with her was conducted on stools outside our threshold. That is how much Mama and Baba cared for Snow Flower. She was my *laotong*, but they loved her as much as they loved me.

THE TENTH MONTH of my thirteenth year arrived. Outside the lattice window the white-hot sky of summer eased into the deep blue of autumn. Only one month remained until Elder Sister's wedding. The groom's family delivered the last round of gifts. Elder Sister's sworn sisters sold one of their twenty-five *jin* of rice, and gifts were bought. The girls came to stay with us for Sitting and Singing in the Upstairs Chamber. Other village women visited to socialize, give advice, and commiserate. For twenty-eight days, we sang songs and told stories. The sworn sisters helped Elder Sister with the last of her quilts and with wrapping the shoes she'd made for the members of her new family. Together we all worked on the third-day wedding books that would be given to Elder Sister. These would introduce her to the women in her new family, and we all struggled with the right words to describe her best attributes and characteristics.

Three days before Elder Sister went to her new home, we had the Day of Sorrow and Worry. Mama sat on the fourth step to the upstairs chamber with her feet on the third step and began a lament.

"Elder Daughter, you were a pearl in my hand," she chanted. "My eyes doubly flood with tears. Twin streams pour down my face. Soon there will be an empty space."

Elder Sister, her sworn sisters, and the village women began to weep upon hearing my mother's sadness. *Ku, ku, ku.*

Aunt sang next, following the rhythm my mother had set. As always, Aunt tried to be optimistic in the midst of sorrow. "I am ugly and not so smart, but I have always tried to have a good nature. I have loved my husband and he has loved me. We are a pair of ugly and not so smart mandarin ducks. We have had much bed fun. I hope you will too."

When my turn came, I lifted my voice. "Elder Sister, my heart cries to lose you. If we had been sons, we would not be torn apart. We would always be together like Baba and Uncle, Elder Brother and Second Brother. Our family is sad. The upstairs chamber will be lonely without you."

Wanting to give her the best gift I could, I sang the knowledge I had learned from Snow Flower. "Everyone needs clothing—no matter how cool it is in summer or how warm it is in winter—so make clothes for others without being asked. Even if the table is plentiful, let your in-laws eat first. Work hard and remember three things: Be good to your in-laws and always show respect, be good to your husband and always weave for him, be good to your children and always be a model of decorum to them. If you do these things, your new family will treat you kindly. In that fine home, be calm of heart."

The sworn sisters followed me. They had loved their sworn sister. She was talented and considerate. When the last girl married out, their treasured sworn sisterhood would dissolve. They would only have memories of embroidering and weaving together. They would only have the words in their third-day wedding books to console them in the years to come. When one of them died, they vowed that the remaining sisters would come to the funeral and burn their writings so the words would travel to the afterworld with her. Even as the sisters were filled with anguish at her departure, they hoped she would be happy.

After everyone had sung and many tears had been shed, Snow Flower made a special presentation. "I will not sing for you," she said. "Instead, I will share the way that your sister and I have found to keep you with us always." From her sleeve, she pulled out our fan, whipped it open, and read the simple couplet we had written together: *"Elder Sister and good friend, quiet and kind. You are a happy memory."* Then Snow Flower pointed out the little pink flower that she had painted in our growing garland at the top of the fan to represent Elder Sister forever and ever.

The next day, everyone gathered bamboo leaves and filled buckets with water. When Elder Sister's new family arrived, we showered them with the leaves as a symbol that the love of the newlyweds would be as eternally fresh as the bamboo; then we tossed the water to tell the groom's family that she was as pure as that clear and vital liquid. Much laughing and good cheer accompanied these pranks.

More hours passed with meals and laments. The dowry was displayed and everyone commented on the quality of Elder Sister's handiwork. All through the day and night, she looked beautiful with her tear-stained eyes. The next morning, she entered the palanquin to go to her new family.

People tossed more water and called out, "Marrying a daughter is just like throwing out water!" We all walked to the edge of the village and watched as the procession crossed the bridge and left Puwei. Three days later, a delivery to Elder Sister's new village was made of glutinous rice cakes, gifts, and all our third-day wedding books, which would be read aloud in her new upstairs chamber. The day after that, as custom required, Elder Brother took the family cart, picked up Elder Sister, and brought her home. Except for conjugal visits a few times a year, she would continue to live with us until the end of her first pregnancy.

Of all the events of Elder Sister's marriage, what I remember most is when she returned after a nuptial visit to her husband's home the following spring. She was usually so peaceful—sitting on her stool in a corner, quietly working with her needle, never causing an argument, always obedient—but now she knelt on the floor with her face buried in Mama's lap, weeping her woes. Her mother-in-law was abusive, always complaining and criticizing. Her husband was unknowledgeable and rough. Her in-laws expected her to haul water and wash clothes for the entire family. See how raw her knuckles were from yesterday's chores? These people did not like to feed her and talked ill of our family for not sending enough food for her when she visited.

Beautiful Moon, Snow Flower, and I huddled together, making clucking sounds of commiseration, but inside, although we were sorry for Elder Sister, we believed this kind of thing would never happen to us. Mama smoothed Elder Sister's hair and patted her trembling form. I expected Mama to tell her not to worry, that these were just temporary problems, but no words came. With helplessness in her eyes, Mama looked to Aunt for guidance.

"I am thirty-eight years old," Aunt said, not with sympathy but with resignation. "I have lived a miserable life. My family was a good one, but my feet and my face made my destiny. Even a woman like me—who is not so smart or beautiful or is deformed or mute—will find a husband, because even a retarded man can make a son. Only a vessel is needed. My father married me to the best family he could find to take me. I cried like you do now. Fate was crueler still. I could not have sons. I was a burden to my in-laws. I wish I could have a son and a happy life. I wish my daughter would never marry out so that I would have her to hear my sorrows. But this is how it is for women. You can't avoid your fate. It is predestined."

These sentiments coming from my aunt—the one person in our household who could always be counted on to say something funny, who always talked about how happy she and Uncle were with their bed fun, who always guided us in our studies with good cheer—were a shock. Beautiful Moon reached over and squeezed my hand. Her eyes filled with tears at this truth, which had not been spoken aloud in the women's chamber until now. Never before had I thought about how hard life had been for Aunt, but now my mind raced over the past years and how she had always put a smiling face on what had clearly been a disappointing life.

Needless to say, these words did not comfort Elder Sister. She sobbed harder, putting her hands over her ears. Mama had to speak, but when she did the words that came out of her mouth slithered from the deepest part of the *yin*—negative, dark, and female.

"You married out," Mama said, in a way that seemed oddly detached. "You go to another village. Your mother-in-law is cruel. Your husband doesn't care for you. We wish you would never leave, but every daughter marries away. Everyone agrees. Everyone goes along with it. You can cry and beg to come home, we can grieve that you have gone, but you—and we—have no choice. The old saying makes this very clear: 'If a daughter doesn't marry out, she's not valuable; if fire doesn't raze the mountain, the land will not be fertile.'"

Hair-Pinning Days

Catching Cool Breezes

SNOW FLOWER AND I TURNED FIFTEEN. OUR HAIR WAS PINNED up in the style of phoenixes as symbols that we were soon to be married. We worked on our dowries in earnest. We spoke in soft voices. We walked on our lily feet in a graceful manner. We were fully literate in *nu shu,* and when we were apart we wrote each other almost daily. We bled each month. We helped around the house, sweeping, picking vegetables from the house garden, preparing meals, washing dishes and clothes, weaving, and sewing. We were considered women, but we didn't have the responsibilities of married women. We still had the freedom to visit when we wanted and spend hours in the upstairs chamber, our heads bent together as we whispered and embroidered. We loved each other in the way I had longed for as a little girl.

That year, Snow Flower came to stay with us for all of Catching Cool Breezes Festival, which takes place during the hottest time of year when the stores from the previous harvest are nearly gone and the new harvest is not yet ready. This means that married-in women, the lowest in any household, are sent back to their natal homes for days or sometimes weeks. We call it a festival, but it is really a series of days that remove unwanted eaters from their in-laws' tables.

Elder Sister had just moved into her husband's home permanently. Her first child was about to be born and there was nowhere else she could possibly be. Mama was visiting her family and had taken Second Brother with her. Aunt had also gone to her natal home, while Beautiful Moon was staying with her sworn sisters across the village. Elder Brother's wife and baby daughter were Catching Cool Breezes with her natal family. Baba, Uncle, and Elder Brother were happy to be left alone. They wanted nothing from Snow Flower and me except hot tea, tobacco, and sliced watermelon. So for three days and nights of the weeks-long Catching Cool Breezes Festival, Snow Flower and I were alone in the upstairs chamber.

On the first night, we lay side by side, wearing our bindings and sleeping slippers, our inner garments, and our outer garments. We pushed our bed under the lattice window, hoping to catch a cool breeze, but there was none, just torrid stillness. The moon would be full soon. The light beams that streamed in reflected off our sweaty faces, making us feel even hotter. The next night, which was even warmer, Snow Flower suggested we shed our outer garments. "No one is here," she said. "No one will know." It brought relief, but we longed for something cooler.

On our third night alone together, the moon was full, and the upstairs chamber was awash in a bright blue glow. When we were sure the men were sleeping, we peeled off our outer and inner garments. We wore nothing but our bindings and our sleeping slippers. We felt air move across our bodies, but it was not a cool breeze and we were still as warm as if we were fully clothed.

"This is not enough," Snow Flower said, stealing my thought right out of my mind.

She sat up and reached for our fan. Slowly she opened it and began to wave it back and forth over my body. As hot as the air was against my skin, it was still a luxurious feeling. But Snow Flower frowned. She closed the fan and set it aside. She searched my face, then let her eyes travel down my neck across my breasts to the flat of my stomach. I should have felt embarrassed by the way she stared, but she was my *laotong*, my old same. There was nothing to be ashamed of.

Looking up, I saw her bring her forefinger to her mouth. The tip of her tongue darted out. In the bright light of the full moon I saw it pink and glistening. In the most delicate gesture, she let the tip of her finger glide across that wet surface. Then she brought her finger down to my stomach. She drew a line to the left, then another in the opposite direction, followed by something like two crosses. The wetness was so cool on my skin that goose bumps rose up. I shut my eyes and let the feeling ripple through me. Then, so fast, the wetness disappeared. When I opened my eyes, Snow Flower was staring into them.

"Well?" But she didn't wait for an answer. "It's a character," she explained. "Tell me which one it is."

Suddenly I understood what she'd done. She'd written a *nu shu* character on my stomach. We had been doing something like this for years, drawing characters in the dirt with sticks or on each other's hands or backs with our fingers.

"I'll do it again," she said, "but pay attention."

She licked her finger and it was no less a fluid movement than the first time she'd done it. As soon as that wetness touched my skin, I couldn't help closing my eyes. The feeling made my body heavy and breathless. A stroke to the left to create a sliver of moon, another sliver below that and in reverse of the first, two strokes to the right to create the first cross, then another two strokes to the left to create the second. Again I kept my eyes closed until the momentary chill left my body. When I opened them, Snow Flower was looking down at me inquisitively.

"Bed," I said.

"That's right," she said, her voice low. "Close your eyes. I will write another."

This time she wrote the character much tighter and smaller in a spot just next to my right hip bone. This one I recognized immediately. It was a verb that meant *to light.*

When I said this, she brought her face down to mine and whispered in my ear, "Good."

The next character swirled across my stomach next to the opposite hip bone.

"Moonlight," I said. I opened my eyes. "The bed is lit by moonlight."

She smiled at my recognition of the opening line to the Tang dynasty poem she had taught me; then we switched positions. As she had done with me, I took time to look at her body: the slenderness of her neck, the small mounds that formed her breasts, the flat expanse of her stomach that was as inviting as a new piece of silk waiting for embroidery stitches, the twin hip bones that protruded sharply, below that a triangle identical to my own, then two slim legs tapering down until they disappeared into her red silk sleeping slippers.

You have to remember that I was not yet married. I still did not know the ways of a man and wife. Only later did I learn that nothing is more intimate for a woman than her sleeping slippers and nothing is more erotic for a man than seeing the white skin of a naked woman against the bright redness of those slippers, but on that night I can tell you that my eyes lingered on them. They were Snow Flower's summer pair. For her embroidery design she had invoked the Five Poisons—centipedes, toads, scorpions, snakes, and lizards. These were the traditional symbols used to counteract the evils brought on by summer—cholera, plague, typhoid, malaria, and typhus. Her stitches were perfect, just as her entire body was perfect.

I licked my finger and looked at the whiteness of Snow Flower's skin. When my wet finger touched her stomach just above her belly button, I felt her intake of breath. Her breasts rose, her stomach hollowed, and goose bumps shimmered across her flesh.

"I," she said. This was correct. I wrote the next character below her belly button. "Think," she said. Then I followed exactly what she had done and wrote on the flesh adjacent to her right hip bone. "Light." Now her left hip bone. "Snow." She knew the poem, so there was no mystery to the words, just the sensations of writing and reading them. I had followed every place that she had written on my body. Now I had to find a new spot. I chose that soft place where the two sides of her ribs came together above her stomach. I knew from my own body that this area was sensitive to touch, to fear, to love. Snow Flower shivered beneath my fingertip as I wrote. "Early."

Just two more words to finish the line. I knew what I wanted to do, but I hesitated. I let my fingertip float along the tip of my tongue. Then, emboldened by the heat, the moonlight, and the way her skin felt against my own, I let my wet finger write on one of her breasts. Her lips parted and her breath came out in a tiny moan. She did not speak the character and I did not demand one. But for my last character in the line, I lay on my side next to Snow Flower so I could see up close the way her skin would respond. I licked my finger, wrote the character, and watched her nipple tighten and pucker. We stayed completely still for a moment. Then, with her eyes still shut, Snow Flower whispered the complete phrase: "I think it is the light snow of an early winter morning."

She rolled on her side to face me. She put her hand tenderly on my cheek as she did every night since we had begun sleeping together all those years ago. Her face glowed in the moonlight. Then she let her hand move down along my neck over my breast down to my hip. "We have two more lines."

She sat up and I rolled onto my back. I thought I was hot these past nights, but now, naked, in the moonlight, I felt as though a fire burned inside me far hotter than anything the gods could inflict on us through the mere cycles of the seasons.

I made myself concentrate when I realized where she was planning on writing the first character. She had moved to the end of the bed and had lifted my feet onto her lap. Just on the inside of my left ankle directly above the edge of my red sleeping slipper she began to write. When she was done, she turned her attention to my right ankle. From there, she alternated from limb to limb, always staying just above the bindings. My feet—those places of so much pain and sorrow, so much pride and beauty—tingled with pleasure. We had been old sames for eight years, yet we had never been this close. The line when she was done: "Looking up, I enjoy the full moon in the night sky."

I was eager for her to experience what I had felt. I held her golden lilies in my hands, then set them to rest on my thighs. I chose the spot that had been most exquisite for me: the shallow between the ankle bone and the tendon that rose up the back of the leg. I wrote the character, which can mean *bending over, kowtowing,* or *prostrating oneself.* On her other ankle I traced the word *I.*

I set her feet down and wrote a character on her calf. After this, I moved to a spot on the inside of her left thigh just above her knee. My last two characters were high up on her thighs. I leaned down to concentrate on writing the most perfect characters possible. I blew on my strokes, knowing the sensation it would cause, and watched as the hair between her legs swayed in response.

Afterward we recited the entire poem together.

"The bed is lit by moonlight.
I think it is the light snow of an early winter morning.
Looking up, I enjoy the full moon in the night sky.
Bending over, I miss my hometown."

We all know that poem is about a scholar who is traveling and missing his home, but on that night and forever after I believed it was about us. Snow Flower was my home, and I was hers.

Beautiful Moon

BEAUTIFUL MOON RETURNED THE NEXT DAY, AND WE GOT BACK to work. Months ago, each of our future in-laws had Delivered the Dates for our weddings, along with the first installments of our official bride-prices—more pork and candy, as well as empty wooden boxes to fill with all the things we would make for our dowries. Finally, and, most important, they sent cloth.

I have told you that Mama and Aunt made cloth for our family, and by now Beautiful Moon and I were adept at weaving ourselves. But the word *homegrown* comes to mind when I think of what we created. The cotton was cultivated by Baba and Uncle, the harvest cleaned by the women in our household, the beeswax we used to create designs and the dyes for turning the fabric blue were used sparingly because we were so frugal.

Other than what we made ourselves, I could only compare my bridal cloth to that used in Snow Flower's tunics, trousers, and headdresses, which had been constructed from beautiful fabrics and sophisticated patterns into a stylish wardrobe. One of my favorite outfits she wore in those days was made from indigo cloth. The intricate design of the indigo and the cut of the jacket were better than anything the married women in Puwei owned or made. Still, Snow Flower wore it with ease until it started to fade and fray. What I'm trying to say is that the cloth and its cut inspired me. I wanted to make clothes for myself that would be suitable for everyday wear in Tongkou.

But the cotton my in-laws sent as part of my bride-price changed all my perceptions. It was soft, without seeds, with complex designs, and dyed in the rich deep indigo so prized by the Yao people. With that gift I realized I still had much to learn and accomplish, but even this cotton was nothing compared to the silk. What arrived for me was not only of fine quality but perfect in color. Red for marriage, but also for anniversaries, New Year's celebrations, and other festivities. Purple and green, both appropriate for a young wife. A bluish gray the color of the sky before a storm and a bluish green the color of a village pond in summer for my years as a matron and later a widow. Black and dark blue for the men in my new home. Some of the silks were plain, while others had been woven to include double-happiness, peony, or cloud patterns.

The rolls of silk and cotton my in-laws sent were not given to me to do with as I pleased. They were to be used in preparing my dowry, just as Beautiful Moon and Snow Flower had to use their gifts to build their dowries. We had to make enough quilts, pillowcases, shoes, and clothes to last a lifetime, since Yao nationality women believe they should never take anything from their in-laws. Quilts! Let me tell you about those. They are boring and hot to make. However, since everyone believes that the more quilts you bring with you to your in-laws' house, the more children you will have, we made as many as possible.

What we loved to make were shoes. We made them for our husbands, our mothers-in-law, our fathers-in-law, and anyone else who lived in our new home, including brothers, sisters, sisters-in-law, and all children. (I was lucky; my husband was the eldest son. He had three younger brothers only. Men's shoes were not ornate, so I could do them quickly. Beautiful Moon had a greater burden. Her new home had one son, plus his parents, five sisters, an aunt, an uncle, and their three children.) We girls also made sixteen pairs for ourselves, four pairs for each of the four seasons. These more than the other things we made would be highly scrutinized, but we were happy with that knowledge because we gave each and every pair the greatest care possible, from creating the soles to the final embroidery stitch. Shoemaking allowed us to display our technical as well as our artistic skills, but it also sent a joyful and optimistic message. In our dialect, the word for *shoe* sounds the same as the word for *child*. Just as with the quilts, the more shoes we made, the more children we would have. The difference is that shoemaking requires delicacy, while quiltmaking is a heavy chore. Because three girls worked side by side, we competed in the friendliest way to compose the most beautiful designs on the outside of each pair of shoes, while giving great strength and support to the inside.

Our future families had sent patterns for their feet. We had not met our husbands and did not know if they were tall or pockmarked, but we knew the size of their feet. We were young girls—romantic as anyone of that age—and we imagined all kinds of things about our husbands from those patterns. Some turned out to be true. Most were not.

We used the patterns to cut pieces of cotton cloth, then glued together three layers of those footprints at a time. We made several sets of these and set them on the windowsill to dry. During Catching Cool Breezes, they dried very quickly. Once dry, we took those layered forms, stacked three together, and sewed them into a thick and sturdy sole. Most people do a simple repeat pattern that looks like rice seeds, but we wanted to impress our new families so we stitched different designs: a butterfly spreading its wings for a husband, a chrysanthemum in bloom for a mother-in-law, a cricket on a branch for a father-in-law. All that work just for the soles, but we saw these as messages to the people we hoped would love us when we married in.

As I said, it was unbearably hot that year during Catching Cool Breezes. We sweltered in the upstairs chamber. Downstairs was only slightly better. We drank tea, hoping it would refresh our bodies, but even in our lightest summer jackets and trousers we suffered. So we talked often about cool memories from our childhoods. I spoke of putting my feet in the river. Beautiful Moon remembered running through the fields during late autumn when the air was crisp against her cheeks. Snow Flower had once traveled north with her father and had experienced the frigid wind that blew in from Mongolia. These things did not soothe us. They were a torment.

Baba and Uncle took pity on us. They knew more than we did how cruel the weather was. They worked in it every day under the brutal sun. But we were poor. We didn't have an inner courtyard to lounge in, or land where we could be carried by bearers to sit under the shade of a tree, or any place where we would be completely shielded from the eyes of strangers. Instead, Baba took some of Mama's cloth and with Uncle's help strung a canopy for us on the north side of the house. Then they laid some padded winter quilts on the ground so we might have something soft to sit on.

"The men are in the fields during the day," Baba said. "They will not see you. Until the weather changes, you girls may do your work here. Just don't tell your mothers."

Beautiful Moon was accustomed to walking to her sworn sisters' houses for embroidery sessions and the like, but I had not been outdoors in Puwei like this since my milk years. Sure,. I had stepped from our threshold into Madame Wang's palanquin and had picked vegetables in our home garden. But beyond that, I was allowed only to look down from the lattice window to the alley that passed by our house. I had not felt the rhythm of the village for too long.

We were gloriously happy—still hot, but happy. As we sat in the shade, actually catching a cool breeze as the festival promised, we embroidered the tops of shoes or did final construction. Beautiful Moon's stitches were concentrated on her red wedding slippers, the most precious of all shoes. Pink and white lotus flowers bloomed, symbolizing her purity and fruit-fulness. Snow Flower had just finished a pair in sky-blue silk with a cloud pattern for her mother-in-law, and they sat next to us on the quilt looking dainty and elegant, a gentle reminder of the high-quality work we should insist on for all our projects. They filled me with happiness, bringing to mind the jacket that Snow Flower had worn on the first day we'd met. But nostalgic thoughts didn't seem to interest Snow Flower; she had simply moved on to a pair for herself, which employed purple silk trimmed with white. When the characters for purple and white were written together they meant *a lot of children*. As was so common with Snow Flower, her embroidery embellishments called upon the sky for inspiration. This time birds and other flying creatures twisted and soared on the tiny swatches. Meanwhile, I was finishing a pair of shoes for my mother-in-law. Her shoe size was slightly larger than my own, and it filled me with pride to know that, based solely on my feet, she would have to consider me worthy of her son. I had not yet met my mother-in-law, so I did not know her likes and dislikes, but during the heat of those days I thought of nothing but coolness. My design wrapped around the shoe, creating a landscape of women taking their ease under willow trees beside a stream. It was a fantasy, but no more so than the mythical birds that adorned Snow Flower's shoes.

We made a pretty picture sitting there on those quilts with our legs tucked under us just so: three young maidens, all betrothed to good families, cheerfully working on our dowries, showing our good manners to those who visited. Small boys stopped to talk to us as they set out to collect firewood or took the family water buffalo to the river. Little girls in charge of their siblings let us hold their baby brothers or sisters. We imagined what it would be like to care for babies of our own. Old widows, whose status and comportment were secure, swayed up to us to gossip, examine our embroidery, and remark on our pale skin.

On the fifth day, Madame Gao paid a visit. She had just returned from Getan Village, where she was negotiating a match. While she was there, she had delivered a set of letters from us to Elder Sister and had picked up a letter from Elder Sister to us. None of us liked Madame Gao, but we had been raised to respect our elders. We offered tea, but she declined. Since there was no money to be made from us, she handed the letter to me and got back into her palanquin. We watched until it turned the corner; then I used my embroidery needle to slice open the rice-paste seal. Because of what happened later that day, and because Elder Sister used so many standard *nu shu* phrases, I think I can reconstruct most of what she wrote:

Family,

Today I pick up a brush, and my heart flies away home.
To my family I write—regards to dear parents, aunt, and uncle.
When I think of past days, my tears cannot stop falling down.
I still feel sad to have left home.
My stomach is big with baby and I am so hot in this weather.
My in-laws are spiteful.
I do all the household work.
In this heat it is impossible to please.
Sister, cousin, take care of Mama and Baba.
We women can only hope that our parents will live many years.
That way we will have a place to return for festivals.
In our natal home, we will always have people who treasure us.
Please be good to our parents.

Your daughter, sister, and cousin

I finished reading the letter and closed my eyes. I was thinking, So many tears for Elder Sister, so much joy for me. I was grateful that we followed the custom of not falling into your husband's house until just before the birth of your first child. I still had two years before my marriage and possibly three years after that before I joined my in-laws permanently.

I was interrupted from these thoughts by something that sounded like a sob. I opened my eyes and looked at Snow Flower. A puzzled expression spread across her face as she stared at something to her right. I followed her gaze to Beautiful Moon, who was brushing at her neck and taking great breaths.

"What's wrong?" I asked.

Beautiful Moon's chest heaved with the effort of drawing in air—*uuuu, uuuu, uuuu*—sounds I will never forget.

She looked at me with her lovely eyes. Her hand stopped brushing and clasped the side of her neck. She did not try to stand. She sat with her legs tucked under her, still looking like a young lady sitting in the shade of a hot afternoon, her needlework in her lap, but I could see that beneath her hand her neck had begun to swell.

"Snow Flower, find help," I said urgently. "Get Baba, get Uncle. Quick!"

Out of the corner of my eye I saw Snow Flower try as best she could to run on her tiny feet. Her voice—unused to being raised—came out unsteady and high-pitched. "Help! Help!"

I crawled across the quilt to Beautiful Moon's side. I saw on her embroidery a bee struggling for life. The stinger had to be in my cousin's neck. I took her other hand and held it in my own. Her mouth opened. Inside, her tongue was growing, engorging.

"What can I do?" I asked. "Do you want me to try to get the stinger out?"

We both knew it was already too late for that.

"Do you want water?" I asked.

Beautiful Moon couldn't answer. She breathed only through her nostrils now, and each breath was more of an effort.

Somewhere in the village I heard Snow Flower. "Baba! Uncle! Elder Brother! Anyone! Help us!"

Those same children who had visited us the last few days gathered around our quilt, their mouths agape as they watched Beautiful Moon's neck, tongue, eyelids, and hands swell. Her skin went from the paleness of the moon she was named for to pink, to red, to purple, to blue. She looked like a creature from a ghost story. A few of Puwei's widows arrived. They shook their heads sympathetically.

Beautiful Moon's eyes locked with mine. Her hand had blown up so much that her fingers were like sausages in my palm, the skin so shiny and taut it looked ready to split. I cradled the monstrous paw in my hand.

"Beautiful Moon, listen to me," I pleaded. "Your baba is coming. Wait for him. He loves you so much. We all love you, Beautiful Moon. Do you hear me?"

The old women began to cry. The children hung on to each other. Village life was hard. Who among us had not seen death? But it was rare to see such bravery, such stillness, such beauty of purpose in the final moments.

"You have been a good cousin," I said. "I have always loved you. I will honor you forever."

Beautiful Moon took another breath. This one sounded like a creaking hinge. It was slow. Almost no air could enter her body.

"Beautiful Moon, Beautiful Moon . . ."

The horrible sound ended. Her eyes were just slits in a face cruelly distorted, but she looked at me with full understanding. She had heard every word I'd said. In the last moment of her life—when no air could enter her body and no air could go out—I felt as though she passed on to me many messages. *Tell Mama I love her. Tell Baba I love him. Tell your parents I am grateful for all they have done for me. Don't let the men suffer for me.* Then her head tipped forward onto her chest.

No one moved. Everything was as still as the panorama I had embroidered on my shoes. Only the sound of weeping and sniffing would have told anyone that something was wrong.

Uncle ran into the alley and pushed through the people to the quilt where Beautiful Moon and I sat. She was so peaceful in her bearing, it gave him hope. But my face and those around us told him otherwise. A horrible cry tore out of him as he sank to his knees. When he saw the condition of Beautiful Moon's face, another dreadful howl. Some of the smaller children ran away. Uncle was so sweaty from working in the fields and then running back to us I could smell him. Tears poured from his eyes, then dripped from his nose, cheeks, and jaw and disappeared into the wetness of his sweaty tunic.

Baba arrived and knelt beside me. A few seconds later, Elder Brother broke through the crowd, panting, Snow Flower on his back.

Uncle kept talking to Beautiful Moon. "Wake up, little one. Wake up. I will get your mama. She needs you. Wake up. Wake up."

His brother, my father, gripped his arm. "No use."

Uncle had a posture eerily similar to Beautiful Moon's, his head tucked down, his legs under him, his hands in his lap—all the same except for the sorrow that dripped from his eyes and the uncontrollable grief that wracked his body.

Baba asked, "Do you want to take her or shall I?"

Uncle shook his head. Wordlessly, he pulled a leg out from under him and planted it on the ground to steady himself; then he lifted Beautiful Moon and carried her into the house. None of us was functioning clearly. Only Snow Flower acted, moving swiftly to the table in the main room and removing the teacups we had set there for the men when they came back from the fields. Uncle laid out Beautiful Moon. Now the others could see how the bee venom had ravaged her face and body. In my mind I kept thinking: It was only five minutes, no more.

Again, Snow Flower took control. "Excuse me, but you need to get the others."

Realizing this meant that Aunt would have to be told about Beautiful Moon's death, Uncle's sobs grew deeper. I could barely think about Aunt myself. Beautiful Moon had been her one true happiness. I had been so shocked by what had happened to my cousin that I hadn't yet had a chance to feel anything. Now my legs lost their strength and tears welled in my eyes in sorrow for my sweet cousin and in pity for my aunt and uncle. Snow Flower wrapped an arm around me and guided me to a chair, giving instructions all the while.

"Elder Brother, run to your aunt's natal village," she directed. "I have some *cash*. Use it to hire a palanquin for her. Then run to your mother's natal village. Bring her back. You will have to carry her like you did me. Maybe Second Brother can help you. But hurry. Your aunt will need her."

Then we waited. Uncle sat on a stool by the table and wept so hard into Beautiful Moon's tunic that stains spread across the fabric like rain clouds. Baba tried to comfort Uncle, but what was the use? He could not be comforted. Anyone who tells you that the Yao people never care for their daughters is lying. We may be worthless. We may be raised for another family. But often we are loved and cherished, despite our natal families' best efforts not to have feelings for us. Why else in our secret writing do you see phrases like "I was a pearl in my father's palm" so frequently? Maybe as parents we try not to care. *I* tried not to care about my daughter, but what could I do? She nursed at my breast like my sons had, she cried her tears in my lap, and she honored me by becoming a good and talented woman fluent in *nu shu*. Uncle's pearl was gone from him forever.

I stared at Beautiful Moon's face, remembering how close we had been. We had had our feet bound at the same time. We had been betrothed to the same village. Our lives had been inexorably linked, and now we were cut from each other forever.

Around us, Snow Flower busied herself. She made tea, which no one drank. She went through the house, looking for white mourning clothes, and set them out for us. She stood at the door, greeting those who had heard the news. Madame Wang arrived in her palanquin and Snow Flower let her in. I might have expected Madame Wang to complain about the loss of her matchmaking payment. Instead, she asked how she could help. Beautiful Moon's future had been in her hands and she felt obliged to see her through this final passage. But her hand shot up to her mouth when she saw Beautiful Moon's distorted face and those frightening monster fingers. And it was so hot. We had no place cool to put her. Things would begin to happen very quickly now to Beautiful Moon.

"How much longer until the mother arrives?" Madame Wang asked.

We did not know.

"Snow Flower, wrap the girl's face in muslin, then dress her in her eternity clothes. Do this now. No mother should see her daughter this way." Snow Flower turned to go upstairs, but Madame Wang grabbed her sleeve. "I will go to Tongkou and bring your mourning clothes. Do not leave this house until I tell you." She released Snow Flower, took one last look at Beautiful Moon, and slipped out the door.

By the time Aunt arrived, Baba, Uncle, my brothers, and I were dressed in plain sackcloth. Beautiful Moon's body had been completely shrouded in muslin, then attired in the clothes for her journey to the afterworld. So many tears in the house that day, but none of them came from Aunt. She swayed in on her lily feet and went straight to her daughter's body. She smoothed the clothes and then placed her hand over what had been her daughter's heart. She stood that way for hours.

Aunt did everything properly for the funeral. She went to the burial on her knees. She burned paper money and clothes at the site for Beautiful Moon to use in the afterworld. She gathered together all of Beautiful Moon's secret writing and burned that too. Afterward, she created a little altar in our house where she made offerings every day. She did not cry in our presence, but I will never forget the sounds that emanated through our house at night when Aunt went to bed. She moaned from some deep, deep part of her soul. None of us could sleep. None of us were any solace. In fact, my brothers and I tried our best to be as quiet—invisible—as possible, knowing that our voices and faces were only bitter reminders of what she had lost. In the mornings, after the men had gone out to the fields, Aunt retreated to her room and wouldn't come out. She lay on her side, her face to the wall, refusing to eat anything more than the bowl of rice that Mama brought her, quiet all day until night enveloped us and that frightening moaning began again.

Everyone knows that part of the spirit descends to the afterworld, while part of it remains with the family, but we have a special belief about the spirit of a young woman who has died before her marriage that goes contrary to this. She comes back to prey upon other unmarried girls—not to scare them but to take them to the afterworld with her so she might have company. The way Beautiful Moon's unhappiness came to us every night in Aunt's otherworldly moans let Snow Flower and me know we were in danger.

Snow Flower came up with a plan. "A flower tower must be made," she said one morning. A flower tower was exactly what was needed to appease Beautiful Moon's spirit. If we provided her with a good flower tower, she would have a place to wander in and entertain herself. If she were happy, Snow Flower and I would be protected.

Some people—those with more money—go to a professional flower tower builder, but Snow Flower and I decided to make our own. We envisioned a tower of many levels, like a seven-tiered pagoda. We put a pair of foo dogs at the entrance. Inside, we painted poems on the walls in our secret writing. We made one level for dancing, another for floating. We made a sleeping room with stars and the moon painted on the ceiling. On another level, we made a women's chamber, with lattice windows done in intricate paper cutouts that provided views in every direction. We constructed a table on which we laid out bits of our favorite threads, some ink, paper, and a brush, so Beautiful Moon might embroider or write letters in *nu shu* to her new ghost friends. We made servants and entertainers out of twisted colored paper and set them about the tower so that every level would provide company, distraction, and amusements. When we weren't working on the flower tower, we composed a lament we would sing to calm my cousin. If the flower tower was for Beautiful Moon's pleasure for all eternity, our words would be a final farewell from the world of the living.

On the day the weather finally broke, Snow Flower and I asked and received permission to go to Beautiful Moon's grave. It was not a long walk to the burial mound, far less than when Snow Flower had gone to the fields to bring back Baba and Uncle when Beautiful Moon died. We sat at the grave for a few minutes. Then Snow Flower set the flower tower on fire. We watched it burn, imagining it being transported to the afterworld and Beautiful Moon drifting through the rooms in delight. Then I pulled out the paper on which we'd written to Beautiful Moon in our secret writing and we began to sing.

"Beautiful Moon, we hope the flower tower brings you peace.
We hope you forget about us, but we will never forget you.
We will honor you. We will clean your grave at Spring Festival.
Do not let your thoughts run wild.
Live in your flower tower and be happy."

Snow Flower and I walked home and went upstairs to the women's chamber. Sitting side by side, we took turns writing the lament onto the folds of our special fan. When we were done, I added to the garland at the top a crescent-shaped moon, as slender and unobtrusive as Beautiful Moon herself.

The flower tower helped protect Snow Flower and me, and it placated Beautiful Moon's restless spirit, but it did nothing for Aunt and Uncle, who could not be consoled. All that was meant to be. We were at the mercy of powerful elements and could do nothing but follow our fates. This can be explained by *yin* and *yang:* There are women and men, dark and light, sorrow and happiness. These things create balance. You take a moment of supreme happiness like Snow Flower and I felt at the beginning of the Catching Cool Breezes Festival, then sweep it away in the cruelest way with Beautiful Moon's death. You take two happy people like Aunt and Uncle, then turn them in an instant into two end-of-the-liners with nothing to live for, who, when my father died, would have to rely on Elder Brother's kindness to care for them and not throw them out. You take a family like mine that is not so well off, then add the pressure of too many weddings in one household. . . . All these things disrupted the balance of the universe, so the gods set things right by striking down a kind-hearted girl. There is no life without death. This is the true meaning of *yin* and *yang.*

The Flower-Sitting Chair

TWO YEARS AFTER BEAUTIFUL MOON DIED, MY HAIR—WHICH
had already been pinned when I was fifteen—was combed into the dragon
style befitting a young woman about to marry. My in-laws sent more
cloth, *cash* so that I might have my own purse, and jewelry—earrings,
rings, necklaces—all in silver and jade. They also gave my parents thirty
bundles of glutinous rice—enough to feed family and friends who would
visit in the days to come—and a side of pork, which Baba sliced and my
brothers delivered to people in Puwei Village to let them know that the
monthlong wedding celebration had officially begun. But what surprised
and pleased Baba most of all—and what showed that our family's hard
work in preparing me for my special future had paid off—was the arrival
of a new water buffalo. With this single gift, my father became one of the
three most prosperous men in our village.

Snow Flower came for the entire month of Sitting and Singing in the
Upstairs Chamber. During those last four weeks as I finished my dowry,
she helped me in many ways and we became even closer. We both had
foolish ideas about what marriage would be, but Snow Flower and I believed nothing would ever come close to the comfort we felt in each
other's arms—the warmth of our bodies, the softness of our skin, the delicate smells. Nothing would ever alter our love, and when we looked
ahead we thought we would have only more to share.

To us, Sitting and Singing in the Upstairs Chamber was the beginning of a deeper commitment between us. After ten years together, our relationship was about to move to new and far more profound levels. Two or three years from now, once I moved to my husband's home permanently and Snow Flower had gone to her husband's home in Jintian, we would visit often. Surely our husbands—both men of wealth and high esteem—would hire palanquins for this purpose.

Since I didn't have sworn sisters to join me during these festivities, my mother, my aunt, my sister-in-law, Elder Sister—who came home, pregnant again—and a few unwed girls from Puwei Village all came to celebrate my good fortune. Madame Wang joined us periodically too. Sometimes we recited favorite stories, or one person would choose a chant that we all followed. Other times we sang of our own lives. My mother—who was satisfied with her fate—recounted "The Tale of the Flower Girl," while Aunt, still in mourning, made us all weep as her words came out in a sorrowful dirge.

One afternoon, as I embroidered the belt to cinch my wedding costume, Madame Wang came to entertain us with "The Tale of Wife Wang." She took a stool next to Snow Flower, who was deep in thought, composing my third-day wedding book and searching for the right words to tell my in-laws about me. The two of them spoke very softly to each other. Every once in a while, I heard Snow Flower's voice saying, "Yes, Auntie" and "No, Auntie." Snow Flower had always shown a kind heart to the matchmaker. I had tried—with only moderate success—to emulate her in this.

When Madame Wang saw we were all waiting, she wiggled her bottom on the stool to get comfortable and began the saga. "There once was a pious woman with few prospects." She had grown quite plump in recent years, which made her slower and more deliberate in her storytelling and in her movements. "Her family married her to a butcher—the lowest possible match for a woman devoted to the Buddhist way. As devout as she was, she was a woman first and gave birth to sons and daughters. Still, Wife Wang did not eat fish or meat. She recited sutras for hours each day, especially the Diamond Sutra. When she wasn't reciting, she begged her husband not to slaughter animals. She warned him of the bad karma that would come to him in the next life if he continued his profession."

The matchmaker put a hand on Snow Flower's thigh in a comforting gesture. I would have found that old woman's hand oppressive, but Snow Flower didn't push it away.

"But Husband Wang told her—and some might say rightly—that his family had been butchers for more generations than anyone could count," Madame Wang continued. " 'You continue to recite the Diamond Sutra,' he said. 'You will be rewarded in your next life. I will keep slaughtering animals. I will buy land in this life and be punished in the next.' "

Wife Wang knew she was doomed for sleeping with her husband, but when he tested her knowledge of the Diamond Sutra and found that she could recite it without flaw, he gave her a room of her own so she could remain celibate for the rest of their married life.

"Meanwhile," Madame Wang went on, and once again her hand traveled to Snow Flower, where it rested lightly on the back of her neck, "the King of the Afterworld sent out spirits to look for those of great virtue. They spied on Wife Wang. Once convinced of her purity, they enticed her to visit the afterworld to recite the Diamond Sutra. She knew what this meant: They were asking her to die. She begged them not to make her leave her children, but the spirits refused to hear her pleas. She told her husband to take a new wife. She instructed her children to be good and obey their new mother. As soon as these words left her mouth, she fell to the floor, dead.

"Wife Wang experienced many trials before she was brought at last to the King of the Afterworld. Through all her tribulations he had been watching her, noting her virtue and piety. Just like her husband, he demanded that she recite the Diamond Sutra. Although she missed nine words, he was so pleased with her efforts—both during her lifetime and in the afterlife—that he rewarded her by allowing her to return to the world of the living as a baby boy. This time she was born into the home of a learned official, but her real name was written on the bottom of her foot.

"Wife Wang had led an exemplary life, but she was only a woman," the matchmaker reminded us. "Now, as a man, she excelled at everything she did. She attained the highest rank as a scholar. She gained riches, honor, and prestige, but as much as she accomplished she missed her family and longed to be a woman again. At last she was presented to the emperor. She told him her story and implored him to let her return to her husband's home village. Just as had happened with the King of the Afterworld, this woman's courage and virtue moved the emperor, but he saw something more—filial piety. He assigned her to her husband's home village as a magistrate. She arrived wearing full scholar regalia. When everyone came out to kowtow, she stunned the gathering by taking off her manly shoes and revealing her true name. She told her husband—now very old—that she wanted to be his wife again. Husband Wang and the children went to her tomb and opened it. The Jade Emperor stepped out and announced that the entire Wang family could transcend this world for nirvana, which they did."

I believed Madame Wang told this story to tell me about my future. My Lu husband and his family, as esteemed and respected as they were in the county, might do things that could be considered offensive or even polluted. Also, it was the nature of a man born under the sign of the tiger to be fiery, spirited, and impulsive. My husband might lash out at society or scoff at binding traditions. (This is not as bad as being a butcher, I admit, but these traits could be dangerous nevertheless.) I, as a woman born under the sign of the horse, could help my husband fight these bad traits. A horse woman should never be afraid to take the lead and steer her mate clear of trouble. To me, this was the true meaning of "The Tale of Wife Wang." Maybe she could not make her husband do what she wanted him to do, but through her piety and good works she not only saved him from the condemnation brought about by his polluted acts, she also helped her whole family reach nirvana. It is one of the few didactic tales told to us that has a happy ending, and on that late autumn day in the month before my marriage it made me happy.

But otherwise my feelings were mixed during Sitting and Singing. I was sad I would be leaving my family, but just as I had with my footbinding I tried to see something bigger—not that tiny slice of life I could see from our lattice window but a panorama like the ones Snow Flower and I saw when we peeked out the window of Madame Wang's palanquin. I was convinced that a new and better future lay ahead of me. Perhaps it was something in my nature; a horse would wander the world if it could. I was happy to be going somewhere new. Naturally, I'd like to say that Snow Flower and I followed our horse natures exactly as the horoscopes outline, but horses—and people—are not always obedient. We say one thing and do another. We feel one way; then our hearts open in another direction. We see one thing but don't understand that blinders hinder our vision. We plod along a well-loved path and then see a road, an alleyway, a river that tempts us. . . .

This is how I felt, and I thought that Snow Flower, my old same, would feel the *same* as I did, but she was a mystery to me. Snow Flower's wedding was a month after mine, but she seemed neither excited nor sad. Instead she was unusually subdued, even as she sang the proper words during our chanting and worked diligently on the third-day wedding book she was making for me. I thought perhaps she was more nervous than I was about the wedding night.

"I'm not afraid of that," she quipped, as we folded and wrapped my quilts.

"I'm not either," I said, but I don't think either of us spoke with much conviction. In my daughter days, when I'd still been allowed to play outside, I'd seen animals do bed business. I knew I was going to do something like that, but I didn't understand how it would happen or what I was supposed to do. And Snow Flower, who usually knew so much more than I did, was no help. We were both waiting for one of our mothers, elder sisters, my aunt, or even the matchmaker to explain how to do this chore as they had taught us how to do so many others.

Since we were both uncomfortable with the topic, I tried to guide the conversation toward our plan for the next few weeks. Instead of returning home immediately after my marriage, I would go straight to Snow Flower's house for her month of Sitting and Singing. I needed to help her with her wedding preparations as she was helping me with mine. I had been wanting to go to her house for ten years now, and in some ways I was more excited about that than in meeting my husband, because I had heard about Snow Flower's home and family for so long, while I knew almost nothing about the man I was going to marry. Still, although I was filled with anticipation—at last I'd be going to Snow Flower's house!—she seemed vague about the details.

"Someone from your in-laws' home will bring you to me," Snow Flower said.

"Do you think my mother-in-law will join us for your Sitting and Singing?" I asked. This would please me, because she would see me with my *laotong*.

"Lady Lu is too busy. She has many duties, just as you will one day."

"But I'll get to meet your mother, elder sister, and . . . who else will be invited?"

I had expected that Mama and Aunt would be part of Snow Flower's rituals. She seemed so much a member of our family that I thought she would want them there.

"Auntie Wang will come," she said.

The matchmaker would probably make several appearances during Snow Flower's Sitting and Singing, just as she had at mine. For Madame Wang, our marrying out was the completion of years of hard work, meaning that her final payments were due. She wouldn't miss any occasion where she could show to other women—the mothers of potential clients—her splendid results.

"Other than Auntie Wang's presence, I don't know what my mother has planned," Snow Flower continued. "Everything will be a surprise."

We were silent as we each folded another quilt. I glanced at her and her features seemed tight. For the first time in many years, my old insecurities bubbled up. Did Snow Flower still feel I was unworthy of her? Was she embarrassed to have the women of Tongkou meet my mother and aunt? Then I remembered that we were talking about *her* Sitting and Singing. It should be *exactly* as Snow Flower's mother wanted it to be.

I took a strand of Snow Flower's hair and tucked it behind her ear. "I can't wait to meet your family. It's going to be a happy time."

She still seemed drawn as she said, "I worry that you'll be disappointed. I've said so much about my mama and baba—"

"And Tongkou and your house—"

"How can they be as good as what you've imagined?"

I laughed. "You're silly to worry. Everything I have in my mind comes from your beautiful word pictures."

THREE DAYS BEFORE my wedding, I began the ceremonies associated with the Day of Sorrow and Worry. Mama sat on the fourth step leading to the upstairs chamber, the women of our village came to witness the laments, and everyone went *ku, ku, ku,* with much sobbing all around. Once Mama and I finished our crying and singing to each other, I repeated the process with my father, my uncle and aunt, and my brothers. I may have been brave and looking forward to my new life, but my body and soul were weak from hunger, because a bride is not allowed to eat for the final ten days of her wedding festivities. Do we follow this custom to make us sadder at leaving our families, to make us more yielding when we go to our husbands' homes, or to make us appear more pure to our husbands? How can I know the answer? All I know is that Mama—like most mothers—hid a few hard-boiled eggs for me in the women's chamber, but these did little to give me strength, and my emotions weakened with each new event.

The next morning, nervousness jolted me awake, but Snow Flower was right beside me, her soft fingers on my cheek, trying to calm me. I would be presented to my in-laws today, and I was so afraid that I couldn't have eaten even if I'd been allowed to. Snow Flower helped me put on the wedding outfit I had made—a short collarless jacket cinched with a belt over long pants. She slipped the silver bangles my husband's family had sent onto my wrist, then helped me put on their other gifts—the earrings, necklace, and hairpins. My bracelets jangled together, while the silver charms I'd sewn onto my jacket tinkled harmoniously. On my feet I wore my red wedding shoes and on my head an elaborate headdress with pearly balls and silver trinkets—all of which quivered when I walked or moved my head or when my feelings broke through. Red tassels hung down in front of my headdress, forming a veil. The only way I could see and still maintain proper decorum was to look straight down.

Snow Flower led me downstairs. Just because I couldn't see didn't mean that I didn't have many emotions tumbling through my body. I heard my mother's ragged footsteps, my aunt and uncle speaking to each other in gentle voices, and the scrape of my father's chair as he rose. Together we walked to Puwei's ancestral temple, where I thanked my ancestors for my life. The whole time, Snow Flower was at my side, guiding me through the alleyways, whispering encouragement and reminding me to hurry if I could because my in-laws would be arriving soon.

When we got home, Snow Flower and I went back upstairs. To keep me still, she held my hands and tried to describe what my new family was doing.

"Close your eyes and picture this." She leaned in close, and my tassels fluttered with each word she spoke. "Master and Lady Lu must be beautifully dressed. They, along with their friends and relatives, have departed for Puwei. They are accompanied by a band, which announces to everyone along the route that on this day they have possession of the roadway." She lowered her voice. "And where is the groom? He waits for you in Tongkou. In just two more days you will see him!"

Suddenly we heard music. They were almost here. Snow Flower and I went to the lattice window. I parted my tassels and looked out. We still couldn't see the band or the procession, but together we watched as an emissary walked down our alleyway, stopped at our threshold, and presented my father with a letter on red paper declaring that my new family had come for me.

Then the band turned the corner, followed by a large crowd of strangers. Once they reached our house, the usual commotion commenced. Down below, people threw water and bamboo leaves on the band, accompanied by the customary laughter and jokes. I was called downstairs. Again, Snow Flower took my hand and guided me. I heard women's voices sing: "Raising a girl and marrying her off is like building a fancy road for others to use."

We went outside, and Madame Wang introduced both sets of parents. I had to be at my most demure at this moment when my in-laws first glimpsed me, so I couldn't even whisper to Snow Flower to describe what they looked like or if she could gauge what they thought of me. Then my parents led the way to the ancestral temple, where my family hosted the first of many celebratory meals. Snow Flower and other girls from our village sat around me. Special dishes were brought out. Alcohol was served. Faces turned red. I was the subject of much teasing by the men and old women. All through the banquet, I sang laments and the women replied. By now I hadn't eaten a real meal for seven days, and the smell of all that food made me dizzy.

The next day—the Day of the Big Singing Hall—featured a formal lunch. My handiwork and all of the third-day wedding books were displayed, accompanied by more singing by Snow Flower, the women, and me. Mama and Aunt led me to the center table. As soon as I was seated, my mother-in-law set before me a bowl of soup that she'd prepared to symbolize the kindness of my new family. I would have given anything to have just a few sips of the broth.

I could not see my mother-in-law's face through my veil, but when I looked down through the tassels and saw golden lilies that seemed as small as my own, I felt a wave of panic. She hadn't worn the special pair of shoes I'd made for her. I could see why. The embroidery on these shoes was far better than anything I had done. I was disgraced. Surely my parents were embarrassed and my in-laws disenchanted.

At this terrible moment, Snow Flower came to my side and took my arm again. Custom dictated that I leave the party, so she escorted me out of the temple and back home. She helped me upstairs, and then lifted off my headdress, removed the rest of my wedding clothes, and buttoned me into a nightdress and my sleeping slippers. I stayed quiet. The perfection of my mother-in-law's shoes gnawed at me, but I was afraid to say anything, even to Snow Flower. I didn't want her to be disappointed in me too.

Very late that night, my family returned home. If I was going to get any advice about bed business, it had to happen now. Mama came into the room and Snow Flower left. Mama looked worried, and for a second I thought she'd come to tell me that my in-laws wanted to back out of the arrangement. She rested her cane on the bed and sat down beside me.

"I have always told you that a true lady lets no ugliness into her life," she said, "and that only through pain will you find beauty."

I nodded modestly, but inside I was practically screaming in terror. She had used these phrases again and again during my footbinding. Could bed business be that bad?

"I hope you will remember, Lily, that sometimes we can't avoid ugliness. You have to be brave. You have promised to be united for life. Be the lady you were meant to be."

And then she stood up, balanced on her cane, and hobbled out of the room. I was not relieved by what she had said! My resolve, my adventurousness, and my strength had completely weakened. I truly felt like a bride—afraid, sad, and very scared now to leave my family.

When Snow Flower came back in and saw I was white with fear, she took my mother's spot on the bed and tried to comfort me.

"For ten years you have trained for this moment," she gently reassured me. "You obey the rules set down in *The Women's Classic*. You are soft in your words but strong in your heart. You comb your hair in a demure manner. You don't wear rouge or powder. You know how to spin cotton and wool, weave, sew, and embroider. You know how to cook, clean, wash, keep tea always warm and ready, and light the fire in the hearth. You take good and proper care of your feet. You remove your old bindings each night before bed. You wash your feet thoroughly and use just the right amount of scent before putting on clean bindings."

"What about . . . bed business?"

"What about it? Your aunt and uncle have been happy doing this thing. Your mama and baba have done it enough to have many children. It can't be as hard as embroidery or cleaning."

I felt a little better, but Snow Flower wasn't done. She helped me into the bed, curled around me, and continued praising me.

"You will be a good mother, because you are caring," she whispered in my ear. "At the same time, you will be a good teacher. How do I know this? Look at all the things you have taught me." She paused for a moment, making sure my mind and body had absorbed what she'd said, before going on in a much more matter-of-fact manner. "And besides, I saw the way the Lus looked at you yesterday and today."

I twisted out of her arms and turned to face her. "Tell me. Tell me everything."

"Remember when Lady Lu brought you the soup?"

Of course I remembered. That was the beginning of what I imagined to be my lifetime of humiliation.

"Your whole body trembled," Snow Flower continued. "How did you do that? The entire room noticed. Everyone commented on your fragility combined with restraint. As you sat there with your head tilted down, showing what a perfect maiden you are, Lady Lu looked over you to her husband. She smiled in approval and he smiled back. You will see. Lady Lu is strict, but her heart is kind."

"But—"

"And the way the whole Lu party examined your feet! Oh, Lily, I'm sure everyone in my village is happy to know that one day you will be the new Lady Lu. Now try to sleep. You have many long days ahead of you."

We lay face-to-face. Snow Flower put a hand on my cheek in her usual way. "Close your eyes," she ordered softly. I did as I was told.

THE NEXT DAY my in-laws arrived in Puwei early enough to pick me up and get me back to Tongkou by late afternoon. When I heard the band on the outskirts of the village, my heart began to race. I couldn't help it, but tears leaked from my eyes. Mama, Aunt, Elder Sister, and Snow Flower all cried as they led me downstairs. The groom's emissaries arrived at the threshold. My brothers helped load my dowry into waiting palanquins. Again I wore my headdress, so I couldn't see anyone, but I heard my family's voices as we went through the final traditional calls and responses.

"A woman will never become valuable if she doesn't leave her village," Mama cried out.

"Goodbye, Mama," I chanted back to her. "Thank you for raising a worthless daughter."

"Goodbye, daughter," Baba said softly.

With the sound of my father's voice, my tears came down in twin streams. I clung to the railing leading to the upstairs chamber. Suddenly I didn't want to go.

"As women, we are born to leave our home villages," Aunt sang out. "You are like a bird flying into a cloud, never to return."

"Thank you, Aunt, for making me laugh. Thank you for showing me the true meaning of sorrow. Thank you for sharing your special talents with me."

Aunt's sobs echoed back to me from her dark place. I couldn't leave her to mourn alone. My tears matched hers.

Looking down, I saw Uncle's sun-browned hands on mine, pulling my fingers away from the railing.

"Your flower-sitting chair waits for you," he said, his voice breaking with emotion.

"Uncle . . ."

Then I heard the voices of my siblings, each of them wishing me farewell. I wanted to see them with my eyes instead of being blinded by those red tassels.

"Elder Brother, thank you for the goodness you have shown me," I chanted. "Second Brother, thank you for letting me care for you when you were a baby in split pants. Elder Sister, thank you for your patience."

Outside, the band played louder. My hands reached out. Mama and Baba took them and helped me over the threshold. As I stepped over it, my tassels swung momentarily back and forth across my face. In little flashes I saw my palanquin covered in flowers and red silk. My *hua jiao*—flower-sitting chair—was beautiful.

Everything I had been told since my betrothal was arranged six years ago flooded my mind. I was marrying a tiger, the best match for me, according to our horoscopes. My husband was healthy, smart, and educated. His family was respected, rich, and generous. I had glimpsed these things already in the quality and quantity of my bride-price gifts, and now I saw them again with my flower-sitting chair. I loosened my grip on my parents' hands and they let go of me.

I took two blind steps forward and stopped. I couldn't see where I was going. I reached out my hands, longing for Snow Flower to take them. As she always had, she came to me. With her fingers wrapped around mine, she led me to the palanquin. She opened the door. All around me I heard crying. Mama and Aunt sang a sorrowful melody—the usual one to say goodbye to a daughter. Snow Flower leaned in close and whispered so no one could hear.

"Remember, we are old sames forever." Then she took something from inside her sleeve and tucked it inside my jacket. "I made this for you," she said. "Read it on your way to Tongkou. I will see you there."

I got into the palanquin. The bearers lifted me up and I was on my way. Mama, Aunt, Baba, Snow Flower, and some friends from Puwei followed my escorts and me to the edge of the village, calling out final good wishes. I sat alone in the palanquin, crying.

Why was I making such a fuss when I would return to my natal home in three days? I can explain it this way: The phrase we use for marrying out is *buluo fujia,* which means not falling into your husband's home immediately. The *luo* means *falling,* like the falling of leaves in autumn or falling in death. And in our local dialect, the word for *wife* is the same as the word for *guest.* For the rest of my life I would be merely a guest in my husband's home—not the kind you treat with special meals, gifts of affection, or soft beds, but the kind who is forever viewed as a foreigner, alien and suspect.

I reached into my jacket and pulled out Snow Flower's package. It was our fan, wrapped in cloth. I opened it, anticipating the happy words she would have written. My eyes scanned the folds until I saw her message: *Two birds in flight—hearts beating as one. The sun shines upon their wings, drenching them with healing warmth. The earth spreads below them—all theirs.* In the garland at the top of the fan, two small birds soared together: my husband and me. I loved that Snow Flower had placed my husband in our dearest possession.

Next I spread open on my lap the handkerchief that had been wrapped around the fan. Looking down, my tassels swinging with the movement of the bearers, I saw she had embroidered a letter to me in our secret language to celebrate this most special moment.

The letter began in the traditional opening to a bride:

I feel knives in my heart as I write to you. We promised each other that we would never be a step apart, that a harsh word would never pass between us.

These words came from our contract, and I smiled at the memory.

I thought we would have our whole lives together. I never believed this day would come. It is sad that we came into this life wrong—as girls—but this is our fate. Lily, we have been like a pair of mandarin ducks. Now everything changes. In the coming days you will learn things about me. I have been restless and filled with apprehension. In my heart and in my mouth I have been weeping, thinking you will no longer love me. Please know that whatever you think of me, my opinion of you will never change.

Snow Flower

Can you imagine how I felt? Snow Flower had been very quiet these past weeks, because she'd been concerned that I would no longer love her. But how could that be? In my flower-sitting chair on my way to my husband, I knew *nothing* would ever change my feelings for Snow Flower. I had a terrible sense of foreboding and wanted to yell to the bearers to take me home so that I could ease my *laotong*'s fears.

But then we arrived at Tongkou's main gate. Firecrackers spit and popped; the band clanged, tooted, and drummed their instruments. People unloaded my dowry. These things had to be taken straightaway to my new home so my husband could change into the wedding clothes I'd made for him. Then I heard a terrible but familiar sound. It was that of a chicken having its neck cut. Outside my flower-sitting chair, someone spattered the chicken's blood on the ground to ward off any evil spirits that might have arrived with me.

At last my door opened, and I was helped out by a woman regarded to be the head of the village. The actual head woman was my mother-in-law, but for this purpose it was the woman in Tongkou with the most sons. She led me to my new home, where I stepped over the threshold and was presented to my in-laws. I knelt before them, touching my head to the ground three times. "I will obey you," I said. "I will work for you." Then I poured tea for them. After this, I was escorted to the wedding chamber, where I was left alone with the door open. I was now just moments away from meeting my husband. I had been waiting for this since the first time Madame Wang came to my house to see my feet, yet I was totally flustered, agitated, and confused. This man was a total stranger, so I was naturally curious about him. He would be the father of my children, so I was anxious about how that business was going to happen. And I had just received a mysterious letter from my old same and I was consumed with worry for her.

I heard people move a table to bar the door. I tilted my head just so, my tassels parted, and I saw my in-laws stack my wedding quilts on the table and place two cups of wine—one tied with green thread, the other with red thread, then both of them tied together—on top of the pile.

My husband entered the anteroom. Everyone cheered. This time I did not try to peek. I wanted to be as conventional as I could in this first meeting. From his side of the table, he pulled the red thread. From my side, I pulled the green thread. Then he jumped up on the table right onto the quilts and leaped into the room. With that action we were officially married.

What could I tell about my husband in the first instant that we stood side by side? I could smell that he had made a general cleaning of his body. By looking down I could see that the shoes I'd made for him were handsome on his feet and that his red wedding trousers were the exact right length. But the moment passed, and we moved on to Teasing and Getting Loud in the Wedding Chamber. My husband's friends burst in, unsteady on their feet and feeble in their words from too much drink. They gave us peanuts and dates so we would have many children. They gave us sweets so we would have a sweet life. But they didn't just hand a dumpling to me like they did to my husband. No! They tied the dumpling with a string and dangled it just above my mouth. They made me jump for it, making sure I never reached my goal. All the while, they made jokes. You know the kind. My husband would be as strong as a bull tonight, or I would be as submissive as a lamb, or my breasts looked like two peaches ready to burst the fabric of my jacket, or my husband would have as many seeds as a pomegranate, or if we used a particular position we would be guaranteed a first son. This is the same everywhere—low-class talk permitted on the first night of any marriage anywhere. And I played along, but inside I was growing more frantic.

I had been in Tongkou for hours. Now it was late at night. Outside on the street, villagers were drinking, eating, dancing, celebrating. A new round of firecrackers was set off, signaling everyone to go home. At long last, Madame Wang closed the door to the wedding chamber and my husband and I were alone.

He said, "Hello."

I said, "Hello."

"Have you eaten?"

"I'm not supposed to eat for another two days."

"You have peanuts and dates," he said. "I won't tell anyone if you want to eat them."

I shook my head and the little balls on my headdress shook and the silver pieces chimed prettily. My tassels parted and I saw that his eyes were cast down. He was looking at my feet. I blushed. I held my breath, hoping to still the tassels so he wouldn't glimpse the emotions on my cheeks. I didn't move and neither did he. I was sure he was still examining me. All I could do was wait.

Finally, my husband said, "I've been told you're very pretty. Are you?"

"Help me with my headdress and find out for yourself."

This came out more tartly than I intended, but my husband just laughed. A few moments later, he set the headdress on a side table. He turned back to face me. We were perhaps a meter apart. He searched my face and I boldly searched his. Everything Madame Wang and Snow Flower had said about him was true. He bore no pockmarks or scars of any kind. He was not as dark-skinned as Baba or Uncle, which told me that his hours in the family fields were few. He had high cheekbones and a chin that was confident but not impudent. An unruly shock of hair fell across his forehead, giving him a carefree look. His eyes sparkled with good humor.

He stepped forward, took my hands in his, and said, "I think we could be happy, you and I."

Could a Yao nationality girl of seventeen hope for better words? Like my husband, I saw a golden future before us. That night, he followed all the correct traditions, even removing my bridal shoes and putting on my red sleeping slippers. I was so accustomed to Snow Flower's gentle touch that I can't really describe how I felt having his hands on my feet, except that this act seemed far more intimate to me than what came next. I didn't know what I was doing, but neither did he. I just tried to imagine what Snow Flower would have done if she were under that strange man instead of me.

ON THE SECOND day of my marriage, I rose early. I left my husband sleeping and stepped out into the hall. You know that feeling when you are sick with worry? This is how I'd felt from the moment I'd read Snow Flower's letter, but I couldn't do anything about it—not during my wedding, last night, or even now. I had to do my best to follow the prescribed course until I saw her again. But it was hard, because I was hungry, exhausted, and my body hurt. My feet were tired and sore from so much walking these last few days. I was uncomfortable in another place too, but I tried to blot out these things as I made my way to the kitchen, where a servant girl about ten years old sat on her haunches, apparently waiting for me. My own servant girl—no one had told me about that. People in Puwei didn't have servants, but I recognized what she was because her feet had not been bound. Her name was Yonggang, which means *brave* and *strong like iron.* (This would prove to be true.) She had already built a fire in the brazier and hauled water to the kitchen. All I had to do was heat the water and take it to my in-laws so they could wash their faces. I also made tea for everyone in the household, and when they came to the kitchen I poured it without spilling a drop.

Later that day, my in-laws sent another round of pork and sweet cakes to my family. The Lus held a big feast in their ancestral temple, yet another banquet where I was not allowed to eat. Before everyone, my husband and I bowed to Heaven and Earth, my in-laws, and the Lu family ancestors. Then we passed through the temple, bowing to everyone who was older than we were. They, in turn, gave us money wrapped in red paper. Then—back to the wedding chamber.

The next day, the third of a marriage, is the one that all brides wait for, because the third-day wedding books that family and friends have made are read. But by now all I could think about was Snow Flower and that I would see her at the event.

Elder Sister and Elder Brother's wife arrived, bringing the books and food I was finally allowed to eat. Many women from Tongkou joined the females of my husband's family to read the words, but neither Snow Flower nor her mother came. This was beyond my comprehension. I was deeply hurt . . . and scared by Snow Flower's absence. There I was at what is considered the happiest of all wedding rites, and I couldn't enjoy it.

My *sanzhaoshu* contained all the usual lines about my family's misery now that I would no longer be with them. At the same time, they extolled my virtues and repeated phrases such as *If only we could persuade that worthy family to wait a few years before taking you*, or *It is sad we are now separated*, while entreating my in-laws to be lenient and teach me their family customs with patience. Snow Flower's *sanzhaoshu* was also what I expected, incorporating her love of birds. It began, *The phoenix mates the golden hen, a match made in heaven*. Again, the usual sentiments, even from my *laotong*.

Truth

IF CIRCUMSTANCES HAD BEEN NORMAL, ON THE FOURTH DAY after my wedding I would have gone back home to my family in Puwei, but I had long planned to go straight to Snow Flower's house for her Sitting and Singing month. Now that I was close to seeing her again, I was more anxious than ever. I dressed in one of my good everyday outfits, a water-green silk jacket and pants embroidered with a bamboo pattern. I wanted to make a favorable impression not only on anyone I passed in Tongkou but also on Snow Flower's family, whom I had heard so much about over these many years. Yonggang, the servant girl, led me through Tongkou's alleyways. She carried my clothes, embroidery thread, cloth, and the third-day wedding book I had prepared for Snow Flower in a basket. I was happy for Yonggang's guidance yet uncomfortable with her company. She was one of many things I would have to get used to.

Tongkou was far bigger and more prosperous than Puwei. The alleyways were clean, with no chickens, ducks, or pigs wandering freely. We stopped before a house that looked exactly how Snow Flower had described it—two stories, peaceful and elegant. I had not been there long enough to know the village's customs, but one thing was exactly the same as in Puwei. We did not yell out greetings or knock to announce our arrival. Yonggang simply opened the main door to Snow Flower's house and stepped inside.

I followed right behind and was immediately assailed by a strange odor, which combined night soil and rotting meat with an overlay of something sickeningly sweet. I had no idea what the source of that could be, except that somehow it seemed human. My stomach roiled, but my eyes rebelled even more, refusing to accept what they were seeing.

The main room was much larger than the one in my natal home, but with far less furniture. I saw a table but no chairs. I saw a carved balustrade leading to the women's chamber, but other than these few things—which showed in their craftsmanship a much higher quality than anything in my natal home—there was nothing. No fire, even. It was late autumn now, and cold. The room was dirty too, with food scraps on the floor. I saw other doors that must have led to bedrooms.

This was not only completely different from what a passerby might have expected from seeing the exterior, but it was vastly different from what Snow Flower had described. I had to be in the wrong place.

By the ceiling were several windows, of which all but one had been sealed. A single ray of light from that window pierced the darkness. In the gloomy shadows, I spotted a woman squatting over a washbasin. She was dressed as a lowly peasant in ragged and dirty padded clothes. Our eyes met and she quickly averted her gaze. Keeping her head down, she stood up into the shaft of light. Her skin was beautiful, as pale and pure as porcelain. She wrapped the fingers of one hand around those of her other hand and bowed.

"Miss Lily, welcome, welcome." She kept her voice low, not out of deference for my newly acquired higher status but at a timbre that seemed tamped down by fear. "Wait here. I will get Snow Flower."

Now I was totally shocked. This had to be Snow Flower's house. But how could it be? As the woman crossed the room to the stairs, I saw she had golden lilies, nearly as small as my own, which to my ignorant eyes seemed remarkable for someone from the servant class.

I listened very hard as the woman addressed someone upstairs. Then my ears heard the impossible—Snow Flower's voice speaking in its most stubborn and argumentative tone. Shocked, that's how I felt, utterly shocked. But beyond this one familiar sound, the house itself was eerily quiet. And in that silence I sensed something lurking like an evil spirit from the afterworld. My whole body resisted this experience. My skin crawled in revulsion. I shivered in my water-green silk outfit, which I'd worn to impress Snow Flower's parents but which offered no protection against the damp wind that blew through the window or the fear I felt to be in this strange, dark, smelly, scary place.

Snow Flower emerged at the top of the stairs. "Come up," she called down to me.

I stood paralyzed, trying desperately to absorb what I was seeing. Something touched my sleeve and I started.

"I don't think the master would want me to leave you here," Yonggang said, her face a mask of worry.

"The master knows where I am," I responded, without thinking.

"Lily." Snow Flower's voice had a quality of sad desperation to it I had never heard before.

Then a memory from just a few days ago flashed in my mind. My mother had told me that as a woman I couldn't avoid ugliness and I had to be brave. "You have promised to be united for life," she'd said. "Be the lady you were meant to be." She hadn't been talking about bed business with my husband. She'd been talking about *this*. Snow Flower was my old same for life. I had a greater and deeper love for her than I could ever feel for the person who was my husband. This was the true meaning of a *laotong* relationship.

I took a step and heard something like a whimper from Yonggang. I didn't know what to do. I had never had a servant before. I patted her shoulder hesitatingly. "Go along." I tried to sound like a mistress should, however that was. "I will be fine."

"If you need to leave for any reason, just step outside and call for help," Yonggang suggested, still concerned. "Everyone here knows Master and Lady Lu. People will take you back to your in-laws' home."

I reached out and took the basket from her hand. When she didn't budge, I nodded at her to move along. She sighed in resignation, bowed quickly, backed herself to the threshold, turned, and left.

With my basket gripped firmly in my hand, I climbed the stairs. As I neared Snow Flower, I saw that her cheeks were streaked with tears. Like the servant woman, she was dressed in gray, ill-fitting, and badly repaired padded clothes. I stopped one stair below the landing.

"Nothing has changed," I said. "We are old sames."

She took my hand, helped me up the final step, and led me into the women's chamber. I could see that it too had been lovely at one time. It was perhaps three times the size of the women's chamber in my natal home. Instead of vertical bars on the lattice window, an intricately carved wooden screen covered the opening. Otherwise, the room was empty but for a spinning wheel and a bed. The beautiful woman I had seen downstairs, her hands folded neatly in her lap, perched gracefully on the edge of the bed. Her peasant clothes couldn't disguise her breeding.

"Lily," Snow Flower said, "this is my mother."

I crossed the room, linked my hands together, and bowed to the woman who had brought my *laotong* into this world.

"You must forgive our circumstances," Snow Flower's mother said. "I can only offer you tea." She rose. "You girls have much to talk over." With that, she swayed out of the room with the sublime grace that comes from feet perfectly bound.

When I left my natal home four days ago, tears had poured down my face. I was sad, happy, and afraid all at the same time. But now, as I sat with Snow Flower on her bed, I saw on her cheeks tears of remorse, guilt, shame, and embarrassment. I longed to yell at her, *Tell me!* Instead, I waited for the truth, realizing that each word from Snow Flower's lips would cause her to lose whatever face she had left.

"Long before you and I met," Snow Flower said at last, "my family was one of the best in the county. You can see"—she gestured around her helplessly—"this once was glorious. We were very prosperous. My great-grandfather the scholar received many *mou* from the emperor."

I listened, my mind spinning.

"When the emperor died, my great-grandfather fell out of favor, so he came home to retire. Life was good. When he died, his son, my grandfather, took over. My grandfather had many workers and many servants. He had three concubines, but they gave him only daughters. My grandmother finally bore a son and secured her place. They married in my mother for that son. People said she was like Hu Yuxiu, who was so talented and charming she had attracted an emperor. My father wasn't an imperial scholar, but he was educated in the classics. People said of him that he would one day be the headman of Tongkou. Mama believed it. Others saw a different future. My grandparents recognized in my father the weakness of having been raised as the only son in a house with too many sisters and too many concubines, while my aunt suspected that he was cowardly and susceptible to vice."

Snow Flower's eyes were distant as she relived a past that no longer existed. "Two years after I was born, my grandparents died," she continued. "My family had everything—stunning clothes, plentiful food, lots of servants. My father took me on trips; my mother took me to the Temple of

Gupo. I saw and learned a lot as a girl. But my father had to take care of Grandfather's three concubines and marry out his four sisters by blood and the five half sisters who had come from the concubines. He also had to provide work, food, and shelter for the field workers and the house servants. Marriages for his sisters and half sisters were arranged. My father tried to show everyone what a big man he was. Each bride-price was more extravagant than the last. He began to sell fields to the big landowner in the west of our province so he could pay for more silk or for another pig to be slaughtered as a bride-price. My mother—you saw her—she is beautiful on the outside but inside she is much like I was before I met you: pampered, sheltered, and ignorant about women's work other than embroidery and *nu shu*. My father . . ." Snow Flower hesitated, then blurted out, "My father took to the pipe."

I remembered back to the day that Madame Gao had made such a nuisance of herself talking about Snow Flower's family. She'd mentioned gambling and concubines but also that Snow Flower's father had taken to the pipe. I was nine years old. I had thought he smoked too much tobacco. Now I realized not only that Snow Flower's father had fallen victim to the opium pipe, but that everyone in the upstairs women's chamber that day, except for me, had known exactly what Madame Gao was talking about. My mother knew, my aunt knew, Madame Wang knew. They had *all* known, yet every one of them had agreed that this common knowledge should not be shared with me.

"Is your father still alive?" I asked tentatively. Surely she would have told me if he'd died, but then again—given all her other lies—maybe not.

She nodded but offered nothing more.

"Is he downstairs?" I asked, thinking of the strange and disgusting smell that had pervaded the main room.

Her features went very still; then she lifted her eyebrows. I took this to mean yes.

"The turning point came with the famine," Snow Flower resumed. "Do you remember that? We hadn't met yet, but there was a particularly bad crop followed by a very cruel winter."

How could I forget? The best we'd eaten was rice gruel flavored with dried turnips. Mama was frugal, Baba and Uncle barely ate, and we had survived.

"My father was not prepared," Snow Flower admitted. "He smoked his pipe and forgot about us. One day my grandfather's concubines left. Maybe they went back to their natal homes. Maybe they died in the snow.

No one knows. By the time spring arrived, only my parents, my two brothers, my two sisters, and I lived in the house. On the surface we still had our elegant life, but in actuality the debt collectors were beginning to visit us regularly. My father sold off more fields. Finally, we had only the house. By then he cared more for his pipe than he did for us. Before he would pawn the furniture—oh, Lily, you can't imagine how pretty everything was—he thought he would sell me."

"Not as a servant!"

"Worse. As a little daughter-in-law."

This had always been the most horrible thing I could imagine: not having your feet bound, being raised by strangers who had to be of such low morals that they didn't want a proper daughter-in-law, being treated lower than a servant. And now that I was married I understood the most terrible aspect of this life. You might be nothing but a bit of bed business for any male who lived in the household.

"We were saved by my mother's sister," Snow Flower said. "After you and I became *laotong*, she arranged a so-so match for my elder sister. She does not come here anymore. Later my aunt sent my elder brother to apprentice in Shangjiangxu. Today my younger brother works in the fields for your husband's family. My younger sister died, as you know—"

But I didn't care about people I had never met and had only heard lies about. "What happened to *you*?"

"My aunt changed my future with scissors, cloth, and alum. My father objected, but you know Auntie Wang. Who's going to say no to her once she's made a decision?"

"Auntie Wang?" My mind reeled. "You mean *our* Auntie Wang, the matchmaker?"

"She is my mother's sister."

I pressed my fingers to my temples. The very first day I met Snow Flower and we went to the Temple of Gupo, she had addressed the matchmaker as Auntie. I thought she'd done this out of courtesy and respect, and from then on I'd also used the honorific when I spoke to Madame Wang. I felt stupid and foolish.

"You never told me," I said.

"About Auntie Wang? That was the one thing I thought you knew."

The one thing I thought you knew. I tried to absorb those words.

"Auntie Wang saw right through my father," Snow Flower went on. "She understood he was weak. She looked at me too. She read in my face that I did not like to obey, that I didn't pay attention, that I was hopeless in the arts of home care, but that my mother could teach me embroidery, how to dress, how to act in front of a man, our secret writing. Auntie is only a woman, but as a matchmaker she is also business-minded. She saw where things were headed for our family and for me. She began looking for a *laotong* match, hoping it would send a good message through the countryside that I was educated, loyal, obedient—"

"And marriageable," I concluded. This was true for me as well.

"She searched the county, traveling far outside her usual matchmaking territory until she heard about you from the diviner. Once she met you, she decided to hitch my fate to yours."

"I don't understand."

Snow Flower smiled ruefully. "You were headed up and I was going down. When you and I first met, I didn't know anything. I was supposed to learn from you."

"But *you're* the one who taught *me*. Your embroidery has always been better than mine. And you knew the secret writing so well. You trained me to live in a home with a high threshold—"

"And you taught me how to haul water, wash clothes, cook, and clean the house. I have tried to teach my mother, but she sees things only as they were."

I had sensed already that Snow Flower's mother held on to a past that no longer existed, but having just heard Snow Flower tell her family story, I think my *laotong* also saw things through the happy veil of memory. Knowing her for all those years, I knew she believed in the idea that the women's inner realm should be beautiful and without worry. Perhaps she thought things would somehow go back to the way they once were.

"From you I learned what I needed to know for my new life," Snow Flower said, "except that I have never been able to clean as well as you."

True, she had never been good at it. I had always thought it was her way of blinding herself to the messiness of the way we lived. Now I realized it was easier for her mind to glide through the air far above the clouds than to acknowledge the ugliness right before her eyes.

"But your house is much larger and harder to clean than mine, and you were just a girl in your hair-pinning years," I argued stupidly, trying to make her feel better. "You had—"

"A mother who could not help me, a father who was an opium addict, and brothers and sisters who left one by one."

"But you're marrying—"

Suddenly I recalled that last day when Madame Gao had come into the upstairs chamber and I witnessed her final argument with Madame Wang. What had she said about Snow Flower's betrothal? I tried to remember what I knew about the arrangement, but Snow Flower rarely if ever talked about her future husband; she rarely if ever showed us any of her bride-price gifts. We had seen bits and pieces of cotton and silk that she was working on, true, but she always said these were everyday projects like shoes for herself. Nothing fancy.

A frightening thought began to formulate in my mind. Snow Flower had to be marrying out into a very low family. The question was, just how low?

Snow Flower seemed to read my thoughts. "Auntie did the best she could for me. I'm not marrying a farmer."

That hurt a little, since my father was a farmer.

"He's a merchant then?" A merchant would have a dishonorable profession, but he might be able to restore some of Snow Flower's lost circumstances.

"I will be marrying out to nearby Jintian Village, just as Auntie Wang said, but my husband's family"—again she hesitated—"they are butchers."

Waaa! This was the worst marriage possible! Snow Flower's new husband would have some money, but what he did was unclean and disgusting. In my mind I replayed everything from the last month as we'd prepared for my wedding. In particular I recalled how Madame Wang had stayed at Snow Flower's side, offering comfort, quietly cajoling. Then I remembered the matchmaker telling "The Tale of Wife Wang." With deep shame I saw that the story had not been meant for me at all but for Snow Flower.

I didn't know what to say. I had heard the truth in snippets, ever since I was nine, but had chosen not to believe or acknowledge it. Now I thought, Isn't it my duty to make my *laotong* happy? Make her forget these troubles? Make her believe that everything will be fine?

I put my arms around her. "At least you will never go hungry," I said, although I turned out to be wrong about that. "There are worse things that can happen to a woman," I said, but I couldn't think what they could be.

She buried her face in my shoulder and sobbed. A moment later, she roughly pushed me away. Her eyes were wet with tears, but I saw not sadness in them but wild ferocity.

"Don't pity me! I don't want it!"

Pity had not entered my mind. I felt sick with confusion and sadness.

Her letter to me had ruined my enjoyment of my wedding. Her not show-ing up for the reading of my third-day wedding books had deeply wounded me. And now this. Under all my turmoil simmered the feeling that Snow Flower had betrayed me. For all our nights together, why hadn't she told me the truth? Was it that she honestly didn't believe what her fate was to be? That because in her mind she was always flying away, she thought this would happen in real life too? Did she truly believe that our feet would leave the ground and our hearts would actually soar with the birds? Or was she just trying to save face by keeping her many secrets, believing this day would never come?

Maybe I should have been angry at Snow Flower for lying to me, but that's not what I felt. I had believed I had been plucked for a special future, which made me too self-centered to see what was directly in front of me. Wasn't it *my* lack as a friend—as a *laotong*—that had prevented me from asking Snow Flower the right questions about her past and her future?

I was only seventeen. I had spent the last ten years almost entirely in the upstairs chamber surrounded by women who saw a specific future for me. The same could be said for the men downstairs. But when I thought about all of them—Mama, Aunt, Baba, Uncle, Madame Gao, Madame Wang, even Snow Flower—the only one I could really blame was my mother. Madame Wang may have duped her in the beginning, but she had eventually learned the truth and decided not to tell me. How I felt about my mother twisted and warped with the realization that her occasional signs of affection, which I now saw as part of her greater lies of omission, had simply been a way to keep me on course to the good marriage that would benefit my entire natal family.

I was at a moment of supreme confusion, and I believe it set the stage for what happened later. I didn't know my mind. I didn't see or under-stand what was important. I was just a stupid girl who thought she knew something because she was married. I didn't know how to resolve any of these things, so I buried them deep, deep, deep inside of me. But my feel-ings didn't—couldn't—disappear. It was as though I'd swallowed the meat of a diseased pig and it slowly began to spoil my insides.

I HAD NOT yet become the Lady Lu who is respected today for her gra-ciousness, compassion, and strength. Still, from the moment I walked into Snow Flower's house, I felt something new inside me. Think again of that diseased piece of pork, and you'll understand what I'm talking about. I had to pretend I wasn't sick or infected, so I used my will to good purpose. I wanted to bring honor to my husband's family by being charitable and kind to people in the lowest of circumstances. Of course, I did not know *how* to do that, because these things were not natural to me.

Snow Flower was getting married in a month, so I helped her and her mother clean the house. I wanted it to be presentable to the groom's party, but no one could deal with the foul odors that permeated the rooms. The sick sweetness came from the opium that Snow Flower's father smoked. And the other rankness, as you have probably guessed, came from his impacted bowels. No incense, no burning of vinegar, no opening of windows even in those cool months could disguise the filthiness of that man and his habits.

I saw the routine of that household, in which two women lived in fear of the man who resided in a room on the ground floor. I experienced their hushed voices and the way they cowered reflexively when he called for them. And I saw the man himself, lying there in his stink and mess. Even in poverty, he was as petulant and quick to anger as a spoiled child. There may have been a time when he'd lashed out physically at his wife and daughter, but now he was just a drug-dazed creature who was better left alone with his vice.

I tried not to let my emotions show. Enough tears had poured in that house without mine being added. I asked to see Snow Flower's bride-price gifts. In my mind I thought: Maybe this butcher family won't be so bad after all. I had seen the silk pieces Snow Flower worked on. These people must be relatively prosperous, even if they were spiritually polluted.

Snow Flower opened a wooden chest and carefully laid out everything she had made on the bed. I saw the sky-blue silk shoes with the cloud pattern she had finished the day Beautiful Moon died. I saw a jacket that used some of that same silk on the front panel; then, in a neat row, Snow Flower propped five pairs of shoes of different sizes in the same fabric but embroidered with additional designs. This all looked familiar to me, and suddenly I understood why. These things had been fashioned from the jacket Snow Flower had worn on the first day we met.

My hands traveled over other items in her dowry. Here was the lavender-and-white material that had made up Snow Flower's traveling outfit when she was nine, now recut and reshaped into vests and shoes. Here was my favorite indigo-and-white cotton weaving that had been slit into panels and strips to be incorporated into jackets, headdresses, belts, and decorations on quilts. Snow Flower's actual bride-price gifts were minimal, but she'd taken pieces from her own clothes to create a unique dowry.

"You will make a remarkable wife," I said, truly awed by what she had accomplished.

For the first time, Snow Flower laughed. I had always loved that sound, so high, so alluring. I joined in, because all of this was . . . beyond—beyond anything I could have imagined, beyond what was fair or right in the universe. Snow Flower's situation and what she'd done with it was horrible and tragic and funny and amazing all at the same time.

"Your things—"

"Not even mine to begin with," Snow Flower answered, as she gulped for air. "My mother recut *her* dowry clothes to make my outfits when I visited you. Now they are recut again for my husband and my in-laws."

Of course! This had to be the case, because now I could remember thinking that a certain pattern seemed too sophisticated for a girl so young, or cutting loose threads from a cuff when Snow Flower wasn't looking. I was stupider than a chicken in a rainstorm. Blood rushed to my face. I clasped my hands over my cheeks and laughed even harder.

"Do you think my mother-in-law will notice?" Snow Flower asked.

"If I was too blind to notice, then . . ." but I couldn't finish because it was all too funny.

Perhaps it is a joke that only girls and women can understand. We are seen as completely useless. Even if our natal families love us, we are a burden to them. We marry into new families, go to our husbands sight unseen, do bed business with them as total strangers, and submit to the demands of our mothers-in-law. If we are lucky, we have sons and secure our positions in our husbands' homes. If not, we are faced with the scorn of our mothers-in-law, the ridicule of our husbands' concubines, and the disappointed faces of our daughters. We use a woman's wiles—of which at seventeen we girls know almost nothing—but beyond this there is little we can do to change our fate. We live at the whim and pleasure of others, which is why what Snow Flower and her mother had done was so *beyond*. They had taken cloth that had once been sent from Snow Flower's family to Snow Flower's mother as a bride-price gift, been shaped into the dowry of a fine maiden, been reshaped again into clothes for a beautiful daughter, and now restructured another time to announce the qualities of a young woman marrying into the house of a polluted butcher. All of it was women's work—the very work that men think is merely decorative—and it was being used to change the lives of the women themselves.

But so much more was needed. Snow Flower had to go to her new home with enough clothes to wear her entire lifetime. Right now, she had very little. My mind raced with things we could do in the month we had left.

When Madame Wang arrived for Snow Flower's Sitting and Singing in the Upstairs Chamber, I took her aside and begged her to go to my natal home. "There are things I need. . . ."

That woman had been critical of me for so long. She had also lied—not to my family but to *me*. I had never cared for her and now I liked her even less for her duplicity, but she did exactly as she was told. (I now outranked her, after all.) She returned from my home several hours later with a basket of my wedding dumplings, some of the sliced pork my in-laws had sent, fresh vegetables from our garden, and another basket filled with cloth that I had planned to cut when I returned home. To see Snow Flower's mother eat that meat was something I'll never forget. She had been raised to be a fine lady and, as hungry as she was, she did not tear into the food as someone in my family might. She used her chopsticks to pull apart slivers of the pork and lift them delicately to her lips. Her restraint and control taught me a lesson I have not strayed from to this day. You may be desperate, but never let anyone see you as anything less than a cultivated woman.

I was not done with Madame Wang. "We will need girls for Sitting and Singing," I said. "Can you bring Snow Flower's elder sister?"

"Her in-laws will not let her come back to this house."

I digested this fact. I had not heard that such a thing was possible.

"We still need girls," I insisted.

"No one will come, Miss Lily," Madame Wang confided. "My brother-in-law's reputation is too bad. No family will allow an unmarried girl to cross this threshold. What about your mother and aunt? They already know the situation—"

"No!" I wasn't ready to deal with them yet, and Snow Flower didn't need their pity. What my *laotong* needed were strangers.

I had *cash* from my wedding. I slipped some of it into Madame Wang's hand. "Do not return until you have found three girls. Pay their fathers whatever you think is the appropriate amount. Tell them I will be responsible for their daughters."

I was sure that my new married status to the best family in Tongkou would be persuasive, yet I could just as easily have been talking out of my behind, for surely my in-laws had no idea I was using their position in this manner. Still, I could see Madame Wang weigh this. She needed to continue to do business in Tongkou and was just about to reap the long-term benefits of bringing me to the Lu family. She did not want to jeopardize her position, but she had already bent many rules to benefit her niece. At last Madame Wang worked out the equation in her mind, nodded once, then left.

A day later, she returned with three daughters of farmers who worked for my father-in-law. In other words, they were girls like me, except they had not had my special advantages.

I *willed* that month. I led the girls in their singing. I helped them find good words to write about Snow Flower—someone they knew not at all—in their third-day wedding books. If they didn't know a character, I wrote it for them myself. If they dawdled in their quiltmaking, I took them aside and whispered that their fathers would be punished if they didn't adequately perform the jobs they had been hired for.

Remember how things were for my elder sister? She was sad to be leaving our home, but everyone believed she was going to a fair marriage. Her songs were neither too tragic nor too blissful, reflecting what was to be her future. I had had mixed emotions about my marriage. I too was sad to leave home, but I was excited that my life would change for the better. I had sung songs to praise my parents for bringing me up and to thank them for their hard work on my behalf. Snow Flower's future, on the other hand, looked bleak. No one could deny or change that, so our songs were filled with melancholy.

"Mama," Snow Flower chanted one day, "Baba failed to plant me on a sunny hill. I will live in the shade forever."

Her mother sang back, "Truly, it is like planting a beautiful flower on a pile of cow dung."

The three girls and I could only agree, raising our voices in unison to repeat both phrases. This is how things were: heavyhearted, but done in the traditional manner.

THE DAYS GREW colder. Snow Flower's younger brother visited one day and glued paper against the lattice window. Still, the damp crept in. Our fingers grew tight and red from the constant chill. The three girls were afraid to say much of anything. We couldn't go on this way, so I suggested that we move downstairs to the kitchen, where we might warm ourselves by the brazier. Madame Wang and Snow Flower's mother deferred to me, showing me once again that I had power now.

Long ago I had made my third-day wedding book for Snow Flower. It was filled with lovely predictions about Snow Flower and her future, but these things no longer pertained. I started again. I cut indigo cloth for the outside, folded it around several sheets of rice paper, and stitched the binding with white thread. Inside the front leaf I pasted red paper cutouts into the corners. The first pages were for me to write my farewell song to Snow Flower, the next were for my introduction of her to her new family, and the rest were left blank so she could use them for her own writings and to store her embroidery patterns. I rubbed ink against stone and enlisted my brush to write the characters in our secret language. I made each stroke as perfect as possible. I couldn't let my hand—so unsteady from the emotions of those days—mar the sentiments.

When the thirty days were over, the Day of Sorrow and Worry began. Snow Flower stayed upstairs. Her mother sat on the fourth stair leading to the women's chamber. Our songs had grown and developed by then. Despite the ominous threat of Snow Flower's father's anger at any noise, I raised my voice to chant my feelings and recommendations, such as they were.

"A good woman should not detest her husband's disadvantage," I sang, remembering "The Tale of Wife Wang." "Help lift your family to a better state. Serve and obey your husband."

Snow Flower's mother and aunt echoed these thoughts. "To be good daughters, we must obey," they sang together. Hearing their voices harmonizing together, no one could doubt the devotion and affection between them. "We must stay in our upstairs rooms, be chaste, be modest, and perfect the womanly arts. To be filial, we must leave home. This is our fate. When we go to our husbands' homes, new worlds unfold—sometimes better, sometimes worse."

"We had our happy daughter days together," I reminded Snow Flower. "Year after year, we were never a step apart. Now we will be together just the same." I recalled things we had written in our first exchanges on the fan and in our *laotong* contract. "We will still speak in whispers. We will still choose our colors, thread our needles, and embroider together."

Snow Flower appeared at the top of the stairs. Her voice floated down to me. "I thought we would soar together—two phoenixes in flight—forever. Now I am like a dead thing sinking to the bottom of a pond. You say we will be together just the same. I believe you. But my threshold will hardly compare to yours."

She slowly descended, stopping to sit by her mother. We expected to see bitter tears, but there were none. She linked arms with her mother and listened politely as the village girls continued their laments. Looking at Snow Flower, I couldn't help wondering at her seeming lack of emotion, when even I—as excited as I'd been to be marrying well—had cried during this ceremony. Were Snow Flower's feelings just as confused as mine had been? She would miss her mother surely, but would she miss that vile father of hers or miss waking up each morning in that empty house, which could only be a constant reminder of everything that had gone wrong with her family? It was terrible to be marrying into a butcher's home, but as a practical matter could it be worse than this? And Snow Flower was born a horse too. The galloping spirit that yearned for adventure was just as strong in her as it was in me. Still, although we were old sames, both of us born under the sign of the horse, my feet were always on the ground— practical, loyal, and obedient—while her horse spirit had wings that wanted to soar and fought against anything that might rein her in, despite having a mind that sought beauty and refinement.

Two days later, Snow Flower's flower-sitting chair arrived. Again she did not weep or struggle against the inevitable. She lingered for a moment in the piteously small crowd that had gathered and then stepped into the sparsely decorated palanquin. The three girls I'd hired didn't even wait for the flower-sitting chair to go around the corner before they set off for their homes. Snow Flower's mother retreated inside, and I was left alone with Madame Wang.

"You must think me an evil old woman," the matchmaker said. "But you should understand that I never lied to your mother or your aunt. There is little a woman can do in this life to change her fate, let alone someone else's, but—"

I held up a hand to prevent her from listing her excuses, because I needed to know something different. "All those years ago when you came to my house and looked at my feet—"

"You're asking me if you really were special?"

When I said yes, she regarded me with hard eyes.

"It is not so easy to find a potential *laotong*," she admitted. "I had several diviners looking throughout the countryside for someone I could match to my niece. True, I would have preferred someone from a higher family, but Diviner Hu found you. Your eight characters matched perfectly to my niece's. But he would have come to me anyway, because, yes, your feet *were* that special. Your fate was destined to change, with or without my niece as your *laotong*. And now I hope *her* fate has been changed because of her relationship to *you*. I told many lies, so she might have a chance at life. I will never apologize to you for that."

I stared into Madame Wang's overly rouged face, considering. I wanted to hate her, but how could I? She had done the best she could for the one person who mattered more to me in the world than any other.

SINCE SNOW FLOWER'S elder sister would not deliver the third-day wedding books, I went in her place. My natal family sent a palanquin, and in a short time I arrived in Jintian. No decorations or raucous sounds of a wedding band gave any hint that anything special was happening in the village on that day. I simply stepped out of my palanquin onto a dirt pathway in front of a house with a low-slung roof and a pile of wood against the wall. To the right of the door was something that looked like a gigantic wok embedded in a brick platform.

A feast should have been prepared for my arrival. It wasn't. The top women in the village should have greeted me. They did, but the coarseness of their dialect, even though only a few *li* from Tongkou, told me a lot about the unsavory quality of the people who lived here.

When the time came to read the *sanzhaoshu,* I was ushered into the main room. On the surface, the house resembled my natal home. Drying chilies hung from the central beam. The walls were of rough unpainted brick. I had hoped these similarities to my home would be reflected in the people who lived there. I did not encounter Snow Flower's husband on this occasion, but I did meet his mother, and she was a dreadful creature. Her eyes were set close together and her lips had the thinness that connotes a narrow mind and a mean spirit.

Snow Flower came into the room, sat on a stool next to the display of her third-day wedding books, and waited quietly. Although I felt I had changed with marriage, she did not look different to my eyes. The women of Jintian clustered around the *sanzhaoshu,* running their dirty fingers over them. They talked among themselves about the stitching on the edges and the paper cutouts, but none of them said a word about the quality of the writing or the thoughts expressed. After a few minutes, the women took positions around the room.

Snow Flower's mother-in-law walked to a bench. Her feet had not been as badly bound as my mother's, but an oddness to her gait marked her class even more than the guttural sounds that spewed from her mouth. She sat down, glanced with distaste at her new daughter-in-law, and then focused her unfeeling eyes on me. "I understand you have married into the Lu family. You are very lucky." The words were polite, but the way she spoke them suggested that I had bathed in offal. "People say that you and my daughter-in-law are well versed in *nu shu*. The women of our village don't value this pastime. We can read it, but we believe it is better to hear it."

I thought otherwise. This woman was like my mother, illiterate in *nu shu*. I glanced around the room, sizing up the other women. They hadn't commented on the writing because they probably knew very little of it themselves.

"We have no need to hide our thoughts in scribbles on paper," Snow Flower's mother-in-law continued. "Everyone in this room knows what I think." When uneasy laughter greeted this comment, she raised three fingers to silence her friends. "It would amuse us to hear you read my daughter-in-law's *sanzhaoshu*. Estimations of my daughter-in-law's worth coming to us from a big-house girl in Tongkou will be most appreciated."

Everything that woman said was a verbal sneer. I reacted as a seventeen-year-old girl might. I picked up the third-day wedding book that Snow Flower's mother had prepared and opened it. I imagined her refined voice and tried to re-create it as I chanted.

"I present this letter to your noble home on this third day after your wedding. I am your mother, and we have now been separated for three days. Misfortune struck our family, and now you marry out to a hard village." As was the custom for a third-day wedding book, the subject shifted, and Snow Flower's mother addressed the new family. *"I hope you will show my daughter compassion for the poverty of her dowry. Even the top layer is plain. Please don't mention it."* It went on in this way, talking about Snow Flower's family's bad luck, their fall from social status, and the poverty they now experienced, but my eyes swept right over these written characters as though they didn't exist. Instead, I made up new words. *"A good woman like our Snow Flower should fall into a good place. She deserves a decent family."*

I set the book down. The room was very quiet. I picked up the third-day wedding book I'd written for Snow Flower and opened it. My eyes sought out Snow Flower's mother-in-law. I wanted her to know that my *laotong* would always have a protector in me.

"People may speak of us as girls who married out," I sang, in the direction of

Snow Flower, *"but we will never be separated in our hearts. You go down; I go up. Your family butchers animals. My family is the best in the county. You are as close to me as my own heart. Our futures are tied together. We are like a bridge over a wide river. We walk side by side."* I wanted Snow Flower's mother-in-law to *hear* me. But her eyes stared back at me suspiciously, her thin lips pressed into a slash of displeasure.

As I came to the end, again I added a few new sentiments. "Don't express misery where others can see you. Don't let sobbing build. Don't give ill-mannered people a reason to make fun of you or your family. Follow the rules. Smooth your anxious brow. We will be old sames forever."

Snow Flower and I were not given an opportunity to speak. I was led back to my palanquin and returned home to my natal family. Once I was alone, I unpacked our fan and opened it. A third of the folds now had writing commemorating moments that were special to us. That seemed about right, for we had lived more than a third of what was considered a long life for women in our county. I looked at all the things that had happened in our lives up to that point. So much happiness. So much sadness. So much intimacy.

I went to the last entry where Snow Flower had written of my marriage into the Lu family. It covered half of a single fold in the fan. I mixed ink and pulled out my finest brush. Just below her good wishes for me, I carefully limned new strokes: *A phoenix soars above a common rooster. She feels the wind around her. Nothing will tether her to the ground.* Only now that I was alone and with those words written did I finally face the truth of Snow Flower's fate. In the garland at the top I painted a wilted flower from which little tears dripped. I waited until the ink dried.

Then I closed the fan.

The Temple of Gupo

MY PARENTS WERE HAPPY TO SEE ME WHEN I RETURNED. THEY were happier still with the sweet cakes that my in-laws sent as gifts. But to be honest, I was not so happy to see them. They had lied to me for ten years, and my insides churned with loathsome emotions. I was no longer the little girl who could let river water wash away unpleasant feelings. I wanted to accuse my family, but for my own welfare I still needed to follow the rules of filial piety. So I rebelled in small ways, isolating myself emotionally and physically as best I could.

At first my family seemed unaware of the change in me. They continued to do and say the customary things and I did my best to refuse their overtures. My mother wanted to examine my private parts, but I denied her this, pleading embarrassment. My aunt inquired about bed business, but I turned away from her, pretending I was too shy. My father tried to hold my hand, but I implied that now I was a married woman this kind of affection was no longer appropriate. Elder Brother sought my company to laugh and share stories; I told him he should do these things with his wife. Second Brother saw my face and kept his distance; I did nothing to change that, suggesting modestly that when he had a wife of his own he would understand. Only Uncle—with his baffled look and nervous hopping—elicited any sympathy from me, but I confided nothing. I did my chores. I worked quietly in the upstairs chamber. I was polite. I held my tongue, because all of them, except my younger brother, were my elders. Even as a married woman, I had no standing to accuse them of anything.

But I could not act like this and go unnoticed for long. To Mama, my behavior—though courteous in every respect—was unacceptable. We were too many people in a small household for one person to take up so much space with what she considered to be my pettiness.

I was home five days when Mama asked Aunt to go downstairs for tea. As soon as Aunt was gone, my mother crossed the room, leaned her cane against the table where I sat, grabbed my arm, and sank her nails into my flesh.

"Do you think you are too good for us now?" She hissed her accusation as I knew she would. "Do you think you are superior because you did bed business with the son of a headman?"

I raised my eyes to hers. I had never shown her disrespect. Now I revealed the anger on my face. She held my gaze, believing she could weaken me with her cold eyes, but I did not look away. Then, in one swift movement, she released my arm, drew back, and hit me hard across the face. My head jolted to the side then came back to center. My eyes sought hers again, which only offended Mama further.

"You dishonor this house with your behavior," she said. "You're beyond disgraceful."

"Beyond disgraceful," I mused in a low tone, knowing that my calm echo would aggravate her even more. Then I grasped her arm and yanked her down so that we were face-to-face. Her cane clattered to the floor.

From downstairs, my aunt called up. "Are you all right, Sister?"

Mama replied lightly. "Yes, just bring the tea when it's ready."

My body shook from the emotions raging beneath my skin. Mama felt them and smiled in her knowing way. I dug my nails into her flesh as she had done to me. I kept my voice low so that no one in the house could hear what I said. "You are a liar. You—and everyone in this family— deceived me. Did you think I wouldn't find out about Snow Flower?"

"We didn't tell you out of kindness to her," she whined. "We love Snow Flower. She was happy here. Why should we have changed the way you saw her?"

"It wouldn't have changed anything. She's my *laotong*."

My mother jutted her chin stubbornly and changed tactics. "Everything we did was for your own good."

I dug my nails deeper. "*Your* good, you mean."

I knew the physical pain I was causing her, but instead of grimacing she now twisted her features into something kind and beseeching. I knew she would try to justify herself, but I never could have imagined the excuse she would conjure up.

"Your relationship to Snow Flower and your perfect feet meant a good marriage, not only for you but for your cousin as well. Beautiful Moon was to be happy."

This diversion from what I was upset about was almost more than I could bear, but I held on to my composure.

"Beautiful Moon died two years ago." My voice came out hoarsely. "Snow Flower came to this house *ten* years ago. Yet you never found the time to tell me of her circumstances."

"Beautiful Moon—"

"This is not about Beautiful Moon!"

"You took her outside. If you hadn't, she would still be here today. You broke your aunt's heart."

I should have expected this manipulation of the facts from my monkey mother. Even so, the accusation was too harsh, too cruel to be believed. But what could I do? I was a filial daughter. I still had to rely on my family until I got pregnant and moved away. How could a girl born under the sign of the horse ever triumph in battle against the devious monkey?

My mother must have sensed her advantage, because she went on. "A proper daughter would thank me—"

"For what?"

"I gave you the life I could never have because of these." She motioned to her deformed feet. "I wrapped and bound your feet, and now you have received the reward."

Her words transported me back to the hours when I experienced the worst pain of my footbinding and she had often repeated a version of that promise. With horror, I realized that during those awful days she had not been showing me mother love at all. In some twisted way, the pain she inflicted on me had to do with her own selfish wants and desires.

The fury and disappointment I felt seemed unbearable. "I will never again expect any kindness from you," I spat out, releasing her arm in disgust. "But remember this. You made it so that one day I would have the power to control what happens to this family. I will be a good and charitable woman, but do not for once think that I will forget what you did."

My mother reached down, picked up her cane, and leaned on it. "I pity the Lu family for having to take you in. The day you leave here will be the most blessed in my life. Until then, do not try this nonsense again."

"Or what? You won't feed me?"

Mama looked at me as though I were a stranger. Then she turned and hobbled back to her chair. When Aunt came upstairs with tea, nothing was said.

And that's how things remained, for the most part. I softened toward the others: my brothers, Aunt, Uncle, and Baba. I wanted to cut Mama out of my life completely, but my circumstances wouldn't allow that. I had to remain in the house until I got pregnant and was ready to give birth. And even when I moved to my husband's home, tradition would require me to travel back to my natal home several times a year. But I tried to keep an emotional distance from my mother—though on most days we were in the same room—by acting as though I'd matured into a woman and no longer needed tenderness. This was the first time I would do this—properly follow customs and rules on the outside, let loose my emotions for a few terrible moments, and then quietly hang on to my grievance like an octopus to a rock—and it worked for everyone. My family accepted my behavior, and I still looked like a filial daughter. Later I would do something like this again, for very different reasons and with disastrous results.

SNOW FLOWER WAS dearer to me than ever. We wrote each other often, and Madame Wang delivered our letters. I worried about her circumstances—if her mother-in-law was treating her well, how she tolerated bed business, and whether things had worsened in her natal home—and she fretted that I no longer cared for her in the same way. We wanted to see each other, but we didn't have the excuse of visiting to work on our dowries, and the only trips we were allowed to take were to our husbands' homes for conjugal visits.

I went to my husband four or five nights a year. Every time I left, the women in my natal household cried for me. Every time I carried my own food, since my in-laws would not provide my meals until I fell permanently into their home. Every time I stayed in Tongkou, I was encouraged by how I was treated. Every time I returned home, my family's emotions were bittersweet, for each night away from them made me seem more precious and made the fact that I would soon leave forever a reality.

With each trip, I became more emboldened, looking out the palanquin window until I knew the route well. I traveled over what was usually a muddy and rutted track. Rice fields and the occasional taro crop bordered the roadway. On the outskirts of Tongkou, a pine tree twisted over the road in greeting. Farther along on the left lay the village's fishpond. Behind me, back where I had come from, the Xiao River meandered. Ahead of me, just as Snow Flower had described, Tongkou nestled in the arms of the hills.

Once the bearers set me down before Tongkou's main gate, I stepped out onto cobblestones that had been laid in an intricate fish-scale pattern. This area was shaped like a horse's hoof, with the village's rice husking room on the right and a stable on the left. The gate's pillars—decorated with painted carvings—held up an elaborate roof with eaves that swept up to the sky. The walls were painted with scenes from the lives of the immortals. The threshold through the front gate was high, letting all visitors know that Tongkou had the highest status in the county. A pair of onyx stones carved with leaping fish flanked the gate for visitors on horseback to dismount.

Just over the threshold lay Tongkou's main courtyard, which was not only welcoming and large but covered with a carved and painted eight-sided dome that was *feng shui* perfect. If I went through the secondary gate to my right, I came to Tongkou's main hall, which was used for greeting common visitors and small gatherings. Beyond this lay the ancestral temple, which was for hosting emissaries and government officials and for festive occasions such as weddings. The village's lesser houses, some of which were built of wood, clustered together just past the temple.

My in-laws' home sat prominently on the other side of the secondary gate to my left. All the houses in this area were grand, but my in-laws' was particularly beautiful. Even today, I am happy to live here. The house has the usual two stories. It is built of brick and plastered on the exterior. Up under the exterior eaves are painted tableaus of lovely maidens and handsome men, studying, playing instruments, doing calligraphy, going over the accounts. These are the kinds of things that have always been done in this house, so those pictures send a message to passersby about the quality of the people who live here and the ways in which we spend our time. The interior walls are paneled in the fine woods of our hills, while the rooms are highly ornamented with carved columns, lattice windows, and balustrades.

When I first arrived, the main room was much as it is now—with elegant furniture, a wood floor, a good breeze from the high windows, and stairs that climbed along the east wall to a wooden balcony embellished with an overlapping diamond pattern. Back then, my in-laws slept in the largest room at the back of the house on the ground floor. Each of my brothers-in-law had his own room that sat on the perimeter of the main room. After a time, wives came to live with them. If they didn't give birth to sons, those wives were eventually moved to other quarters and concubines or little daughters-in-law took their places in my brothers-in-law's beds.

During my visits, nighttime was devoted to bed business with my husband. We needed to make a son, and we both tried very hard to do what was necessary for that to happen. Other than that, my husband and I didn't see each other much—he spent his days with his father, while I spent mine with his mother—but over time we got to know each other better, which made our evening task more bearable.

As in most marriages, the most important person for me to build a relationship with was my mother-in-law. Everything Snow Flower had told me about Lady Lu following the usual conventions was true. She watched over me as I did the same chores that I did in my natal home—making tea and breakfast, washing clothes and bedding, preparing lunch, sewing, embroidering, and weaving in the afternoon, and finally cooking dinner. My mother-in-law ordered me about freely. "Dice the melon into smaller cubes," she might say, as I made winter melon soup. "The pieces you have cut are fit only for our pigs." Or "My monthly bleeding escaped onto my bedding. You must scrub hard to get out the stains." As for the food I brought from home, she would sniff and say, "Next time bring something less smelly. The odors of your meal ruin the appetites of my husband and sons." As soon as the visit was over, I was sent back home with no thank-you or goodbye.

That about sums up how things were for me—not too bad, not too good, just the usual way. Lady Lu was fair; I was obedient and willing to learn. In other words, we each understood what was expected of us and did our best to fulfill our obligations. So, for example, on the second day of the first New Year after my wedding, my mother-in-law invited all of Tongkou's unmarried girls and all of the girls who, like me, had recently married into the village to pay a visit. She provided tea and treats. She was polite and gracious. When everyone left, we went with them. We visited five households that day, and I met five new daughters-in-law. If I hadn't already been Snow Flower's *laotong,* I might have searched their faces, looking for those who might want to form a post-marriage sworn sister-hood.

THE FIRST TIME Snow Flower and I met again was for our annual visit to the Temple of Gupo. You would think we would have had much to say, but we were both subdued. I believed her to be remorseful—about having lied to me all those years and about her low marriage. But I too felt un-comfortable. I didn't know how to discuss my feelings about my mother without reminding Snow Flower of her own deceit. If these secrets weren't enough to stifle conversation, we now had husbands and did things with them that were very embarrassing. It was bad enough when our fathers-in-law listened at the door or our mothers-in-law checked the bedding in the morning. Still, Snow Flower and I had to discuss some-thing, and it felt safer to talk about our duty to get pregnant than to delve into those other thorny subjects.

We spoke delicately about the essential elements that must be in place for a baby to take hold and whether or not our husbands obeyed these rit-uals. Everyone knows that the human body is a miniature version of the universe—the eyes and ears are the sun and moon, breath is air, blood is rain. Conversely, those elements play important roles in the development of a baby. Since this is so, bed business shouldn't take place when rain pours off the roof, because it will cause a baby to feel trapped and con-fined. It shouldn't take place during thunderstorms, which will cause a baby to develop feelings of destruction and fear. And it shouldn't take place when the husband or wife is distressed, which will cause those dark spirits to carry over to the next generation.

"I have heard that you should not do bed business after too much hard work," Snow Flower told me, "but I don't believe that my mother-in-law has heard that." She looked exhausted. I felt the same way after visiting my husband's home—from the nonstop labor, from being polite, and from al-ways being watched.

"This is the one rule my mother-in-law doesn't respect either," I com-miserated. "Haven't they heard an exhausted well yields no water?"

We shook our heads at the nature of mothers-in-law, but we also wor-ried that if we did become pregnant we might not have healthy or intelli-gent sons.

"Aunt told me the best time to get pregnant," I said. Although all her babies had died except for Beautiful Moon, we still trusted Aunt's expertise in this regard. "There can be no unpleasantness in your life."

"I know." Snow Flower sighed. "When water is still, the fish breathes with ease; when wind is gone, the tree stands firm," she recited.

"We each need a quiet night when the moon is full and bright, which suggests both the roundness of a pregnant belly and the purity of the mother."

"And when the sky is clear," Snow Flower added, "which tells us that the universe is calm and ready."

"And we and our husbands are happy, which will let the arrow fly to its target. Under these circumstances, Aunt says, even the most deadly of insects will come out to mate."

"I know what needs to occur"—Snow Flower sighed again—"but these things are hard to align at one time."

"But we must try."

And so, on our first visit to the Temple of Gupo after our marriages, Snow Flower and I made offerings and prayed that these things would come to pass. However, despite following the rules, we didn't become pregnant. You think it's easy to get pregnant after doing bed business only a handful of times a year? Sometimes my husband was so eager that his essence did not go inside.

During our second visit to the temple after becoming wives, our prayers were deeper and our offerings greater. Then, as was our custom, Snow Flower and I visited the taro man for our special chicken lunch followed by our favorite dessert. As much as we both loved that dish, neither of us ate with enjoyment. We compared notes and tried to come up with new tactics to become pregnant.

Over the following months, I did my best to please my mother-in-law when I visited the Lu household. In my natal home, I tried to be as congenial as possible. But no matter where I was, people were beginning to give me looks that I read as admonishments for my lack of fertility. Then, a couple of months later, Madame Wang delivered a letter from Snow Flower. I waited until the matchmaker left before unfolding the paper. In *nu shu,* Snow Flower had written:

I am pregnant. I am sick to my stomach every day. My mother tells me this means the baby is happy in my body. I hope it is a boy. I want this to happen to you.

[142]

I couldn't believe that Snow Flower had beaten me. I was the one with the higher status. I should have gotten pregnant first. So deep was my humiliation that I didn't tell Mama or Aunt the good news. I knew how they would react. Mama would criticize me, while Aunt would be too joyous on Snow Flower's behalf.

The next time I visited my husband and we did bed business, I wrapped my legs around his and held him on top of me with my arms until he was done. I held him for so long that he fell asleep limp inside of me. I lay awake for a long time, breathing calmly, thinking of the full moon outside and listening for any rustling in the bamboo beside our window. In the morning, he had rolled away from me and was sleeping on his side. By now I knew what had to be done. I reached under the quilt and placed my hand around his member until it was hard. When I was certain he was about to open his eyes, I withdrew my hand and closed my own eyes. I let him do his business again, and when he rose and dressed to begin his day I stayed very still. We heard his mother in the kitchen, beginning the tasks that I should have done already. My husband looked at me once, sending a loud message: If I didn't get up soon and begin my chores, there would be serious consequences. He didn't yell at me or hit me as some husbands might, but he left the room without saying goodbye. I heard the low murmurs of his and his mother's voices a few moments later. No one came for me. When I finally rose, dressed, and went into the kitchen, my mother-in-law smiled happily, while Yonggang and the other girls exchanged knowing glances.

Two weeks later, back in my own bed in my natal home, I woke up feeling as though fox spirits were shaking the house. I made it to the half-filled chamber pot and threw up. Aunt came into the room, knelt down beside me, and wiped away the dampness on my face with the back of her hand. "Now you really will be leaving us," she said, and for the first time in a very long while the great cave of her mouth spread into a wide grin.

That afternoon I sat down with my ink and brush and composed a letter to Snow Flower. "When we see each other this year at the Temple of Gupo," I wrote, "we will both be as round as the moon."

MAMA, AS YOU can imagine, was as strict with me during those months as she had been during my footbinding. It was her way, I think, to consider only the bad things that could happen. "Don't climb hills," she chastised me, as though I had ever been allowed to do that. "Don't cross a narrow bridge, stand on one foot, watch an eclipse, or bathe in hot water." I was never in danger of doing any of those things, but the food restrictions were a different matter. In our county we are proud of our spicy food, but I was not permitted to eat anything seasoned with garlic, chilies, or pepper, which could delay the delivery of my placenta. I was not allowed to eat any part of a lamb, which could cause my baby to be born sickly, or eat fish with scales, since this would cause a difficult labor. I was denied anything too salty, too bitter, too sweet, too sour, or too pungent, so I couldn't eat fermented black beans, bitter melon, almond curd, hot and sour soup, or anything remotely flavored. I was permitted bland soups, sautéed vegetables with rice, and tea. I accepted these limitations, knowing that my worth was based entirely on the child growing inside of me.

My husband and in-laws were delighted, of course, and they began to prepare for my arrival. My baby was due at the end of the seventh lunar month. I would visit the annual festival at the Temple of Gupo to pray for a son and then travel on to Tongkou. My in-laws agreed to this pilgrimage— they would do everything they could to ensure a male heir—on condition that I spend the night at an inn and not overtax myself. My husband's family sent a palanquin to pick me up. I stood outside my family's threshold and accepted everyone's tears and embraces; then I got in the palanquin and was carried away, knowing I would return again and again in coming years for the Catching Cool Breezes, Ghost, Birds, and Tasting festivals, as well as any celebrations that might happen in my natal family. This was not a final goodbye, just a temporary farewell, as it had been for Elder Sister.

By this time, Snow Flower, who was further along in her pregnancy than I, already lived in Jintian, so I picked her up. Her stomach was so big, I couldn't believe her new family was allowing her to travel at all, even if it was to pray for a son. We were funny, standing in the dirt, trying to hug each other with our big bellies between us, laughing the whole while. She was more beautiful than in all the years I had known her, and true happiness seemed to pulsate from her.

Snow Flower talked during the entire trip to the temple, speaking of how her body felt, how she loved the baby inside her, and how kind everyone had been to her since she'd moved into her husband's home. She clutched a piece of white jade that hung around her neck to help give the baby's skin the clear pale color of the stone, instead of the ruddy complexion of her husband. I also wore white jade, but unlike Snow Flower, I hoped it would protect my child not from my husband's skin tone but from my own, which, even though I spent my days inside, was naturally darker than the creamy white of my *laotong*'s.

In years past we'd quickly visited the temple, bowing and putting our heads to the floor as we made supplications to the goddess. Now we walked in proudly, sticking out our round baby bellies, glancing at the other mothers-to-be to see who was larger, who carried high and who carried low, yet always mindful that our minds and tongues should carry only noble and benevolent thoughts so these attributes would be passed on to our sons.

We made our way to the altar, where perhaps a hundred pairs of infant shoes were lined up. Both of us had written poems on fans as offerings to the goddess. Mine spoke of the blessings of a son, how he would carry on the Lu line and cherish his ancestors. I ended with, *Goddess, your goodness graces us. So many come to you to beg for sons, but I hope you will hear my plea. Please grant my desire.* That had seemed appropriate when I had written it, but now I imagined what Snow Flower had done with her fan. It had to be filled with lovely words and memorable decorations. I prayed that the goddess would not be too swayed by Snow Flower's offering. "Please hear me, please hear me, please hear me," I chanted under my breath.

Together Snow Flower and I laid our fans on the altar with our right hands, while with our left hands we each snatched a pair of the baby shoes from the altar and hid them in our sleeves. We then left the temple quickly, hoping not to be caught. In Yongming County, all women who want a healthy child steal outright—but with the pretense of covertness—a pair of shoes from the goddess's altar. Why? As you know, in our dialect the word for *shoe* sounds the same as the word for *child*. When our babies are born we return a pair of shoes to the altar—which explains the supply that we stole from—and make offerings as thanks.

We stepped back outside into the beautiful day and made our way to the thread kiosk. As we had for twelve years, we searched for colors that we felt would capture the ideas for the designs we had in our minds. Snow Flower held out a selection of greens for me to examine. Here were greens bright as spring, dry as withered grass, earthy as leaves at the end of summer, vibrant as moss after a rain, dull as that moment before the yellows and reds of fall begin to set in.

"Tomorrow," Snow Flower said, "let's stop by the river on our way home. We'll sit and watch the clouds drift by overhead, listen to the water wash the stones, and embroider and sing together. In this way our sons will be born with elegant and refined tastes."

I kissed her cheek. Away from Snow Flower I sometimes let my mind ramble into dark places, but now I loved her as I always had. Oh, how I had missed my *laotong*.

Our visit to the Temple of Gupo would not have been complete without lunch at the taro stand. Old Man Zuo grinned toothlessly when he saw us with our baby bellies. He made a special meal for us, taking care that he followed all the dietary requirements for our condition. We savored every bite. Then he brought our favorite dish, the deep-fried taro coated in caramelized sugar. Snow Flower and I were like two girls in our giddiness, rather than two married ladies about to give birth.

That night in the inn after we had slipped into our nightclothes, Snow Flower and I lay in bed facing each other. This would be our last night of togetherness before we became mothers. We had learned so many lessons about what we should or shouldn't do and how these things would affect our unborn children. If my son could respond to hearing profane language or the touch of white jade against my skin, then certainly he had to feel my love for Snow Flower in his little body too.

Snow Flower put her hands on my stomach. I did the same to hers. I had grown accustomed to the way my baby kicked and pushed against my skin from the inside, especially at night. Now I felt Snow Flower's baby moving inside her against my hands. We were in that moment as close as two women could be.

"I am happy we are together," she said, then let a finger trace a spot where my baby was reaching out an elbow or a knee to her.

"I'm happy too."

"I feel your son. He's strong. Just like his mother."

Her words made me feel proud and full of life. Her finger stopped, and once again she held my belly in her warm hands.

"I'll love him as much as I love you," she said. Then, as she had since the time she was a little girl, she trailed one hand up to my cheek and let it rest there until we both fell asleep.

I would turn twenty in a couple of weeks, my baby would come soon, and my real life was about to begin.

Rice-and-Salt Days

Sons

Lily,

I write to you as a mother.
My baby was born yesterday.
A boy with black hair.
He is long and thin.
My childbearing pollution days are not over.
For one hundred days my husband and I will sleep apart.
I think of you in your upstairs room.
I await word of your baby.
Let it be born alive.
I pray for the Goddess to protect you from any problems.
I long to see you and know you are well.
Please come to the one-month celebration.
You will see what I wrote about my son on our fan.

Snow Flower

I WAS HAPPY THAT SNOW FLOWER'S SON WAS BORN HEALTHY
and hoped he would remain so, because life in our county is very fragile.
We women hope to have five children who reach adulthood. For that to
happen, we must get pregnant every one or two years. Many of those

babies die through miscarriages, at childbirth, or from illnesses. Girls—so susceptible to weakness from poor food and neglect—never outgrow their vulnerability. We either die young—from footbinding as my sister died, in giving birth, or from too much work with too little nourishment—or we outlive those we love. Baby boys, so precious, can die just as easily, their bodies too young to have taken root, their souls too tempting for spirits from the afterworld. Then, as men, they are at risk from infection from cuts, food poisoning, problems in the fields or on roads, or hearts that can't stand the stress of watching over an entire household. This is why there are so many widows. But no matter what, the first five years of life are insubstantial for boys and girls.

I worried not only for Snow Flower's son but for the baby I carried as well. It was hard to be afraid and have no one to encourage or comfort me. When I was still in my natal home, my mother had been too busy enforcing oppressive traditions and customs to offer me any practical advice, while my aunt, who had lost several unborn children, tried to avoid me completely so that her bad luck would not touch me. Now that I was in my husband's home, I had no one. My in-laws and my husband had concern for the baby's well-being, of course, but none of them seemed troubled that I might die delivering their heir.

Snow Flower's letter felt like a good omen. If childbirth had gone easily for her, surely my baby and I would survive it too. It gave me strength to know that even though we were in new lives, our love for each other had not diminished. If anything, it was stronger as we embarked on our rice-and-salt days. Through our letters we would share our ordeals and triumphs, but as with everything else we needed to follow certain rules. As married women who had fallen into our husbands' homes, we had to abandon our girlish ways. We wrote stock letters, with accepted formats and formalized words. In part, this was because we were foreigners in our husbands' homes, busy learning the ways of new families. In part, it was because we did not know who might read our letters.

Our words had to be circumspect. We could not write anything too negative about our circumstances. This was tricky, since the very form of a married woman's letter needed to include the usual complaints—that we were pathetic, powerless, worked to the bone, homesick, and sad. We were supposed to speak directly about our feelings without appearing ungrateful, no-account, or unfilial. Any daughter-in-law who lets the real truth of her life become public brings shame to both her natal and husband's families, which, as you know, is why I have waited until they were all dead to write my story.

At first I was lucky, because I didn't have anything bad to report. When I became betrothed, I'd learned that my husband's uncle was a *jinshi,* the highest level of imperial scholar. The saying I had heard as a girl—"If one person becomes an official, then all of his family's dogs and cats go to heaven"—now became clear. Uncle Lu lived in the capital and left the care of his holdings to Master Lu, my father-in-law, who was out most days before dawn, walking the land, speaking with farmers about crops, supervising irrigation projects, and meeting with other elders in Tongkou. All accounts and responsibility for what happened on the land rested on his shoulders. Uncle Lu spent the money with no concern for how it arrived in his coffers. He had done so well that his two youngest brothers lived in their own nearby houses—though not as fine as this one. They often visited with their families for dinner, while their wives called almost daily to our upstairs women's chamber. In other words, everyone in Uncle Lu's family—the dogs and cats, all the way down to the five big-footed servant girls who shared a room off the kitchen—benefited from his position.

Uncle Lu was the ultimate master, but I secured my place by being the first daughter-in-law and then by giving my husband his first son. As soon as my baby was born and the midwife put him in my arms, I was so blissful that I forgot the pain of childbirth and so relieved that I didn't worry about all the bad things that could still happen to him. Everyone in the household was happy and their gratitude came to me in many forms. My mother-in-law made me special soup with liquor, ginger, and peanuts to help my milk come in and my womb shrink. My father-in-law sent through his concubines blue brocaded silk so that I might make his grandson a jacket. My husband sat and talked to me.

For these reasons I have told the young women who have married into the Lu family, and the others I eventually reached through my teaching of *nu shu,* that they should hurry to have a baby boy. Sons are the foundation of a woman's self. They give a woman her identity, as well as dignity, protection, and economic value. They create the link between her husband and his ancestors. This is the one accomplishment a man cannot achieve without the aid of his wife. Only she can guarantee the perpetuation of the family line, which, in turn, is the ultimate duty of every son. This is the supreme way he completes his filial duty, while sons are a woman's crowning glory. I had done all this and I was ecstatic.

Snow Flower,

My son is here beside me.
My childbearing pollution days are not over.
My husband visits in the morning.
His face is happy.
My son has eyes that stare at me in question.
I can't wait to see you at the one-month party.
Please use your best words to put my son on our fan.
Tell me of your new family.
I don't see my husband very often. Do you?
I look out the lattice window to yours.
You are always singing in my heart.
I think of you every day.

Lily

Why do they call these rice-and-salt days? Because they are composed of common chores: embroidery, weaving, sewing, mending, making shoes, cooking meals, washing the dishes, cleaning the house, washing the clothes, keeping the brazier going, and being ready at night to do bed business with a man you still do not know well. They are also days filled with the anxiety and drudgery of being a young mother with your first baby. Why does it cry? Is it hungry? Is it getting enough milk? Will it ever sleep? Does it sleep too much? And what of fevers, rashes, bug bites, too much heat, too much cold, colic, not to mention all the illnesses that sweep through the county taking babies each year, despite the best efforts of herbal doctors, offerings on family altars, and the tears of mothers? Quite apart from the baby who suckles at your breast, you have to worry on a deeper level about the true responsibility of womanhood: to have more sons and ensure the next generation and generations after that. But during the first few weeks of my son's life I had another concern, which had nothing to do with my daughter-in-law, wife, or mother duties.

When I asked my mother-in-law to invite Snow Flower to my son's one-month party, she said no. This slight is something people in our county consider a terrible insult. I was crushed and confused that she would do this but powerless to change her mind. The day turned out to be one of the most important and festive occasions of my life, and I experienced it without Snow Flower at my side. The Lu family visited the ancestral temple to place my son's name on the wall with all their other family members. Red eggs—a symbol of life dyed red for celebration—were given to the guests and relatives. A grand banquet was served with birds-nest soup, salted birds that had been pickled for six months, and wine-fed duck stewed with ginger, garlic, and fresh red and green hot peppers. Through it all I missed Snow Flower horribly and later wrote to her as many details as I could recall, not thinking that they might remind her of the dreadful oversight. Apparently she accepted the lapse, because she sent a gift of an embroidered baby jacket and a hat decorated with small charms.

When my mother-in-law saw these, she said, "A mother must always be careful whom she chooses to let into her life. Your son's mother cannot associate with a butcher's wife. Filial women raise filial sons, and we expect you to obey our wishes."

With her words I realized that my in-laws not only did not want Snow Flower to come to the party, they didn't want me to see her at all. I was horrified, terrified, and, since I'd just had the baby, crying all the time. I didn't know what to do. I would have to fight my in-laws on this matter, not realizing how dangerous it would be.

In the meantime, Snow Flower and I secretly wrote to each other nearly every day. I had thought I knew all about *nu shu* and that men should never touch or see it, but now that I lived in the Lu household, where all the men knew men's writing, I saw that our secret women's writing wasn't much of a secret. Then it dawned on me that men throughout the county had to know about *nu shu*. How could they not? They wore it on their embroidered shoes. They saw us weaving our messages into cloth. They heard us singing our songs and showing off our third-day wedding books. Men just considered our writing beneath them.

It is said that men have hearts of iron, while women are made of water. This comes through in men's writing and women's writing. Men's writing has more than 50,000 characters, each uniquely different, each with deep meanings and nuances. Our women's writing has perhaps 600 characters, which we use phonetically, like babies, to create about 10,000 words. Men's writing takes a lifetime to learn and understand. Women's writing is something we pick up as girls, and we rely on context to coax meaning. Men write about the outer realm of literature, accounts, and crop yields; women write about the inner realm of children, daily chores, and emotions. The men in the Lu household were proud of their wives' fluency in *nu shu* and dexterity in embroidery, though these things had as much importance to survival as a pig's fart.

Since the men deemed our writing insignificant, they paid no attention to the letters I wrote or received. My mother-in-law was another story. I had to skirt the edges of her awareness. For now she didn't demand to know to whom I was writing, and over the next several weeks Snow Flower and I perfected a delivery system. We used Yonggang to run between our villages to transport our notes, embroidered handkerchiefs, and weaving. I liked to sit at the lattice window and watch her. I thought, so many times, I could make the trip myself. It was not that far away and my feet were strong enough to make it, but we had rules governing such things. Even if a woman can walk a great distance, she should not be seen alone on the road. Kidnapping by low types was a danger, while reputations were under even greater threat if a woman did not have the proper escort—her husband, her sons, her matchmaker, or her bearers. I could have walked to Snow Flower, but I never would have risked it.

Lily,

You ask about my new family.

I am very lucky.

In my natal home, there was no happiness.

My mother and I had to be quiet all day, all night.

The concubines, my brothers, my sisters, and the servants were gone.

My natal home felt empty.

Here I have my mother-in-law, my father-in-law, my husband, and his younger sisters.

There are no concubines or servants in my husband's home.

Only I fill those roles.

I do not mind the hard work.

Everything I needed to know came from you, your sister, your mother, your aunt.

But the women here are not like your family.

They do not like fun.

They do not tell stories.

My mother-in-law was born in the year of the rat.

Can you imagine anyone worse for someone born in the year of the horse?

The rat believes the horse is selfish and thoughtless, though I am not.

The horse believes the rat is scheming and demanding, which she is.

But she does not beat me.

She does not yell at me beyond what is customary for a new daughter-in-law.

Have you heard about my mother and father?
Within days of my falling into my husband's home,
Mama and Baba sold off the last of their belongings.
They took the *cash* and slipped away into the night.
As beggars, they will not have to pay taxes or other debts.
But where are they?
I worry about my mother.
Is she still alive?
Is she in the afterworld?
I do not know.
Perhaps I will never see her again.
Who would have guessed that my family was so unlucky?
They must have done bad deeds in former lives.
But if they did, then what about me?
Do you hear any words you can tell me?
And you, are you happy?

Snow Flower

Now that I knew this tragic news about Snow Flower's parents, I began to listen more carefully to the household gossip. Word began to filter in from merchants and salesmen who roamed the county that they had seen Snow Flower's parents sleeping under a tree, begging for food, or wearing dirty and tattered clothes. I thought often of how my *laotong*'s family had once been powerful in Tongkou and how her beautiful mother must have felt to be marrying into the family of an imperial scholar. Now look how low she had been brought. I feared for her with her lily feet. Without influential friends, Snow Flower's parents had been reduced to the mercy of the elements. Without a natal home, Snow Flower was worse than an orphan. I believed it was better to have dead parents, whom you could worship and honor as ancestors, than parents who had disappeared into the transient life of beggars. How would she know when they died? How would she be able to provide a proper funeral, clean their graves at New Year, or appease them when they fretted in the afterworld? That she was sad and without me to hear her thoughts was hard for me and had to be unbearable for her.

As for Snow Flower's last question—was I happy?—I wasn't sure how to respond. Should I write about the women in my new home? My new upstairs chamber housed too many women who did not like one another. I was the first daughter-in-law, but not long after I arrived in Tongkou the second son's wife came to live in the house. She had gotten pregnant right away. She was barely eighteen and cried nonstop for her family. She gave birth to a daughter, which upset my mother-in-law and made matters worse. I tried to befriend Second Sister-in-law, but she kept to a corner with her paper, ink, and brush, constantly writing to her mother and sworn sisters, still in her home village. I could have told Snow Flower about the unseemly ways Second Sister-in-law tried to impress Lady Lu by constantly kowtowing, whispering obsequious words, and maneuvering for position, while Master Lu's three concubines bickered among themselves, their petty jealousies pinching their faces and turning their stomachs sour, but I dared not put these sentiments on paper.

Could I have written to Snow Flower about my husband? I suppose I could have, but I didn't know what to say. I rarely saw him, and when I did he was usually talking to someone else or engaged in important tasks. During daylight hours, he went out to survey the fields and oversee projects on the land, while I embroidered or did other chores in the upstairs room. I served him at breakfast, lunch, and dinner, remembering to be as demure and quiet as Snow Flower had been at my family's table. He did not speak to me on those occasions. He sometimes came to our room early to visit our son or to do bed business. I assumed we were like any other married couple—even Snow Flower and her husband—so there was nothing of interest to write.

How could I answer Snow Flower's question about my happiness when the main conflict I had in my life had to do with her?

"I admit you have learned well from Snow Flower," my mother-in-law said one day, when she caught me writing to my *laotong,* "and we are grateful for that. But she is no longer a member of our village, nor is she under Master Lu's protection. He cannot and should not try to change her fate. As you know, we have codes governing wives that have to do with war and other border disagreements. As female guests, wives are not to be harmed during feuds, raids, or wars, because we are seen as belonging to both our husbands' villages and our natal villages. You see, Lily, as wives we have protection and loyalty from both places. But if something happened to you in Snow Flower's village, anything we might do could lead to retaliation and possibly even an ongoing fight."

I listened to Lady Lu's excuses, but I knew her reasons were far more base. Snow Flower's natal family was disgraced and she'd married a polluted man. My in-laws simply didn't want me to associate with her.

"Snow Flower's fate was preordained," my mother-in-law went on, venturing closer to the truth, "and it does not meet yours in any way. Master Lu and I would look favorably on a daughter-in-law who decided to break contract with someone who is no longer a true old same. If you need companionship, I will remind you of the young married women in Tongkou to whom I introduced you."

"I remember them. Thank you," I mumbled haplessly, while inside I was screaming in terror. *Never, never, never!*

"They would like you to join a post-marriage sworn sisterhood."

"Again, thank you—"

"You should consider their invitation an honor."

"I do."

"I'm just saying that you need to discharge Snow Flower from your thoughts," my mother-in-law said, and finished with a variation of her usual admonition. "I don't want memories of that unfortunate girl influencing my grandson."

The concubines snickered behind their fingers. They enjoyed seeing me suffer. In moments like these, their status rose and mine fell. But other than this continued criticism, which the others relished and which frightened me deeply, my mother-in-law was kinder to me than my own mother had been. She followed all the rules, just as Snow Flower had said. "When a girl, obey your father; when a wife, obey your husband; when a widow, obey your son." I had heard this my entire life, so I was not intimidated. But my mother-in-law taught me another axiom one day, when she was aggravated with her husband: "Obey, obey, obey, then do what you want." For now, my in-laws could prevent me from seeing Snow Flower, but they could never stop me from loving her.

Snow Flower,

My husband treats me well.

I don't even know where all our family fields are.

I also work hard.

My mother-in-law watches everything I do.

The women in my household are well educated in *nu shu*.

My mother-in-law has taught me new characters.

I will show them to you when we next meet.

I do embroidery, weaving, and shoemaking.

I spin cloth and prepare meals.

I have a son.

I pray to the Goddess that one day I'll have another son.

You should too.

Please listen to me.

You must obey your husband.

You must listen to your mother-in-law.

I ask you not to worry so much.

Instead, remember when we embroidered together and whispered at night.

We are two mandarin ducks.

We are two phoenixes flying across the sky.

Lily

In her next letter, Snow Flower mentioned nothing about her new family other than that her son had learned to sit. When she came to the end, she inquired again about my life:

Tell me about your meals and what is discussed.

Do they recite the classics when they eat?

Does your mother-in-law entertain the men with stories?

Does she sing to them to aid in their digestion?

I tried to answer truthfully. The men in my household discussed finances: what extra piece of land they could lease, who would till it, how much they should seek in rents, the cost of taxes. They had a desire to "get higher," to "get to the top of the mountain." Every family says these things at New Year, incorporating special dishes that invoke these wishes— knowing that this is exactly what they are. But my in-laws worked very hard to make them happen. It made for boring conversation that I did not understand, nor did I care to understand. They already had more than anyone in Tongkou. I could not imagine what else they could desire, yet their eyes never wavered from the top of the mountain.

I hoped that Snow Flower was happier now, conforming—as all wives must—to circumstances completely different from anything she had known before. Then, one dark afternoon as I nursed my son, I heard Madame Wang's palanquin stop outside our threshold. I expected to see her come up the stairs. Instead, my mother-in-law entered the room and with a disapproving frown dropped a letter on the table beside me. As soon as my son was asleep, I pulled the oil lamp closer and opened it. I noticed right away that the format was different. With a feeling of trepidation I began to read.

Lily,

I sit upstairs and cry. Outside I hear my husband killing a pig. He compounds his violation of the pollution laws.

When I first married in, my mother-in-law made me stand on the platform outside the house and watch as a pig was killed so I could see where our livelihood comes from. My husband and father-in-law brought the pig to our threshold. He was carried upside down on a pole strung between my father-in-law's and my husband's shoulders. The pig was between them, crying, crying, crying. He knew what was coming. I have heard this many times now, because they all know what is about to happen and their cries echo through our village much too often.

My father-in-law held the pig down next to a large wok filled with boiling water. (Do you remember that wok outside my house? The one embedded in the platform? Below that is a place to burn coal.) My husband slit the pig's throat. First, he collected the blood for blood custard, then he shoved the body in the wok. The pig was boiled to soften its skin. My husband asked me to scrape the hairs off the hide. I cried and cried, but not as noisily as the pig had done. I told them I would never watch or be a part of this pollution again. My mother-in-law condemned me for being so weak.

Every day I become more and more like Wife Wang. Do you remember when my aunt told us that story? I have become a vegetarian. My in-laws don't care. It leaves more meat for them.

I am alone in the world but for you and my son.

I wish I had never lied to you. I promised I would always tell you the truth, but I don't like you knowing of my ugly life.

I sit at the lattice window and look across the fields to my home village. I imagine you at your window looking back at me. My heart flies across the fields to you. Are you sitting there? Do you see me? Do you feel me?

Without you I am sad. I urge you to write or visit me.

Snow Flower

This was horrible! I looked out the lattice window toward Jintian, wishing that I could at least see Snow Flower. I felt terrible knowing that she was suffering and I couldn't put my arms around her to comfort her. In front of my mother-in-law and the other women in the upstairs chamber I pulled out a piece of paper and mixed ink. Before I picked up the brush, I reread Snow Flower's letter. The first time I had taken in only her sadness. Now I realized she'd broken from the traditional stylized lines used by wives in their letters and was using her *nu shu* to write more candidly and forthrightly about her life.

With her bold act, I realized the true purpose of our secret writing. It was not to compose girlish notes to each other or even to introduce us to the women in our husbands' families. It was to give us a voice. Our *nu shu* was a means for our bound feet to carry us to each other, for our thoughts to fly across the fields as Snow Flower had written. The men in our households never expected us to have anything important to say. They never expected us to have emotions or express creative thoughts. The women—our mothers-in-law and the others—put up even greater blockades against us. But from here on out, I hoped Snow Flower and I would be able to write the truth of our lives, whether we were together or apart. I wanted to drop the set phrases that were so common among wives in their rice-and-salt days and express my real thoughts. We would write as we had talked when we were huddled together in the upstairs chamber of my natal home.

I had to see Snow Flower and tell her things would be better. But if I visited her against my mother-in-law's wishes, I would be committing one of the worst crimes possible. Sneaking around to write or read letters paled in comparison to this, but I had to do it if I wanted to see my *laotong*.

Snow Flower,

I cry to think of you in that place. You are too good to have such ugliness in your life. We must see each other. Please come to my natal home for Expel Birds Festival. We will bring our sons. We will be happy again. You will forget your troubles. Remember that beside a well one does not thirst. Beside a sister one does not despair. In my heart I am forever your sister.

Lily

Sitting in the upstairs chamber, I planned and schemed, but I was scared. Simplicity seemed best—I would pick up Snow Flower in my palanquin on my way home—but it would also be the easiest way to get caught. The concubines might look out the lattice window and see my palanquin veer to the right toward Jintian. Even more dangerous, the roads would be busy with many women—including my mother-in-law—

returning to their natal homes for the festival. Anyone might see us; anyone might report us, if only to curry favor with the Lu family. But by the time the festival arrived, I had built up my bravery to the point I thought we might succeed.

THE FIRST DAY of the second lunar month marked the beginning of farming season, hence the Expel Birds Festival. Inside, on that morning, the women in our household rose early to make sticky rice balls; outside, birds waited for the men to begin planting rice seeds. I worked next to my mother-in-law, squeezing together the balls, using this rice to protect more rice, that most precious of daily foods. When the time came, Tongkou's unmarried women carried the bird feast outside and set the balls on sticks in the fields to attract the birds, while the men sprinkled poisoned grain along the edges of the fields for the birds to continue gorging themselves. Just as the birds pecked at their first deadly mouthfuls, Tongkou's married women stepped into palanquins, got on carts, or climbed onto the backs of big-footed women to be taken through the fields back to their natal villages. The old women tell us that if we don't leave, the birds will eat the rice seeds our husbands are about to sow and we won't be able to give them any more sons.

As planned, my bearers stopped in Jintian. I did not get out of the palanquin for fear someone might see me. The door swung open and Snow Flower, with her son asleep on her shoulder, joined me. It had been eight months since I'd seen her at the Temple of Gupo. With all the work she did, I had imagined that whatever plumpness she had gained during her pregnancy would be gone, but she was still shapely beneath her tunic and skirt. Her breasts were larger than mine, although I could see that her son was scrawny compared to my own. Her stomach also bulged, which was why she'd placed her son on her shoulder instead of cradled in her arms.

She gently turned her son so I could see him. I pulled my son from my breast and lifted him so the babies were face-to-face. They were now seven and six months old. They say all babies are beautiful. My son was, but her boy, despite his thick black hair, was as thin as a river reed, with sickly yellow skin and features scrunched into a scowl. But of course I complimented her on him and she did the same to me.

As our bodies swayed, bumped, and lurched to the bearers' gait, we talked about our new projects. She was weaving a piece of cloth that incorporated a line from a poem—a very difficult and taxing undertaking. I was learning how to make pickled birds—a relatively easy task except that it needed to be done correctly to prevent spoilage. But these were simple pleasantries; we had serious things to talk about. When I asked her how things were going, she did not hesitate for a moment.

"When I wake up in the morning, there is no joy except what I feel for my son," she confessed, her eyes locked onto mine. "I like to sing when I wash the clothes or bring in the firewood, but my husband gets angry if he hears me. When he is displeased, he won't permit me to cross over the threshold for anything other than my chores. If he is happy, in the evening he lets me sit outside on the platform where he kills his pigs. But when I'm there, I can only think of the animals that have died. When I fall asleep at night, I know I will rise again, but there will be no dawn, only darkness."

I tried to reassure her. "You say these things because you are a new mother and it has been winter." I had no right to compare my loneliness to hers, but even I was enveloped by melancholy on those occasions, when I missed my natal family or the cold shadows of the shortened days dampened my heart. "Spring is here," I offered, both to her and myself. "We'll be happier with the longer days."

"My days are better when they are short," she replied matter-of-factly. "Only when my husband and I go to bed do the complaints stop. I don't hear my father-in-law grumble about the weakness of his tea, my mother-in-law chastise me for the softness of my heart, my sisters-in-law demand clean clothes, my husband order me to be less of an embarrassment in the village, or my son demand, demand, demand."

I was appalled that my old same's situation was this bad. She was miserable and I didn't know what to say, though just a few days ago I'd promised myself that we would be more candid with each other. In my confusion and awkwardness I let myself be bound up by convention.

"I have tried to accommodate my husband and mother-in-law and it has made my life better," I offered. "You should do the same. You suffer now, but one day your mother-in-law will die and you will be the lady of the household. All number-one wives who are mothers of sons conquer in the end."

She smiled ruefully, and I thought over her complaint about her son. I truly didn't understand it. A son was a woman's life. It was her job and her fulfillment to meet his every demand.

"Soon your son will be walking," I said. "You'll be chasing him everywhere. You'll be very happy."

She tightened her arms around her baby. "I am already with child again."

I beamed my congratulations, but my brain was in turmoil. This explained her swollen breasts and bulging stomach. She had to be pretty far along. But how could she have gotten pregnant so soon? Was this the pollution she had written about in her letter? Had she and her husband done bed business before the hundred days were complete? It had to be so.

"I wish you another son," I managed to say.

"I hope so." She sighed. "Because my husband says it is better to have a dog than a daughter."

We all knew the truth of those words, but who would say that to his pregnant wife?

The feel of the palanquin setting down and the whoops of joy and greeting coming from my brothers saved me from trying to come up with an appropriate response. I was home.

How the household had changed! Elder Brother and his wife now had two children. She had gone back to her natal home for the Expel Birds Festival, but had left the youngsters for us to see. My younger brother had not yet married in, but preparations for his wedding were well under way. He was officially a man. Elder Sister had arrived with her two daughters and a son. She was growing old before our eyes, though I still thought of her as a girl in her hair-pinning days. Mama could not criticize me as easily, although she tried. Baba was proud, but even I could see the burden he felt by having so many mouths to feed for even these few days. Altogether, there were seven children aged six months to six years under our roof. The household rattled with the sounds of tiny footsteps running across the floor, pleas for attention, and songs to quiet. Aunt was happy with all the children about; a house full of children had been her lifelong dream. Still, every once in a while I saw her eyes tear up. If the world were fairer, Beautiful Moon would have been there with her children too.

We spent three days chatting, laughing, eating, and sleeping—none of us arguing, backbiting, condemning, or accusing. For Snow Flower and myself, the best times were at night in the upstairs chamber. We placed our sons on the bed between us. Seeing the two of them side by side, the differences between them were even more apparent. My son was fat with a shock of black hair that stood straight up like his father's. He loved to nurse and gurgled at my breast until he was drunk with my milk, pausing only to look up at me and smile. Snow Flower's son had a difficult time with his mother's milk, spitting it out on her shoulder when she burped him. He was fussy in other respects as well—crying late in the afternoon, his face red with anger, his bottom pink and blistered with rash. But once the four of us snuggled beneath the quilt, both babies quieted, listening to our whispers.

"Do you like bed business?" Snow Flower asked, when she was sure everyone was asleep.

For so many years we had heard the bawdy jokes told by old women or the offhand remarks made by Aunt about the bed fun she and Uncle had. All of that had been very confusing, but now I understood that there was nothing confusing about it.

"My husband and I are like two mandarin ducks," Snow Flower prompted, when I didn't respond right away. "We find mutual felicity in soaring together."

I was taken aback by what she said. Was she lying again, as she had for so many years? Into my bewildered silence, she spoke again.

"But as much as we both enjoy it," Snow Flower went on, "I am disturbed that my husband doesn't obey the rules about bed business after giving birth. He waited only twenty days." She paused again, then admitted, "I don't blame him. I agreed. I wanted it to happen."

Though completely bewildered by her desire to do bed business, I was relieved. She had to be telling me the truth, because no one would lie to cover a worse truth. What could be more shameful than committing a polluted act?

"This is a bad thing," I whispered back. "You must follow the rules."

"Or what? I'll become as polluted as my husband?"

This thought had already come to me, but I said, "I don't want you to get sick or die."

She laughed into the darkness. "No one gets sick from bed business. It only gives you pleasure. I work hard all day for my mother-in-law. Do I not deserve the delights of night? And, if I have another son, I will be happier still."

That last part I knew to be true. The one who slept between us was both difficult and weak. Snow Flower needed to have another son . . . just in case.

Too soon, our three days were over. My heart felt lighter. My palanquin dropped Snow Flower back in front of her house; then I went home. No one had spotted my diversion on the road, and the *cash* I paid my bearers guaranteed their silence. Emboldened by my success, I knew I would be able to see Snow Flower more often. Many festivals throughout the year required married women to return to their natal homes, and we also had our annual visit to the Temple of Gupo. We might be married ladies, but we were still old sames, no matter what my mother-in-law said.

OVER THE FOLLOWING months, Snow Flower and I continued to write each other, our words flying back and forth over the fields as free as two birds floating on a high breeze. Her complaints lessened and so did mine. We were young mothers and our lives were bright with the day-to-day adventures of our sons—new teeth coming in, first words spoken, steps taken. To my mind, we were both content as we settled into the rhythms of our new homes, learned how to please our mothers-in-law, and adjusted to the duties of being wives. I even grew more accustomed to writing Snow Flower about my husband and our intimate moments. By now I understood the old instruction: "Ascend the bed, act like a husband; descend the bed, act like a gentleman." I preferred my husband when he descended the bed. By day, he followed the Nine Considerations. He was clearheaded, listened carefully, and appeared affable. He was modest, loyal, respectful, and righteous. When in doubt, he asked his father questions, and on those rare occasions when he got angry, he was careful not to let it show. So by night, when he ascended the bed, I was happy for his enjoyment but relieved when he finished with me. I did not understand what my aunt had talked about when I was in my hair-pinning days, and I truly didn't comprehend Snow Flower's pleasure in bed business. But no matter how deep my ignorance, I knew one thing: You cannot break the pollution laws without paying a heavy toll.

Lily,

My daughter was born dead. She left without planting roots, so she knew nothing of the sorrows of life. I held her feet in my hands. They would never know the agony of footbinding. I touched her eyes. They would never know the sadness of leaving her natal home, of seeing her mother for the last time, of saying goodbye to a dead child. I put my fingers over her heart. It would never know pain, sorrow, loneliness, shame. I think of her in the afterworld. Is my mother with her? I don't know either of their fates.

Everyone in my household blames me. My mother-in-law says, "Why did we marry you in if not to bear sons?" My husband says, "You are young. You will have more children. Next time you will bring me a son."

I have no way to vent my sorrow. I have no one to listen to me. I wish I could hear you coming up the stairs.

I imagine myself as a bird. I would soar in the clouds, and the world below would seem very far away.

The piece of jade I wore around my neck to protect my unborn child weighs upon me. I cannot stop thinking about my dead baby girl.

Snow Flower

Miscarriages were common occurrences in our county, and women were not supposed to care if they had one, especially if the child was a girl. Stillbirths were considered dreadful only if the baby was a son. If a still-born child was a girl, parents were usually thankful. No one needed another worthless mouth to feed. For me, while I'd been petrified when I was pregnant that something might happen to my baby, I honestly didn't know how I would have felt if he had been a daughter and had died before breathing the air of this world. What I'm trying to say is that I was bewildered that Snow Flower felt the way she did.

I had begged her to tell me the truth, but now that she had I didn't know how to respond. I wanted to reply with sympathy. I wanted to give her comfort and solace. But I was scared for her and didn't know what to write. Everything that had happened in Snow Flower's life—the reality of her childhood, her terrible marriage, and now this—was beyond my understanding. I had just turned twenty-one. I had never experienced real misery, my life was good, and these two things left me with little empathy.

I searched my mind for the right words to write the woman I loved, and to my great shame I let the conventions I'd grown up with wrap around my heart as I'd done that day in the palanquin. When I picked up my brush, I retreated to the safety of the formal lines appropriate for a married woman, hoping this would remind Snow Flower that our only real protection as women was the placid face we presented, even in those moments of greatest distress. She had to try to get pregnant again—and soon—because the duty of all women was to keep trying to give birth to sons.

Snow Flower,

I am sitting in the upstairs chamber thinking deeply.
I write to console you.
Please listen to me.

Dear one, quiet your heart.
Think of me beside you—my hand on yours.
Imagine me crying at your side.
Our tears form four streams that run forever.
Know this.
Your sorrow is deep but you are not alone.
Do not grieve.
This was preordained, just as riches and poverty are preordained.
Many babies die.
This is a mother's heartbreak.
We cannot control these things.
We can only try again.
Next time, a son. . . .

Lily

Two years passed during which our sons learned to walk and talk. Snow Flower's son did these things first; he should have. He was six weeks older, but his legs weren't sturdy trunks like my son's. His thinness stayed with him, and it seemed a thinness of personality. This is not to say he wasn't smart. He was very clever, but not as clever as my son. By age three, my son already wanted to pick up the calligraphy brush. He was magnificent, the darling of the upstairs chamber. Even the concubines showered him with attention, bickering over him as they did over new pieces of silk.

Three years after my first son was born, my second son arrived. Snow Flower did not share the good luck of my destiny. She may have enjoyed bed business with her husband, but it produced nothing—except a second stillborn daughter. After this loss, I recommended she go to the local herbalist to procure herbs to help her conceive a son and enhance her husband's strength and frequency in his below-the-belt region. Thanks to my advice, Snow Flower informed me, she and her husband had been satisfied in numerous ways.

Joy and Sorrow

WHEN MY ELDER SON REACHED FIVE YEARS, MY HUSBAND started to talk about bringing in a traveling tutor to begin our boy's formal education. Since we lived in my in-laws' home and had no resources of our own, we had to ask them to bear the expense. I should have been ashamed of my husband's desires, but I never regretted that I wasn't. For their part, my in-laws could not have been more pleased than the day the tutor moved in and my son left the upstairs chamber. I wept to see him go, but it was one of the proudest moments of my life. I secretly harbored the hope that perhaps one day he might take the imperial exams. I was only a woman, but even I knew that these exams provided a stepping-stone for even the poorest scholars from the most wretched circumstances to a higher life. Nevertheless, his absence in the upstairs chamber left me with a black emptiness that was not filled by my second son's amusing antics, the squawking of the concubines, the bickering of my sisters-in-law, or even my periodic visits with Snow Flower. Happily, by the first month of the new lunar year, I found myself pregnant again.

By this time, the upstairs chamber was very crowded. Third Sister-in-law had moved in and given birth to a daughter. She was followed by Fourth Sister-in-law, whose complaining grated on everyone. She, too, had a daughter. My mother-in-law expended particular cruelty on Fourth Sister-in-law, who later lost two sons in childbirth. So it is fair to say that the other women in the household greeted my news with envy. Nothing caused more consternation in the upstairs chamber than the monthly arrival of one of the wives' bleeding. Everyone knew; everyone talked about it. Lady Lu always noted these events and loudly cursed the young woman in question for all to hear. "A wife who does not bear a son can always be replaced," she might say, though she hated with her entire soul her husband's concubines. Now, when I looked around the women's chamber, I saw jealousy and smoldering resentment, but what could the other women do but wait and see if another son came out of my body? I, however, had experienced a change of heart. I wanted a daughter, but for the most practical reason. My second son would leave me for the world of men very shortly, while daughters did not leave their mothers until they married out. My secret ambition flamed with news that Snow Flower was also with child. I cannot tell you how much I wanted her to have a daughter too.

Our first and best opportunity to meet to share our aspirations and expectations arrived with the Tasting Festival on the sixth day of the sixth month. After five years of living with the Lus, I knew my mother-in-law had not reversed her position on Snow Flower. I suspected that she was aware that we saw each other during festivals, but so long as I didn't flaunt the relationship and kept up with my household duties, my mother-in-law left the subject alone.

As it had always been, Snow Flower and I found pleasure in the upstairs chamber of my natal home, but our old intimacy couldn't be shown, not when we had our children in our bed or in cots around us. Still, we whispered together. I confessed to her that I longed for a daughter who would be my companion. Snow Flower smoothed her hands over her belly and in a small voice reminded me that girls were but worthless branches unable to carry on their fathers' lines.

"They will not be useless to us," I said. "Could we not make a *laotong* match for them now—before they are born?"

"Lily, we *are* worthless." Snow Flower sat up. I could see her face in the moonlight. "You know that, don't you?"

"Women are the mothers of sons," I corrected her. This had secured my place in my husband's home. Surely Snow Flower's son had secured her place too.

"I know. The mothers of sons . . . but—"

"So our daughters will be our companions."

"I've already lost two—"

"Snow Flower, don't you want our daughters to be old sames?" The thought that she might not crushed against my skull.

She looked at me with a sad smile. "Of course, *if* we have daughters. They could carry our love for each other even after we go to the afterworld."

"Good, that's settled. Now, lie down beside me. Smooth your brow. This is a happy moment. Let us be happy together."

We returned to Puwei with newborn daughters the following spring. Their birthdays did not match. Their birth months did not match. We peeled away their swaddling and held their feet sole to sole. Even as infants, their foot size did not match. I may have looked at my daughter, Jade, with mother eyes, but even I could see that Snow Flower's daughter, Spring Moon, was beautiful in comparison to mine. Jade's skin was too dark for the Lu family, while Spring Moon's complexion was like the flesh of a white peach. I hoped Jade would be as strong as the stone she was named for and wished that Spring Moon would be heartier than my cousin, whom Snow Flower had honored in her daughter's name. None of the eight characters corresponded, but we didn't care. These girls would be old sames.

We opened our fan and looked at our lives together. So much happiness had been recorded there. Our match. Our marriages. The births of our sons. The births of our daughters. Their future match. *"One day two girls will meet and become* laotong," I wrote. *"They will be as two mandarin ducks. Another pair—their hearts glad—will sit together on a bridge and watch them soar."* Above the garland at the top, Snow Flower painted two small sets of wings flying toward the moon. Two other birds, nesting side by side, looked up.

When we were done, we sat together, cradling our daughters. I felt so much joy, yet I didn't stop to consider that by ignoring the rules governing the match of two girls, we were breaking a taboo.

TWO YEARS LATER, Snow Flower sent me a letter announcing that she had finally given birth to a second son. She was jubilant and I was elated, believing that her status would rise in her husband's home. But we hardly had time to rejoice, because just three days later our country received sad news. Emperor Daoguang had gone to the afterworld. Our county was plunged into mourning, even as his son, Xianfeng, became the new emperor.

I had learned, from Snow Flower's family's bitter experience, that when an emperor dies his court falls out of favor so that with every imperial transition come disorder and disharmony, not just in the palace but across the country. At dinner when my father-in-law, my husband, and his brothers discussed what was happening outside of Tongkou, I absorbed only what I could not ignore. Rebels were causing trouble somewhere and landowners were pressing for higher rents from their tenant farmers. I felt for people—like those in my natal family—who would suffer, but truly these things seemed far removed from the comforts of the Lu household.

Then Uncle Lu lost his position and returned to Tongkou. When he stepped out of his palanquin, we all kowtowed, putting our heads to the ground. When he told us to rise, I saw an old man dressed in silk robes. He had two moles on his face. All people cherish the hair on their moles, but Uncle Lu's were splendid. He had at least ten hairs—coarse in texture, white in color, and a good three centimeters long—sprouting from each mole. As I got to know him, I saw that he loved to play with those hairs, pulling them slightly to encourage them to grow even more.

His clever eyes looked from face to face before settling on my first son. My boy had lived eight years now. Uncle Lu, who should have greeted his brother first, reached out a veined hand and laid it on my son's shoulder. "Read a thousand books," he said, in a voice resonant with education yet twisted by many years in the capital, "and your words will flow like a river. Now, little one, show me the way home." With that, the most esteemed man in the family took the hand of my son, and together they passed through the village gate.

ANOTHER TWO YEARS passed. I had recently given birth to a third son, and we were all working hard to keep things as they'd been, but anyone could see that between Uncle Lu's loss of favor and the rebellion against the rent increase, life was not the same. My father-in-law began to cut back on his tobacco and my husband spent longer days in the fields, sometimes even picking up tools himself and joining our farmers in their labors. The tutor left and Uncle Lu took over my eldest son's lessons. And in the upstairs chamber, the bickering between the wives and concubines increased as the usual gifts of silk cloth and embroidery thread diminished.

When Snow Flower and I met at my natal home that year, I barely spent any time with my family. Oh, we had our meals together and sat outside at night as we had when I was a girl, but Mama and Baba weren't the reason I visited. I wanted to see and be with Snow Flower. We had turned thirty and had been *laotong* for twenty-three years. It was hard to believe that so much time had gone by and harder still to believe that once she and I had been heart-to-heart close. I loved Snow Flower as my *laotong,* but my days were filled with children and chores. I was now the mother of three sons and a daughter, while she had two sons and a daughter. We had an emotional relationship that we believed would never be broken and was deeper than the binds we had with our husbands, but the passion of our love had faded. We didn't worry about this, since all deep-heart relationships must endure the practical realities of rice-and-salt days. We knew that when we reached our days of sitting quietly we would once again be together in the old way. For now, all we could do was share as much of our daily lives as possible.

In Snow Flower's household, the last of her sisters-in-law had married out, eliminating the chores she had once needed to do for them. Her father-in-law had also died. A pig he was slaughtering had twisted so strongly at the final moment that the knife slipped in his hand and sliced his arm down to the bone; he bled to death on the family's threshold as so many pigs had done. Now Snow Flower's husband was the master, though he—and everyone who lived under that roof—was still very much under the control of his mother. Knowing Snow Flower had nothing and no one, her mother-in-law stepped up her needling, while her husband lowered his protection of her against it. Still, Snow Flower found joy in her second son, who had already grown from a baby into a robust toddler. Everyone loved this child, believing that the first son would not make his tenth birthday, let alone age twenty.

Although Snow Flower's circumstances were not as high as my own, she paid attention and listened far more deeply than I did. I should have expected this. She had always been more interested in the outer realm than I. She explained that the rebels I'd heard about were called Taipings and that they sought a harmonious order. They believed—as do the Yao people—that ghosts, gods, and goddesses have an influence on crops, health, and the birth of sons. The Taipings forbade wine, opium, gambling, dancing, and tobacco. They said property should be taken away from the landlords, who owned 90 percent of the land and received up to 70 percent of the crop, and that those who worked on the land should share equally. In our province, hundreds of thousands of people had left their homes to join the Taipings and were taking over villages and cities.

She talked about their leader, who believed he was the son of a famous god, about something he called his Heavenly Kingdom, about his abhorrence of foreigners and political corruption. I did not comprehend what Snow Flower was trying to tell me. To me, a foreigner was someone from another county. I lived within the four walls of my upstairs chamber, but Snow Flower had a mind that flew to faraway places, looking, seeking, wondering.

When I returned home and asked my husband about the Taipings, he answered, "A wife should worry about her children and making her family happy. If your natal family disquiets you so, next time I will not give you permission to visit."

I did not say another word about the outer realm.

A LACK OF rain and what that did to the crops made everyone in Tongkou hungry—from the lowest fourth daughter of a farmer to the revered Uncle Lu—yet I still didn't concern myself until I saw our storeroom begin to empty. Soon my mother-in-law disciplined us over spilled tea or too large a fire in the brazier. My father-in-law refrained from taking much meat from the central dish, preferring that his grandsons eat this precious resource first. Uncle Lu, who had lived in the palace, did not complain as he might have, but as the truth of his circumstances sank in, he became more demanding of my son, hoping that this small boy would be the family's passage back to better circumstances.

This challenged my husband. At night when we were in bed and the lamps turned low, he confided in me. "Uncle Lu sees something in our son, and I was happy when he took over the boy's lessons. But now I look ahead and see we might have to send him away to pursue his studies. How can we do that when the whole county knows we will soon have to sell fields if we are to eat?" In the darkness, my husband took my hand. "Lily, I have an idea and my father thinks it is a good one, but I worry about you and our sons."

I waited, afraid of what he would say next.

"People need certain things to live," he continued. "Air, sun, water, and firewood are free, if not always abundant. But salt is not free, and everyone needs salt to live."

My hand tightened around his. Where was this leading?

"I have asked my father if I can take the last of our savings," he said, "travel to Guilin, buy salt, and bring it back here to sell. He has granted me permission."

There were more dangers than I could name. Guilin was in the next province. To get there, my husband would have to pass through territory occupied by the rebels. Those who weren't rebels were desperate farmers who'd lost their homes and had turned into bandits who stole from those who dared travel the roads. The salt business itself was perilous, which was one reason it was always in such short supply. Men who controlled salt in our province had their own armies, but my husband was just one man. He had no experience dealing with either warlords or wily merchants. If all this were not enough, my female mind imagined my husband encountering many beautiful women in Guilin. If he were successful in his venture, he might bring one or more of them home as concubines. My weakness as a woman came out of my mouth first.

"Don't pluck at wildflowers," I begged, using the euphemism for the types of women he might meet.

"A wife's value is in her virtues, not her face," he reassured me. "You have given me sons. My body will travel a great distance, but my eyes will not look at what they shouldn't see." He paused, then added, "Remain faithful, avoid temptation, obey my mother, and serve our sons."

"I would do no less," I promised. "But I don't worry about myself."

I tried to tell him of my other concerns, but he responded, "Do we stop living because a few people are unhappy? We must continue to use our roads and rivers. They belong to all Chinese people."

He said he might be gone for a year.

FROM THE MOMENT my husband left, I worried. As the months wore on, I grew increasingly anxious and frightened. If something happened to him, what would become of me? As a widow, I would have very few options. Since my children were too young to take care of me, my father-in-law could sell me away to another man. Knowing that under those circumstances I might never see my children again, I understood why so many widows killed themselves. But crying day and night about the possibilities was no way for me to go. I tried to maintain a serene facade in the upstairs chamber, even as I agonized over my husband's safety.

Longing to be comforted by the sight of my first son, I did something I had not done before. I volunteered many times a day to fetch tea for the women in the upstairs chamber; then, once downstairs, I sat quietly within earshot of his lessons with Uncle Lu.

"The three most important powers are Heaven, Earth, and Man," my son recited. "The three luminaries are the Sun, the Moon, and the Stars. Opportunities given by Heaven are not equal to the advantages afforded by Earth, while the advantages of Earth do not match the blessings that come from harmony among men."

"Any boy can memorize the words, but what do they mean?" Uncle Lu was strident in his correctness.

Do you think my son could give a wrong answer? No, and I'll tell you why. If he didn't answer a question correctly or made a mistake in his recitations, Uncle Lu gave him a whack on his open palm with a bamboo slat. If he got it wrong the next day, twice the punishment.

"Heaven gives Man weather, but without the fertile soil of the Earth, it is worthless," my son answered. "And rich soil is useless without harmony among men."

From my shadowed corner I beamed with pride, but Uncle Lu did not conclude the lesson because of one right answer.

"Very good. Now let's talk about empire. If you strengthen the family and follow the rules that are written in the Book of Rites, then order will be found in a household. This spreads from one household to the next, building the security of the state until you reach the emperor. But one rebel begets another rebel and soon there is disorder. Little one, pay attention. Our family owns land. Your grandfather ruled over it while I was gone, but now the people know I no longer have court connections. They see and hear the rebels. We must be very, very careful."

But the terror he was so afraid of did not arrive in the form of the Taipings. The last thing I heard before the death spirits descended on us was that Snow Flower was pregnant again. I embroidered her a handkerchief wishing her health and happiness in the coming months, then decorated it with silvery fish jumping from a pale-blue stream, believing that this was the most benign—and cool—image I could create for one who would be pregnant during summer.

THAT YEAR THE big heat came early. It was too soon to go back to our natal homes, so we women and children languished in our upstairs chambers, waiting, waiting, waiting. When the temperature continued to go up, the men in Tongkou and in the villages around us took the children to the river to wade and swim. This was the same river where I had cooled my feet as a girl, so I was delighted when my father-in-law and my brothers-in-law offered to treat the children in this way. But it was also the same river where the big-footed girls did the washing and—as the village wells soured with insect larvae—hauled water for drinking and cooking.

The first case of typhoid struck in the best village in the county—my Tongkou. It fell upon the precious first son of one of our tenant farmers, then swept through that household, killing everyone. The disease arrived as a fever, followed by a severe headache, then sickness in the stomach. Sometimes a hoarse cough came next, or a rash of rose-colored spots. But once the diarrhea hit, it was only a matter of hours before death brought a merciful end. As soon as we heard a child had taken ill, we knew what would happen next. First the child died, then the other brothers and sisters, then the mother, then the father. It was a pattern that we heard again and again, for a mother cannot turn away from a sick child and a husband cannot abandon a dying wife. Soon every village in the county had cases.

The Lu family retreated from village life and shut its doors. The servants disappeared, perhaps sent away by my father-in-law, perhaps running away out of fear. To this day, I still don't know. The women in our household gathered the children into our upstairs chamber, believing we would be safest there. Third Sister-in-law's infant son was the first to show symptoms. His forehead became dry and hot. His cheeks flushed a deep pink. I saw this and took my children to my sleeping chamber. I called for my eldest son. Without my husband here, I should have surrendered to his desire to stay with his great uncle and the rest of the men, but I did not give him a choice.

"Only I will leave this room," I told my children. "Elder Brother is in charge of you when I am not here. You are to obey him in all ways."

Each day during that dreadful season, I left the room once in the morning and once at night. Knowing the way that this disease discharged itself from the people it attacked, I carried out the chamber pot and dumped it myself, being careful that nothing from the night soil storage area touched my hands, my feet, my clothes, or our pot. I drew brackish water from the well, boiled it, and then strained it so it was as clear and clean as possible. I was afraid of food, but we had to eat. I didn't know what to do. Should we eat food raw, straight from the garden? But when I thought about the night soil we used in our fields and how the sickness had poured from so many bodies, I knew that couldn't be right. I remembered back to the one thing my mother always cooked when I was sick—*congee.* I made it twice a day.

The rest of the time we were locked in my room. During the day, we heard people running back and forth. At night, the fitful cries of the ill and the anguished cries of mothers came to us. In the morning, I put my ear against the door and listened for news of who had gone to the afterworld. With no one to care for them except each other, the concubines died agonized and alone, but for the very women whom they'd conspired against.

Whether it was day or night I worried about Snow Flower and my husband. Was she trying the same safeguards I was following? Was she well? Had she died? Had that pathetic first son of hers succumbed? Had the entire family perished? And what of my husband? Had he died in another province or on the road? If anything happened to either of them, I didn't know what I would do. I felt caged in by my fear.

My sleeping chamber had one window, too high for me to see out of. The smells of the bloating and diseased dead set before houses permeated the humid air. We covered our noses and mouths, but there was no escape—just a foul odor that stung our eyes and spoiled our tongues. In my mind I ticked off all of the jobs I had to do: Pray constantly to the Goddess. Swathe the children in dark red cloth. Sweep the room three times a day to frighten any ghost spirits hunting for prey. I also listed all the things from which we should refrain: no fried food, no sautéed food. If my husband had been home, then no bed business. But he was not home, and I had only myself to be vigilant.

One day as I cooked the rice porridge, my mother-in-law entered the kitchen with a dead chicken hanging from her fingers.

"There's no point in saving these any longer," she said gruffly. As she disjointed the bird and chopped garlic, she warned, "Your children will die without meat and vegetables. You will starve them to death before they can even get sick."

I stared at the chicken. My mouth salivated and my stomach grumbled, but for the first time in my married life I turned a deaf ear. I did not answer. I just poured the *congee* into bowls and placed them on a tray. On my way to my room, I stopped before Uncle Lu's door, knocked, and left a bowl for him. I had to do this, don't you see? He was not only the oldest and most respected member of our family but my son's teacher as well. The classics tell us that, in relationships, the one between teacher and student comes second only to the one between parent and child.

The other bowls I delivered to my children. When Jade protested that there were no scallions, no slivers of pork, not even any preserved vegetables, I slapped her hard across the face. The other children swallowed their complaints, while their sister bit her lower lip and fought back tears. I paid no attention to any of it. I simply picked up my broom and went back to sweeping.

Days passed and still no symptoms in our room, but the heat was fully upon us now, worsening the smells of illness and death. One evening, when I went to the kitchen, I found Third Sister-in-law standing like a wraith in the middle of the darkened room dressed head to toe in the white of mourning. I guessed from her appearance that her children and her husband must be dead. I was frozen in place by the empty, soulless look in her eyes. She did not move, nor did she acknowledge that she saw me just a meter in front of her. I was too scared to back away and too scared to move forward. Outside I heard the night birds calling and the low moan of a water buffalo. In my alarm, a stupid thought entered my brain. Why weren't the animals dying? Or were they dying and there was no one left to tell me?

"The useless pig lives!" A voice rang out virulent and bitter behind me.

Third Sister-in-law did not blink, but I turned to face the source. It was my mother-in-law. Her hairpins had been pulled out and her hair fell in oily strings around her face. "We should never have let you into this house. You are destroying the Lu clan, you polluted, filthy pig."

My mother spat at Third Sister-in-law, who did not have the will to wipe the mess from her face.

"I curse you," my mother-in-law swore, her face red with anger and grief. "I hope you die. If you don't die—but please, Goddess, make her suffer—Master Lu will marry you out by fall. But if I had my way, you would not live to see daylight."

With that my mother-in-law, who had not once acknowledged my presence, spun away, grabbed the wall for support, and staggered out of the room. I turned back to my sister-in-law, who still seemed lost to this world. Everything told me that what I was about to do was wrong, *wrong*, but I reached out, put my arms around her, and guided her to a chair. I set water to heat, then with all the courage I could find I dipped a cloth in a bucket of cool water and wiped my sister-in-law's face. I threw the cloth in the brazier and watched it burn. Once the water boiled, I made a pot of tea, poured a cup for my sister-in-law, and set it before her. She did not pick it up. I did not know what more I could do, so I began to make the *congee*, patiently stirring the bottom of the pan so the rice wouldn't stick or burn.

"I strain to hear my children's cries. I look everywhere for my husband,"

Third Sister-in-law murmured. I turned to face her, thinking she was speaking to me. Her eyes told me she wasn't. "If I remarry, how can I meet my husband and children in the afterworld?"

I had no comforting words to offer, for there were none. She had no great tree for protection and no faithful mountain standing behind her. She stood and swayed out of the kitchen on her delicate lily feet, as frail as if she were a lantern that had been released during the lantern festival and was drifting away. I went back to my stirring.

The next morning when I went downstairs, it seemed as though there had been a shift. Yonggang and two other servants had returned and were cleaning the kitchen and restocking the pile of firewood. Yonggang informed me that Third Sister-in-law had been found dead earlier that morning. She had killed herself by swallowing lye. I often wonder what might have happened if she had waited a few more hours, because by lunchtime my mother-in-law was down with fever. She must have already been sick the night before when she had been so cruel.

Now I had a terrible choice to make. I had kept my children protected in my room, but my duty as my husband's wife was to his parents above all else. To serve them did not just mean bringing them tea in the morning, washing their clothes, or accepting criticism with a smiling face. Serving them meant that I should esteem them above everyone else—above my parents, above my husband, above my children. With my husband away, I had to forget my fear of the disease, expel all feelings for my children out of my heart, and do the correct thing. If I didn't and my mother-in-law died, my shame would have been too great.

But I didn't abandon my children easily. My other sisters-in-law were with their own families in their own rooms. I didn't know what was happening behind their closed doors. They might have already taken sick. They might have already died. I couldn't trust my father-in-law with the care of my children either. Had he not spent the night beside his wife? Wouldn't he be the next to get sick? And I had not seen Uncle Lu since the epidemic began, although he left his empty bowl outside his room each morning and evening for me to refill.

I sat in the kitchen, twisting my fingers with worry. Yonggang came over, knelt before me, and said, "I will watch your children."

I remembered how she had escorted me to Snow Flower's house just after my wedding, how she had cared for me after I'd given birth to my babies, and how she had turned out to be loyal and discreet in carrying my letters to my *laotong*. She had done all this for me, and along the way, without my noticing, she had grown from a ten-year-old girl into a big-boned, big-footed young woman of twenty-four. To me, she was still as ugly as a pig's genitals, but I knew she had not yet fallen ill and that she would care for my children as though they were her own.

I gave her exact instructions for how I wanted their water and food prepared, and I gave her a knife to keep with her in case things got worse and she had to guard the door. With that, I left my children in the hands of the fates and turned my attention to my husband's mother.

For the next five days, I cared for my mother-in-law in all the ways a daughter-in-law can. I cleaned her lower half when she no longer had the strength to use the chamber pot. I made her the same *congee* that I had made my children; then I cut my arm as I had seen my mother do so that my vital fluid could be stirred into the porridge. This is a daughter-in-law's supreme gift and I gave it, hoping that through some miracle what had given me vitality would replenish hers.

But I don't have to tell you how terrible this disease is. You know what happens. She died. She had always been fair, and often kind, to me, so it was hard to say goodbye. When her last breath seeped out, I knew I couldn't do everything that should be done for a woman of her stature. I washed her soiled and desiccated body in warm water scented with sandalwood. I dressed her in her longevity clothes and tucked her *nu shu* writing in her pockets, sleeves, and tunic. Unlike a man, she had not written to leave a good name for a hundred generations. She had written to tell her friends of her thoughts and emotions, and they had written her in the same way. Under other circumstances, I would have burned these things at her grave site. But with the heat and the epidemic, bodies had to be buried quickly with little thought given to issues of *feng shui, nu shu,* or filial duty. All I could do was make sure my mother-in-law would have the comfort of her friends' words for reading and singing in the afterworld. As soon as I was done, her body was carted away for a hasty burial.

My mother-in-law had lived a long life. I could be happy for her in that regard. And, because my mother-in-law died, I became the head woman of the household, though my husband was still away. Now the sisters-in-law would have to answer to me. They would need to remain in my good graces to receive favorable treatment. With the concubines also dead, I looked forward to more harmony, because on one thing I was very clear: There would be no more concubines under this roof.

Just as the servants had intuited, the disease was leaving our county. We opened our doors and took stock. In our household, we had lost my mother-in-law, my third brother-in-law, his entire family, and the concubines. Brothers Two and Four survived, as did their families. In my natal family, Mama and Baba died. Of course I regretted that I had not spent more time with them on my last visit, but Baba and I had stopped having much of a relationship after I had my feet bound, and things had never been the same with Mama after our argument over the lies she had kept about Snow Flower. As a married-out daughter, my only obligation was to mourn my parents for a year. I tried to honor my monkey mother for what she had done to and for me, but I was not heartsick with grief.

All in all, we were lucky. Uncle Lu and I did not exchange words. That would have been improper. But when he came out of his room he was no longer a benign uncle idling away his retirement years. He drilled my son with such intensity, focus, and dedication that we never had to hire an outside tutor again. My son never shirked in his studies, buoyed by the knowledge that the night of his wedding and the day his name appeared on the emperor's golden list would be the most glorious of his life. In the former, he would be fulfilling his role as a filial son; in the latter, he would leap from the obscurity of our little county to such fame that the whole of China would know him.

But before any of that happened, my husband came home. I cannot begin to explain the relief I felt as I saw his palanquin come up the main road, followed by a procession of oxen-pulled carts loaded with bags of salt and other goods. All the things I had worried about and cried about were not going to happen to me—at least not yet. I was swept up in the happiness that all of Tongkou's women showed as our men unloaded the carts. We all cried, releasing the burdens, fear, and grief we had been carrying. For me—for all of us—my husband was the first good sign that any of us had seen in months.

The salt was sold throughout the county to desperate but grateful people. The extravagance of these sales washed away our financial worries. We paid our taxes. We bought back the fields we'd had to sell. The Lu family's standing and wealth abounded. That year's harvest turned out to be bountiful, which made autumn even more celebratory. Having weathered dark days, we could not have been more relieved. My father-in-law hired artisans to come to Tongkou and paint additional friezes under our eaves that would tell our neighbors and all those who would visit our village in the future of our prosperity and good luck. I could walk outside today and see them now: my husband in his jacket boarding the boat to take him downriver, his dealings with the Guilin merchants, the women of our household wearing flowing gowns and doing our embroidery as we waited, and my husband's joyous return.

Everything is painted under our eaves just as it happened, except for the portrait of my father-in-law. In the frieze he sits in a high-backed chair, surveying all he owns and looking proud, but in reality he missed his wife and no longer had the heart to care for worldly things. He died quietly one day, walking the fields. Our first duties were to be the best mourners the county had ever seen. My father-in-law was laid in a coffin and placed outside for five days. With our new money, we hired a band to play music, all day and all night. People from around the county came to kowtow before the coffin. They brought with them gifts of money wrapped in white envelopes, silk banners, and scrolls decorated with men's writing praising my father-in-law. All the brothers and their wives went on their knees to the grave site. The people of Tongkou plus others from neighboring villages followed behind us on foot. We were a river of white in our mourning clothes as we inched our way through the green fields. At every seven paces, everyone kowtowed, foreheads to the ground. The grave site was a kilometer away, so you can imagine how many times we stopped on that rocky road.

Young and old wailed their grief, while the band blared their horns, trilled their flutes, crashed their cymbals, and banged their drums. As the eldest son, my husband burned paper money and set off firecrackers. The men sang; the women sang. My husband had also hired several monks, who performed rites to help lead my father-in-law—and, we hoped, all those who had died in the epidemic—to a happy existence in the spirit world. Following the burial, we hosted a banquet for the entire village. As the guests went home, high-ranking Lu cousins gave each person a good-luck coin in paper, a piece of candy to wash away the bitter taste of death, and a washing towel for body cleansing. That took care of the first week of rites. Altogether we had forty-nine days of ceremonies, offerings, banquets, speeches, music, and tears. By the end—although my husband and I were not yet done with our official mourning period—everyone in the county knew that we were, at least in name, the new Master and Lady Lu.

Into the Mountains

I STILL DID NOT KNOW WHAT HAD HAPPENED TO SNOW FLOWER and her family during the typhoid outbreak. In my concern for my children, in my duties to my mother-in-law, and in the joy of my husband's return, followed by my father-in-law's death and funeral, and finally by my husband and I becoming Master and Lady Lu sooner than perhaps we were ready, I had—for the first time in my life—forgotten about my *lao-tong*. Then she sent me a letter.

Dear Lily,

I hear you are alive. I am sorry about your in-laws. I am sadder still to hear of your mama and baba. I loved them very much.

We survived the epidemic. In the early days, I miscarried—another girl. My husband says it is just as well. If I had carried all my children to term, I would have four daughters—a disaster. Still, three times to hold a dead child in your hands is three too many.

You always tell me to try again. I will. I wish I could be like you and have three sons. As you say, sons are a woman's worth.

Many people died here. I would tell you things are quieter now, but my mother-in-law lives. She says bad things about me every day, turning my husband against me.

I invite you to visit. My lowly gate hardly compares to yours, but I long to put our troubles behind us. If you love me, please come. I want to be together before we begin binding our daughters' feet. We have much to talk about in this regard.

Snow Flower

With my mother-in-law in the afterworld, I thought constantly of what she had told me about a wife's duty: "Obey, obey, obey, then do what you want." Without my mother-in-law's watchful eyes, I could finally see Snow Flower openly.

My husband had plenty of objections: Our sons were now eleven, eight, and one-and-a-half, our daughter had recently turned six, and he liked me to be at home. I eased his concerns over several days. I sang to him to calm his mind. I gave each of the children projects, which soothed their father's heart. I prepared all his favorite dishes. I washed and massaged his feet each night after he came in from roaming the fields. I attended to his below-the-belt area. He still did not want me to go, and I wish I had listened.

On the twenty-eighth day of the tenth month, I put on a lavender silk tunic I had embroidered with a chrysanthemum pattern appropriate for fall. I had once thought that the only clothes I would ever wear were the ones I had made during my hair-pinning days. I hadn't considered that my mother-in-law would die and leave behind her untouched bolts or that my husband would make enough riches that I would be able to buy unlimited quantities of the very best Suzhou silk. But knowing I was going to Snow Flower and remembering the way she had worn my clothes when we were girls, I took nothing else for the three nights I would be away.

The palanquin dropped me before Snow Flower's house. She sat waiting on the platform outside her threshold, dressed in a tunic, pants, apron, and headdress of soiled, worn, and poorly dyed indigo and white cotton. We did not go inside right away. Snow Flower was pleased to have me beside her in the cooling afternoon air. As she chattered on about this and that, I saw clearly for the first time the giant wok where the pig carcasses were boiled to remove their hair and loosen their skin. Inside the open door of an outbuilding, I glimpsed meat hanging from beams. The smell turned my stomach. But what was worse was the mother pig and her babies who kept coming up onto the platform, looking for food. After Snow

Flower and I finished our lunch of steamed water grass and rice, she took our bowls and set them at our feet so the sow and her babies could eat what we'd left behind.

When we saw the butcher returning home—pushing a cart loaded with four baskets, each containing a pig stretched out full length on its belly— we went upstairs, where Snow Flower's daughter embroidered and her mother-in-law cleaned cotton. The room was musty and gloomy. Snow Flower's lattice window was even smaller and less decorated than the one in my natal home, though I could see through it to my window in Tongkou. Even up here we could not escape the smell of pig.

We sat down and spoke of what was foremost in our minds—our daughters.

"Have you thought about when we should start their footbinding?" Snow Flower asked.

It was right and proper for it to begin this year, but I hoped from Snow Flower's question that she and I were of the same mind.

"Our mothers waited until we were seven, and we have been happy together ever since," I ventured carefully.

Snow Flower's face broke into a broad grin. "This is exactly what I thought. You and I had our eight characters matched so perfectly. Should we not only match our daughters' eight characters but also match those eight characters to ours as much as possible? They could start their binding on the same day and at the same age as we did."

I looked over at Snow Flower's daughter. Spring Moon had her mother's beauty at that age—silken skin and soft black hair—but her demeanor seemed resigned as she sat with her head down, squinting at her embroidery as she assiduously tried not to eavesdrop on her fate.

"They will be like a pair of mandarin ducks," I said, relieved that we had come to such an easy agreement, though I'm sure we were both hoping that our matched characters would make up for the fact that the girls' eight characters were not so perfectly in accord.

Snow Flower was truly lucky to have Spring Moon; otherwise she would have been left alone all day with her mother-in-law. Let me say this: That woman was still as biting and mean-spirited as I remembered. She had but one refrain: "Your oldest son is no better than a girl. He's a weakling. How will he ever have the strength to slaughter a pig?" I thought something not befitting Lady Lu: Why couldn't the spirits have taken her in the epidemic?

Our evening meal brought back tastes from my childhood before my dowry gifts began to arrive—preserved long beans, pigs' feet in chili sauce, wok-fried slivers of pumpkin, and red rice. Every meal when I was in Jintian was the same in the sense that we always had some part of the pig. Pig fat in black beans, pig ears in a clay pot, flaming pig intestines, pig penis sautéed with garlic and chili. Snow Flower ate none of it, quietly eating her vegetables and rice.

After dinner, her mother-in-law retired for the night. Although tradition says that two old sames should share a bed when visiting—meaning the husband sleeps elsewhere—the butcher announced that he would not remove himself to other quarters. His excuse? "There is nothing so evil as a woman's heart." This was an old saying and probably true, but it was not a gracious thing to say to Lady Lu. Nevertheless, it was his house and we had to do what he said.

Snow Flower took me back upstairs to the women's chamber, where she made a bed with some of her clean, though frayed, dowry quilts. On the cabinet she placed a low bowl filled with warm water for me to wash my face. Oh, how I wanted to dip a cloth into that water and wipe away the cares that played across my *laotong*'s features. As I thought this, she brought out an outfit almost identical to hers—*almost,* because I remembered when she had pieced it together from one of her mother's dowry treasures. Snow Flower leaned forward, kissed my cheek, and whispered in my ear, "Tomorrow we will have all day together. I will show you my embroidery and what I have done on our fan. We will talk and remember." Then she left me alone.

I blew out the lantern and lay beneath the quilts. The moon was nearly full, and the blue light that came through the lattice window transported me back many years. I buried my face in the folds where Snow Flower's scent was as fresh and delicate as when we had been in our hair-pinning years. The memory of low moans of pleasure filled my ears. Alone in that dark room I blushed at things perhaps best forgotten. But the sounds didn't go away. I sat up. The noises were not in my head but coming up to me from Snow Flower's room. My *laotong* and her husband were doing bed business! My *laotong* may have become a vegetarian, but she was no Wife Wang of the story. I covered my ears and tried to fall asleep, but it was hard. My good fortune had made me impatient and intolerant. The polluted and polluting nature of that place and the people who lived there rasped against my senses, my flesh, my soul.

The next morning, the butcher left for the day and his mother went back to her room. I helped Snow Flower wash and dry the dishes, bring in firewood, haul water, slice the vegetables for the midday meal, go to the shed where the sides of pork were kept to fetch meat, and attend to her daughter. Once all this was done, Snow Flower set water to heat that we could use for bathing. She carried the kettle back upstairs to the women's chamber and shut the door. We had never had any inhibitions. Why would we now? The air in that little house was surprisingly warm even though it was the tenth month, but goose bumps rose on my skin behind the path of Snow Flower's wet cloth.

But how do I say this without sounding like a husband? When I looked at her I saw that her pale skin—always so beautiful—had begun to thicken and darken. Her hands—always so smooth—felt rough on my skin. Lines were etched above her lip and at the corners of her eyes. Her hair was pinned back in a tight bun at the nape of her neck. Strands of gray threaded through it. She was my age—thirty-two. Women in our county often do not live beyond forty years, but I had just seen my mother-in-law go to the afterworld, and she had still looked very handsome for a woman who had reached the remarkable age of fifty-one.

That night, more pig for dinner.

I DIDN'T REALIZE it then, but the outer realm—that tumultuous world of men—was pushing its way into Snow Flower's and my lives. During my second night at her house, we were awakened by terrible sounds. We met in the main room and huddled together, all of us, even the butcher, terrified. Smoke filled the room. A house—maybe a whole village—was burning somewhere. Dust and ash settled on our clothes. The clatter of clanging metal and the beat of horses' hooves pounded into our heads. In the dark of night, we had no idea what was happening. Was it a catastrophe in just one village or was this something much worse?

A big disaster was coming. The people who lived in villages behind us began to flee, leaving their farms for the safety of the hills. From Snow Flower's window the next morning, we saw them—men, women, and children—on hand-drawn or oxen-pulled carts, on foot, on ponies. The butcher ran to the edge of the village and shouted to the stream of refugees.

"What's happened? Is it war?"

Voices called back.

"The Emperor has sent word to Yongming City that our government must take action against the Taipings!"

"Imperial troops have arrived to drive out the rebels!"

"There's fighting everywhere!"

The butcher cupped his hands and yelled, "What should we do?"

"Run away!"

"The battle will be here soon!"

I was petrified, overwhelmed, and dazed with panic. Why didn't my husband come for me? Again and again I berated myself for choosing this time—after all these years—to visit Snow Flower. But this is the nature of fate. You make choices that are good and sound, but the gods have other plans for you.

I helped Snow Flower assemble bags for her and the children. We went to the kitchen and gathered together a large sack of rice, tea, and liquor for drinking and to treat injuries. Finally, we rolled four of Snow Flower's wedding quilts into tight bundles and set them by the door. When everything was ready, I dressed in my silk traveling outfit, went outside to stand on the platform, and waited for my husband, but he didn't come. I looked up the road to Tongkou. A stream of people were leaving there too, only instead of going up into the hills behind the village they were crossing the fields, going toward Yongming City. The two trails of people—one going into the hills, the other going to town—confused me. Hadn't Snow Flower always said that the hills were the arms that embraced us? If so, why were the people of Tongkou going the opposite direction?

In the late afternoon, I saw a palanquin leave the Tongkou group and veer toward Jintian. I knew it was coming for me, but the butcher refused to wait.

"It's time to go!" he bellowed.

I wanted to remain behind and wait for my family to get me. The butcher said no.

"Then I will walk out and meet the palanquin," I said. So many times sitting at my lattice window I'd imagined walking here. Couldn't I now go toward my family?

The butcher chopped his hand through the air to prevent me from saying another word. "Many men are coming. Do you know what they will do to a lone woman? Do you know what your family will do to me if anything happens to you?"

"But—"

"Lily," Snow Flower cut in, "come with us. We'll be gone for only a few hours, then we'll send you to your family. It is better to be safe."

The butcher lifted his mother, his wife, the youngest children, and me into the cart. As he and the eldest son began to push us, I looked back across the fields behind Jintian. Flames and plumes of smoke billowed into the air.

Snow Flower kept passing water to her husband and eldest son. It was deep into fall now, and when the sun set the chill came down on all of us, but Snow Flower's husband and son sweated as if it were the middle of a summer day. Without being asked, Spring Moon hopped down from the cart, taking her little brother with her. She carried the boy on her hip, then on her back. Finally, she set him on the ground, took his hand, and kept her other hand on the cart.

The butcher assured his wife and mother that we would be stopping soon, but we didn't stop. We were part of a trail of misery that night. At the time of the most forbidding darkness just before dawn, we hit the first steep hill. The butcher's face strained, his veins bulged, his arms shook with the effort of trying to push the cart up the hill. Finally he gave out, collapsing behind us. Snow Flower slid to the edge of the cart, hung her legs over the side for a moment, then let them drop to the ground. She looked at me. I looked back. The sky behind Snow Flower was red with fire. The sounds that traveled on the wind pushed me out of the cart. Snow Flower and I tied two quilts apiece to our backs. The butcher slung the sack of rice over his shoulder and the children carried as much of the other food as possible. I realized something. If we were only going to be gone for a few hours, why had we brought so much food? I might not see my husband and children for several days. In the meantime, I'd be out here in the elements, with the butcher. I put my hands over my face to collect myself. I could not let him see my weakness.

On foot we joined the others. Snow Flower and I took the butcher's mother's arms and pulled her up the hill. She weighed us down, but how like her rat personality this was! When Buddha wanted the rat to spread his word, the wily creature tried to get a free ride from the horse. The horse wisely said no, which is why the two signs have not been a good match ever since. But on that terrible path on that hideous night, what could we two horses do?

The men around us wore grim faces. They had left behind their homes and livelihoods, and now they wondered if they would return to piles of ash. The women's faces were streaked with tears of fear and from the pain of walking farther in one night than in their entire lives since footbinding. The children did not complain. They were too frightened. We had only just begun our escape.

Late the next afternoon—and we had not stopped once—the road narrowed to a path that wound up steeper and steeper. Too many sights bruised our eyes. Too many sounds scratched our ears. Sometimes we passed old men or women who had sat down to rest, never to get up again. In our county I could not have imagined that I would see parents abandoned in this way. Often, as we went by, we heard mumbled requests, last words spoken to a son or daughter and repeated now as final sustenance: "Leave me. Come back tomorrow when this is over." Or, "Keep going. Save the sons. Remember to set an altar for me at Spring Festival." Every time we passed someone like that, my thoughts traveled to my mother. She could not have made this journey with only her cane for support. Would she have asked to be left behind? Would Baba have deserted her? Would Elder Brother?

My feet hurt as they had during my footbinding and pain shot up my legs with each step. But I was lucky in my suffering. I saw women my age and younger—women in their rice-and-salt years—whose feet had broken under the stress of walking so far or had fractured into bits against a rock. From the ankle up they were unhurt, but they were completely crippled. They lay there, not moving, only crying, waiting to die from thirst, starvation, or cold. But we kept going, never looking back, burying shame in our empty hearts, shutting out the sounds of agony and sorrow as best we could.

When the second night fell and our world grew black, despondency enveloped all of us. Belongings were abandoned. People got separated from their families. Husbands searched for wives. Mothers called out for their children. It was late fall, the season when footbinding begins, so many times we encountered young girls whose bones had recently broken and who were now left behind, as had food, extra clothes, water, traveling altars, dowry gifts, and family treasures. We also saw little boys—third, fourth, or fifth sons—who begged anyone who passed for help. But how can you help others when you have to keep moving while holding tightly to your favorite child's hand with your husband's hand tightly grasping yours? If you are afraid for your life, you don't think about others. You think only about the people you love, and even that may not be enough.

We had no bells to tell us what time it was, but it was dark and we were beyond tired. We had been walking now for more than thirty-six hours—without rest, without food, and with only the occasional sip of water. We began to hear horrible long screams. We could not imagine what they were. The temperature dropped. Around us leaves and branches collected frost. Snow Flower wore her indigo cotton and I was in my silk. Neither of our outfits would be much protection against what was to come. Beneath our shoes, the rocks became slippery. I was sure my feet were bleeding, because they felt oddly warm. Still, we kept walking. The butcher's mother staggered between us. She was a weak old woman, but her rat personality had a will to live.

The path narrowed to a third of a meter. To our right, the mountain—I cannot call it a hill any longer—rose so steeply it touched our shoulders as we trudged single file. To our left, the mountain fell away into blackness. I could not see what was down there. But on the trail ahead of me and behind me were many bound-footed women. We were like flowers in a gale. Our feet were not our only weakness. Our leg muscles—which had never worked this hard—ached, quivered, shook, and spasmed.

For an hour, we followed a family—father, mother, and three children—until the woman slipped on a rock and fell into that pit of darkness below us. Her scream was loud and long, until it abruptly ended. We'd been hearing this kind of death all night. From there on, I passed one hand over the other, grabbing at weeds, allowing my hands to be torn by the jagged rocks that poked from the cliff to my right. I would do anything to keep from becoming another scream in the night.

We came to a sheltered bowl. The mountains were silhouetted against the sky around us. Small fires burned. We were up high, yet with this dip in the landscape the Taipings could not see the glow from the fires, or at least we hoped they couldn't. We edged our way down into the bowl.

Perhaps because I was without my family I saw only children's faces in the firelight. Their eyes had a glazed and empty look. Perhaps they had lost a grandmother or a grandfather. Perhaps they had lost a mother or a sister. They were all frightened. No one should see a child in that condition.

We stopped when Snow Flower recognized three families from Jintian who had found a relatively sheltered spot under a large tree. They saw the butcher had a sack of rice on his back and scooted over to make room for us by the fire. Once I sat with my feet and hands close to the flames, they began to burn, not from the heat but from the frozen bones and flesh beginning to thaw.

Snow Flower and I rubbed her children's hands. They wept quietly, even the eldest boy. We pushed the three children together and covered them with a quilt. Snow Flower and I nestled together under another, while the mother-in-law took an entire quilt for herself. The last was for the butcher. He waved at us dismissively. He pulled one of the men from

Jintian aside, whispered a few words, and nodded. He knelt down beside Snow Flower.

"I'm going to look for more firewood," he announced.

Snow Flower gripped his arm. "Don't go! Don't leave us."

"Without a fire, we won't last the night," he said. "Don't you feel it? Snow is coming." He gently pried Snow Flower's fingers from his arm. "Our neighbors will look after you while I'm gone. Do not be afraid. And"—here he lowered his voice—"if you have to, push these people away from the fire. Make room for yourself and your friend. You can do it."

And I thought, Maybe she can't, but I couldn't allow myself to die up here without my family.

As tired as we all were, we were too scared to sleep or even close our eyes. And we were all hungry and thirsty. In our little circle around the fire, the women—who I learned later were post-marriage sworn sisters—distracted us from our fears by singing a story. It's a funny thing that although my mother-in-law was extremely literate in *nu shu*—perhaps *because* she was so familiar with such a variety of characters—singing and chanting had not been very important to her. She was more interested in composing a perfect letter or a lovely poem than in the entertaining or consoling qualities of a song. Because of this, my sisters-in-law and I had forsaken many of the old chants we had grown up with. In any event, the tale sung that night was familiar but one I hadn't heard since childhood. It told of the Yao people, their first home, and their brave fight for independence.

"We are Yao people," Lotus, a woman perhaps ten years older than I, began. "In antiquity, Gao Xin, a kind and benevolent Han emperor, was under attack by an evil and ambitious general. Panhu—a mangy, unwanted dog—heard of the emperor's problems and challenged the general to battle. He won and was given the hand of one of the emperor's daughters. Panhu was happy, but his betrothed was embarrassed. She did not want to marry a dog. Still, her duty was clear, so she and Panhu fled into the mountains, where she gave birth to twelve children, the very first Yao people. When they grew up, they built a town called Qianjiadong—the Thousand-Family Grotto."

This first part of the story finished, another woman, Willow, took up the chant. Next to me, Snow Flower shivered. Was she remembering our daughter days, when we listened to Elder Sister and her sworn sisters or Mama and Aunt as they sang this story of our beginnings?

"Could there be a place of so much water and such good land?" Willow asked in the song. "Could it be safer from intruders when it was hidden from sight, the only access through a cavernous tunnel? Qianjiadong held much magic for the Yao people. But such a paradise cannot remain undisturbed forever."

I began to hear verses sung by women sitting around other fires in the bowl. The men should have stopped our chanting, for certainly the rebels could hear us. But the purity of the women's voices gave us all strength and courage.

Willow continued. "Many generations later, in the Yuan dynasty, someone from the local government, bold in his explorations, walked through the tunnel and found the Yao people. Everyone was dressed resplendently. Everyone was fat from the wealth of the land. Hearing of this tantalizing place, the emperor—greedy and without gratitude—demanded high taxes from the Yao people."

Just as the first snowflakes fell on our hair and faces, Snow Flower linked her arm through mine and raised her voice to recount the next part of the story. "Why should we pay? the Yao people wanted to know." Her voice trilled with the cold. "On top of the mountain that blocked their village from intruders, they built a parapet from stone. The emperor sent three tax collectors into the cavern to negotiate. They did not come out. The emperor sent another three—"

The women around our fire joined in. "They did not come out."

"The emperor sent a third contingent." Snow Flower's voice gathered power. I had never heard her this way. Her voice floated out clear and beautiful across the mountains. If the rebels had heard her, they would have run away, fearing a fox spirit.

"They did not come out," we women called our response.

"The emperor sent troops. A bloody siege occurred. Many Yao people—men, women, and children—died. What to do? What to do? The headman took a water buffalo horn and divided it into twelve pieces. These he gave to different groups and told them to scatter and live."

"Scatter and live," we women repeated.

"This is how the Yao people came to be in the valleys and in the mountains, in this province and in others," Snow Flower wound down.

Plum Blossom, the youngest woman in our group, finished the tale. "They say that in five hundred years, Yao people, wherever they are, will walk through the cavern again, put the horn back together, and rebuild our enchanted home. That time comes to us soon."

It had been many years since I'd heard the story, and I didn't know what to think. The Yao had believed they were secure, hidden behind the safety of the mountain, their parapet, and the secret cavern, but they were not. Now I wondered who would come into our mountainous bowl first and what would happen when they did. The Taipings might try to win us over, while the Great Hunan Army might mistake us for rebels. Either way, would we fight a losing battle and be like our ancestors? Would we ever be able to return home? I considered the Taipings, who—like the Yao people—had revolted against high taxes and rebelled against the feudal system. Were they right? Should we join them? Were we violating our ancestors by not honoring that?

That night none of us slept.

Winter

THE FOUR FAMILIES FROM JINTIAN STAYED TOGETHER UNDER the protection of the large tree with its spreading branches, but the ordeal didn't end—not after two nights or even a week. We suffered worse snow that year than had been in our province in anyone's memory. We endured freezing temperatures at every moment. Our breaths became clouds of steam that were swallowed by the mountain air. We were always hungry. Each family hoarded its food, unsure of how long we would be away. Coughs, colds, and sore throats swept back and forth across the camp. Men, women, and children continued to die from these ailments and from the relentlessly frigid nights.

My feet—and those of most of the women in these mountains—had been badly hurt during our escape. We did not have privacy, so we had to unwrap, clean, and rewrap our feet in front of the men. And we overcame our embarrassment about other body functions, learning to do our business behind a tree or in the common latrine, once it was dug. But unlike most women up here, I was without my family. I desperately missed my eldest son and the rest of my children. I worried constantly about my husband, his brothers, my sisters-in-law, their children, even the servants—and if they had reached the protection of Yongming City.

It took almost a month for my feet to heal enough to walk on them again without restarting the bleeding. At the beginning of the twelfth lunar month, I decided I would go every day in search of my brothers and their families and Elder Sister and her family. I hoped they were safe up here, but how could I locate them when we were ten thousand people spread out across the mountains? Each day I draped one of the quilts over my shoulders and gingerly set out, always marking my progress, knowing that if I didn't find my way back to Snow Flower's family I would surely perish.

One day—perhaps two weeks into my searching—I came across a group from Getan Village huddled under a rocky overhang. I asked if they knew Elder Sister.

"Yes, yes, we do!" one of the women chirped.

"We were separated from her on the first night," her friend said. "Tell her, if you find her, to come be with us. We can shelter one more family."

Yet another—the one who appeared to be their leader—cautioned that they only had space for people from Getan, in case I got any ideas.

"I understand," I said. "But if you see her, could you tell her I'm looking for her? I'm her sister."

"Her sister? Are you the one known as Lady Lu?"

"Yes," I responded warily. If they thought I had anything to give them, they were mistaken.

"Men came looking for you."

My stomach jumped at these words. "Who were they? My brothers?"

The women looked at each other, then at me, sizing me up. Their leader spoke again. "They were mindful not to say who they were. You know how things are up here. One among them was the master. I would say he had a good build. His shoes and clothes were of good quality. His hair came down on his forehead like this."

My husband! It had to be!

"What did he say? Where is he now? How—"

"We don't know, but if you are Lady Lu, know that a man is looking for you. Don't worry." The woman reached up and patted my hand. "He said he would come back."

But as much as I searched, I never heard another story like this. Soon I came to believe that those women had used their own bitterness against me, but when I returned to the spot where I had met them, a different set of families huddled under the rocky shelf. After that discovery, I went back to my camp feeling nothing but deep despair. Supposedly I was Lady Lu, but looking at me no one would know it. My lavender silk with the expertly embroidered chrysanthemum pattern was filthy and torn, while my shoes were blackened with my blood and scuffed from daily wear in the outdoors. I could only imagine what the sun, wind, and cold were doing to my face. From my age of eighty, I can look back now and say with certainty that I was a frivolous and stupid young woman to think of vanity when the lack of food and the unrelenting cold were our true villains.

Snow Flower's husband became a hero to our small band of people. By being in an unclean profession, he did many things that needed to be done, without complaint and without thanks. He was born under the sign of the rooster—handsome, critical, aggressive, and deadly if required. It was in his nature to look to the earth for survival; he could hunt, clean an animal, cook it over an open fire, and dry the skins for us to use for warmth. He could carry heavy loads of firewood and water. He never tired. Up here, he wasn't a polluter; he was a guardian and champion. Snow Flower was proud of him for being such a leader, and I was—and am—forever grateful that his actions kept me alive.

Aiya! But that rat mother of his! She was always skulking and slinking about. In these most desperate circumstances, she continued to denounce and complain, even over the most unimportant things. She always sat closest to the fire. She never released the quilt she had been handed that first night and at every opportunity took one of the others until we demanded it back. She hid food in her sleeves, pulling it out when she thought we weren't looking to shove bits of burnt flesh into her mouth. You often hear that rats are clannish. We saw this every day. She constantly wheedled and manipulated her son, but she didn't have to. He did what any filial son would do. He obeyed. So when that old woman went on and on about how she needed more food than her daughter-in-law, he made sure that she, and not his wife, ate. Being filial myself, I couldn't argue with the logic of that, so Snow Flower and I began to share my portion. Then one day, after we had reached the bottom of our rice sack, the butcher's mother said that the eldest son shouldn't be given food that the butcher had hunted or scavenged.

"It's too precious to waste on someone so weak," she said. "When he dies, we will all be relieved."

I looked at the boy. He was eleven that year, the same age as my eldest son. He stared at his grandmother with sunken eyes, too pathetic to fight for himself. Certainly Snow Flower would say something on his behalf. He was the first son after all. But my old same did not love that boy the way she should have. Her eyes, even in that terrible moment when he was being consigned to certain death, were not on him but on her second son.

As clever, resilient, and strong as the second boy was, I could not let this happen to an eldest son. It went against all tradition. How would I answer my ancestors when they asked how I had let the child die? How would I greet that poor boy when I saw him in the afterworld? As the eldest son, he deserved more food than any of us, including the butcher. So I began sharing my portion with Snow Flower and her son. When the butcher realized what was happening, he slapped the boy and then his wife.

"That food is for Lady Lu."

Before either of them could respond, his rat mother jumped in. "Son, why give food to that woman anyway? She is just a stranger to us. We must think of our own blood: you, your second son, and me."

No mention, of course, of the first son or Spring Moon, both of whom had survived this far on scraps and had become frailer with each passing day.

But for once the butcher didn't buckle under his mother's pressure.

"Lady Lu is our guest. If I bring her back alive, there may be a reward."

"Money?" his mother asked.

Such a typical rat question. That woman could not hide her greed and acquisitiveness.

"There are things Master Lu can do for us that go beyond money."

The old woman's eyes narrowed to slits as she considered this. Before she could speak, I said, "If there is to be a reward, I will need a larger portion. Otherwise"—and here I twisted my face into one of the spoiled grimaces I remembered from my father-in-law's concubines—"I will say that I found no hospitality from this family, only avarice, inconsideration, and vulgarity."

Such a tremendous risk I took that day! The butcher could have thrown me out of the group right then. Instead, despite his mother's never-ending complaints, I received the largest amount of food, which I was able to share with Snow Flower, her eldest son, and Spring Moon. Oh, but how hungry we were. We became little more than corpses—lying still all day, our eyes closed, breathing as shallowly as possible, trying to harness whatever resources we had left. Maladies considered mild at home continued to reduce our numbers. With little food, energy, hot cups of tea, or fortifying doses of herbs, no one had the strength to fight these nuisances. As more succumbed, few among us had the strength to move the bodies.

Snow Flower's eldest son sought my side whenever possible. He was unloved, true, but he was not as stupid as his family believed. I thought of the day that Snow Flower and I had gone to the Temple of Gupo to pray for sons and how we wanted them to have elegant and refined tastes. I could see these things lay dormant in the boy, though he had received no formal education. I could not help him learn men's writing, but I could repeat what I had overheard Uncle Lu teach my son. "The five things the Chinese people respect the most are Heaven, Earth, the emperor, parents, and teachers. . . ." When I ran out of lessons I could remember, I told him a didactic tale carried by the women in our county about a second son who becomes a mandarin and returns home to his family, but I changed it to fit this poor boy's circumstances.

"A first son runs by the river," I began. "He is as green as bamboo. He knows nothing of life. He lives with his mama, baba, younger brother, and younger sister. The younger brother will follow his father's trade. The younger sister will marry out. Mama's and Baba's eyes never rest upon their eldest son. When they do, they beat his head until it is as swollen as a melon."

The boy shifted beside me, moving his eyes from the fire to my face as I went on.

"One day the boy goes to the place where his father keeps his money. He takes some *cash* and hides it in his pocket. Then he goes to where his mother keeps food. He fills a satchel with as much as he can carry. Then, without a single goodbye, he walks away from his house and through the fields. He swims across the river and walks some more." I thought of a far-away place. "He walks all the way to Guilin. You think this journey into the mountains was hard? You think living outside in winter is hard? This is nothing. Out on the road, he had no friends, no benefactors, and only the clothes on his back. When he ran out of food and money, he survived by begging."

The boy colored, not from the heat of the fire but from shame. He must have heard that his maternal grandparents had been reduced to this life.

"Some people say this is disreputable," I continued, "but if it is the only way to live, then it takes great courage."

From the other side of the fire, the butcher's mother grunted. "You're telling the story wrong."

I paid no attention. I knew how the story went, but I wanted to give this child something to hold on to.

"The boy wandered through the streets of Guilin, looking for people who were dressed as mandarins. He listened to how they spoke and shaped his mouth to make the same sounds come out. He sat outside tea-houses and tried to speak to the men who entered. Only when his speech became refined did someone look his way."

Here I broke with the story. "Boy, there are people who are kind in the world. You may not believe it, but I have met them. You should always be on the lookout for someone who can be a benefactor."

"Like you?" he asked.

His grandmother snorted. Once again, I ignored her.

"This man took the boy in as a servant," I resumed. "As the boy served him, the benefactor taught him everything he knew. When he could teach no more, he hired a tutor. After many years the boy, now a grown man, took the imperial exam and became a mandarin—only at the lowest level," I added, believing that such a thing was possible even for Snow Flower's son.

"The mandarin returned to his home village. The dog before his family home barked three times in recognition. Mama and Baba came out of the house. They did not recognize their son. The second brother came out. He did not recognize his sibling. The sister? She had married out. When he told them who he was, they kowtowed, and very shortly thereafter they asked him for favors. 'We need a new well,' his father said. 'Can you hire someone to dig it for us?' 'I have no silk,' his mother said. 'Can you buy some for me?' 'I have taken care of our parents for many years,' the younger brother said. 'Will you pay me for the time I have spent?' The mandarin remembered how badly they had treated him. He climbed back into his palanquin and went back to Guilin, where he married, had many sons, and lived a very happy life."

"*Waaa!* You tell these stories and ruin an already ruined boy's life?" The old woman spat into the fire one more time and glared at me. "You give him hope when there is none? Why do you do that?"

I knew the answer, but I would never tell it to that old rat woman. We were not under normal circumstances, I know, but away from my own family I needed someone to care for. In my mind, I saw my husband as this boy's benefactor. Why not? If Snow Flower could help me when we were girls, couldn't my family change this boy's future?

SOON ANIMALS IN the hills around us became scarce, driven from their homes by the presence of so many people or dead—as so many of us died—from the cruelty of that winter. Men—farmers all—weakened. They had brought only what they could carry; when that ran out, they and their families starved. Many husbands asked their wives to go back down the mountain for supplies. In our county, as you know, women are not to be hurt in wartime, which is why we are often sent to find food, water, or other supplies during upheavals. Harming a woman during hostilities always leads to an escalation of fighting, but neither the Taipings nor the soldiers in the Great Hunan Army were from around here. They did not know the ways of the Yao people. Besides, how were we women, weak from hunger and frail on our bound feet, to go down the mountain in winter and carry back provisions?

So a small band of men set out, treading carefully down the mountain, hoping to find food and other necessities in the villages we had evacuated. Only a few made it back, and they told of seeing their friends decapitated and the heads mounted on stakes. The new widows, unable to bear the news, committed suicide: throwing their bodies over the cliff they had worked so hard to climb, swallowing burning embers from the evening fire, cutting their own throats, or slowly starving themselves. Those who didn't take this path dishonored themselves even more by seeking new lives with other men around other fires. It seemed that in the mountains some women forgot the rules about widowhood. Even if we are poor, even if we are young, even if we have children, it is better to die, remain true to our husbands, and keep our virtue than to bring shame on their memories.

Separated from my children, I observed Snow Flower's closely, seeing how they had been influenced by her, learning more about her through them, and—because I missed my own so terribly—comparing mine to hers. In my home, our eldest son had already taken his rightful place and a bright future stretched before him. In this family, Snow Flower's eldest son had a position even lower than hers. No one loved him. He seemed adrift. Yet to me he was the most like my *laotong*. He was gentle and delicate. Perhaps this was why she had turned away from him with such a hard heart.

My second son was a good and smart boy, but he did not have the inquisitiveness of my first son. I imagined him living with us for his entire life, marrying in a bride, siring children, and working for his older brother. Snow Flower's second son, on the other hand, was the bright light of this family. He had his father's build, short and stocky, with strong arms and legs. The child never showed fear, never shivered from cold, never whined with hunger. He followed his father like a shadow spirit, even going on hunting expeditions. He must have been a help in some way or else the butcher would not have allowed such a thing. When they returned with an animal carcass, the boy sat on his haunches next to his baba, learning how to prepare the meat for cooking. This similarity to his father told me a lot about Snow Flower. Her husband may have been crude, stinky, and beneath my old same in every way, but the love she showed the boy told me that she also cared very much for her husband.

Spring Moon's face and manner were everything that my daughter's were not. Jade carried my so-so family's coarseness in her features, which was why I was so hard on her. Since the moneys made from the salt business would provide her with a generous dowry, she would marry well. I believed Jade would make a good wife, but Spring Moon would become an extraordinary wife, if she were given the chances I'd been given.

All of them made me miss my family.

I was lonely and scared, but this was softened by the nights with Snow Flower. But how do I tell you this? Even here, even under these circumstances, with so many people about, the butcher wanted to do bed business with my *laotong*. In the cold and open space right next to the fire, they did it under their quilt. The rest of us averted our eyes, but we could not close our ears. Thankfully he was quiet, with only the occasional grunt, but a few times I heard sighs of enjoyment—not from the butcher but from my *laotong*. I did not understand this thing. After that business was over, Snow Flower would come to me and wrap her arms around me as we had done as girls. I could smell the sex on her, but with the freezing temperatures I was grateful for her warmth. Without her body next to mine I would have been just another woman who died in the night.

Naturally, with all that bed business, Snow Flower got pregnant again, though I hoped that between the cold, the hardship, and our lack of nourishment that her monthly bleeding had simply paused as had mine. She did not want to hear that kind of talk.

"I've been pregnant before," she said. "I know the signs."

"Then I wish for you another son."

"This time"—her eyes gleamed with a combination of happiness and certainty—"I will have one."

"Indeed, sons are always a blessing. You should be proud of your eldest son."

"Yes," she responded mildly, then added, "I have watched you two together. You like him. Do you like him enough for him to become your son-in-law?"

I liked the boy, but this proposal was out of the question.

"There can be no man-woman match between our families," I said. I owed Snow Flower a great deal for what I had become. I wanted to do the same for Spring Moon, but I would never allow my daughter to stoop so low. "A true-heart match between our daughters is far more important, don't you agree?"

"Of course you are right," Snow Flower responded, unaware, I think, of my true feelings. "When we get home we will meet with Auntie Wang as planned. As soon as the girls' feet have settled into their new shapes, they will go to the Temple of Gupo to sign their contract, buy a fan to write of their lives together, and eat at the taro stand."

"You and I should meet in Shexia too. If we are discreet, we can watch them."

"Do you mean spy on them?" Snow Flower asked, incredulous. When I smiled, she laughed. "I always thought I was the wicked one, but look who's scheming now!"

Despite the privations of those weeks and months, our plan for our daughters gave us hope and we tried to remember life's goodness with each passing day. We celebrated Snow Flower's younger son's fifth birthday. He was such a funny little boy and we were entertained watching him with his father. They acted like two pigs together—nosing about, foraging, jostling their strong bodies against each other, both of them streaked with dirt and grime, both of them delighting in each other's company. The older son was content to sit with the women. Because of my interest in the boy, Snow Flower began paying attention to him too. Under her eyes, he smiled readily. In his expression, I saw his mother's face at that age— sweet, guileless, intelligent. Snow Flower looked back at him—not with mother love exactly, but as though she liked what she saw more than she had previously thought.

One day as I was teaching him a song, she said, "He shouldn't learn our women's songs. We learned some poetry as girls—"

"Through your mother—"

"And I'm sure you've learned more in your husband's home."

"I have."

We were both excited, rattling off titles of poems we knew.

Snow Flower took her boy's hand. "Let's teach him what we can to be an educated man."

I knew this would not be so very much since we were both illiterate, but that boy was like a dried mushroom dropped into boiling water. He soaked up everything we gave him. Soon he could recite the Tang dynasty poem that Snow Flower and I had loved so well as girls and whole passages from the classical book for boys that I had memorized to help my son in his lessons. For the first time, I saw true pride in Snow Flower's face. The rest of the family did not feel the same, but for once Snow Flower did not cower or cede to their demands that we stop. She had remembered the little girl who used to pull back the curtain on the palanquin so we could peek out.

Those days—cold and uncomfortable and as filled with fear and hardship as they were—were wonderful in the sense that Snow Flower was happy in a way I had not seen her for many years. Pregnant, without much food, she seemed to glow from inside as though she were lit by an oil lamp. She enjoyed the company of the three sworn sisters from Jintian and relished not being locked up solely with her mother-in-law. Sitting with those women, Snow Flower sang songs I hadn't heard for a long time. Out here in the open, away from the confines of her dark and dreary little house, her horse spirit was free.

Then, on a freezing night after we had been up there for ten weeks, Snow Flower's second son went to sleep curled by the fire and never again woke up. I don't know what killed him—sickness, hunger, or the cold—but in the early morning light we saw that frost covered his body and his face had gone icy blue. Snow Flower's keening echoed through the hills, but the butcher took it hardest. He held the boy in his arms, tears running down his cheeks, their wetness sending trails through the many weeks of dirt that were ground into his face. He would not be comforted. He would not release the boy. He had no ears for his wife or even his mother. He hid his face in his son's body, trying to block out their entreaties. Even when the farmers in our group sat around him, shielding him from our view and comforting him in low whispers, he did not yield. Every once in a while he lifted his face and cried to the sky, "How could I have lost my precious son?" The butcher's brokenhearted question was one that appeared in many *nu shu* stories and songs. I glanced at the faces of the other women around the fire and saw their unspoken question: Could a man—this butcher—feel the same despair and sadness that we women feel when we lose a child?

He sat that way for two days, while the rest of us sang mourning songs. On the third day, he rose, hugged the child to his chest, and dashed away from our fire, through the clusters of other families, and into the woods that he and his son had ventured into so many times before. He returned two days later, empty-handed. When Snow Flower asked where her son was buried, the butcher turned and hit her with such ferocity that she flew back a couple of meters and landed with a thud onto the hard-packed snow.

He proceeded to beat her so badly that she miscarried in a violent gush of black blood that stained the icy slopes throughout our campsite. She was not very far along, so we never found a fetus, but the butcher was convinced that he'd rid the world of another girl. "There is nothing so evil as a woman's heart," he recited again and again, as though none of us had heard that saying before. We just kept to our ministrations of Snow Flower—stripping off her pants, melting water to wash them, cleaning her thighs of bloodstains, and taking the stuffing from one of her wedding quilts to stanch the putrid ghastliness that continued to flow from between her legs—and never raised our eyes or voices to him.

When I look back, I think it was a miracle that Snow Flower survived those last two weeks in the mountains as she passively accepted beating after beating. Her body weakened from the loss of blood from the miscarriage. Her body bruised and tore from the daily punishment her husband rained down on her. Why didn't I stop him? I was Lady Lu. I had made him do what I wanted before. Why not this time? *Because* I was Lady Lu, I could not do more. He was a physically strong man, who did not shy away from using that strength. I was a woman, who, despite my social standing, was alone. I was powerless. He was well aware of that fact, as was I.

At the time of my *laotong*'s lowest moment, I realized how much I needed my husband. To me, so much of my life with him had been about duty and the roles we were required to play. I regretted all the occasions when I had not been the wife he deserved. I vowed that if I made it down from that mountain I would become the kind of woman who might actually earn the title of Lady Lu and not be just an actor in a pageant. I wished for this and willed it to come true, but not before I would reveal myself to be far more brutal and cruel than Snow Flower's husband.

The women under our tree continued to watch over Snow Flower. We tended to her cuts, using boiled snow to douse away potential infections, wrapping them in cloth torn from our own bodies. The women wanted to make her soup from the marrow of the animals the butcher brought to feed us. When I reminded them that Snow Flower was a vegetarian, we took turns walking in groups of two to forage in the forest for bark, weeds, and roots. We made a bitter broth and spoon-fed it to her. We sang songs of comfort.

But our words and deeds did nothing to ease her mind. She would not sleep. She sat by the fire, her knees drawn up, her arms wrapped around them. Her whole body rocked with gut-wrenching despair. None of us had clean clothes, but we had tried to remain neat in appearance. Snow Flower no longer cared. She neglected to wash her face with clumps of snow or rub her teeth with the hem of her tunic. Her hair hung loose, reminding me of the night my mother-in-law sank into illness. She became more and more like Third Sister-in-law on that same evening—barely present with us at all, her mind floating, floating, floating away.

There came a point every day when Snow Flower wrested herself away from the fire to wander the snowy mountains. She walked as if in a dream, lost, uprooted, untethered. Every day I went with her, unasked, holding on to her arm, the two of us tottering over the icy rocks on our lily feet as she wound her way to the edge of the cliff, where she wailed into the great expanse, the sound flying away on the strong northern wind.

I was terrified, always thinking back to our terrible escape into the hills and the hideous sounds of the women's screams as they fell to their deaths so many meters below. Snow Flower did not share my trepidation. She looked out over the cliffs, watching snow hawks soar on the mountain winds. I thought of all of the times Snow Flower had talked about flying. How easy it would have been for her to take one step out and over the cliff. But I never left her side, never let go of her arm.

I tried to talk to her about things that would tie her to earth. I might say something like, "Would you prefer to approach Madame Wang about our daughters or shall I?" When she didn't respond, I would try something else. "You and I live so close. Why should we wait for the girls to become old sames before they meet? The two of you should come for a long visit. We will bind their feet together. Then they will have those days to remember too." Or, "Look at that snow flower. Spring is coming and soon we will leave this place." For ten days she answered only in monosyllables.

Then, on the eleventh day, as she veered to the edge of the cliff, she finally spoke. "I have lost five children, and my husband has blamed me each time. He always takes his frustration and stuffs it in his fists. When those weapons need to find their release, they find me. I used to think he was angry that I'd been pregnant with girls. But now, with my son . . . Was it grief all along that my husband felt?" She paused and tilted her head as she tried to work things out in her mind. "Either way, he has to put his fists somewhere," she concluded despairingly.

Which meant that these beatings had been going on since the first year she'd fallen permanently into the butcher's house. Although her husband's actions were common and accepted in our county, it hurt that she had hidden this from me so well and for so long. I had thought she would never again lie to me and that we would no longer have secrets, but I wasn't upset about that. Instead, I felt guilty for having ignored the signs of my *laotong*'s unhappy life for too long.

"Snow Flower—"

"No, listen. You think my husband has evil in his heart, but he is not an evil man."

"He treats you as less than human—"

"Lily," she cautioned, "he is my husband." Then her thoughts plunged to an even darker place. "I've wanted to die for a long time, but someone is always around."

"Don't say such things."

She ignored me. "How often do you think about fate? I think about it nearly every day. What if my mother had not married out to my father's house? What if my father had not taken to the pipe? What if my parents had not married me out to the butcher? What if I had been born a son? Could I have saved my family? Oh, Lily, I have been so ashamed of my circumstances before you. . . ."

"I never—"

"Ever since you first entered my natal home I have seen your pity." She shook her head to prevent me from speaking. "Don't deny it. Just hear me." She paused for a moment before continuing. "You see me and you think I fell so far, but what happened to my mother was far worse. As a girl, I remember her crying all day and all night in sorrow. I'm sure she wanted to die, but she wouldn't abandon me. Then, after I went to my husband permanently, she wouldn't abandon my father."

I saw where this was heading, so I said, "Your mother never allowed herself an embittered heart. She never gave up—"

"She went with my father on the road. I'll never know what happened to them, but I'm sure she did not allow herself to die until he was gone first. It's been twelve years now. So often I've wondered if I could have helped her. Could she have come to me? I'll answer this way. I dreamed I'd get married and find happiness away from the sickness of my father and the sadness of my mother. I did not know I would be a beggar in my husband's home. Then I learned how to get my husband to bring home food I would eat. You see, Lily, there are things they don't tell us about men. We can make them happy if we show them pleasure. And, you know, it is fun for us too, if we let it be."

She sounded like one of those old women who are always trying to frighten girls before they marry out with that kind of talk.

"You don't have to lie. I'm your *laotong*. You can be truthful."

She pulled her eyes away from the clouds and for the briefest moment looked at me as though she didn't recognize me. "Lily"—her voice came out sad and sympathetic—"you have *everything,* and yet you have nothing."

Her words cut me, but I couldn't think about them now as she confessed. "My husband and I didn't follow the rules concerning the pollution of a wife after childbirth. We both wanted more sons."

"Sons are a woman's worth—"

"But you've seen what happens. Too many girls come into my body."

To this undeniable problem I had a practical response.

"It wasn't their destiny to live," I said. "Be thankful, for something was probably wrong with them. We women can only try again—"

"Oh, Lily, when you talk like that my head feels empty. I hear only the wind rushing through the trees. Do you feel how the ground wants to give way beneath my feet? You should go back now. Let me be with my mother. . . ."

Many years had passed since Snow Flower lost her first daughter. Then, I hadn't been able to understand her grief. But by now I'd experienced more of life's miseries and saw things very differently. If it is perfectly acceptable for a widow to disfigure herself or commit suicide to save face for her husband's family, why should a mother not be moved to extreme action by the loss of a child or children? We are their caretakers. We love them. We nurse them when they are sick. In the case of sons, we prepare them to take their first steps into the men's realm. In the case of daughters, we bind their feet, teach them our secret writing, and train them to be good wives, daughters-in-laws, and mothers, so they will fit into the upstairs chambers of their new homes. But no woman should live longer than her children. It is against the law of nature. If she does, why wouldn't she wish to leap from a cliff, hang from a branch, or swallow lye?

"Every day I come to the same conclusion," Snow Flower admitted, as she looked out over the deep valley below. "But then your aunt comes into my mind. Lily, think how she suffered and how little we cared for her suffering."

I responded with the truth. "She hurt terribly, but I think we were a comfort to her."

"Remember how sweet Beautiful Moon was? Remember how demure she was even in death? Remember when your aunt came home and stood over her body? We'd all been concerned about her feelings, so we wrapped Beautiful Moon's face. Your aunt never saw her daughter again. Why were we so cruel?"

I could have said that Beautiful Moon's corpse was too horrible a memory to place in a mother's mind. Instead, I said, "We will visit Aunt at the first chance. She will be happy to see us."

"You perhaps," Snow Flower said, "but not me. I remind her too much of herself. But know this. She reminds me every day to endure." She thrust her chin forward, took one last look out across the misty hills, and said, "I think we should go back. I can see you are cold. And besides, there's something I want you to help me write." She reached into her tunic and pulled out our fan. "I brought it with me. I was afraid the rebels might burn my house and it would be lost." Her eyes stared into mine. She was fully back now. She let out her breath and shook her head. "I said I'd never again lie to you. The truth is, I thought we'd die up here. I didn't want us to be without it."

She pulled on my arm.

"Come away from the edge, Lily. Seeing you stand there like that scares me."

We walked back to our camp, where we improvised ink and a brush. We took two half-burned logs from the fire and let them cool; then we scraped at the charred parts with rocks, carefully preserving what came off. This we mixed with water in which we boiled some roots. It wasn't as black or opaque as ink, but it would work well enough. Then we loosened the edge of a basket, extracted a length of bamboo, and sharpened it as best we could. This we used for our brush. We took turns recording in our secret language our journey here, the loss of Snow Flower's little boy and unborn baby, the cold nights, and the blessings of friendship. When we were done, Snow Flower gently closed the fan and tucked it back inside her tunic.

That night the butcher did not beat my *laotong*. Instead he wanted and got bed business. Afterward she came to my side of the fire, slipped under her wedding quilt, curled up beside me, and rested her palm on my face. She was tired from so many sleepless nights and I felt her body soften quickly. Just before she drifted off, she whispered, "He loves me as best he can. Everything will be better now. You'll see. He has had a change of heart." And I thought, Yes, until the next time he throws his grief or his anger into the loving person beside me.

THE NEXT DAY we received word it was safe to return to our villages. After three months in the mountains, I'd like to say we'd seen the last of death. We had not. We had to pass all those who'd been left behind during our escape. We saw men, women, children, babies—all badly decomposed from exposure to the elements, from animal feasts, and from the natural decomposition of flesh. White bones flashed at us in the bright sunlight. Garments brought back instant identification, and too often we heard cries of recognition and remorse.

If all this were not enough, many of us were so weak that death was inevitable—now, at this last stage, when we were almost home. Mostly it was women who died on the way down the mountain. Balancing on our lily feet, we were top-heavy. We were *pulled* toward the abyss that fell away to our right. This time, in daylight, we not only heard the screams but saw the flapping of women's arms as they futilely fought the air. A day earlier, I would have worried for Snow Flower, but her face was set in concentration as she carefully placed one foot after the other before her.

The butcher carried his mother on his back. Once, when Snow Flower faltered, drawing back uncertainly at the sight of a mother wrapping the decayed remains of a child to take home for a proper burial, he stopped, set his mother down, and took Snow Flower's elbow. "Please keep walking," he pleaded with her softly. "We will be at our cart soon. You will ride the rest of the way back to Jintian." When she refused to tear her eyes away from the mother and her child, he added, "I will come back in the spring and bring his bones home. I promise we will have him nearby."

Snow Flower straightened her shoulders and forced herself to step reluctantly around the woman with her tiny bundle.

The hand-drawn cart was no longer where we'd left it. This and so many things that had been discarded three months ago had been taken, either by the rebels or by the Great Hunan Army. But as the land flattened we were drawn to our homes, forgetting our aching, bleeding, starving bodies. Jintian was unscathed, as far as I could tell. I helped the butcher's mother into the house and went back outside. I wanted to go home. I had come so far that I knew I could walk the last few *li* to Tongkou, but the butcher ran to tell my husband I was back and to come and get me.

As soon as he set off, Snow Flower grabbed me. "Come," she said. "We don't have much time." She pulled me into the house, even as my eyes yearned to watch the butcher as he loped up the road to my village. When we got upstairs, she said, "Once you did me a great kindness by helping me with my dowry. Now I can repay a small portion of that debt." She opened a trunk and pulled out a dark blue jacket with a pale blue silk panel woven in a cloud pattern on the front. That silk panel I remembered from the jacket Snow Flower had worn on the first day we met. She offered it to me. "I would be honored if you would wear this when you see your husband again."

I saw how terrible Snow Flower looked, but I hadn't considered how I might appear to my husband. I had worn my lavender silk jacket with the chrysanthemum embroidery for three solid months. Not only was it filthy and torn, but looking at myself in the mirror as water heated so I could bathe, I saw three months of living in the mud and snow under an unforgiving sun at high altitude upon my face.

I had time to wash only those places that he would see or smell first—my hands, arms, face, neck, armpits, and that place between my legs. Snow Flower did the best she could with my hair, pinning the grimy matted mass into a bun and then wrapping it in a clean headdress. Just as she helped me step into her dowry pants, we heard a pony's hooves and the creaking wheels of a cart coming near. Quickly she buttoned me into the tunic. We stood face-to-face. She placed the palm of her hand on the square of sky-blue silk on my chest.

"You look beautiful," she said.

I saw before me the person whom I loved above all others. Still, I was troubled by what she had said before we came down the mountain about my pitying her for her circumstances. I didn't want to leave without explaining myself.

"I never thought you were"—I struggled to find tactful words and gave up—"less than I was."

She smiled. My heart beat against her hand. "You said no lies."

Then, before I could say anything else, I heard my husband's voice calling me. "Lily! Lily! Lily!"

With that, I ran—yes, ran—downstairs and outside. When I saw him, I fell to my knees and put my head at his feet, so embarrassed I was by how

I must have looked and smelled. He lifted me up and enfolded me in his arms.

"Lily, Lily, Lily . . ." My name came out muffled as he kissed me again and again, oblivious that others watched our reunion.

"Dalang . . ." I had never before spoken his name.

He took me by the shoulders and pushed me back so he could see my face. Tears glistened in his eyes; then he pulled me close again, crushing me to him.

"I had to get everyone out of Tongkou," he explained. "Then I had to see our children safely on their way. . . ."

These actions, which I didn't fully understand until later, were what changed my husband from the son of a good and generous headman to a much-respected headman in his own right.

His body trembled as he added, "I looked for you many times."

So often in our women's songs, we say, "I had no feelings for my husband" or "My husband had no feelings for me." These are popular lines, used in chorus after chorus, but on that day I had deep feelings for my husband, and he for me.

My last moments in Jintian went by in a blur. My husband paid the butcher a handsome reward. Snow Flower and I embraced. She offered me the fan to take home, but I wanted her to keep it, for her sorrow was still near and all I felt was happiness. I said goodbye to Snow Flower's son and promised I would send him some notebooks to study men's writing. Finally, I bent down to Snow Flower's daughter. "I will see you very soon," I said. Then I got on the cart and my husband flicked the reins. I looked back to Snow Flower, waved, and turned toward Tongkou—toward my home, my family, my life.

Letter of Vituperation

THROUGHOUT THE COUNTY PEOPLE WENT ABOUT REBUILDING their lives. Those of us who survived that year had experienced too much, first with the epidemic and then with the rebellion. We were depleted—emotionally, and by the numbers of those we'd lost—but grateful to be alive. Slowly we gained weight. Men went back to the fields and sons returned to the main hall for study, while women and girls retired to their upstairs rooms to embroider and weave. We all moved forward, invigorated by our good fortune.

Sometimes in the past I had wondered about the outer realm of men. Now I vowed I would never venture into it again. My life was meant to be spent in the upstairs chamber. I was happy to see my sisters-in-law's faces and looked forward to long afternoons spent with them in needlework, tea, song, and story. But this was nothing to how I felt upon seeing my children. Three months was forever, in their eyes and in mine. They had grown and changed. My eldest son had turned twelve while I was away. Safe in the county seat during the chaos, protected by the emperor's troops, he had studied very hard. He had learned the supreme lesson: All scholars, no matter where they lived or what dialect they spoke, read the same texts and took the same exams so that loyalty, integrity, and a singular vision would be maintained across the realm. Even far from the capital, in remote counties like ours, local magistrates—all trained in an identical manner—helped people to understand the relationship between themselves and the emperor. If my son stayed on this track, one day he would surely sit for the examinations.

I saw Snow Flower more that year than since we were girls. Our husbands did not try to stop us, even though the rebellion still raged in other parts of the country. After all that had happened, my husband believed I would be safe in the butcher's care, while the butcher encouraged his wife's visits to my home, knowing she always returned with gifts of food, books, and *cash*. We shared a bed in each other's homes, while our husbands moved to other rooms to allow us time together. The butcher dared not object, following my husband's lead in this regard. But how could they have stopped any of it—our visits, our nights together, our whispered confidences? We had no fear of sun or rain or snow. "Obey, obey, obey, then do what you want."

Snow Flower and I continued to meet in Puwei for festivals as we always had. It was good for her to see Aunt and Uncle, whose lifetime of goodness within the family had earned them love and respect. Aunt was beloved as a grandmother to all her "grandchildren." At the same time, Uncle was also in a better position than he had been when my father was alive. Elder Brother needed Uncle's advice in the fields and in keeping the accounts, and Uncle was honored to give it. Aunt and Uncle had found a happy ending that no one could have imagined.

That year when Snow Flower and I went to the Temple of Gupo, our thanks were profound and deep. We made offerings, kowtowing in thanks that we had survived the winter. Then, arm in arm, we walked to the taro stand. Sitting there, we planned our daughters' futures and discussed the methods of footbinding that would ensure perfect golden lilies. Back in our own homes, we made bindings, purchased soothing herbs, embroidered miniature shoes to place at the altar of Guanyin, formed glutinous rice balls to present to the Tiny-Footed Maiden, and fed our daughters red-bean dumplings to soften their feet. Separately, we spoke with Madame Wang about our daughters' match. When Snow Flower and I met again, we compared conversations, laughing at how her aunt was still the same, with her powdered face and wily ways.

Even now, looking back at those months of spring and early summer, I see how blithely happy I was. I had my family and I had my *laotong*. As I said, I moved forward. This was not the case with Snow Flower. She did not regain the weight she had lost. She picked at her food—a few grains of rice, two bites of vegetable—preferring instead to drink tea. Her skin became pale again, while her cheeks refused to fill out. When she came to Tongkou and I suggested that we visit her old friends, she politely declined, saying, "They wouldn't want to see me" or "They won't remember me." I nagged her until she agreed she would come with me next year to the Sitting and Singing ceremony of a Lu girl here in Tongkou, who was Snow Flower's second cousin twice removed and my next-door neighbor.

In the afternoons Snow Flower sat with me as I did my embroidery, but she gazed out the lattice window, her mind elsewhere. It was as though she had jumped off the cliff after all, on our last day in the mountains, and was in a soundless fall. I saw her sadness but refused to accept it. My husband warned me several times about this. "You are strong," he said one night after Snow Flower had returned to Jintian. "You came back from the mountains and you make me more proud every day with the way you manage our household and set a good example for the women of our village. But you—and please, do not get angry with me—are blind when you look at your old same. She is not your *same* in every way. Maybe what happened last winter was too much for her. I do not know her well, but surely you can see she puts a brave face on a bad situation. It has taken you many years to understand this, but not every man is like your husband."

That he would confide this to me embarrassed me deeply. No, that's not right. Rather, I was irritated that he dared to interfere in the inner-realm affairs of women. But I did not argue with him, because it wasn't my place. Still, in my own mind I had to prove him wrong and myself right. So I looked more closely at Snow Flower when she next visited. I listened, really listened. Life had degenerated for Snow Flower. Her mother-in-law had cut back on her food, allowing her only one-third of the rice required for subsistence.

"I eat only clear porridge," she said, "but I accept it. I'm not so hungry these days."

Far worse, the butcher had not stopped beating her.

"You said he wouldn't do it again," I protested, not wanting to believe what my husband had seen so clearly.

"If he assaults me, what can I do? I can't fight back." Snow Flower sat across from me, her embroidery lying in her lap as limp and wrinkled as tofu skin.

"Why didn't you tell me?"

She answered with a question of her own. "Why should I trouble you with things you cannot change?"

"We can shift fate if we try hard enough," I said. "I changed my life. You can too."

She stared at me with mouse eyes.

"How often does it happen?" I asked, trying to keep my voice calm but frustrated that her husband was still using his fists against her, angry that she accepted it so passively, and hurt that she hadn't confided in me—again.

"The mountains changed him. They changed all of us. Don't you see that?"

"How often?" I pressed.

"I fail my husband in many ways—"

In other words, it happened more often than she cared to admit.

"I want you to come and live with me," I said.

"Desertion is the worst thing a woman can do," she responded. "You know that."

I did. For a woman it was an offense punishable by death by her husband's hand.

"Besides," Snow Flower went on, "I would never leave my children. My son needs protection."

"But to protect him with your own body?" I asked.

What response could she give?

I look back now and see with the clarity of eighty years that I showed far too much impatience with Snow Flower's despondency. In the past, whenever I had been unsure of how to react to my *laotong*'s unhappiness I had pressured her to follow the rules and traditions of the inner realm as a way of combating the bad things that happened in her life. This time I went further by launching a campaign for her to take control of her rooster husband, believing that as a woman born under the sign of the horse she could use her willfulness to change the situation. With only a useless daughter and an unloved first son, she should try to get pregnant again. She needed to pray more, eat the proper foods, and ask the herbalist for tonics—all to guarantee a son. If she presented her husband with what he wanted, he would remember her worth. But this was not all. . . .

By the time the Ghost Festival arrived on the fifteenth day of the seventh month, I had peppered Snow Flower with many questions that she should have understood were suggestions for her to improve the overall situation. *Why* couldn't she try to be a better wife? *Why* couldn't she make her husband happy in the ways I knew she could? *Why* didn't she pinch her cheeks to bring back the color? *Why* didn't she eat more so she would have more energy? *Why* couldn't she go home right now and kowtow to her mother-in-law, make her meals, sew for her, sing to her, do what she had to do to make that old woman happy in her old age? *Why* didn't she try harder to make things right? I thought I was giving practical advice, but I had nothing like Snow Flower's worries and concerns. Still, I was Lady Lu and I thought I was right.

So when I ran out of things Snow Flower could do in her home, I questioned her about her time spent in mine. Wasn't she happy to be with me? Didn't she like the silk clothes I gave her? Didn't she present the gifts the Lu family sent to her husband for our continued gratitude with enough deference that he would be pleased with her? Didn't she appreciate that I had hired a man to teach reading and writing to boys her son's age in Jintian? Didn't she see that by making our daughters *laotong* we would be changing Spring Moon's fate, much as mine had been changed?

If she truly loved me, why couldn't she do as I had done—wrap herself in the conventions that protected women—to make her bad situation better? To all these queries she just sighed or nodded. Her reaction made me even more impatient. I stepped up my questions and well-considered reasons, until she surrendered, promising to do as I'd instructed. But she didn't, and the next time my frustration with her was even more pointed. I didn't understand that the bold horse of Snow Flower's childhood had been broken in spirit. I was stubborn enough to believe I could fix a horse that had gone lame.

MY LIFE CHANGED forever on the fifteenth day of the eighth lunar month of the sixth year of Xianfeng's reign. Mid-Autumn Festival had arrived. A few days remained before our daughters' footbinding began. This year, Snow Flower and her children were to visit us for the holiday, but they were not who came to my threshold. It was Lotus, one of the women who'd lived under our tree in the mountains. I invited her to have tea with me in the upstairs chamber.

"Thank you," she said, "but I am in Tongkou to visit my natal family."

"A family likes to welcome home a married-out daughter," I replied, with the customary nicety. "I'm sure they will be happy to see you."

"And I to see them," she said, as she reached into the basket of moon cakes that hung on her arm. "Our friend has asked me to give you something." She pulled out a long slender package, wrapped in a fragment of celadon-colored silk I had recently given Snow Flower. Lotus handed it to me, wished me good fortune, and swayed down the alley and around the corner.

I knew from the shape what I was holding, but I couldn't fathom why Snow Flower hadn't come and had sent the fan instead. I took the bundle upstairs and waited until my sisters-in-law set out together to drop off moon cakes to our friends in the village. I sent my daughter with them, saying she should enjoy these last few days outside while she could. Once they left, I sat in my chair by the lattice window. Hazy light filtered through the latticework, casting a design of leaves and vines across my worktable. I stared at the package for a long time. How did I know to be afraid? Finally, I peeled back one edge, then another, of the green silk until our fan was fully exposed. I picked it up. Then I slowly clicked open one fold after another. Next to the charcoal-ink characters we had written the night before we came down from the mountains I saw a new column of characters.

I have too many troubles, Snow Flower had written. Her calligraphy had always been finer than mine, the legs of her mosquito lines so thin and delicate that the ends wisped into nothing. *I cannot be what you wish. You won't have to listen to my complaints anymore. Three sworn sisters have promised to love me as I am. Write to me, not to console me as you have been doing, but to remember our happy girl-days together.* And that was it.

I felt like a sword had thrust into my body. My stomach leaped at the surprise of it, then contracted into an uneasy ball. *Love?* Was she really talking about love with sworn sisters in *our* secret fan? I read the lines again, puzzled and confused. *Three sworn sisters have promised to love me.* But Snow Flower and I were *laotong,* which was a marriage of emotions strong enough to cross over great distances and long separations. Our bond was supposed to be more important than marriage to a man. We had pledged to be true and faithful until death parted us. That she seemed to be abandoning our promises in favor of a new relationship with sworn sisters hurt beyond reason. That she was suggesting that somehow we could still be friends literally took my breath away. To me, what she had written was ten thousand times worse than if my husband had walked in and announced he'd just taken his first concubine. And it wasn't as though I hadn't been given the opportunity to join a post-marriage sisterhood myself. My mother-in-law had pushed me very hard in that direction, but I had schemed and plotted to keep Snow Flower in my life. Now she was tossing me aside? It seemed that Snow Flower—this woman for whom I had deep-heart love, whom I treasured, and to whom I'd committed myself for life—did not care for me in the same way.

Just when I thought my devastation could go no deeper, I realized that the three sworn sisters she had written about had to be the ones from her village whom we'd met in the mountains. In my mind, I replayed everything that had happened last winter. Had they been conspiring to steal her away from me from that first night with their singing? Had she been attracted to them, like a husband to new concubines who are younger, prettier, and more adoring than a loyal wife? Were the beds of those women warmer, their bodies firmer, their stories fresher? Did she look at their faces and see no expectations and no responsibilities?

This pain was unlike anything I had felt before—plunging, searing, excruciating, far worse than childbirth. Then something shifted in me. I began to react not as the little girl who had fallen in love with Snow Flower but as Lady Lu, the woman who believed that rules and conventions could provide peace of mind. It was easier for me to begin picking at Snow Flower's faults than to feel the emotions raging inside of me.

I had always made allowances for Snow Flower out of love. But once I began to focus on her weaknesses, a pattern of deceit, deception, and betrayal began to emerge. I thought about all the times Snow Flower had lied to me—about her family, about her married life, even about her beatings. Not only had she not been a faithful *laotong*, she had not even been a very good friend. A friend would have been honest and forthright. If all this were not enough, I let memories of the recent weeks wash over me. Snow Flower had taken advantage of my money and position to gain better clothes, better food, and a better situation for her daughter, while ignoring all my help and suggestions. I felt duped and immensely foolish.

And then the strangest thing happened. An image of my mother came to my mind. I remembered that as a child I'd wanted her to love me. I'd thought if I did everything she asked during my footbinding, I would earn her affection. I believed I'd won it, but she had no feeling for me at all. Just like Snow Flower, she had looked out only for her own selfish interests. My first reaction to my mother's lies and lack of regard for me had been anger, and I never forgave her, but over time I gradually stepped farther and farther away from her until she no longer had an emotional hold over me. To protect my heart, this was what I would have to do with Snow Flower. I couldn't let anyone know I was dying from anguish that she no longer loved me. I also had to hide my anger and distress, because these were not good qualities for a proper woman.

I folded the fan and put it away. Snow Flower had asked me to write back. I didn't. A week went by. I did not start my daughter's footbinding on our agreed-upon date. Another week passed. Lotus came to my door again, this time delivering a letter, which Yonggang brought to me in the upstairs chamber. I unfolded the paper and stared at the characters. Always those strokes had seemed like caresses. Now I read them as daggers.

Why have you not written? Are you ill or has good fortune smiled on your door again? I began my daughter's binding on the twenty-fourth day, just as you and I began ours. Did you begin on that date too? I look out my lattice window to yours. My heart soars out to you, singing happiness for our daughters.

I read it once, then set one corner of the paper into the flame of the oil lamp. I watched the edges curl and the words become smoke. In the coming days—as the weather cooled and I began my daughter's footbinding— more letters arrived. I burned them too.

I was thirty-three years old. I would be lucky to live another seven years, luckier still to get seventeen. I could not endure the sick feeling in my stomach for another minute, let alone a year or more. My torment was great, but I summoned the same discipline that had gotten me through my footbinding, the epidemic, and the winter in the mountains to help me. I began what I called Cutting a Disease from My Heart. Anytime a memory came into my mind, I painted over it with black ink. If my sight fell upon a memory, I drove it away by closing my eyes. If a memory came in the form of a scent, I buried my nose in the petals of a flower, threw extra garlic in the wok, or conjured up the smell of starvation in the mountains. If a memory grazed my skin—in the form of my daughter's touch against my hand, my husband's breath against my ear at night, or the feel of a limp breeze across my breasts as I bathed—I scratched or rubbed or pounded it away. I was as ruthless as a farmer after harvest, yanking out every last remnant of what last season had been his most prized crop. I tried to clear everything down to bare earth, knowing this was the only way I could protect my damaged heart.

When memories of Snow Flower's love continued to torment me, I constructed a flower tower like the one we had built to ward off Beautiful Moon's spirit. I had to excise this new ghost, prevent her from ever again preying on my mind or tormenting me with broken promises of deep-heart love. I purged my baskets, trunks, drawers, and shelves of gifts Snow Flower had made for me over the years. I sought every letter she had written in our lifetime together. I had a hard time finding everything. I couldn't find our fan. I couldn't find . . . let's just say many things were missing. But what I found I pasted or placed in the flower tower; then I composed a letter:

You who once knew my heart, now know nothing of me. I burn all your words, hoping they will disappear into the clouds. You, who betrayed and abandoned me, are gone from my heart forever. Please, please leave me alone.

I folded the paper and slipped it through the tiny lattice window and into the upstairs chamber of the flower tower. Then I set fire to the foundation, adding oil when necessary to burn through the handkerchiefs, weavings, and embroideries.

But Snow Flower was persistent in her haunting. When I bound my daughter's feet, it was as if Snow Flower were in the room with me, a hand on my shoulder, whispering in my ear, "Make sure there are no folds in the bindings. Show your daughter your mother love." I sang to drown out her words. Sometimes at night I felt her imagined hand resting upon my cheek and I could not fall asleep. I lay there awake, furious with myself and with her, thinking, I hate you, I hate you, I hate you. You broke your promise to be true. You betrayed me.

Two people bore the brunt of my suffering. The first, I'm ashamed to admit, was my daughter. The second, I'm sorry to say, was old Madame Wang. My mother love was very strong, and when I bound Jade's feet you will never know just how careful I was, remembering not only what had happened to Third Sister but also all the lessons my mother-in-law had instilled in me about how to do this job properly, with the least chance of infection, deformity, or death. But I also transferred the pain I felt about Snow Flower out of my body and into my daughter's feet. Weren't my lily feet the source of all my pains and gains?

Though my daughter's bones and disposition were pliant, she wept piteously. I could not stand it, though we had only just begun. I took my feelings and harnessed them, driving my daughter back and forth across the floor of our upstairs room, wrapping her bindings ever tighter on those days that her feet were rewrapped, and chastising her—no, crying bitterly at her—with what my mother had drilled into me. "A true lady lets no ugliness into her life. Only through pain will you have beauty. Only through suffering will you find peace. I wrap, I bind, but you will have the reward." I hoped that through my actions I might reap a little of that reward and find the peace my mother had promised.

Under the guise of wanting the best for Jade, I spoke with other women in Tongkou who were binding their daughters' feet. "We all live here," I said. "We all have good families. Shouldn't our daughters become sworn sisters?"

My daughter's feet came out nearly as small as my own. But before I knew the final outcome of that, Madame Wang paid me a call in the fifth month of the new lunar year. In my mind, she had never changed. She had always been an old woman, but on this day I looked at her with a more critical eye. She was far younger than I am now, which meant that when I'd first met her all those years ago, she was forty years old at most. But then my mother and Snow Flower's mother were dead by that age—give or take—and had been considered long-lived. Thinking back on it, I believe that Madame Wang, as a widow, did not want to die or go to another man's home. She chose to live and fend for herself. She would not have succeeded if she had not been exceedingly smart and business-minded. But she still had her body to contend with. She let people know she was unassailable by wearing powder to cover what beauty may have lain in her face and dressing in gaudy clothes to set her apart from the married women in our county. Now, in what I guessed must have been her late sixties, she no longer had to hide behind powder and garish silk. She was an old woman—still smart, still business-minded, but with one flaw that I knew too well. She loved her niece.

"Lady Lu, it's been too long," she said, as she plopped down in a chair in the main room. When I did not offer tea, she looked around anxiously. "Is your husband here?"

"Master Lu will be home later, but you get ahead of yourself. My daughter is too young for him to negotiate a marriage match."

Madame Wang slapped her thigh and chortled. When I didn't join in, she sobered. "You know I am not here for that. I have come to discuss a *laotong* match. This business is for women only."

I slowly began to tap the nail of my index finger against the teak arm of my chair. The sound was loud and unnerving even to me, but I did not stop.

She reached into her sleeve and pulled out a fan. "I brought this for your daughter. Perhaps I can give it to her."

"My daughter is upstairs, but Master Lu would not consider it proper for her to see something that he has not examined first."

"But, Lady Lu," Madame Wang confided, "this is in our women's writing."

"Then give it to me." I reached out my hand.

The old matchmaker saw my hand shaking and hesitated. "Snow Flower—"

"No!" The syllable came out harsher than I intended, but I could not bear to hear that name spoken. I calmed myself, then said, "The fan, please."

She reluctantly gave it to me. Inside my head I had an army of brushes with black ink, obliterating the thoughts and memories that kept popping up. I called upon the hardness of the bronzes in the ancestral temple, the hardness of ice in winter, and the hardness of bones dried out under an unrelenting sun to give me strength. In one swift movement I opened the fan.

I understand there is a girl of good character and women's learning in your home. These were the first characters Snow Flower had written to me so many years ago. I looked up and saw Madame Wang's gaze upon me, watching for my reaction, but I kept my features as placid as the surface of a pond on a still night. *Our two families plant gardens. Two flowers bloom. They are ready to meet. You and I are of the same year. Shall we not be old sames? Together we will soar above the clouds.*

I heard Snow Flower's voice in every carefully drawn character. I snapped the fan shut and held it out to Madame Wang. She did not take it from my outstretched hand.

"I think, Madame Wang, there has been a mistake. The eight characters of these two girls do not match. They were born on different days in different months. More importantly, their feet did not match before binding began, and I doubt they will match when they are done. And"—I waved my hand idly to take in the main room—"family circumstances do not match. All of this is common knowledge."

Madame Wang's eyes narrowed. "You think I don't know the truth of these things?" She snorted. "Let me tell you what I know. You have severed your bond with no explanation. A woman—your *laotong*—weeps in confusion—"

"Confusion? Do you know what she did?"

"Speak to her," Madame Wang went on. "Don't disrupt a plan that was

agreed upon by two loving mothers. Two girls have a bright future together. They can be as happy as their mothers."

I couldn't possibly agree to the matchmaker's suggestion. I was weak
with sorrow, and too many times in the past I'd let myself be taken in—
diverted, influenced, convinced—by Snow Flower. I also couldn't risk seeing Snow Flower with her sworn sisters. My mind was already tormented
enough imagining their whispered secrets and physical intimacies.

"Madame Wang," I said, "I would not bring my daughter so low as to
match her to the spawn of a butcher."

I was intentionally spiteful, hoping the matchmaker would abandon
the subject, but it was as though she hadn't heard me, because she said, "I
remember the two of you together. Crossing a bridge, you were mirrored
in the water below—same height, same size feet, same courage. You
pledged fidelity. You promised you would never be a step apart, that you
would be together forever, never separated, never distant—"

I'd done all of those things with an open heart, but what about Snow
Flower?

"You do not know of what you speak," I said. "On the day your niece
and I signed our contract, you said, 'No concubines allowed.' Do you remember that, old woman? Now go ask your niece what she has done."

I tossed the fan into the matchmaker's lap and turned my face away, my
heart as chilled as the river water that used to run over my feet. I felt that
old woman's eyes on me, weighing, wondering, questioning, but she did
not have the will to go on. I heard her rise unsteadily. Her eyes continued
to bore into me, but I did not waver in my steadfastness.

"I will relay your message," she said at last, her voice filled with kindness and a deep understanding that agitated me, "but know this. You are a
rare person. I saw that long ago. Everyone in our county envies your good
luck. Everyone wishes you longevity and prosperity. But I see you breaking two hearts. It is so sad. I remember the little girl you were. You had
nothing but a pretty pair of feet. Now you have abundance in your life,
Lady Lu—an abundance of malice, ingratitude, and forgetfulness."

She hobbled out the door. I heard her get into her palanquin and order
her bearers to take her to Jintian. I could not believe that I had allowed her
to have the last word.

A YEAR WENT by. The day of Snow Flower's cousin's Sitting and Singing
in the Upstairs Chamber next door approached. I was still devastated, my

mind beating a never-ending rhythm—*ta dum, ta dum, ta dum*—like a heart or a woman's chant. Snow Flower and I had planned to go to the celebration together. I didn't know if she would still come. If she did, I hoped we could avoid a confrontation. I didn't want to fight her as I'd fought my mother.

The tenth day of the tenth month arrived—a good and propitious date for the neighbor girl to begin her wedding activities. I walked next door and went to the upstairs chamber. The bride was pretty in a wan sort of way. Her sworn sisters sat around her. I spotted Madame Wang and, next to her, Snow Flower: clean, her hair pulled back in the style befitting a married lady, and dressed in one of the outfits I had given her. That sensitive spot where my ribs came together above my stomach constricted. The blood seemed to drain from my head and I thought I might faint. I didn't know if I could sit through this event with Snow Flower in the room and still maintain my dignity as a woman. I quickly glanced at the other faces. Snow Flower had not brought Willow, Lotus, or Plum Blossom with her for companionship. I let my breath out in a *whoosh* of relief. If one of them had been there, I would have run away.

I took a seat across the room from Snow Flower and her aunt. The celebration had all of the usual singing, complaints, stories, and jokes. Then the mother of the bride asked Snow Flower to tell us of her life since leaving Tongkou.

"Today I will sing a Letter of Vituperation," Snow Flower announced.

This was not at all what I had anticipated. How could Snow Flower possibly want to make a public grievance against me when I was the one who had been wronged? If anything, I should have prepared a chant of accusation and retaliation.

"The pheasant squawks and the sound carries far," she began. The women in the room turned to her upon hearing the familiar opening for this traditional type of communication. Then Snow Flower began to sing in that same *ta dum, ta dum, ta dum* rhythm I had been hearing for months. "For five days I burned incense and prayed to find the courage to come here. For three days I boiled fragrant water to cleanse my skin and my clothing so I would be presentable to my old friends. I have put my soul into my song. As a girl, I was prized as a daughter, but everyone here knows how hard my life has been. I lost my natal home. I lost my natal family. The women in my family have been unlucky for two generations. My husband is not kind. My mother-in-law is cruel. I have been pregnant seven times, but only three babies breathed the air of this world. Now only a son and a daughter live. It seems I am cursed by fate. I must have done bad deeds in a former life. I am seen as less than others."

The bride's sworn sisters wept in sympathy as they were supposed to. Their mothers listened attentively—*oohing* and *aahing* over the sad parts, shaking their heads at the inevitability of a woman's fate, and admiring the way that Snow Flower drew upon our language of misery.

"I had but one happiness in my life, my *laotong*," Snow Flower went on—*ta dum, ta dum, ta dum.* "In our contract we wrote there would never be a harsh word between us, and for twenty-seven years this was so. We always spoke true words. We were like long vines, reaching out to each other, forever entwined. But when I told her of my sadness, she had no patience. When she saw how poor I was in spirit, she reminded me that men farm and women weave, that industriousness brings no hunger, believing I could change my destiny. But how can there be a world without the poor and ill-fated?"

I watched the women in the room cry for her. I was beyond stunned.

"Why have you turned away from me?" she sang out, her voice high and beautiful. "You and I are *laotong*—together in our souls even when we couldn't be together in our daily lives." Abruptly she brought in a new subject. "And why have you hurt my daughter? Spring Moon is too young to understand why, and you will not say. I did not expect you to have a malicious heart. I beg you to remember that once our good feeling was as deep as the sea. Do not make a third generation of women suffer."

At this last bit, the air in the room changed as the others took in this final injustice. Life was hard enough for girls without my making it harder for someone far weaker than myself.

I drew myself up. I was Lady Lu, the woman with the greatest respect in the county, and I should have risen above this. Instead, I listened to that inner music that had been pounding in my head and heart for months now.

"The pheasant squawks and the sound carries far," I said, as a Letter of Vituperation began to form in my mind. I still wanted to be reasonable, so I addressed Snow Flower's last and most unfair accusation first. I looked from woman to woman as I sang. "Our two girls cannot be *laotong*. They are not the same in any way. Your old neighbor wants something for her daughter, but I won't break the taboo. In saying no, I have done what any mother would do."

Then, "All the women in this room know hardship. As girls, we are raised as useless branches. We may love our families, but we are not with them for long. We marry out into villages we do not know, into families we do not know, to men we do not know. We work endlessly, and if we complain we lose what little respect our in-laws have for us. We bear children; sometimes they die, sometimes we die. When our husbands tire of us, they take in concubines. We have all faced adversity—crops that don't come in, winters that are too cold, planting seasons with no rain. None of this is so special, but this woman seeks special attention for her woes."

I turned to Snow Flower. Tears stung my eyes as I sang to her, and I regretted the words as soon as they left my mouth. "You and I were matched as a pair of mandarin ducks. I always remained true, but you've shunned me to embrace sworn sisters. A girl sends a fan to one girl, not writing new ones to many. A good horse does not have two saddles; a good woman is not unfaithful to her *laotong*. Perhaps your perfidy is why your husband, your mother-in-law, your children, and, yes, the betrayed old same before you, do not cherish you as they might. You shame us all with your girlish fancies. If my husband came home today with a concubine, I would be thrown from my bed, neglected, dismissed from his attentions. I—as all the women here—would have to accept it. But . . . from . . . you . . ."

My throat closed in on itself and the tears I'd been holding back escaped from my eyes. For a moment I thought I couldn't go on. I shifted away from my own pain and tried to bring this back to something all the women in the room would understand. "We might expect this loss of affection from our husbands—they have a right, and we are only women— but to endure this from another woman, who by her very sex has experienced much cruelty just by living, is merciless."

I went on, reminding my neighbors of my status, of my husband who had brought salt to the village, and of the way he had made sure that all of the people of Tongkou were transported to safety during the rebellion.

"My doorstep is clean," I declared, then turned to Snow Flower. "But what about yours?"

At that moment, an untapped spring of anger came bubbling to the surface, and not one woman in that room stopped me from expressing it. The words I used came from such a dark and bitter place that I felt as though I'd been sliced open with a knife. I knew *everything* about Snow Flower, and I proceeded to use it against her under the guise of social correctness and the strength of my being Lady Lu. I humiliated her in front of the other women, revealing every weakness. I held nothing back, because I had lost all control. Unbidden, a long-ago memory came to me of my younger sister's leg flailing and her loose bindings twirling around her.

With each invective I threw out, I felt as though my bindings had come loose and I was finally free to say what I really thought. It took me many years to realize that my perceptions at this time were completely wrong. The bindings weren't flying through the air and slapping at my *laotong*. Rather, they were whirling tighter and tighter around *me,* trying to squeeze away the deep-heart love I'd longed for my entire life.

"This woman who was your neighbor took with her a dowry that was made from her mother's dowry, so that when that poor woman went out onto the street she had no quilts or clothes to keep her warm," I proclaimed. "This woman who was your neighbor does not keep a clean house. Her husband carries on a polluted business, killing pigs on a platform outside her front door. This woman who was your neighbor had many talents, but she squandered them, refusing to teach the women in her husband's household our secret language. This woman who was your neighbor lied about her circumstances as a girl in her daughter days, lied as a young woman in her hair-pinning days, and continues to lie as a wife and mother in her rice-and-salt days. She has lied not only to all of you but to her *laotong* as well."

I paused, gauging the women's faces around me. "How does she spend her time? I'll tell you how! Her lust! Animals go into heat seasonally, but this woman is always in heat. Her rutting causes the whole household to go silent. When we were in the mountains running from the rebels"— I rocked forward and the others leaned toward me—"she did bed business with her husband rather than be with me—her *laotong*. She says she must have done bad deeds in a former life, but I, as Lady Lu, tell you that her bad deeds in *this* life made her fate."

Snow Flower sat across from me, tears running down her cheeks, but I was so desolate and confused that I could show only my anger.

"We wrote a contract as girls," I concluded. "You made a promise, which you broke."

Snow Flower took a deep quivering breath. "You once asked that I always tell you the truth, but when I tell it to you, you misunderstand or you don't like what you hear. I have found women in my village who do not look down on me. They do not criticize me. They do not expect me to be someone I am not."

Every word she spoke reinforced everything I had suspected.

"They do not humiliate me in front of others," Snow Flower went on. "I have embroidered with them, and we console one another when we are troubled. They do not pity me. They visit me when I have not been well. . . . I am lonely and alone. I need women to comfort me every day, not just at the times of your choosing. I need women who can hear me as I am and not how they remember me or wish me to be. I feel like a bird flying alone. I cannot find my mate. . . ."

Her soft words and gentle excuses were just what I was afraid of. I closed my eyes, trying to block my feelings. To protect myself I had to hold on to this grievance as I had with my mother. When I opened my eyes, Snow Flower had lifted herself to her feet and was delicately swaying toward the stairs. When Madame Wang did not follow her, I felt a pang of sympathy. Even her own aunt, the only one among us who made a living and survived on her wits, would not offer solace.

As Snow Flower disappeared step-by-step down the stairs, I promised myself I would never see her again.

WHEN I LOOK back on that day, I know that I failed terribly in my duties and obligations as a woman. What she had done was unforgivable, but what I said was despicable. I had let my anger, hurt, and ultimately my desire for revenge take control of my actions. Ironically, the very things that embarrassed me and that I later felt much regret over completed my passage to becoming Lady Lu. My neighbors had seen me be brave when my husband was away in Guilin. They knew how I'd cared for my mother-in-law during the epidemic and shown proper filial piety at my in-laws' funerals. After I survived the winter in the mountains, they'd watched as I'd sent teachers to outlying villages, attended ceremonies in nearly every home in Tongkou, and generally acquitted myself well as the wife of the headman. But on that day, I truly earned the respect that came with being Lady Lu by doing what all women are supposed to do for our country but can rarely accomplish. A woman must set an example of decorum and right thinking in the inside realm. If she is successful, these things will travel from her door to the next, making not only women and children behave properly but inspiring our men to make the outside realm as safe and settled as possible so the emperor can look out from his throne and see peace. I did all that in the most public way possible by showing my neighbors that Snow Flower was a low and base woman who should not be a part of our lives. I had succeeded even as I destroyed my *laotong*.

My Song of Vituperation became known. It was recorded on handkerchiefs and fans. It was taught to girls as a didactic lesson and sung during the month of wedding festivities to warn brides of life's pitfalls. In this way, Snow Flower's disgrace spread throughout the county. As for me, all that had happened crippled me. What was the point of being Lady Lu if I didn't have love in my life?

Into the Clouds

EIGHT YEARS PASSED. DURING THAT TIME, EMPEROR XIANFENG died, Emperor Tongzhi assumed power, and the Taiping Rebellion ended somewhere in a distant province. My first son married in and his wife got pregnant, fell into our home, and had a son—the first of many precious grandsons. My son also passed his exams to become a *shengyuan* district scholar. He immediately began studying to become a *xiucai* scholar, from the province. He did not have much time for his wife, but I think she found comfort in our upstairs chamber. She was a young woman of good learning and home skills. I liked her very much. My daughter, a girl of sixteen well into her hair-pinning days, was betrothed to the son of a rice merchant in faraway Guilin. I might never see Jade again, but this alliance would further protect our ties to the salt business. The Lu family was wealthy, well respected, and without bad fortune. I was forty-two years old, and I had done my very best to forget about Snow Flower.

On a day late in fall in the fourth year of Emperor Tongzhi's reign, Yonggang came into the upstairs room and whispered in my ear that someone wanted to see me. I asked her to show the guest upstairs, but Yonggang's eyes went to my daughter-in-law and daughter, who were embroidering together, and shook her head no. This was either impertinence on Yonggang's part or something more serious. Without a word to the others, I went downstairs. As I entered the main room, a young girl in worn clothes dropped to her knees and put her forehead to the floor. Beggars like this came to my door often, for I was known to be generous.

"Lady Lu, only you can help me," the girl implored, as she shuffled her crumpled form toward me until her forehead rested on my lily feet.

I reached down and touched her shoulder. "Give me your bowl and I'll fill it."

"I have no beggar's bowl and I don't need food."

"Then why are you here?"

The girl began to weep. I asked her to rise and when she didn't I tapped her shoulder again. Next to me, Yonggang stared at the floor.

"Get up!" I ordered.

The girl lifted her head and looked up into my face. I would have recognized her anywhere. Snow Flower's daughter looked exactly like her mother at that age. Her hair fought against the restriction of her pins and fell in loose tendrils about her face, which was as pale and clear as the spring moon she was named for. I wistfully remembered this girl before she was born. Through the mists of memory I saw Spring Moon as a beautiful baby, then during those terrible days and nights of our Taiping winter. Once this pretty little thing would have been my daughter's *laotong*. Now here she was, her forehead dropping back to my feet, begging for my help.

"My mother is very sick. She will not last the winter. We can do nothing for her now except settle her fretful mind. Please come to her. She calls out to you. Only you can answer."

Even five years earlier the depth of my pain would have still been so great that I might have sent the girl on her way, but I had learned a lot in my duties as Lady Lu. I could never forgive Snow Flower for all the sadness she had caused me, but for my own position in the county I had to show my face as a gracious lady. I told Spring Moon to go home and promised that I would arrive there shortly; then I arranged for a palanquin to take me to Jintian. Riding there, I buttressed myself against seeing Snow Flower and the butcher, their son, who I realized must have married in by now, and, of course, the sworn sisters.

The palanquin set me down before Snow Flower's threshold. The place had not changed. A pile of wood rested against the side of the house. The platform with its embedded wok waited for fresh kill. I hesitated, taking it all in. The butcher's form loomed in the dark doorway, and then he was before me—older, stringier, but the same in so many ways.

"I cannot bear to see her suffer" were the first words he spoke to me after eight years. He roughly wiped the dampness at his eyes with the back of his hand. "She gave me a son, who has helped me do better at my business. She gave me a good and useful daughter. She made my house more beautiful. She cared for my mother until she died. She did everything a wife should do, but I was cruel to her, Lady Lu. I see that now." Then he brushed past me, adding, "She is better off in the company of women." I watched him stalk toward the fields, the one place where a man can be alone with his emotions.

It is hard for me to think about this even after all these years. I thought I had erased Snow Flower from my memory and cut her from my heart. I had truly believed I would never forgive her for loving sworn sisters more than me, but the moment I saw Snow Flower on her bed, all those thoughts and emotions fell away. Time—*life*—had brutalized her. I stood there, an older woman, true, but my skin was still smooth from creams, powders, and nearly a decade protected from the sun, while my clothes spoke to the whole county about the person I was. In the bed across the room lay Snow Flower, an aged crone dressed in rags. Unlike her daughter, whose face had been immediately familiar to me, I would not have recognized Snow Flower if I had seen her on the street outside the Temple of Gupo.

And yes, the other women were there—Lotus, Willow, and Plum Blossom. As I suspected all those years ago, Snow Flower's sworn sisters were the women who'd lived with us under the tree in the mountains. We did not exchange greetings.

As I approached the bed, Spring Moon rose and stepped aside. Snow Flower's eyes were closed and her skin was deathly pale. I looked at her daughter, unsure of what to do. The girl nodded and I took Snow Flower's cold hand in my own. She stirred without opening her eyes, then licked her cracked lips.

"I feel . . ." She shook her head as though trying to rid her mind of a thought.

I called her name softly, then gently squeezed her fingers.

My *laotong*'s eyes blinked open and she tried to focus, at first not believing who was before her. "I felt your touch," she murmured at last. "I knew it was you." Her voice was weak, but when she spoke, the years of pain and horror fell away. Behind the ravages of disease, I saw and heard the little girl who invited me to become her *laotong* all those years ago.

"I heard you call for me," I lied. "I came as fast as I could."

"I was waiting."

Her face contorted in anguish. Her other hand clutched her stomach and she pulled up her legs reflexively. Snow Flower's daughter wordlessly dipped a cloth into a bowl of water, wrung it out, and handed it to me. I took it and wiped away the sweat that had collected on Snow Flower's forehead during the spasm.

Through her agony she spoke. "I'm sorry for everything, but you should know I never wavered in my love for you."

As I accepted her apology, another spasm hit, this one worse than the first. Her eyes shut against the pain, and she did not speak again. I refreshed the cloth and put it back on her forehead; then I once again took her hand and sat with her until the sun went down. By that time, the other women had left and Spring Moon had gone downstairs to make dinner. Alone with Snow Flower, I pulled back her quilt. Her disease had eaten the flesh around her bones and fed it to a tumor that had grown to the size of a baby inside her belly.

Even now I can't explain my emotions. I had been hurt and angry for so long. I thought I would never forgive Snow Flower, but instead of dwelling on that my mind tumbled with the realization that my *laotong*'s womb had betrayed her again and that the tumor inside her must have been growing for many years. I had a duty to care. . . .

No! That's not it. The whole time I was hurt it was *because* I still loved Snow Flower. She was the only one ever who saw my weaknesses and loved me in spite of them. And I had loved her even when I hated her most.

I tucked the quilt back around her and began plotting. I had to get a proper doctor. Snow Flower should eat, and we needed a diviner. I wanted her to fight as I would fight. You see, I *still* didn't understand that you cannot control the manifestations of love, nor can you change another person's destiny.

I lifted Snow Flower's cold hand to my lips; then I went downstairs. The butcher slouched at the table. Snow Flower's son, a grown man now, stood next to his sister. They looked at me with expressions that came directly from their mother—proud, enduring, long-suffering, beseeching.

"I'm going home now," I announced. Snow Flower's son's face crumpled in disappointment, but I held up my hand placatingly. "I will be back tomorrow. Please arrange a place for me to sleep. I will not leave this place until . . ." I couldn't go on.

I thought that once I settled in we would win this battle, but two weeks were all we had. Two weeks out of what would turn out to be my eighty years to show Snow Flower all the love I felt for her. Not once did I leave that room. Whatever went into my body, Snow Flower's daughter brought. Whatever went out of my body, Snow Flower's daughter took away. Every day I washed Snow Flower, then used the same water to wash myself. A shared bowl of water many years before was how I knew Snow Flower loved me. Now I hoped she would see my actions, remember the past, and know that nothing had changed.

At night, after the others left, I moved from the cot the family had prepared for me and into the bed next to Snow Flower. I wrapped my arms around her, trying to bring warmth to her shriveled form and alleviate the torment that so wracked her body that she whimpered even in her dreams. Each night I fell asleep wishing my hands were sponges that would absorb the growth in her belly. Each morning I woke to find her hand upon my cheek, her hollowed eyes staring at me.

For many years, Jintian's doctor had attended to Snow Flower. Now I sent for my own. He took one look and shook his head.

"Lady Lu, a cure is not possible," he said. "All you can do now is wait for the onset of death. You can see it already in the purple tint of her flesh just above her bindings. First, her ankles; then her legs will come next, swelling and turning the skin purple as her life force slows. Soon, I suspect, her breathing will change. You'll recognize it. An inhale, an exhale, then nothing. Just when you think she is gone she will take another breath. Do not cry, Lady Lu. At that time the end will be very near, and she will not even be aware of her pain."

The doctor left packets of herbs for us to brew into a medicinal tea; I paid him and vowed I would never use him again. After he left, Lotus, the eldest of the sworn sisters, tried to comfort me. "Snow Flower's husband brought in many doctors, but one doctor, two doctors, three doctors could do nothing for her now."

The old fury threatened to rise up in me, but I saw the sympathy and compassion in Lotus's face, not just for Snow Flower but for me as well.

I remembered that bitter was the most *yin* of flavors. It caused contractions, reduced fevers, and calmed the heart and spirit. Convinced that bitter melon was something that would stall Snow Flower's disease, I called upon her sworn sisters to help by making sautéed bitter melon with black bean sauce and bitter melon soup. The three women did as I asked. I sat on Snow Flower's bed and fed her spoonful after spoonful. At first she ate without arguing. Then she clamped her mouth shut and looked away from me as though I weren't there.

The middle sworn sister pulled me aside. At the top of the stairs, Willow took the bowl from my hands, and whispered, "It's too late for this. She doesn't want to eat. You must try to let her go." Willow patted my face kindly. Later that day, she would be the one who cleaned up Snow Flower's bitter-melon vomit.

My next and final plan was to bring in the diviner. He came into the room and announced, "A ghost has attached itself to your friend's body. Do not worry. Together we will drive it from this room and she will be cured. Miss Snow Flower," he said, bending over the bed, "here are some words for you to chant." Then to the rest of us, he ordered, "Kneel and pray."

So Spring Moon, Madame Wang—yes, the old matchmaker was there through most of it—the three sworn sisters, and I dropped to our knees around the bed and began praying and singing to the Goddess of Mercy, while Snow Flower's voice weakly repeated her lines. Once the diviner saw us busy with our tasks, he took a piece of paper from his pocket, wrote some incantations on it, set it on fire, and ran back and forth across the room, trying to drive away the hungry ghost. Next he used a sword to slice through the smoke: *swish, swish, swish.* "Ghost out! Ghost out! Ghost out!"

But this did not help. I paid the diviner and from Snow Flower's lattice window watched as he got into his pony-drawn cart and trotted off down the road. I vowed that from here on I would use diviners only to find propitious dates.

Plum Blossom, the third and youngest of the sworn sisters, came to stand next to me. "Snow Flower is doing everything you ask of her. But I hope you see, Lady Lu, that she only does these things for you. This torment has gone on too long. If she were a dog, would you keep her suffering so?"

Pain exists at many levels: the physical agony that Snow Flower endured, the sorrow at seeing her suffer and believing that *I* couldn't bear another moment, the torturous regret I felt for the things I had said to her eight years ago—and to what purpose? To be respected by the women of my village? To hurt Snow Flower as she had hurt me? Or had it come down to my pride—that if she wouldn't be with me, she shouldn't be with anyone? I'd been wrong on every count, including the last one, because during those long days I saw the solace that the other women brought to Snow Flower. They had not come to her just at this final moment as I had; they had watched over her for many years. Their generosity—in the form of little bags of rice, cut vegetables, and gathered firewood—had kept her alive. Now they came every day, neglecting their duties at home. They did not crowd in on our special relationship. Instead, they hovered like benign spirits, praying, continuing to light fires to scare away ghosts eager for Snow Flower, but always leaving us to ourselves.

I must have slept, but I don't remember it. When I wasn't attending to Snow Flower, I was making burial shoes for her. I chose colors I knew she would love. I threaded my needle and embroidered one shoe with a lotus blossom for *continual* and a ladder for *climbing* to suggest that Snow Flower was on a continual climb to heaven. On the other, I embroidered tiny deer and curly-winged bats, symbols that meant long life—the same ones that you see on wedding garments and hang as celebratory notices at birthdays—to let Snow Flower know that, even after her death, her blood would continue through her son and her daughter.

Snow Flower deteriorated. When I had first arrived and washed and rewrapped her feet, I saw that her curled toes had already turned dark purple. As the doctor said it would, that horrible death color crept up to her calves. I tried to make Snow Flower fight the disease. In the early days I begged her to call on her horse nature to kick away those spirits who wanted to claim her. Now, I knew, all that was left was to ease her way to the afterworld as best we could.

Yonggang saw all this when she came to see me each morning, bringing fresh eggs, clean clothes, and messages from my husband. She had been obedient and loyal to me for many years, but at this time I discovered that she had once broken faith with me in a way for which I will be forever grateful. Three days before Snow Flower died, Yonggang arrived for one of her early morning visits, knelt before me, and laid a basket at my feet.

"I saw you, Lady, many years ago," she said, her voice cracking in fear. "I knew you couldn't mean what you were doing."

I didn't know what she was talking about or why she had chosen this moment to confess. Then she pulled the cloth from the top of the basket, reached in, and took out letters, handkerchiefs, embroideries, and Snow Flower and my secret fan. These were things I'd looked for when I was burning our past, but this servant had risked being thrown into the street to save them, during those days of Cutting a Disease from My Heart, and then kept them protected all these years.

Seeing this, Spring Moon and the sworn sisters scurried around the room, digging into Snow Flower's embroidery basket, rifling through drawers, and reaching under the bed to find secret hiding places. Soon I had before me all the letters I had ever written Snow Flower and everything

I had ever made for her. In the end, everything—except what I had once destroyed—was there.

For the last days of Snow Flower's life, I took us on a journey through our lives together. We had both memorized so much that we could recite whole passages, but she weakened quickly and spent the rest of the time just holding my hand and listening.

At night, in bed together under the lattice window, the moonlight bathing us, we were transported back to our hair-pinning days. I wrote *nu shu* characters on her palm. *The bed is lit by moonlight. . . .*

"What did I write?" I asked. "Tell me the characters."

"I don't know," she whispered. "I can't tell. . . ."

So I recited the poem and watched as tears dripped from the edges of Snow Flower's eyes, ran down her temples, and lost themselves in her ears.

During the last conversation we had, she asked, "Could you do one thing for me?"

"Anything," I said, and I meant it.

"Please be an aunt to my children."

I promised that I would.

Nothing helped or relieved Snow Flower's suffering. In the final hours, I read her our contract, reminding her how we had gone to the Temple of Gupo and bought the red paper, sat down together, and composed the words. I read again the letters we had sent each other. I read happy parts from our fan. I hummed old melodies from our childhood. I told her how much I loved her and said I hoped she would be waiting for me in the afterworld. I talked her all the way to the edge of the sky, not wanting her to go yet yearning to release her into the clouds.

Snow Flower's skin went from ghostly white to golden. A lifetime of worries melted from her face. The sworn sisters, Spring Moon, Madame Wang, and I listened to Snow Flower's breathing: an inhale, an exhale, then nothing. Seconds passed; then an inhale, an exhale, then nothing. More excruciating seconds, then an inhale, an exhale, then nothing. The whole time I kept my hand on Snow Flower's cheek, as she had done for me throughout our entire lives together, letting her know that her *laotong* was there until that final inhale, exhale, and then truly nothing.

SO MUCH OF what happened reminded me of the didactic story that Aunt used to chant about the girl who had three brothers. I now understand that we learned those songs and stories not just to teach us how to behave but because we would be living out variations of them over and over again throughout our lives.

Snow Flower was carried down to the main room. I washed her and dressed her in her eternity clothes—all of them ragged and faded, but in patterns I remembered from our childhood. The oldest sworn sister combed Snow Flower's hair. The middle sworn sister patted Snow Flower's face with powder and painted her lips. The youngest sworn sister decorated her hair with flowers. Snow Flower's body was placed in a coffin. A small band came to play mourning music as we sat next to her in the main room. The oldest sworn sister had enough money to buy incense to burn. The middle sworn sister had enough money to buy paper to burn. The youngest sworn sister had no money for incense or paper, but she did a very good job crying.

Three days later, the butcher, his son, and the husbands and sons of the sworn sisters carried the coffin to the grave site. They walked very fast, as if they were flying across the ground. I took almost all of Snow Flower's *nu shu* writing, including much of what I had sent her, and burned it so she would have our words in the afterworld.

We returned to the butcher's house. Spring Moon made tea, while the three sworn sisters and I went upstairs to clean away all signs of death.

It was through them that I learned of my greatest shame. They told me that Snow Flower was not their sworn sister. I didn't believe it. They tried to convince me otherwise.

"But the fan?" I cried out in frustration. "She wrote that she was joining you."

"No," Lotus corrected. "She wrote that she didn't want you to worry about her anymore, that she had friends here to console her."

They asked if they could see the words for themselves. Snow Flower, I learned, had taught these women how to read *nu shu*. Now they crowded over the fan like a gaggle of hens, exclaiming and pointing out to one another hallmarks that Snow Flower had told them about over the years. But when they came to the last entry, they turned serious.

"Look," Lotus said, pointing to the characters. "There is nothing here about her becoming our sworn sister."

I snatched the fan away and took it to a corner where I could examine it myself. *I have too many troubles,* Snow Flower had written. *I cannot be what you wish. You won't have to listen to my complaints anymore. Three sworn sisters have promised to love me as I am—*

"You see, Lady Lu?" Lotus said to me from across the room. "Snow Flower wanted us to listen to her. In exchange she taught us the secret language. She was our teacher, and we respected and loved her for that. But she didn't love us, she loved you. She wanted that love returned, unburdened by your pity and your impatience."

That I had been shallow, stubborn, and selfish did not alter the gravity and stupidity of what I had done. I had made the greatest mistake for a woman literate in *nu shu*: I had not considered texture, context, and shades of meaning. More than that, my belief in my own self-importance had made me forget what I had learned on the first day I'd met Snow Flower: She was always more subtle and sophisticated in her words than this mere second daughter of a common farmer. For eight years, Snow Flower had suffered because of my blindness and ignorance. For the rest of my life—which has been nearly as many years as Snow Flower was when she died—I have lived with the regret.

But they were not done with me.

"She tried to please you in every way," Lotus said, "even by doing bed business with her husband too soon after giving birth."

"*That's* not true!"

"Every time she lost a baby, you offered no more sympathy than her husband or mother-in-law," Willow went on. "You always said that her only worth was from giving birth to sons, and she believed you. You told her to try again, and she obeyed."

"This is what we are supposed to say," I answered indignantly. "This is how we women give comfort—"

"But do you think those words were a consolation when she had lost another baby?"

"You weren't there. You didn't hear—"

"Try again! Try again! Try again!" Plum Blossom taunted. "Can you deny you said these things?"

I couldn't.

"You demanded that she follow your advice on this and many other things," Lotus picked up. "Then when she did, you criticized her—"

"You're changing my meaning."

"Are we?" Willow asked. "She talked about you all the time. She never said a bad word against you, but we heard the truth of what happened."

"She loved you as a *laotong* should for everything that you were and everything you were not," Plum Blossom concluded. "But you had too much man-thinking in you. You loved her as a man would, valuing her only for following men's rules."

Finished with one cycle, Lotus began another.

"Do you remember when we were in the mountains and she lost the baby?" she asked, in a tone that made me dread what was coming.

"Of course I remember."

"She was already sick."

"That's not possible. The butcher—"

"Maybe her husband brought it on that day," Willow admitted. "But the blood that burst from her body was black, stagnant, dying, and none of us saw a baby in that mess."

Again, Plum Blossom finished. "We were here with her for many years, and this thing happened several more times. She was already quite sick when you sang your Letter of Vituperation."

I hadn't been able to argue successfully with them before. How could I argue this point now? The tumor had to have been growing for a very long time. Other things from back then fell into place: Snow Flower's loss of appetite, her skin going so pale, and her loss of energy at the very moment when I was nagging her to eat better, pinch her cheeks to lure in more color, and do all of her expected chores to bring harmony to her husband's home. And then I remembered that just two weeks back when I'd first arrived in this house, she'd apologized. I hadn't done the same— not even when she was in her worst pain, not even when her death was imminent, not even when I was smugly telling myself I still loved her. Her heart had always been pure, but mine had been as shriveled, hard, and dry as an old walnut.

I sometimes think about those sworn sisters—all dead now, of course. They had to be careful in what they said to me, because I was Lady Lu. But they were not going to let me walk away from that house without knowing the truth.

I went home and retired to my upstairs chamber with the fan and a few saved letters. I ground ink until it was as black as the night sky. I opened the fan, dipped my brush into the ink, and made what I thought would be my final entry.

You who always knew my heart now fly above the clouds in the warmth of the sun. I hope one day we will soar together. I would have many years to consider those lines and do what I could to change all the harm I had caused to the person I loved most in the world.

Sitting Quietly

Regret

I AM NOW TOO OLD TO USE MY HANDS TO COOK, WEAVE, OR embroider, and looking at them I see the spots brought by living too many years, whether you work outside under the sun or are sheltered your whole life in the women's chamber. My skin is so thin that pools of blood collect just under the surface where I bump into things or things bump into me. My hands are tired from grinding ink against the inkstone, my knuckles swollen from holding my brush. Two flies sit on my thumb, but I'm too weary to shoo them away. My eyes—the watery eyes of a very old lady—have been watering too much these past days. My hair—gray and thin—has fallen from the pins that should hold it in place beneath my headdress. When visitors come, they try not to look at me. I try not to look at them either. I have lived too long.

After Snow Flower died, I still had half of my life ahead of me. My rice-and-salt days were not over, but in my heart I began my years of sitting quietly. For most women, this begins with their husband's death. For me, it began with Snow Flower's death. I was "the one who has not died," but things kept me from being completely still or quiet. My husband and family needed me to be a wife and mother. My community needed me to be Lady Lu. And then there were Snow Flower's children, whom I needed—so that I could make amends to my *laotong*. But it's hard to be truly generous and behave in a forthright manner when you don't know how.

The first thing I did in the months immediately following Snow Flower's death was to take her place in all her daughter's wedding traditions and ceremonies. Spring Moon seemed resigned to the prospect of marriage, sad to be leaving home, uncertain—having seen the way her father treated her mother—about what lay in store for her. I told myself these were the kinds of things all girls worry about. But on her wedding night, after her new husband fell asleep, Spring Moon committed suicide by throwing herself in the village well.

"That girl not only polluted her new family but the entire village's drinking water," gossips whispered. "She was just like her mother. Remember that Letter of Vituperation?" That I had composed the letter that had ruined Snow Flower's reputation raked across my conscience, so I hushed this talk whenever I heard it. Through my words, I became known as someone who was forgiving and charitable to the unclean, but I knew that in my first attempt to make things right with Snow Flower I had failed miserably. The day I wrote that girl's death onto the fan was one of the worst of my life.

I next focused my efforts on Snow Flower's son. Despite the lowest of circumstances and no support from his father, he had picked up a bit of men's writing and was good at numbers. Nevertheless, he worked at his father's side and had no more joy in his life than he had when he was younger. I met his wife, who still lived with her natal family. This time a good choice had been made. The girl became pregnant, but the thought that she would be falling into the butcher's house pained me. Although it is not my way to interfere with the outer realm of men, I prevailed upon my husband—who had not only inherited Uncle Lu's vast holdings but had added to them from the salt business profits and now had fields that stretched all way to Jintian—to find something for this young man to do besides slaughter pigs. He hired Snow Flower's son to collect rents from the farmers and gave him a house with its own kitchen garden. Eventually the butcher retired, moved in with his son, and began doting on his grandson, who brought big joy to that home. The young man and his family were happy, but I knew that I still had not done enough to earn my way back to Snow Flower.

AT AGE FIFTY, when my monthly bleeding stopped, my life changed again. I experienced a shift from waiting on others to having others wait on me, though I certainly watched what they did and corrected them for anything not done to my satisfaction. But as I said, in my heart I was already sitting quietly. I became a vegetarian and abstained from such warm foods as garlic and wine. I contemplated religious sutras, practiced cleansing rituals, and hoped to renounce the polluting aspects of bed business. Although I had conspired my entire married life for my husband never to bring in a concubine, I looked at him and felt sympathy for him. He deserved the rewards of a lifetime of hard work. I did not wait for him to act—perhaps he never would have—but took it upon myself to find and bring into our home not one but three concubines to entertain him. By choosing them myself, I was able to prevent many of the jealousies and petty disagreements that usually arrive with pretty young women. I did not mind when they gave birth. And, in truth, my husband's esteem grew in the village. He had proved that he could not only afford the women but that his *chi* was stronger than any man's in the county.

My relationship with my husband turned into one of great companionship. He often came to the women's chamber to drink tea and talk with me. The solace that he found in the quiet of the inner realm caused his worries about the chaos, instability, and corruption of the outer realm to melt away. We were more content together at this time than perhaps at any other in our entire lives. We had planted a garden, and it bloomed around us in so many ways. All of our sons married in. All of their wives proved to be fertile. Our home was merry with the sounds of grandchildren. We loved them, but there was one child not of my blood who interested me most of all. I wanted her near me.

In a little house in Jintian, the rent collector's wife had given birth to a girl. I wanted that child—Snow Flower's granddaughter—to become my eldest grandson's wife. Age six is not too early for Contracting a Kin, if both families want to seal a betrothal for a prized couple, if the groom's family is willing to begin delivering bride-price gifts, and if the bride's family is poor enough to need them. I felt that we met all the conditions, and my husband—after thirty-two years of marriage, during which I had never caused him to be embarrassed or ashamed of me—was generous enough to grant me this request.

I sent for Madame Wang just as the girl's feet were about to be bound. The old woman was escorted into the main room by two big-footed girls, which told me that even though other matchmakers now had more business, she had put away enough money to live well. Still, the years had not been kind to Madame Wang. Her face had wizened. Her eyes were white with blindness. She was toothless. She had very little hair. Her body had shrunk as her back hunched. She was so frail and deformed she could barely walk on her lily feet. I knew then that I didn't want to live so long, yet here I am.

I offered tea and sweetmeats. We made small talk. I believed she didn't remember who I was. I thought I could use this to my advantage. We chatted some more, then I came to the point.

"I'm looking for a good match for my grandson."

"Shouldn't I be speaking to the boy's father?" Madame Wang asked.

"He is away and requested that I negotiate on his behalf."

The old woman closed her eyes as she thought about this. Either that or she drifted off to sleep.

"I hear there is a good prospect in Jintian," I went on loudly. "She is the daughter of the rent collector."

What Madame Wang said next told me that she knew exactly who I was.

"Why not bring in the girl as a little daughter-in-law?" she asked. "Your threshold is very high. I'm sure your son and daughter-in-law would be happy with that arrangement."

Actually, they were quite displeased with what I was doing. But what could they do? My son was a scholar. He had just passed the next level of the imperial examinations to become a *juren* at the very young age of thirty. Either his head was in the clouds or he was traveling the countryside. He rarely came home, and when he did it was with outlandish stories of what he'd seen: tall, grotesque foreigners with red beards, who had wives with waists so constricted that they couldn't breathe and huge feet that flip-flopped like just-caught fish. These tales aside, my son was filial and did what his father wanted, while my daughter-in-law had to obey me. Nevertheless, she had removed herself from these discussions entirely and retired to her room to weep.

"I'm not looking for a big-footed girl," I said. "I want to marry in a girl who has the most perfect feet in the county."

"This child has not begun that process. There are no guarantees—"

"But you have seen these feet, am I correct, Madame Wang? You are a good judge. What do you think the result will be?"

"The child's mother may not know how to do a good job—"

"Then I will see to it myself."

"You can't bring the girl into *this* house if you intend a marriage," Madame Wang said querulously. "It would be improper for your grandson to see his future wife."

She had not changed, but then neither had I.

"You are right, Madame. I will visit the girl's home."

"That is hardly appropriate—"

"I will be visiting often. I have many things to teach her." I watched Madame Wang mull that over. Then I leaned forward and covered the old woman's hand with my own. "I believe, Auntie, that the girl's grandmother would have approved."

Tears welled in the matchmaker's eyes.

"This girl will need to learn the womanly arts," I continued hurriedly. "She will need to travel—not so far as to give her ambitions outside the women's realm, but I think you would agree that she should visit the Temple of Gupo every year. They tell me there once was a man who made a special taro treat. I hear his grandson continues the legacy."

I persisted in the negotiation, and Snow Flower's granddaughter came under my protection. I personally bound her feet. I showed her all the mother love I could possibly give as I made her walk back and forth across the upstairs chamber of her natal home. Peony's feet came to be perfect golden lilies, identical in size to my own. During the long months that Peony's bones set, I visited her nearly every day. Her parents loved her very much, but her father tried not to think about the past and her mother did not know it. So I talked to the girl, weaving stories about her grandmother and her *laotong,* about writing and singing, about friendship and hardship.

"Your grandmother was born of an educated family," I told her. "You will learn what she taught me—needlework, dignity, and, most important, our secret women's writing."

Peony was diligent in her studies, but one day she said to me, "My writing is crude. I hope you will be forgiving of me and it."

She was Snow Flower's granddaughter, but how could I not see myself in her too?

I SOMETIMES WONDER which was worse, watching Snow Flower or my husband die. Both suffered greatly. Only one had a funeral procession in which three sons went on their knees all the way to the grave site. I was fifty-seven when my husband went to the afterworld, too old for my sons to think about having me marry out again or even worry about whether or not I would be a chaste widow. I was chaste. I had been for many years, only now I was doubly a widow. I have not written much about my husband in these pages. All of that is in my official autobiography. But I will say this: He gave me reasons to continue day after day. I had to make sure his meals were provided. I had to think of clever things to amuse him. With him gone, I ate less and less. I no longer cared to be an exemplar of womanhood in the county. Days drifted into weeks. I forgot about time. I ignored the cycles of the seasons. Years folded into decades.

The problem with living so long is that you see too many people pass before you. I outlived nearly everyone—my parents, my aunt and uncle, my siblings, Madame Wang, my husband, my daughter, two of my sons, all of my daughters-in-law, even Yonggang. My eldest son became a *gongsheng* and then a *jinshi* scholar. The emperor himself read his eight-legged essay. As a court official, my son is away most of the time, but he has secured the Lu family's position for generations to come. He is filial, and I know he will never forget his duties. He has even bought a coffin—big and lacquered—for me to rest in after I die. His name—along with those of his great-uncle Lu and Snow Flower's great-grandfather—hangs in proud men's characters in Tongkou's ancestral temple. Those three names will be there until the building crumbles.

Peony is now thirty-seven, six years older than I was when I became Lady Lu. As the wife of my eldest grandson, she will become the new Lady Lu when I die. She has two sons, three daughters, and may yet have more children. Her eldest son married in a girl from another village. She recently gave birth to twins, a boy and a girl. In their faces I see Snow Flower, but I also see myself. As girls we are told that we are useless branches, because we will not carry on our natal family names but only the names of the families we marry out to, if we are lucky enough to bear sons. In this way, a woman belongs to her husband's family forever, whether she is alive or dead. All of this is true, and yet these days my contentment comes from knowing that Snow Flower's and my blood will soon rule the house of Lu.

I have always believed the old saying that cautions, "A woman without knowledge is better than a woman with an education." My entire life I tried to shut my ears to what happened in the outside realm and I didn't aspire to learn men's writing, but I did learn women's ways, stories, and *nu shu*. Years ago, when I was in Jintian teaching Peony and her sworn sisters the strokes that make up our secret code, many women asked if I would copy down their autobiographies. I could not say no. Of course, I charged them a fee—three eggs and a piece of *cash*. I didn't need the eggs or the money, but I was Lady Lu and they needed to respect my position. But it went beyond that. I wanted them to place a value on their lives, which for the most part were dismal. They were from poor and ungrateful families, who married them out at tender ages. They suffered the heartache of separation from their parents, the loss of children, and the indignities of having the lowest position in their in-laws' homes, and far too many of them had husbands who beat them. I know a lot about women and their suffering, but I still know almost nothing about men. If a man does not value his wife upon marriage, why would he treasure her after? If he sees his wife as no better than a chicken who can provide an endless supply of eggs or a water buffalo who can bear an endless amount of weight upon its shoulders, why would he value her any more than those animals? He might appreciate her even less, since she is not as brave, strong, tolerant, or able to scavenge on her own.

Having heard so many stories, I thought of my own. For forty years, the past only aroused regret in me. Only one person ever truly mattered to me, but I was worse to her than the worst husband. After Snow Flower asked me to be an aunt to her children, she said—and these were the last words she ever spoke to me—"Though I was not as good as you, I believe that heavenly spirits joined us. We will be together forever." So many times I've thought back on that. Was she speaking the truth? What if the afterworld has no sympathy? But if the dead continue to have the needs and desires of the living, then I'm reaching out to Snow Flower and the others who witnessed it all. Please hear my words. Please forgive me.

Author's Note and Acknowledgments

ONE DAY IN THE 1960S, AN OLD WOMAN FAINTED IN A RURAL
Chinese train station. When the police searched her belongings in an effort to identify her, they came across papers with what looked to be a
secret code written on them. This being the height of the Cultural
Revolution, the woman was arrested and detained on suspicion of being a
spy. The scholars who came to decipher the code realized almost at once
that this was not something related to international intrigue. Rather, it was
a written language used solely by women and it had been kept a "secret"
from men for a thousand years. Those scholars were promptly sent to
labor camp.

I first came across a brief mention of *nu shu* when I wrote a review of
Wang Ping's *Aching for Beauty* for the *Los Angeles Times*. I became intrigued
and then obsessed with *nu shu* and the culture that rose up around it. I discovered that few *nu shu* documents—whether letters, stories, weavings, or
embroideries—have survived, since most were burned at grave sites for
metaphysical and practical reasons. In the 1930s, Japanese soldiers destroyed many pieces that had been kept as family heirlooms. During the
Cultural Revolution, the zealous Red Guard burned even more texts,
then banned the local women from attending religious festivals or making
the annual pilgrimage to the Temple of Gupo. In the following years, the
Public Security Bureau's scrutiny further diminished interest in learning

or preserving the language. During the last half of the twentieth century, *nu shu* nearly became extinct, as the primary reasons that women used it disappeared.

After I chatted about *nu shu* in an e-mail with Michelle Yang, a fan of my work, she very sweetly took it upon herself to look up and then forward to me what she found on the Internet about the subject. That was enough for me to begin to plan a trip to Jiangyong (previously called Yongming) County, where I went in the fall of 2002, with the help of the brilliant and prudent planning of Paul Moore of Crown Travel. When I arrived, I was told I was only the second foreigner to go there, although I knew of a couple of others who had apparently flown under the radar. I can honestly say that this area is still as remote as ever. For this reason, I must thank Mr. Li, who not only was a great driver (which is hard to find in China) but who also proved to be very patient when his car got stuck in one muddy track after another as we traveled from village to village. I was extremely lucky to have Chen Yi Zhong as my interpreter. His friendly manner, eagerness to walk unannounced into houses, subtlety with the local dialect, familiarity with classical Chinese and history, and enthusiastic interest in *nu shu*—something that he had not known existed—helped make my journey especially fruitful. He translated conversations in alleys and kitchens, as well as *nu shu* stories that had been collected by the *nu shu* museum. (Let me now offer my appreciation to the director of that museum, who most generously opened display cases and let me peruse the collection.) I have relied on Chen's colloquial translation of many things, including the Tang dynasty poem that Lily and Snow Flower wrote on each other's bodies. Since this region is still closed to foreigners, it was necessary to travel in the company of a county official, also named Chen. He opened many doors, and his relationship with his bright, beautiful, and cherished daughter showed me more than any article or speech how the status of little girls has changed in China.

Together, Messieurs Li, Chen, and Chen took me by car, pony-pulled cart, sampan, and foot to see and do everything I wanted. We went to Tong Shan Li Village to meet Yang Huanyi, who was then age ninety-six and the oldest living *nu shu* writer. Her feet had been bound when she was a girl and she told me about that experience, as well as her wedding ceremonies and festivities. (Although anti-footbinding activities began in the late nineteenth century, the practice lingered in rural areas well into the twentieth. Only in 1951, when Mao Zedong's armies finally liberated Jiangyong County, did the practice end in the *nu shu* region.)

Recently, the People's Republic of China reversed its previous stance and now considers *nu shu* to be an important element of the Chinese people's revolutionary struggle against oppression. To that end, the government is making an effort to keep the language alive by opening a *nu shu* school in Puwei. It was there that I met and interviewed Hu Mei Yue, the new teacher, and her family. She shared with me tales about her grandmothers and how they taught her *nu shu*.

Even today, the village of Tongkou is an extraordinary place. The architecture, paintings on the houses, and what remains of the ancestral temple all attest to the high quality of life that was once enjoyed by the people who lived there. Interestingly, although today the village is poor and remote by any measure, the temple lists four men from this area who became imperial scholars of the highest rank during the reign of Emperor Daoguang. Beyond what I learned in the public buildings, I would like to thank the many people of Tongkou who let me wander freely in their homes and answered endless questions. I'm also grateful to the people of Qianjiadong—believed to be the Thousand Family Village of Yao lore rediscovered by Chinese scholars in the 1980s—who also treated me as an honored guest.

On my first day back home, I sent an e-mail to Cathy Silber, a professor at Williams College, who in 1988 did field research on *nu shu* for her dissertation, to say how impressed I was that she had lived for six months in such an isolated and physically uncomfortable area. Since then, we have spoken by phone and through e-mail about *nu shu,* the lives of the women writers, and Tongkou. I was also helped tremendously by Hui Dawn Li, who answered countless questions about ceremonies, language, and domestic life. I am immensely grateful for their knowledge, openness, and enthusiasm.

I am deeply indebted to the works of several other scholars and journalists who have written about *nu shu:* William Chiang, Henry Chu, Hu Xiaoshen, Lin-lee Lee, Fei-wen Liu, Liu Shouhua, Anne McLaren, Orie Endo, Norman Smith, Wei Liming, and Liming Zhao. *Nu shu* relies heavily on standard phrases and images—such as "the phoenix squawks," "a pair of mandarin ducks," or "the heavenly spirits matched the two of us"—and I, in turn, have relied on the translations of those listed above. However, since this is a novel, I did not use the customary pentasyllabic and heptasyllabic rhyming scheme used in *nu shu* letters, songs, and stories.

For information on China, the Yao people, Chinese women, and footbinding, I would like to acknowledge the work of Patricia Buckley Ebrey,

Benjamin A. Elman, Susan Greenhalgh, Beverley Jackson, Dorothy Ko, Ralph A. Litzinger, and Susan Mann. Finally, Yue-qing Yang's evocative documentary, *Nu-shu: A Hidden Language of Women in China,* helped me to understand that many women in Jiangyong County are still living with the fallout of arranged, loveless marriages. All these people have their own well-established opinions and conclusions, but please remember *Snow Flower and the Secret Fan* is a work of fiction. It doesn't purport to tell everything about *nu shu* or explain all its nuances. Rather, it is a story that has been filtered through my heart, my experience, and my research. Put another way, all mistakes are my own.

Bob Loomis, my editor at Random House, once again showed himself to be patient, insightful, and thorough. Benjamin Dreyer, copy editor extraordinaire, offered some early and very good advice for which I am greatly obliged. Thank you to production editor Vincent La Scala, who shepherded the novel, and Janet Baker, who carefully read the manuscript. None of my work would see the light of day if it weren't for my agent, Sandy Dijkstra. Her faith in me has been unwavering, while everyone in her office has been wonderful to work with, especially Babette Sparr, who handles my foreign rights and was the first person to read the manuscript.

My husband, Richard Kendall, gave me the courage to keep moving forward. This time around he also had to field questions from numerous people who, while I was away, kept asking him, "You let her go there by herself?" He had not thought twice about letting me follow my heart. My sons, Christopher and Alexander, who were physically apart from me during the writing of this book, continued to be as inspired and inspiring as a mother could ever wish for.

A final thank-you goes out to Leslee Leong, Pam Maloney, Amelia Saltsman, Wendy Strick, and Alicia Tamayac—all of whom took very good care of me when I was housebound with a serious concussion and drove me around Los Angeles to doctors' appointments and on other errands during the three months I couldn't drive. They are a living example of a sworn sisterhood and I truly could not have finished *Snow Flower* without them.

A Note on the Author

LISA SEE is the author of *Flower Net* (an Edgar Award nominee), *The Interior*, and *Dragon Bones*, as well as the widely acclaimed memoir *On Gold Mountain*. The Organization of Chinese American Women named her the 2001 National Woman of the Year. She lives in Los Angeles.

Visit the author's website: www.LisaSee.com

A Note on the Type

This book was set in Bembo, a typeface based
on an old-style Roman face that was used for
Cardinal Bembo's tract *De Aetna* in 1495. Bembo
was cut by Francisco Griffo in the early sixteenth
century. The Lanston Monotype Machine
Company of Philadelphia brought the
well-proportioned letterforms of Bembo to the
United States in the 1930s.